D0355948

Received On:

JUN 12 2018

Ballard Branch

SEASON
OF THE
WITCH

NO LONGER PROPERTY OF
SEATTLE PUBLIC LIBRARY

SEASON
OF THE
WITCH

ARNI THORARINSSON

Translated by Anna Yates

amazon crossing

The characters and events portrayed in this book are fictitious. Any similarity to real persons, living or dead, is coincidental and not intended by the author.

Text copyright © 2005 by Arni Thorarinsson
English translation copyright © 2012 by Anna Yates

All rights reserved.
Printed in the United States of America.

No part of this book may be reproduced, or stored in a retrieval system, or transmitted in any form or by any means, electronic, mechanical, photocopying, recording, or otherwise, without express written permission of the publisher.

Season of the Witch was first published in 2005 by Forlagid as Tími nornarinnar. Translated from Icelandic by Anna Yates. Published in English by AmazonCrossing in 2012.

Published by AmazonCrossing
P.O. Box 400818
Las Vegas, NV 89140

ISBN-13: 978-1611091038
ISBN-10: 1611091039
Library of Congress Control Number: 2011963581

At the very moment that his head crashed onto the rocky ground, I was putting down the remote control and thinking about the love people have for their pets.

The context is inappropriate, of course. Yet it happened like that—just like that, and at the same time as I was considering whether love for pets arises from the power of the lover over the loved. And vice versa: whether the person who loves a pet is at the same time in the pet's power. The things you can think of. One time, two places. Is there a context?

1 SATURDAY

"Wilderness tour?"

Ásbjörn's blabbing is drowned out by the background noise. "What?" I shout into the phone. It's the brand-new goddamned cell phone he forced on me with this new assignment up north. I hate a gadget that means people can get hold of me anytime, anywhere; it's a disadvantage. It enables me to get hold of people anytime, anywhere; that's an advantage. So what is gained? Continuous contact with the outside world. And what is lost? Peace. Freedom from contact with the outside world.

"What?" Ásbjörn yells back.

"What did you say?"

"I said there was an accident on a wilderness..."

He falls silent.

"Accident?" I ask.

Silence.

"An accident where?"

No answer. I've been cut off. I place the phone in my lap and pull over. I read somewhere that cell phones have made life much easier for criminals, but much harder for writers of crime fiction, because the thrill and risk of being out of touch is almost a thing of the past. But couldn't there be more thrill and risk in being in touch than out?

"What's up?" asks Jóa, our photographer. She looks at me sideways from the passenger seat, chunky in her thick blue quilted parka. Although I say "chunky," Jóa is to me a beautiful young woman, with her kind face and constant smile. The *Afternoon News* venture of opening a branch in Northern Iceland with me as the only reporter has been made just bearable by her presence. Exile with her, if only for the time being, is a considerably more pleasant thought than exile with just Ásbjörn.

I light a cigarette. "Ásbjörn was going on about an accident somewhere around here that he probably wants us to cover. Then I was cut off."

Jóa looks around. "We're surrounded by mountains, Einar."

I wind the window down and blow smoke out into the damp air. Immediately raindrops start falling. Was that an objection? Is there someone up there who wants to put out the fire?

"High technology," I grumble.

"Not much use up here in the north," remarks Jóa. "The mountains block the signal."

She's misunderstood me. I was talking about the celestial fire service. The Almighty's antismoking police.

"I don't think that's it," I reply, looking around. "Hjaltadalur valley doesn't look narrow enough to block reception. These peaks aren't all that high." I try to mimic an actor's pompous delivery: "They have the shape of freshly filled silicone breasts on the body of the land."

"You never change!" laughs Jóa, with an overtone of disdain. Then she glances around and adds: "Actually, you're quite right, although your prose isn't exactly original. They're quite shapely, these breasts."

Nature has decreed that Jóa and I have similar preferences in feminine beauty.

"Maybe the land simply doesn't like the perpetual electronic stimulus," I sigh. "And who can blame it?"

I pick up the damned cell phone and call Ásbjörn.

He is pissed. "Why did you hang up on me?"

"I didn't hang up on you. You must have touched a button by accident."

"I did not touch any button."

"Yes, you did," I say.

"*You* must have touched a button by accident. You're hopeless with cell phones."

I give Jóa a wink. "OK, OK. Enough. Were you saying something about an accident?"

"A woman fell into the Jökulsá River. She may have drowned. Can you cover it?"

"Yeah, yeah."

"Where are you?" Ásbjörn asks.

"In the Hjaltadalur valley. We've just left Hólar after interviewing the high school students from Akureyri."

"You're not far from the scene. Ambulance and police are on the way from here, or they may already have gotten to Varmahlíd. I gather the people from the tour drove down in their SUVs to meet the ambulance."

"What were you saying about a wilderness tour?"

"Yes," he says, "it's a group from a company here in Akureyri, on a wilderness tour."

"One of those trips that are supposed to strengthen corporate bonding? A booze-fest presented as team building?"

"I wouldn't know. You and your condescending humor, Einar. We've got a good chance of a scoop, with photos and interviews. So shut up and put the pedal to the metal."

I'm not backing down. "It sounds to me, Ásbjörn, as if our little Akureyri newspaper branch could do with its own team-building excursion. To improve morale, strengthen solidarity, and enhance motivation and mutual care."

He says nothing.

"What do you say? A venture into the wilderness? Under your bold, strong leadership?"

He still says nothing. He's hung up. Or accidentally touched the button.

"Riding home from Hólar," I sing absently, recalling the old nursery rhyme as we pass a roadside sign: *Home to Hólar.* The rain is letting up. The grass fields are yellow and mucky under the gray sky. In the middle of nowhere a cross stands up out of the ground, all alone. Horses have huddled together and stand stock-still, pensive, stoic. In the rearview mirror I see the belfry of Hólar Cathedral sticking up like a sharpened pencil, separate from the old cathedral, which reminds me of an eraser.

Optimistic students from Akureyri High School had intended to premiere their production of the play *Loftur the Sorcerer* in the cathedral. When I interviewed the kids they told me the plan had not worked out. It sounded like a cool idea to me, since the action of the old play actually takes place at Hólar and in the cathedral itself. But what do I know? I haven't even read the play or seen it staged. And I'm no ecclesiastical authority, so the impropriety of staging on hallowed ground a play about a man who sells his soul to the devil isn't that obvious to me. As a compromise they've been permitted to use the Hólar College gym, in among the small campus's eclectic buildings, which include all sorts of modern structures and even an old turf farmhouse. Icelandic architectural history in a nutshell. Not to mention impeccable Icelandic taste.

I wonder if I'd be more at peace with myself if I'd studied something like horse breeding at Hólar College? Would it have given me the balance, stoicism, and thoughtfulness I notice in the horses that are rushing past like hairy statues along the roadside as we drive up through Skagafjördur?

"Why don't you make an effort?" Jóa suddenly asks.

I'm taken aback. "At horse breeding?"

"No, idiot. To get along with poor old Ásbjörn. I mean, the two of you have got to work closely together up here in the north. Why not make the effort?"

"I really don't think I want to. If I get along with Ásbjörn I'll be a completely different person. He is who he is. I am who I am."

I can feel her looking at me in surprise. Even disapprovingly. "Maybe a change of personality would do you good," she mutters.

"The man is just so fucking boring," I add to make my point. "Or do you like him?"

She is silent for a while. "He is who he is."

"See. We're in agreement."

"No, we are not in agreement," she says. "You're a pain in the ass too. And he's pretty much a broken man. Losing his news editor job..."

"Yes, fortunately sometimes the right decisions are made," I interject.

"...and being sent up north to the back of beyond with you, of all people."

"It's a tough punishment, I'll grant you. For both of us." I think of the horses again: *You can lead a horse to water, but you can't make it drink.* The media group that just bought 50 percent of the *Afternoon News* may be assholes. But at least they realized that Ásbjörn was not up to his job as news editor. Making him head of a new Akureyri office instead is another matter. So was giving his old job to ex-television personality Trausti Löve. Both decisions are supposed to make the paper more in touch with modern times. And my role in all of this modernization? Well, like I said, they probably are assholes.

Jóa shakes her head. "You're like two little boys. Two little boys who've been sent to the corner for fighting and keep on fighting there, long after you've forgotten what it was about."

She's absolutely right, as usual. But how the hell am I going to go about serving my time when she goes back down south?

As we drive over the bridge across the Héradsvötn River we see a crowd of people outside the roadside café in Varmahlíd, on the other side of the river. Four big SUVs are surrounded by other vehicles in the parking lot, and a police car and ambulance are parked in front of the building.

"Well, well," I remark. "Surely all these people don't live here at Varmahlíd, do they?"

"They're probably vacationers, spending the Easter holiday in bucolic bliss," Jóa replies. "And presumably the people on the wilderness tour."

"The ones wearing the ponchos."

A number of the people in the crowd look like blimps in blue dry suits, and two or three of them are also wearing life vests over the top. Some have red safety helmets on their heads. They must have set off in a hurry, without taking time to change. As we approach it's obvious that they are upset. Most are standing in three clusters around the ambulance, either crying or comforting the weepers. Inside the ambulance I spot two people in blue, along with a man and woman in white coats.

We pull up and Jóa reaches into the back for her camera.

"She simply fell overboard. Quite suddenly. I don't understand it," says Sigurpáll.

Sigurpáll is a tall, heavyset man, middle-aged and weather-beaten, with bushy red hair and beard. On his craggy face the beard is just beginning to gray. Sigurpáll Einarsson, the owner of *Sigurpáll Einarsson Wilderness Tours Ltd*, appears to be power-fully built inside his bulky dry suit. But his lips are trembling.

"This has never happened to me before. Never. And every-thing had been going so well. The group was getting along fine."

I've cornered him by the ambulance. "Were you in charge?" I ask him.

He slowly nods his shaggy head. Then shakes it, just as slowly, as if he has lost sight of his place in reality. There is so much dis-tress all around that no one else seems likely to be more capable of providing information. I must try and get a clearer picture of what happened.

"What happened before the accident? What kind of trip was it?"

He is quiet for a while. "A wilderness tour. I've organized doz-ens, even hundreds of them, over the past five years. Exactly the same. We were going over the rapids on the Jökulsá River when she fell overboard from the raft. Just like that."

"Isn't it rather early in the year for white-water rafting? It's a summer activity, isn't it?" I ask.

"Yes, we don't usually start till May. But the weather's been so good. It's been fine and windless, so two or three weeks either way doesn't make any difference. The conditions today were perfect.

That wasn't it. I was asked to organize a tour for the company, and I did it in the usual way. Team building, food and drink, white-water rafting on the glacial river, cliff-jumping, and so on. And the Jökulsá is tailor-made for beginners."

"Drink? Alcoholic drinks?"

Sigurpáll sniffs. "We serve hot cocoa."

I wait for him to go on. When he doesn't, I ask: "Were they drunk?"

Sigurpáll is startled. There is suspicion in his brown eyes. "Who are you, anyway?"

"I'm Einar. I'm a journalist on the *Afternoon News*. We've opened an office in Akureyri."

"Why don't you stick to the scandals down south? Isn't there enough dirt for you there?" he growls.

I don't like the look of this. "The *Afternoon News* wants to improve its coverage of the drastic changes now being experienced in the regions," I quote from an article published a few days ago in the paper by the editor, Hannes, "and provide a better service to the people who live there."

"You're not going to sensationalize this, are you?" he asks.

Now his voice is trembling, along with his lips.

"Not at all," I reply, trying to appear cool. He's clearly losing it. "I'm just looking for accurate information about this accident. The name of the company, for instance." I look around at the gaggle of distressed people. Nobody looks intoxicated to me. I notice that Jóa is busy taking photos, but keeping a low profile.

"They're from the Yumm candy factory in Akureyri," says Sigurpáll reluctantly.

"How big was the group?"

"Nearly thirty people. Some brought their husbands or wives along."

"Isn't that unusual, on these team-building trips?" I ask.

"Yes, kind of. But it was also supposed to be their annual staff party ending with a dinner in Akureyri this evening." He goes on: "I don't know if that dinner is going to happen."

"Yeah, well, it's not as if anyone died, is it?"

Now Sigurpáll is shaking from head to foot.

"Who is the woman who fell in the river?" I ask.

"She's the boss's wife. I don't remember her name."

"What about him?"

"Ásgeir Eyvindarson. He's in the ambulance. Unconscious, like her."

"What?" I ask. "What happened to him?"

"He jumped in after her," Sigurpáll replies. And it's as if the floodgates are opened. "I was in the boat ahead of them, and I didn't see what happened until too late. He jumped in, but he couldn't reach her. She was swept downstream, and then him too. It was a few minutes before we could fish them out."

"How many minutes, do you think?"

"I don't know. Five, maybe. Perhaps more. It all happened so fast."

"Weren't they wearing life vests?"

He gives me a scornful look. "Of course they were." Then he looks down and violently kicks a pebble toward the river before slouching off toward the café.

Jóa is in the doorway devouring an ice cream. *Some people are cooler than others*, I think. But I'm not laughing. I try to get into conversation with two police officers who are sitting in their squad car.

"We're just off," says the driver. "You can get in touch with the station at Akureyri later today. Or the hospital."

Suddenly a man's roar of pain resounds from the ambulance. I can't tell if the distress is mental or physical. Everyone turns in shock to look. At that very moment the ambulance backs up and sharply turns around. The police car drives off, followed by the ambulance. I watch them cross the river. The sirens start to wail, and the chilling noise, which you can never get used to, echoes out over the peaceful countryside.

2 SATURDAY

The mountains and ridges, which from the air look as sharp and forbidding as razor blades on end, appear quite harmless, a little rusty and worn, when seen from the ground. When I flew into Akureyri nearly a week ago, the snow in the ravines resembled pure white stripes on a gray woolen sweater. Now, as we drive down the Öxnadalur valley toward Akureyri, nothing is left of the snow but grubby patches here and there at the foot of the mountain slopes. We pass the occasional farmhouse. Rolls of hay in their white plastic packaging, scattered in the withered grass fields, are the only sign of habitation.

Most of the farms will probably soon be taken over by the banks or by the wealthy of Iceland, who see the future as opportunities for larger production units, enhanced profitability, and glossy annual reports.

The old stone cairns that used to mark the route through the mountains fly by, symbols of times long gone, an Iceland that will never return.

I am brought out of my musings by Jóa, who produces a plastic bag from the roadside café in Varmahlíd. She takes from it two small chocolate eggs and offers me one.

"It's a bit early, isn't it? A week before Easter. Aren't they for Easter Sunday?"

"That's so last century," answers Jóa like a continuation of my thoughts at the wheel. "Now everything is allowed, always."

She has already started on her egg. I make it clear to her that I can't drive and open the chocolate egg at the same time. She breaks it open and passes me the slip of paper with the proverb.

"What does it say?" she inquires.

"*What goes around comes around.*"

Jóa chuckles, inadvertently blowing bits of chocolate out of her mouth. "Gotcha!"

I grunt and chuck the proverb out the window. "What does yours say?"

"*You must be strong to endure the good times.*"

"Remember that, Jóa honey," I say with a smile. "Remember that your days of wine and roses with Ásbjörn and me in the north start today, but they won't last forever. You must be strong. Oh, yes, indeed."

She shakes her head gleefully. "At least I don't have a phobia about everywhere outside the city—not like some people."

"Do you mean me?" I ask, pretending to be offended. "I don't even know what that means. All I know is I'm a town mouse at heart."

And I also know in my heart of hearts, although I'm not about to say so to Jóa, that being exiled might do me good. I didn't say so to Hannes either, when he informed me of what had been decided. Yep, *informed.* I argued for the sake of arguing, without even knowing why. Hannes leaned over his scratched,

12

carved wooden desk at the *Afternoon News*, holding a thick cigar between the index and middle fingers of his right hand, knocked the ash off into the ashtray, turned his steady blue gaze upon me, stuck out his jaw, and said:

"My dear Einar."

When he addresses me like that, I know I've gotten to the point where I have no choice but to do what Hannes has decided for me.

"My dear Einar. I want you to do this..."

And that was that. I was to abandon my old beat, crime reporting in the capital area, to be transferred for an indefinite period up north to Akureyri, where Ásbjörn and I would be in charge of "strengthening the newspaper's position in the north and east of the country, during the period of rapid change and development that is now taking place there," as Hannes had put it in his editorial in the paper. I was to be responsible for the news side, while Ásbjörn would run the office, along with sales and distribution. Jóa would be assigned to us for the time being as our photographer.

Hannes is well aware that Ásbjörn and I don't get along. Ásbjörn is submissive and hesitant when he should be bold and decisive, stubborn and rigid where he should be open-minded and flexible. And he gets his panties in a twist if you tell him so. We're not a good combination.

"The Odd Couple?" Hannes had commented. "Yes, admittedly. But Ásbjörn was born and brought up in the east, and he went to Akureyri High School. He's familiar with the area. And you're our best newshound..."

Goddamn it.

"...and the one I trust best for real news content. And you've been sorting out your, how shall I put it, sir? Your lifestyle?"

Son of a bitch.

"And you will have plenty to keep you busy, which will be helpful to you in your battle with your demons. That is how I dealt with my own similar problems, sometime in the last century."

Fucking shit.

"Hermann and I are in agreement."

Oh my God. I thought of the new CEO of the *Afternoon News* and vice-chair of the board, Hermann Gudfinnsson. He attained that position after Hannes had cleverly maneuvered a merger with the Icelandic Media Company—the group owned by the wealthy Ölver Margrétarson Steinsson—to form the Icelandic Media Corporation. Hermann was a rich and respected economist when he was convicted, twenty years ago, of killing his wife, and now he's a reformed worker in the vineyard of the Lord. What I still don't get is what particular god Hermann is toiling for, in deed rather than word. But I suppose that's not my business.

Hannes went on, puffing at his cigar: "There is no way, at this time, when the pillars of society are creaking, not least in the media market, that we can take account of some old personal conflict between you and Ásbjörn. We've got a battle on our hands, and in this battle, all of us, and I mean *all*, must stand together. Anyone who doesn't has no place on our team. Ásbjörn was, as you are well aware, not a good news editor, not my cup of tea in that job. So he's not doing it anymore..."

"I'm not at all sure that his successor is any better," I interjected.

Hannes fumed: "You were offered the job yourself and turned it down."

The best decision I've ever made, I thought.

Hannes went on regardless. "I believe that Ásbjörn's abilities, his attention to detail, and his organizational skills will prove more useful in this important task, rather than handling paper clip purchasing and taxi receipts here at the head office. You and he, sir, are going north."

"And into the outer darkness," I added.

But I wasn't sure I meant it. I wasn't sure of anything. Except that it might be good to try something you haven't tried before. And tried again. And again.

I'm thinking of the biggest loss entailed by my exile: my daughter, Gunnsa. My only consolation is that she's planning to visit me at Easter. And I can always make the odd flying visit to the south.

It's close to six o'clock when we drive up Eyjafjördur, past the Hlídarbær community center, which, once, long ago, before the days of pubs and clubs in Iceland, fulfilled its function, but now seems to be an empty shell.

I switch the radio on for the evening news.

When I look out my window,
Many sights to see.
And when I look in my window,
So many different people to be
That it's strange, so strange...

The lyrics of the old pop song seep into my consciousness in the silence between me and Jóa, who is dozing next to me. She stirs as the singer belts out the final notes.

"*Season of the Witch*, from Donovan," says the DJ, speaking from Akureyri, capital of north Iceland. "The song was played for Skarphédinn and the other kids in the Akureyri High School Drama Group, who will be giving their first performance of *Loftur the Sorcerer* at Hólar on Holy Thursday. And for our last song on this Saturday before Palm Sunday, here's Donovan again. We'll be here again next week at the same time. Thank you for listening, and good-bye."

"Thanks to you too," mumbles Jóa.

And the gentle voice begins, as if chanting a rhyme, first with a quiet guitar accompaniment; then a touch of piano is added:

> *The continent of Atlantis was an island*
> *Which lay before the great flood*
> *In the area we now call the Atlantic Ocean.*
> *So great an area of land, that from her western shores*
> *Those beautiful sailors journeyed*
> *To the South and the North Americas with ease,*
> *In their ships with painted sails…*

Nice image, I think, losing myself in it.

"People are always claiming to have found traces of Atlantis here and there," Jóa suddenly remarks. "I remember there was some American who said he'd discovered ruins using sonar soundings on the floor of the Mediterranean, off the coast of Cyprus. And there was a German scholar who revealed Atlantis, using satellite photographs, on the salt plains of southern Spain. And a Swede said that the descriptions were more consistent with Ireland. It's only a question of time until someone finds Atlantis here in Iceland. We're always claiming to find what we want to find."

"I don't have a lot of luck with that," I remark.

"That's because you don't know what you want to find."

"Oh, yeah. But what descriptions do you mean? Are there accounts of Atlantis? Wasn't the whole place supposed to have sunk into the ocean without a trace more than twelve thousand years ago?"

"Er, it's a legend, Einar," Jóa replies, in rather too motherly a tone for my taste. "So far as I remember, in Greek mythology the gods are supposed to have been so enraged by the greed, immorality, and iniquity of those who lived in this land of milk and honey that they sent a tidal wave to destroy Atlantis. And since then people have always been searching for the lost island."

"How come you know so much about Greek mythology?"

"Hail Atlantis!" exclaims Jóa with the vocalist, and the music swells. "I know about all sorts of things, if you haven't noticed. I've even read Plato. Have you?"

"Yes, actually, I read him in high school," I haughtily reply. "He was an ancient Greek philosopher. I know these things. But what's he got to do with Atlantis?"

"He was the first person to give an account of Atlantis. And he was one of us."

"One of us?" I ask as we pass a sign welcoming us to Akureyri. "Or one of you?"

"Both!" chortles Jóa.

There is nothing on the evening news about an Akureyri woman being unconscious after having fallen into the glacial waters of the Jökulsá River.

Ásbjörn has found office accommodations for us in the heart of the town. The *Afternoon News* has its offices—three offices, reception, break room, and bathroom—on the upper floor of an old wooden building clad in red corrugated iron on Ráðhústorg, the Town Hall Square itself, at the corner of Hafnarstræti and Brekkugata. Ásbjörn, naturally, didn't waste money on renovations. When they open a new club, they rip out all the fixtures and start again, but Ásbjörn doesn't see the *Afternoon News* premises as a place of entertainment, but a workplace. So we move straight into the old offices of a wholesaler, with ocher-yellow paint peeling off the walls. Ásbjörn and his wife live on the floor above. Town Hall Square is an expanse of concrete with the odd leafless tree and deserted benches. The few people who venture out into the square appear to be kids on skateboards—much the same as in Reykjavík. Our competitors, the *Morning News* and the state radio station, both have their offices in a modern glass-and-concrete structure rather like a fish tank on the corner of Kaupvangsstræti and Glerárgata, at the southern end of the harbor. They have a breathtaking view of the fjord, and an American fast-food chain is conveniently located in the same building. Next to us, on the contrary, is one of the many travel agencies offering wilderness tours and all sorts of trips in the quest for what we want to find, without knowing what it is. The view from my office window is the cracked wall of the building next door.

All's quiet on the Akureyri front on a Saturday evening: the weekend edition has long been delivered to anyone who's interested. Nonetheless Ásbjörn is hanging over his computer in his office.

"How did it go?" he asks without looking up when I knock on the doorframe.

"Jóa got some pictures, and I did a rather uncomfortable interview with the organizer of the trip. He may be a great outdoorsman, but I think he needed trauma counseling as much as the rest of them."

"You can talk to Trausti about it, anyway," he curtly remarks over his shoulder. "He phoned and asked you to get in touch."

If I don't have a very high opinion of Ásbjörn, I'm not yet sure what I think of his successor in the news editor's chair: Trausti Löve—who in another lifetime worked with Ásbjörn and me as a temporary summer employee, when he and I, by pure chance, started out on our journalistic careers together on the late, lamented *People's Times*. Later he became a TV reporter and was once chosen "Iceland's Sexiest Man" in a popularity poll. I hear the office door open, followed by shrill barking. "Ásbjörn!" calls a husky female voice. "Ásbjörn Grímsson!" He turns off the computer and struggles to his feet, a stocky figure with a sagging ass. He quickly takes off his green slippers, which he has unfortunately brought with him from the head office in Reykjavík, and thrusts his feet into black fur-lined boots. Sometimes Ásbjörn reminds me of an overripe tomato on two legs, wearing green slippers. For a moment I feel a twinge of pity for him. Even sympathy.

His face is puffy and tired. His black hair, greasy and disheveled. He looks at me and says, in a not-unfriendly manner, "Please keep your cell phone turned on. I don't want to have to speak to Trausti about it. I've got enough on my plate."

I nod and accompany him out to the tiny reception area. Jóa is sitting drinking coffee as she watches the news on *Vision 2*, the *Afternoon News*'s new sister station. Karólína, Ásbjörn's wife, is hovering at the reception desk, where she sometimes helps out, and flicking through the Sunday edition of the *Morning News*, which is printed and distributed on Saturday evening. The couple's lapdog, a little white mutt with its body hair trimmed short but a sort of bouffant puff on his head, is tethered to the leg of the coffee table in the waiting area. The dog's name is Pal. He's keeping his mouth shut for the moment, but his stubby little tail wags when his other owner approaches.

"Look, Pal," says Karólína. "Daddy's here."

If Ásbjörn had a tail it would definitely be wagging now— the little dog's enthusiastic barking and tongue waving certainly cheer him up.

"Daddy's going to take Mommy and Pal out to the Bautinn Grill," remarks the Lady Wife from behind the *Morning News* to anyone who's listening. "Pal will get a treatie-weatie."

"Anything about that woman on *Vision 2*?" I ask Jóa.

"Not a peep," she answers, with a twinkle toward doggy and Dad.

"Thanks for the tip," I say to Ásbjörn, who's untying the dog from the table. "How did you hear about it?"

"I have my contacts," he replies self-importantly.

Out of the corner of my eye I see that Karólína has put the paper down and is looking at us with a surprised look on her face. I don't know much about their marriage, except that it is childless. I haven't really gotten to know the Lady Wife. Just shaken her hand at the paper's annual dinner-dance, my ability to stand upright permitting. Like her husband and me, she's on the wrong side of thirty-five. Her flat voice doesn't fit her appearance. She is tall and she must once have been slender, but she's getting a little softer and plumper at the waist. She has a long neck and a curved nose, so she looks a little like a bird, with pretty features and shoulder-length straight hair, bleached white. I've always had the impression that Karólína is about to explode from some internal tension, like a bird caught in a trap and longing to take flight.

When Mommy, Daddy, and the dog have gone I tell Jóa I must just quickly call the new news editor. She grunts and switches over to the news on the state TV station.

My office is an oversize closet. Although I've only been here a week it already has that lived-in look. Three shelves on one wall, laden with newspapers, books and papers, computer disks, old diaries, and all sorts of junk. My tattered old poster with the words of wisdom *A tidy desk is a sign of a sick mind* is on the wall, along with an old photograph, which was there when I arrived, of fishing vessels in Akureyri Harbor. That's all the view I have, other than the wall of the neighboring building.

I dig my phone out of the junk on my desk and call Trausti's cell phone. I'm pretty sure he'll be eating out with some other Beautiful People.

"Trausti," he answers. In the background is a hubbub of chatter and the clink of glasses.

"It's Einar," I say, lighting up a cigarette. "You wanted to talk to me."

"Hello, buddy," replies the news editor.

Yet another word I really loathe.

I can just see him in my mind's eye, in his trendy clothes, feasting on red wine and a steak marinated in brandy, as tan as a freshly minted chocolate Easter egg. I wonder what maxim this egg will produce. Could it be the old *Afternoon News* slogan— which has as yet survived the disruptions and merger, and which Ásbjörn has emblazoned on the outside of our outpost in the north: *Truth Be Told*?

The resonant and—in the opinion of TV viewers at least— confidence-inspiring voice continues: "Tomorrow I want you and Jóa to go east to Reydargerdi. Things got wild there last night, and it will probably be the same tonight. It may get out of hand at any time. *Riots in Reydargerdi* and all that."

"Are you talking about more fights? It's just the usual Icelandic weekend binge, Trausti. It's been going on ever since our Viking ancestors first got here."

"No, it hasn't. These are fights between Icelanders and immigrants. If you can't see the difference, you're just not competent, buddy."

Although I feel an almost overwhelming urge to stick my tongue out at the receiver, I resist it, since inanimate objects can't be held responsible. "You may not be aware that once upon a time everyone in Iceland was an immigrant," I remark with icy politeness. "You yourself are descended from immigrants of olden times. *Löve* doesn't sound like an Icelandic name to me. Or is there a difference I'm not seeing?"

There's a brief silence. Either he's considering what I've said or he's taking another bite of his steak.

"The difference," he finally says, "is that one is the past and the other is the present. Your job is to reflect the present, where you are."

"I've still got to write up the piece on the woman who fell in the glacial river..."

"That will be featured on all the radio and TV news bulletins tomorrow."

"I'm sure drunken reveling at Reydargerdi will be too. And Jóa's got exclusive pictures..."

"You can do that over the phone, while you're on the other story..."

"Couldn't I cover the Reydargerdi story by phone, then?" I continue to argue.

It would have been nice to have a leisurely Sunday stroll around "the town of prosperity and good fortune, the town of education, culture, and flowers," as Akureyri was called by local poet Davíd Stefánsson. To breathe in the sea air at the harbor, look out over the still waters of the fjord, walk up and down the Hafnarstræti pedestrian street, admire the botanical gardens, the high school, the picturesque old wooden houses, sneer at the modern concrete ones, have a cup of coffee in the artists' quarter, and go to morning service with Jóa in Akureyri Church, which stands on its hilltop site with its two towers, at the top of the stairway to heaven.

Or something. A bit too romantic, maybe. But something other than driving all the way to Reydargerdi. Maybe even just getting to know the route from my new home to my new workplace.

"I knew you were difficult, but I won't put up with this bullshit. You get over to the east with Jóa, and by dinnertime tomorrow I want an article with interviews and photos, and a mood piece, for Monday's paper. You can't do that by phone."

I know he's right. "Well, since you ask so nicely," I say. "But I'll have to send the article in on Monday morning. It will take eight or nine hours just to drive there and back."

The news editor laughs. "Buddy! We're a high-tech modern media company. You can take your laptop, write the piece at Reydargerdi, send it in with the photos, and then set off back to Akureyri."

The fucking slave driver is right again. Apart from the modern technology stuff, I'm having trouble getting used to the new press time of the newspaper, 9:00 a.m. instead of 11:00. "As in the neighboring countries" was the phrase Hannes used: always a favorite with those who want to justify some pointless change. In the case of the *Afternoon News* it means that the paper is put to bed the evening before, with hardly a chance of getting a new story on the front page in the morning. It also means that the name of the *Afternoon News* now makes no sense at all.

"OK. But then you'll have to allow me a bit more time after the weekend on the story about the high school students' production of *Loftur the Sorcerer* at Hólar. The first performance is on Holy Thursday."

"Hahahaha! Nice one!" Trausti Löve howls with laughter so the restaurant echoes with it. "Schoolkids performing What's-His-Face the Sorcerer! Oh, yeah, you can have plenty of time for a big news story like that. Of course! Why not? Ahahahahahaha!"

I don't let him throw me. "And I want some time to investigate the growing market in illegal drugs here in the north, as I told you before." He says nothing. Probably not listening. But I hear him laughing with a woman, who's suggesting he ought to be out of range, except hers.

"Everything all right then, buddy?" says Trausti cheerfully when he comes back on the line.

"I have a right to days off, like other people. Like you, for instance."

"Whatever," he says. "Whatever."

After Jóa and I have ordered a pizza and watched the weekly satirical news show—which I sometimes think is closer to the truth than the "real" news—we turn in to our separate bedrooms around ten. And I go to sleep, with my lorikeet by my side.

3 SUNDAY

Don't get me wrong about the lorikeet.

Ásbjörn had managed to arrange inexpensive furnished accommodations for me, the intrepid Akureyri reporter for the *Afternoon News*, in a row house in Hlídar, one of the new districts beyond the Glerá River. It's a lot bigger than my little basement pad back in Reykjavík—really quite luxurious. The kitchen is on the right of the entrance hall, then there's a large living/dining room with a TV and sound system, and, on the left, three bedrooms and a bathroom. Jóa has made herself at home in the first bedroom, and I'm in the back one. I envisage Gunnsa having the middle room. I can't begin to say how much I'm looking forward to her visit over Easter. Sometimes I think Gunnsa's more grown-up than her old dad. And one thing's for sure: if I'd had her scary experiences on our beach vacation last summer, I certainly wouldn't be as well balanced as she is now. I just don't know where she gets her mental strength. Definitely not from me, and hardly from her mother, Gulla. Sometimes it seems that genes simply mutate, through the grace of God.

But my accommodations aren't a bed of roses.

The apartment belongs to an old friend of Ásbjörn's who has gone abroad for postgraduate study. The advantage of this arrangement is that the apartment has everything you could possibly need in a home. But the disadvantage is that it has more than you could possibly need in a home. Never mind the cupboard in the middle bedroom crammed with broken toys, the piles of garments in my bedroom cabinets, and the no-smoking rule—which I was quick to violate. And never mind the shelves laden with glass geese, porcelain angels, and pottery cats, which I have clumsily knocked over, breaking necks and amputating wings and tails, and then inexpertly tried to glue back together. Never mind all that. No, it's the yellow lorikeet that shares my room. This little creature, which is the size of my hand, is alive and kicking. It lives in a gilded cage on a small table in one corner of the room. I have been entrusted with the important task of keeping this bundle of fluff in the land of the living. I'm required to feed it morning seed and evening seed, seed bars and seed clusters; give it fresh water regularly; and change the sand in the bottom of the cage. I'm even supposed to give the bird a bath in the sink now and then. In addition, several times a week I must close all windows and other exits, open the cage, and allow the bird to fly around the apartment at will, so that it will feel for a while as if it's actually free. In the life of this little bird, I am cast in the role of God Almighty. It's not a role I relish, maintaining such delusions. I have enough trouble maintaining the idea that I'm free myself.

Truth be told, I'm a little annoyed with Ásbjörn for foisting this responsibility upon me. When I suggested that maybe he and his wife could take the bird in, he snapped back: "It's that parrot's home. Do you want it to die of culture shock? And how on earth do you think Pal would react? You should just be grateful I took all the potted plants that have to be watered."

Hadn't thought of that. It crossed my mind to ask whether the relationship between the parrot and Pal might be something like the relationship between him and me. But that would get me nowhere.

Instead I have to follow the instructions on the daily checklist and listen to the bird chirping and whistling all day long and occasionally angrily shrieking with a noise like a machine gun.

I don't know whether my unwelcome roommate is male or female, or what its name is. But as I am forced into the role of God, I've decided the bird is a girl, named Polly. I felt a little better once that decision had been made.

Maybe Gunnsa will enjoy taking care of the bird when she comes to visit me.

Anyway, that's the whole story about the lorikeet.

The early morning silence between Jóa and me gradually wears off as the sun rises. It's a dry, relatively warm day.

"Yeah, apparently they're planning some kind of industrial production there. The raw material will be unhealthy people, and the end product will be healthy ones," I remark in answer to Jóa's question about the future of the community around Lake Mývatn since the mining of silica from the lake floor came to an end.

We've driven across the Víkurskard pass, past Ljósavatn Lake and Godafoss Falls, over the Reykjaheidi moors, and up Reykjadalur valley. We're leaving the Mývatn district to cross the mountain wilderness to Egilsstadir. Jóa points her finger at the map to guide me. I can find my way around all the bars in Reykjavík with my eyes closed, but all these place names simply confuse me.

"Well, well," says Jóa. "Environmentally friendly industry replacing pollution. Isn't that what they call it? Being green instead of destroying nature?"

I nod as I drive. "They're just as likely to go for an aluminum plant or steelworks or some such infernal monstrosity. That crowd in Reydargerdi had ideas about regenerating the local economy by some kind of nature resort for tourists. I went there last winter on another story, or maybe in the end it was the same story. I met the mayor and the leader of the council, and they said they had high hopes of attracting investors to their nature resort scheme, along with the pillar of the local community, Ásgrímur Pétursson. The development was supposed to be built on his family's land. And what came out of it?"

Jóa seems to be waiting for me to answer my own question. I recall reading the *Afternoon News* a few months later on a plane to a sunny destination with Gunnsa. Banner headline: *CONTRACT COMPLETED!* "A thousand new jobs in two years," the finance minister at the time, Ólafur Hinriksson, was quoted as saying, as he rejoiced over successful negotiations with Industria, an American conglomerate, to build an aluminum smelter in the East Fjords, along with the necessary hydroelectric development to power the plant. By a typical Icelandic coincidence, Ólafur happens to be married to Ásgrímur Pétursson's daughter—but that, of course, has nothing to do with anything.

"So the outcome is the same as ever," I continue to expound to Jóa. "Reydargerdi and the nearby communities are being overwhelmed by foreign laborers who come to Iceland for the thousands of jobs building hydro plants and factories, which are beneath the dignity of Icelanders themselves."

"But things are booming over there, aren't they?" Jóa interjects.

"A boom tends to entail a bust, though, doesn't it?"

"Come on, you know what I mean. That region was in terminal decline. You couldn't depend on the fisheries anymore, and people were leaving in droves. And now investment capital is pouring in."

"But is this really the end of the population drain?" I object, probably more to keep the conversation going than because I actually disagree with her. "Isn't it simply a question of foreigners coming in to replace the Icelanders who've left for the capital?"

"Have you got something against foreigners?"

"Not at all," I hasten to reply, recalling the arguments I had put to Trausti Löve on the phone. "All I mean is that a new regional imbalance takes over from the old one. So do we want a regional imbalance here in Iceland, or a global one?"

It's not so very long since I had an encounter with bigots, and it opened my eyes to my own prejudices. My new insight into my own position led me to a better understanding of where other people stand. I'm doing my best to grow up, but I take care not to rush the process.

Jóa seems to be reading my mind. "Is Gunnsa's black boyfriend still around?"

"Raggi? Oh, yes. Thank goodness. He's a fine young man."

"But it was a shock at first, wasn't it?"

"Yep, a serial shock," I admit ruefully. "First that my little Gunnsa was a fourteen-year-old adolescent. Then that she, as an adolescent, had started smoking. Then that she had a boyfriend. And finally that he was black. How much more could I be expected to take?"

"And then you had a crush on Rúna, his mom?"

I don't know what to say. "Yeah...something like that. I don't know..."

"So is it over?"

"Mind your own business! I don't know. I suppose so. I haven't spoken to Rúna for a while. I've found it hard to settle things in my mind. I'm still growing up."

So much for growing up.

"You can't have been that into her. When you can't make up your mind, that's usually what it's about."

"Maybe that's it. Perhaps somewhere in my unconscious I had a midlife fantasy of a nice little nuclear family. A bit unconventional and cobbled together, but a nuclear family all the same."

We don't speak for a while. There isn't much traffic on the mountain road. The landscape through the car windshield grows gradually more monotonous, reminiscent of a velvety black carpet with specks of dust here and there.

"Are you seeing anyone at the moment?" I ask.

"Not at this precise moment," replies Jóa, firmly ending that line of conversation.

I switch the radio on. On Channel 1 a church service is in progress. The pastor proclaims:

Today is Palm Sunday. And who was feted with palm leaves on this day, more than two thousand years ago? Jesus rode into Jerusalem as the triumphant Messiah. All around him people waved their palm leaves, giving him a hero's welcome. But a week later that had all changed, and the crowds encircled him shouting, "Crucify him!"

He goes on expatiating about Christ's final days in this life, which we recall now, during the most important week of the church year.

Holy Week is not a period of self-indulgence and gluttony, but of prayer and penitence. We are called to join Christ on his final journey and share his pain, for suffering is part of human life. And his story assures us that suffering is not pointless—not his, not our own. Jesus said: "Father, forgive them, for they know not what they do." And those words have meaning for all of us sinners—not only for those who crucified Christ at Golgotha. And also the words that, if we wish to be disciples of Christ, we too must shoulder his cross and follow every day in his footsteps. The cross of suffering is an indispensable aspect of the life of all Christians. The events of Holy Week serve to help us understand the suffering in our own lives...

"Thanks for that contribution, Einar." Jóa reaches out to turn the radio off. "I think that's enough suffering for now."

The first time I went to Reydargerdi, it was the middle of winter; the sun vanished from the sky shortly after midday, as if a light had been switched off. The little village by the sea huddled in the freezing whiteness, threatened by the snow-laden mountain slopes above. Paths had been trodden in the snow between buildings, and I saw the occasional person out and about. At the hotel, I was the only guest.

Now, as then, Hotel Reydargerdi reminds me strongly of a 1960s school building. But the array of national flags on flagpoles at the entrance, which limply drooped on my last visit, now flutter proudly.

The old concrete building that houses the municipal offices, across the main road from the hotel, and the plain boxy structure where Ásgrímur Pétursson runs his business, have both had a facelift: a paint job and repairs. The place is humming with life: cars, heavy machinery. Meaning: money. So this is what an Icelandic hamlet in the back of beyond, with a population numbering in the hundreds, looks like after an Extreme Makeover.

It's nearly one o'clock. "Since when do a journalist and a photographer get sent on a five-hour drive across moor and mountain just to cover a drunken weekend brawl?" I ask Jóa when I have squeezed the car into the hotel's packed parking lot.

"Since yesterday," she replies.

"And the only difference," I continue, "between this weekend brawl and the ones that have taken place in Iceland every weekend for decades, or maybe centuries, is that this time the fighting is between groups who speak different languages or have skins of different colors or eyes that look different. What the hell is happening?"

"I think your argument may be a tiny bit contradictory, dear boy," says Jóa as she steps out of the car toting her camera bag and adjusting her dirty-blond ponytail.

I turn the engine off and open my door. "Surely that comes as no surprise?" I ask with an injured look. "I can't keep up with all the contradictions that are constantly being forced upon me. And there were enough of them to begin with."

Reydargerdi Police Station occupies one end of the ground floor of the municipal offices. Access is from the far end. The "station" apparently comprises a shabby reception desk and two offices. Somewhere beyond them, I suppose there must be some cells. After all, what's a police station without cells?

The beautification of the village has not yet reached in here. Gray paint is peeling off the walls, which are cracked and dented, as if they might have been kicked by a horse. Nor, apparently, has it had any effect on Chief of Police Höskuldur Pétursson, who offers us a seat in an office that's about twice the size of my little closet in Akureyri. Höskuldur is a squat man in his late fifties, with bristling gray hair and a general grayness about him. Below his heavy-lidded eyes are deeply marked circles, dark as bruises against his square, good-humored countenance. There's something familiar about that face.

I start my tape recorder.

"Well, yes, it's been quite a difficult weekend," he sighs, "but nothing to make a big fuss about. Just people out having fun, really."

"Where was this?"

"At the new bar, Reydin, just down the road here."

I restrain myself from making a silly remark about Rage at Reydin. But it will do for a headline.

"So the village has a bar now?"

Höskuldur becomes animated: "Oh, yes, indeed. And another one's due to open soon. The hotel simply can't cope with all the new customers who are coming in."

"Well, that's excellent news," I comment. "But how did this 'fun' start, if that's what you call the fight?"

"Well, it's never easy to say how these things start. It's easier to say how they end. They end up here. With us." His chuckle is strained.

"So who was fighting?"

"That's not easy to say either. When you have a free-for-all, it's not easy to say who's fighting and who's not."

There's a lot here that's not easy to say.

"Were they locals?"

Höskuldur shrugs his beefy shoulders. "It's not easy to say these days who's a local and who isn't."

Yawn. I glance at Jóa, who's sitting in the corner with a wry expression on her face. She starts taking pictures of the chief, who responds by sitting up straight in his chair and assuming a serious expression.

"I see," I lie. "Was anyone seriously hurt?"

"One fractured hand, one concussion, two black eyes, one nasty kick to the groin, a selection of abrasions and bruises. That's about it, in the end."

"So nobody was armed? No knives, broken bottles, anything like that?"

He leans back in his chair. Jóa has put her camera down.

"Oh, yes, now you mention it. A few cuts here and there. A few stitches here and there."

"What about arrests?"

"Just some guests we put up here for the night."

"Last night and the night before?"

"Five the night before last. Two last night. Nothing more than that."

"So the police have no concerns about a dangerous and uncontrollable situation arising when two groups come into conflict? The locals and the incomers?"

Höskuldur hesitates. "Of course we're concerned about violence and drunkenness. We always have been. Nothing's changed."

"And hasn't the problem gotten worse since so many people moved into the area to work on the construction projects?"

"You listen to me, young man," says the chief, leaning across his desk toward me. "Of course there are more problems when the population of a little place like this suddenly increases. There are more people, more jobs, and that means more tasks for us. That's what we prefer to call them, not 'problems.' And we deal with our tasks as they come up. And I hope we are going to be left alone to deal with them. It's never a good idea to add fuel to the flames."

"Oh? Is something on fire here then?"

Höskuldur's friendly expression has been steadily wearing thin since the start of the interview. Now he is the picture of distrust. "Please, I would ask you, as a responsible reporter, not to take my remarks out of context. I admit that these are sensitive times here. But in such delicate situations, it's necessary to act responsibly. And that applies to the media too."

"I couldn't agree more," I reply. "But isn't it sometimes a fine line between acting responsibly and presenting a false, or at least edited, version of the truth? Isn't that a matter of responsibility too?"

He stands up behind his desk and extends a meaty hand to shake mine. "I hope I can trust you to do the former without doing the latter," he says, his friendliness restored. "I hope you will live up to that trust."

The reception area of the hotel, on the opposite side of the street, is as neat and tidy as before. But the bare and unadorned interior has given way to a riot of flowers and potted plants in every corner. Behind the desk is the long-faced, sunken-cheeked man I remember from my previous visit, who owned and ran the place with his Thai wife. Still long-faced and sunken-cheeked, he is now better dressed and groomed.

I introduce Jóa and myself, mentioning that I stayed at the hotel last winter.

"Yes, I think I remember you," says the man, whose name is Óskar. "From the *Afternoon News*, weren't you?"

"That's right," I say, looking around and glancing into the crowded restaurant. "Things have changed a bit since last year. There was hardly anyone here then. Including me."

"Yes, it's extraordinary."

"So you and your wife are still running the hotel? Finally cashing in?"

"Unfortunately not. We leased the business from the municipality, as you may remember. We'd been running it for three years. But the village authorities revoked the agreement and sold the hotel to Ásgrímur Pétursson—lock, stock, and barrel. We just work here now."

"What a bummer! When business finally picked up!"

"There's no point thinking about that. We get our wages. And we don't have to worry anymore."

"But you wouldn't have to anyway, would you, now that things are looking up?"

Apparently stoical, he replies: "So be it." Then adds: "Fortunately we're Buddhists."

Jóa says she's going out to take some pictures of village life. I explain to the innkeeper why we have come to the village and tell him about our conversation with the chief of police.

"Höskuldur isn't Ásgrímur Pétursson's brother for nothing," he remarks with a smile.

Now I realize why I thought there was something familiar about Chief Höskuldur.

"He's all right, apart from that. And I think it's better to play these things down rather than making a fuss. They can get out of control."

"What really happened?"

"You can't quote me on this. Not a word. I don't want any trouble."

"No, not a word. I'm just looking for information."

He ushers me into his office behind the reception desk. We sit side by side in two armchairs in front of his desk.

"When you get a melting pot of people of various origins," he says, "Poles, Portuguese, Chinese, Dutch, Latvians, Estonians, and the rest—it can make a curious cocktail. People bring with them all their different cultures, beliefs, social backgrounds, education, and experience. Not to mention languages. And they generally don't know much about Icelandic culture and natural conditions, or the weather. Everybody must be aware of that, or at least they should be. But the problems start to arise when you add the Icelanders into the mix. My wife and I knew all about that long before people started flooding into the village. My wife's from Thailand, as you may recall."

I nod. I had observed some prejudice against her. "So are the Icelanders responsible for this drunken violence on the weekends?"

"That's how it started. But it's not necessarily the case now. After a while everyone gets to feel insecure and tense and angry. The mixture gets shaken up."

"And becomes a Molotov cocktail?"

"No, not at all. It's nowhere near that bad. Not yet. And the good things here far outweigh the bad. So far."

"Have you had any problems with gangs?"

He glances around as if to ensure that no one is eavesdropping. "There are a few guys, maybe four or five of them, who seem to get something out of it." He speaks softly. "They egg each other on, with insults, insinuations, and aggression. Usually it's about women or some form of racial slur. Or just xenophobia, if there's no racial angle. It's as stupid as you can imagine."

"Icelanders?"

"Well, oddly enough…most of them are Icelanders, but one of them is the son of a man who came in from somewhere in the Baltic or the Balkans or wherever. I don't remember exactly. They've formed a gang, for their own entertainment. But these troublemakers, whatever their ethnicity, seem to seek each other out. I've actually heard that they're getting bored with starting fights here in the village, so they go over to Akureyri now and then for a bigger thrill. The night before last, it was one of the Icelanders who suffered the most damage. I hear he's rather sore around the crotch today."

"Who is he?"

"A young man of about twenty. Agnar Hansen."

"Not, perchance, related to Jóhann Hansen, leader of the local council?"

"His son, as a matter of fact. The boy's an alcoholic, of course. Or worse."

"Where can I find him?"

"They hang out at Reydin. But I shouldn't think they'll be welcome there much longer. The owner's not happy about the reputation his place is getting. Naturally enough. There's a lot at stake for everyone here. But especially for some individuals."

"Who's the owner?"

"Who?" echoes Óskar in surprise. "The Owner, of course. With a capital O."

"Really?" I exclaim. "But Ásgrímur's hardly likely to kick out the son of his best friend and ally, Mr. Big, the local boss?"

"There's only one boss here. And bosses know which side their bread is buttered on. Isn't that what it's all about?"

"Ah, yes. What happened about that planned nature resort that was supposed to be developed on Ásgrímur's land outside the village?"

"That came to nothing. Ásgrímur has leased the land to Industria Corporation and their subcontractors for accommodations for their workers. Made a very sweet deal too."

Well, I never.

Reydin looks as if it may have started life as a warehouse. The wood has been polished up. Posts and beams support a lofty roof over the long, narrow room. On either side are wooden tables and chairs in two rows and, at the end of the space, a big, solid wood bar. I wonder briefly whether it's due to growing multicultural influence that the bar is open on one of the high holy days of the Christian calendar, Palm Sunday. In the old Lutheran Iceland of my youth, no business could open its doors on that day. There are about twenty customers in the bar, scattered at six tables, most drinking beers. A few have opted for coffee. The majority are male and Icelandic, but other languages can be heard through the babble. Over the loud-speakers, rock veteran Bubbi Morthens is singing one of his classic songs about a life of toil in the fishing industry.

Jóa and I have agreed that she will sit in a corner with her camera and keep a low profile. I approach the bar. I don't feel I'm attracting any particular attention. The bartender is a gorgeous young girl who asks with a smile what I would like.

"I'll have a Coke, please."

When she's finished serving me, I say quietly, but without whispering, that I'm looking for Agnar Hansen.

Without hesitation, she calls out "Agnar!" toward two young men sitting at a table with glasses of beer. "There's someone here looking for you."

I go over to their table. "Hi. I'm Einar, from the *Afternoon News*. Which of you is Agnar?"

I see at once that the answer is obvious.

"Me," mumbles one of them. He wears his blond hair in a po-nytail. He looks as if he was once fit and healthy, but he is clearly declining physically and mentally. His face is dull and flushed, marked with abrasions and bruises. On his right wrist is a filthy bandage, and he has a cut on the back of his left hand. He is wear-ing a sleeveless blue top and jeans. No tattoos. No swastikas.

There's something odd about Agnar's posture in his chair. As if his crotch may be hurting.

"Sorry to disturb you. May I sit down for a minute?"

The other kid, who looks a little younger than Agnar, gets up and walks off. Agnar offers me his chair.

"Are you going to write about this brutal attack on me on Friday?" he asks hoarsely. He has long, protruding front teeth, on which he wears a retainer.

"That's right," I answer, smiling sweetly. "Will you tell me about it?"

"Absolutely," he replies, looking at me from bloodshot blue eyes.

I turn my tape recorder on. He recounts all the aggression, violence, and abuse to which he, in his innocence, was subjected that evening. "Just look at me," he remarks, scandalized, pointing out his injuries.

"Yes, I see."

"But you're only seeing part of it."

"What started it?" I inquire.

He drinks deeply from his beer. "I don't remember, man. But look at me!"

"Wasn't it you and your friends that started it?"

He shakes his head, and slams his fist down on the table so the beer glasses rattle and my Coke spills. "These people—you can't say anything to them!"

"What people?"

"Look, you put a photo of me in the paper looking like this. Then they'll see what these people are capable of."

I give Jóa a wave. I'm not going to get anything useful out of Agnar Hansen. I take my leave, but he doesn't seem to notice. While Jóa is taking pictures of the unspecified damage inflicted by unspecified thugs, I go back to the bartender, who is polishing glasses with a practiced hand.

"You're new around here," she smiles. I introduce myself yet again and explain what I'm doing in Reydargerdi.

She says her name is Elín. She's lived here all her life.

"I was intending to take off and head for the city, but then the money came pouring in."

"So you're going to stay on in Reydargerdi?"

"I'm not planning to stay here till I die," says Elín. "But at least now I won't be broke when I leave."

"Take the money and run?"

She gives me a sweet smile. "Pretty much. Can I offer you a beer? On the house?"

I stop dead in my tracks. Not so long ago I'd have jumped at such an offer and wondered if she had anything more in mind. But not now. "No, thank you. Got to keep a clear head on the job." I gesture toward the shelves laden with alcohol behind her. "You must know all about that?"

She nods and returns to polishing the glasses.

"It's rather hard to get a clear idea of what happened," I say. "Can you help me at all?"

Without hesitation, she replies: "Just Agnar, out for a good time. Blind drunk as usual. And he'd probably smoked a few joints too and maybe sniffed something. He and two of his friends were pestering a Portuguese couple, coming on to the woman. The man tried to get them to go away and leave them alone. But they just got more agitated, and then the woman burst into tears. Three Poles from the next table intervened, and that's when everything got out of hand."

"So it's not a question of racial conflict or xenophobia or any-thing like that?"

"Superficially, maybe. But one of Agnar's gang is a foreigner. I've known Agnar since we were kids. He was a nice boy, a good kid. But he had a rough time in his teens. Children of powerful people tend to get bullied. And he was victimized because of his dad and his buck teeth. They used to call him the Hansen Hare. Agnar's been using since he was fifteen, and he's getting worse and worse. His only real problem is that he hates himself."

So, equipped with all I've learned and quotations from Chief of Police Höskuldur Pétursson, I do my best to write a responsible article about the "Turmoil in Reydargerdi." The innkeeper generously allows me to sit in his office, polishing my piece on the computer screen, moving sentences back and forth, changing emphasis here, adding a proviso there. It's nearly 8:00 p.m. when I reach my final destination.

My headline isn't, after all, *Rage at Reydin*. It is:

SENSITIVE TIMES IN REYDARGERDI
says chief of police
Seven in custody on the weekend after bar brawl

I submit my piece online, and Jóa sends her photos in. I'm not looking forward to the four-hour drive in the dark across the highlands back to Akureyri. Then I remember the woman who fell into the river. I phone Akureyri District Hospital. The patient is still unconscious. It appears that she suffered a severe blow to the head, although she was wearing a safety helmet. She is believed to have hit the rocks face-first when she fell into the icy water. They can give no information about the woman's prognosis, but I learn that the husband regained consciousness soon after the incident and was discharged. He is as well as can be expected and is with his wife.

So we employ the latest technology to send our account and photos of the trip that ended so tragically. And finally Jóa and I embark on our own journey into the wilderness.

4 MONDAY

I am jolted awake as I sit in my closet with my feet on the desk, dozing. Someone's shaking me and shouting. What's up? Is this, finally, the End of the World?

I swing around in my chair. Ásbjörn is standing there, his bloated face deathly pale with distress. I'm still confused.

Are we under attack by terrorists?

"Pal's missing! Einar! Pal's missing!"

I rub my eyes. I'm dog-tired. Jóa and I took turns at the wheel on the way home. We didn't get back to Akureyri until almost two o'clock last night. Jóa's probably still fast asleep in bed.

I glance at my watch. It's nearly 1:00 p.m.

"Sorry, Ásbjörn. Would you mind saying that again?"

"Pal is missing."

I've never seen him so upset. I want to laugh, but I can't find the energy. So I say:

"I'm sorry to hear that. What happened?"

Ásbjörn paces back and forth across the floor, two steps each way. "Karólína took him for his walk this morning as usual and let him off the leash for a run on the hillside below the church.

She's been doing it every day since we came here, and there's never been any problem. Pal's well brought up. He knows what's allowed and what isn't. He always comes back, and he always obeys when we call him. But this time…"

He takes out a polka-dot handkerchief and blows his nose.

"What happened this time?" I inquire.

"Some woman stopped Karólína to ask for directions. When she was gone, and my wife started looking around for Pal, he wasn't there. Disappeared. Into thin air."

Ásbjörn repeats the fact, as if unable to believe it.

"She called and called and searched and searched…"

"And Pal had simply vanished? Into thin air?" I remark.

He shakes his head, over and over again. "You may find this amusing, Einar. But it isn't, not for Karólína. It isn't amusing for us."

I stand up and pat him on the shoulder. "No. I understand that it's been a shock for you. But have you contacted the police? Perhaps someone's found Pal and taken him down to the station?"

He doesn't seem to hear me. "We've been all over the town center, and we've driven all around the suburbs. It's as if…"

"As if the earth had swallowed him?"

He gazes soulfully at me.

"I say again, Ásbjörn—and please listen to me—what about the police? Have you called the police?"

"Yes, I have an old friend on the force here, and he's been asking around. But no one has contacted them. In fact, he's even exceeded his authority and asked the police officers on the beat to keep their eyes open. But nothing…"

"Hang on. When did this happen?"

"Nine o'clock this morning."

"But that's only four hours ago. You must be patient. Of course the dog will turn up."

"You don't understand, Einar. Pal's no ordinary dog. He's very sensitive to change. New people. New places…"

He's not the only one, I think to myself. I don't know what to say next.

I lead Ásbjörn to the break room and pour us both a coffee, black without sugar. We stand there for a while, sipping at our drinks.

"Where's Karólína?" I ask.

"She's out looking for him. She's absolutely devastated. I don't know…she might…I don't know." He shakes his head again, as if he hopes to shake something loose.

"I suppose Pal has a collar with his name and address?"

"Only for our address in Reykjavík. During the move, we forgot to update it."

"Is there anything I can do to help?" I cautiously offer.

He hesitates, then summons up courage. "Could you do a short interview with Karólína for tomorrow's paper, with a photo of Pal? Maybe someone will recognize him."

I'm lost for words.

"It would make her feel so much better," he adds with an expression that combines embarrassment and entreaty in about equal proportions.

"Well, Ásbjörn, that would hardly count as news. You know that as well as I do."

He looks down. "I know. Of course. But I was hoping you could find an angle. Human interest. Something like that. For the inside pages."

I think about it. *Dog Goes Missing* isn't much of a headline. Then I have an idea.

"Maybe we could place Pal in a wider context. The move to a new home, getting lost. We could see Pal as a newcomer here, just like us. Or the outsiders in Reydargerdi…"

Ásbjörn flings up his hands in delight and smiles from ear to sticking-out ear. Quite unprecedented, and more than a little disquieting.

"Brilliant! Abso-fucking-lutely brilliant!"

Never before have I heard this overgrown Boy Scout use such language. He's clearly beside himself.

"Einar!" he exclaims. "That's pure genius! Thank you, with all my heart."

I think I spot a tear in his eye.

And when I've created a little canine drama, with an interview with a woman on the verge of a nervous breakdown, and sent it south to the head office accompanied by a photo of the Missing Mutt, I find myself at a loss. What on earth am I doing here? What have I got myself into? Has the world become a madhouse? And am I the maddest, baddest of them all?

I have the impression that news editor Trausti Löve would have answered *yes* to the last of my questions. "Excuse me, but do you think we've launched an Akureyri branch, at vast expense, just so that we can advertise for lost dogs?" he snapped.

But I'd got all my ducks in a row. I'd called Hannes and explained the situation.

"I feel we should do this as a favor to Ásbjörn, my dear sir," he said. "But it will be up to you to ensure the paper is not flooded with more stories of lost dogs, or cats, in Akureyri. We can't allow this to become a precedent. We have more important uses for our column space. Such as the article from Reydargerdi you and Jóa contributed to today's paper. Excellent work."

I thanked him, on both counts. Then I went on: "I have my doubts about this Akureyri business, Hannes. I'm not at all sure it's going to work. I don't like…"

"Nonsense!" replied Hannes. "Things are progressing in the right direction. We're already seeing increased sales in the north and east of the country—subscriptions are up, and also retail sales and advertising. It's all going as planned. You must give it time, sir, time."

In my case, giving it time is largely a matter of hanging in here until my daughter comes to visit me.

What are those naked people up to?

I gaze up at the painted ceiling of the whitewashed Café Amor on Town Hall Square. But I soon get a stiff neck, so instead I look at the view from the window, at the *Afternoon News* offices across the square, and the National Bank next door, like a miniature version of their Reykjavík headquarters. And the square itself seems like a miniaturized version of Ingólfstorg square in Reykjavík.

Then I swing my head back again to contemplate the naked people on the ceiling.

The café takes its name from the god of love. Are the naked people Doing It? Nope. They're dropping glasses and cups… I make no more progress in my critique of the ceiling art. Jóa sweeps in and joins me at the table.

"What are you having?"

"Cappuccino. You want one?"

"Not now. I'm going to take a look around town and take some pics for our files. Can I have the car?"

"No problem," I reply, handing her the keys and pointing out my heap of rust, parked outside a shop on the left of the square.

It is four o'clock this Monday afternoon. The weather has warmed up, overcast and windless. I should think the locals may be worried about the lack of snow on the ski slopes. They've been advertising for weeks that ski conditions would be excellent on the Akureyri pistes over Easter.

"But I really think we should be allowed to go home early, after all the rushing around we did over the weekend."

"I agree," says Jóa. "When shall I pick you up?"

"Oh, about five thirty. Ásbjörn's on his way over here. Asked me to meet him. Don't know why. He's awfully upset about the mutt."

"Poor guy. His wife's a bit odd, don't you think?"

I shrug and light a cigarette.

Jóa stands up. "Have you stopped drinking completely, Einar?"

I make a face. "I don't know. How do you ever know whether anything's stopped completely?"

"But why did you stop?"

"Well, Hannes made it clear to me that the paper's tolerance quota had run out."

"Surely that wasn't the first time?"

"No, not at all. But somehow I couldn't go on like that. I'd had enough of myself. I didn't feel I could spend the rest of my life with Jim Beam as my only companion. You know, Jim once said to me: *I'm good company along the way, but I'm not good at being in charge.* I wanted to show Ole Jim that I'm in charge, not him. I suppose that was it…"

"But why didn't you go into rehab, like everyone else?"

"Oh, I can't do what everyone else does. I loathe uniforms. Can you imagine me in regulation pajamas, robe, and slippers?"

She grins. "Maybe not."

"It's OK. I'm doing fine."

Lying through my teeth.

"Good," says Jóa with a farewell salute.

As I order another cappuccino I see Ásbjörn bustling across the square toward me. *Is he feeling like I did last summer, when Gunnsa went missing on our vacation?* I wonder.

He orders a beer and takes a seat next to me, sweaty and shaky.

"I just want to thank you again, Einar, for being so helpful to Karólína and me."

"I'm glad to help, Ásbjörn. I just hope it leads to something."

He sits in silence and drinks deeply of his beer before changing his mind and returning most of it to the glass.

I wait for him to speak.

He takes another drink, a big one, swallowing this time. "I, um...," he mumbles, then clears his throat. "I...Something odd is happening, Einar. I know we haven't been close friends—far from it. I know you find me...how can I put this..."

"Not necessarily the best company?"

"Yes, that'll do. And the feeling is mutual. But I want to ask your views on something..." He hesitates. "Something odd is happening. I'm getting mysterious phone calls. At work and at home. Sometimes at night."

"Ah," I remark. I lean toward him across the table, my curiosity aroused. "What's so mysterious about these calls?"

"The person always hangs up when I answer. Karólína has answered twice, and those were hang-ups too. It's driving her crazy."

"Do you have caller ID?"

"Yes, but it just says *unknown number.*"

"Isn't it possible that you're using a phone number that someone else had before? That the caller's trying to reach another person?"

Ásbjörn takes another sip of his beer.

"And it could be more than one person trying to reach them?"

"Yes, I've considered that. Thousands of times. But it doesn't make sense. Then I wouldn't be getting calls at work too. Those phone numbers are new."

I have a thought. "That's true. Have you spoken to your policeman buddy?"

He shakes his head.

"Have you any idea who it could be? Can you think of anyone?"

As I finish speaking, the café door is flung open, and the good ship Karólína steams over to our table. I don't like the expression on her face, but Ásbjörn has his back to her and doesn't notice the trouble heading our way.

"What is the meaning of this!" she shrieks.

Taken aback, Ásbjörn awkwardly struggles to his feet.

"Little Pal's missing, and you sit here at the bar enjoying a beer! I just don't know..."

"But Karó dear, it's only a half-pint of beer..."

I haven't heard his nickname for his wife before.

"...and I haven't even drunk half..."

"You half-wit! You're coming with me right now, Ásbjörn Grímsson, to help me search. I'm speechless..."

And with that, Ásbjörn Grímsson is led away in custody.

I've just gotten back to my desk, and I'm about to pick up the phone to call the hospital when the goddamned cell phone starts yapping at me.

"Listen, great doggy detective," cackles Trausti Löve, "are you forgetting *Question of the Day*? It was supposed to be in an hour ago."

Son of a bitch.

"Ohhh," I groan. "Yes, I'd forgotten that ridiculous bullshit. I've been toiling away all weekend and all day. Can't you let me off...?"

"Nope. You can't get out of it. It was discussed and decided. Once a week, on Tuesdays to be precise, the *Question of the Day* comes from Akureyri. Or wherever you happen to be at the time. It's all part of the deal, buddy."

"And what on earth am I supposed to ask them?"

"Not my problem. *What's your favorite place to party?* for instance. That should be easy enough for you. Get to it."

I call Jóa's cell phone.

"Hello," she says. There's something odd about her voice.

"Hi. Look, apparently we've got to go out on the street and do *Question of the Day*. I'd forgotten all about it. Can you come right away?" I turn around.

"OK." Jóa is standing in the doorway with her phone to her ear.

Fortunately for us, the passers-by in Town Hall Square are in a good mood.

All looking forward to participating in the sufferings of Christ over Easter, no doubt. Within ten minutes we have our answers to the urgent question *What's your favorite place to party?*

The Sjallinn disco. Café Akureyri. The Vélsmidjan bar. Glaumbær.

Glaumbær? In Reykjavík? But it burned down thirty years ago. *That's right. No other place has ever been as good.* I don't suppose I have to specify the age of the person who gave that answer.

Now all I need is one more victim.

Three young girls walk into the square from Hafnarstræti, apparently in high spirits. They are convulsed with laughter when

I stop them and ask if they would mind answering the *Question of the Day*.

"Who's going to answer?"

They keep on giggling. I wonder if they've been smoking funny cigarettes.

All three are wearing low-riding jeans, exposing bare midriffs.

"Sólrún, you answer it," says one of them.

"Yeah, Sólrún," adds the other. "Answer what you said before."

Sólrún is a pretty girl, a little bit chubby. Under her jacket she is wearing a sweater so low-cut that I very nearly forget what the *Question* is.

"All right," says Sólrún, raising a clenched fist as if taking part in a political demonstration. "I'll answer."

"And your last name?"

"Bjarkadóttir."

"What do you do, Sólrún?"

"I'm a student at the high school."

Jóa takes a photo and goes off to send her pics in.

"What's your favorite place to party?"

"Kjartan Arnarson's dick."

All three girls burst out laughing.

"What's your favorite food?" I ask without a smile.

"Same answer!" gasps Sólrún. They fall about in gales of laughter.

"And your favorite drink?" But they have moved on, spluttering with giggles.

The news editor is in a ferocious temper. No doubt he's late for his next gourmet dinner. "Einar, it isn't rocket science. Even you ought to be able to cope with it. There are five answers to the

Question of the Day. Not four, not three, not two, not one. Five. F-I-V-E. I've got five photos here and only four answers. Where's the fifth?"

"It's not fit to print," I reply.

"Oh? Why not?"

"Believe me. It isn't."

"You mean the answer given by high school student Sólrún Bjarkadóttir?"

"Yes, that's the one I mean."

"So what did she say?"

"She said her favorite place to party was Kjartan Arnarson's dick."

A choking gasp from the news editor. "Who's Kjartan Arnarson?"

"I don't know, and I don't want to know."

"Come on, Einar. It's just some high school joke. It's fun. A young, plain-speaking voice in the paper. Of course we'll print it."

I feel sweat beading on my brow.

"Are you crazy? It's out of the question."

"It's not for you to say. It's my decision, buddy."

"But…but…whoever he is, that poor guy…and I think the girl was high."

"So? That's her problem. Not ours. Really, the things I have to deal with…," grumbles Trausti Löve as he hangs up.

The woman who fell into the glacial river is dead. She never regained consciousness. Her name was Ásdís Björk Gudmundsdóttir. Fifty-five years old, she is survived by her husband and a grown son.

Jóa has been in bed for ages by midnight when I abandon my attempts to drop off. I get up, check on Polly—who is fast asleep with her head under her wing—and go into the living room to consult the telephone directory.

Kjartan Arnarson is listed in Akureyri. Profession: high school teacher.

Holy fucking shit.

5 TUESDAY

A jolly little family is waiting for me in the newspaper offices when I arrive there around midday after a sleepless night. As I step across the threshold, I'm greeted with applause and cheerful barking. In the reception area Ásbjörn stands with Karólína, cradling Pal in her arms. All are wreathed in smiles. In the corner, Jóa is smirking.

"It worked!" exclaims Ásbjörn. "A girl brought Pal in just now. Her mother noticed the article in the paper this morning."

"Where did they find him?" I ask, patting the excited little creature.

"He'd gotten lost down on the docks, and the girl spotted some boys about to throw him in the sea. She just managed to rescue him." Ásbjörn concludes his account with a melodramatic shudder.

With her free hand, Karólína dries her eyes. "How can such boys have been raised? How could anyone treat such a sweet little doggie that way?"

I seem to remember her subjecting her husband to not-dissimilar treatment only yesterday.

"Sometimes humans are the only beasts that deserve the name," remarks Ásbjörn as emphatically as before, before continuing more cheerfully: "Anyway. All's well that ends well."

Karólína kisses the dog right on the snout. "Mommy and Daddy have got their Pal back."

"Oh, yes, indeed," I say, entering my closet. I don't expect things to be quite so rosy there.

And I'm right. On top of the piles of papers on my desk are three message slips. The first is from a man named Kjartan Arnarson, asking me to call. The second from Hannes, telling me to call. And the third from some woman. I shut my door, open the window with the view of the neighboring wall, and light up. Then I summon up courage and call Kjartan Arnarson.

A youthful male voice answers, "Kjartan."

"This is Einar, from the *Afternoon News*. I had a message to call you. I think I know why."

Silence. He takes a deep breath. "You think you know why, do you? You think you know what you've done to me?"

"I think I know what harm the comments have done you. And I can hardly express how much I deplore it."

"Goddamned hypocrite. Fucking duplicity." He does not raise his voice, in spite of the intemperate language. "Why on earth did you print that nonsense?"

"I know I can hardly expect you to believe me, but the comments were published against my wishes."

"No, you can't expect me to believe that. I just thank God that I'm not married and haven't any children. Can you imagine the damage such an affair would do to a man's marriage and family?"

"Yes, I can."

I've been debating whether my loyalty to the *Afternoon News* extends as far as Trausti Löve. I've reached the conclusion that it doesn't. Trausti betrayed me. I owe him nothing.

"I told the news editor in Reykjavík what the girl said and made it clear that it wasn't fit to print. But he decided to publish it anyway."

Kjartan laughs sarcastically. "You're all the same, passing the buck. Oh, yes, you're men of honor."

"So you've already spoken to Trausti Löve?"

"Yes. He told me all the Akureyri content comes from you."

"That is so. But I don't decide what is printed and what isn't."

He says nothing.

"Will you give me an hour? I must speak to the editor of the paper. The buck stops with him. Can I call you back?" I say.

"Tell him I'm lucky not to lose my job. And tell him Sólrún Bjarkadóttir was suspended for a month. I interceded with the principal on her behalf, and he agreed to withdraw the suspension. She received a reprimand instead, for now."

"So the principal believed you?"

"Sólrún admitted at once that it had been a joke that went too far. She's a wreck. She's just a young girl, trying to be cool. That anyone could do such a thing to a kid…"

We say our good-byes, coolly on his side. Now for Hannes.

"Hannes, do you understand now why I was unhappy about Trausti being appointed news editor?" I ask, temper fraying.

"Calm down, sir, calm down. I saw that awful blunder this morning, and I wanted to hear your side before going any further."

I explain what happened.

"Is this our new news-gathering policy?" I angrily expostulate. "Am I supposed to put up with this unprincipled clown, who's been thrown off TV? He's allowed to run amok, playing stupid tricks, and with no idea of the bigger picture. He can only do harm to the paper and its staff. And—most important of all—destroy the lives of innocent people. Just to put himself in the limelight and sell a few more papers."

"I'm sure Trausti meant well. He is supposed to make sure that the paper always takes people by surprise, and raise our profile," Hannes feebly counters.

"If it had been a news item, or an important article, it might have been acceptable to take chances. But this…"

"I know what you're saying, my good sir, but…"

"Look, Hannes," I interrupt, "if we don't publish an apology on the front page tomorrow…"

"On the front page?"

"Yes. On the front page. If we don't publish an apology there tomorrow, signed by the news editor, taking personal responsibility for the error, you'll have my resignation. And I assure you, I'm not bluffing."

"Now, now…"

"No, *now nows* won't help. If you don't do this, I might as well give up and go home. How do you think I would be able to get interviews and information after such a scandal? Gain people's confidence, make contacts?"

I hear Hannes light a cigar, puff, and exhale. "All right, my good sir. We'll do as you say. Trausti will learn his lesson."

"I doubt it."

I've got a grip on myself, but I'm as angry as ever.

"Anything else of interest?" Hannes inquires, signaling a change of subject.

"Yes, actually, really good news," I reply. "Pal has turned up. Joy is unconfined in the domain of the former news editor—and actually I'm beginning to feel Ásbjörn would have been preferable to Trausti."

Once I've filled him in on the details of Pal's rescue, Hannes comments:

"Indeed. Well, I think such good news calls for a follow-up. An interview with the girl who saved the little dog, a photo of them together. It will be a feel-good human interest story for people in Akureyri, and other readers, in tomorrow's paper. In the first place it will counteract any negative impact of the matter we were discussing earlier. Secondly, it's a story that everyone can identify with. Thirdly, it will be a justification for our unprecedented Missing Dog story in today's paper. And fourthly, it will demonstrate that the *Afternoon News* can help people with their everyday problems. So what do you say to that?"

I think about what he has said. I must admit he has a point. "OK, I'll do it. And you'll rake Trausti over the coals?"

"As good as done, my good sir. As good as done."

Kjartan Arnarson is far from thrilled when I tell him about my dealings with Hannes.

"I'll believe it when I see it," he says. "And I may still take other action to regain my good name."

In reception Karólína is working, and Pal is once again tethered to the desk by his leash. Karólína is singing in a whiny voice like someone playing a saw, humming something undefined as she works. Her singing voice is nothing like her throaty speaking voice. I ask after Jóa. Karólína tells me she's gone out with her camera bag. Ásbjörn is at his desk in his office. I can see he has shaken off his worries. I tell him about Hannes's idea.

"Excellent," he says. "Good for everyone."

"I suppose you made a note of the girl's name, address, and phone number?"

"Of course. Karó and I are going to send her a little something today, to say thank you."

He takes a piece of paper from his pants pocket and hands it to me. I make a note of the information, then pass it back to him.

I get hold of Jóa on her cell phone, and before long we are on our way to meet the intrepid canine rescuer, Björg Gudrúnardóttir, who was quick to agree to an interview. In the backseat Pal sits quietly, tethered to the door handle.

"Where were you?" I ask as I struggle to find my way to Holtagata using a map of the town.

"I looked in at the *Akureyri Post*. Their offices are just near ours, on Skipagata."

"The *Akureyri Post*? I've been intending to drop by, but I haven't had time. Remarkable, the way they've managed to publish a local weekly paper year after year. We really need to establish a good relationship with them."

"I met the editor. I suggested the three of us get together some evening at one of these fine local restaurants that I'm always hearing about. The Easter break has started, and I think we deserve a little fun, Einar, after our hard toil and pizza diet. Do you agree?"

"Absolutely. I love the idea. And it's about time I made some use of my expense account," I say.

Holtagata is a picturesque little street overlooking the town center, not far from the church and the high school, where Björg lives in a charming old house. Pal apparently recognizes the place and greets it with a low bark.

Björg lets us in. She's a smiling, shy girl of about seventeen, with long, dark hair parted in the middle, green almond eyes, and full, unpainted lips. She wears a ring in one nostril. Of average height, she is slender, dressed in tight-fitting black pants and a black blouse. She bends down over Pal, who greets her with enthusiastic wagging of his stubby tail and licks her hand. She invites us into the living room, on the left of the entrance hall, and offers us something to drink. I accept a Coke and Jóa, a glass of water. Björg goes to the kitchen across the hall to fetch them. As we enter the living room, we are briefly struck dumb. The room is neat as a pin, with hardwood parquet flooring and white furniture. But it is also crammed with cacti: big cacti, little cacti, tall and short, and of all possible varieties I cannot identify.

"You've got a whole lot of cacti here" is my scintillating remark when Björg enters the living room with our drinks.

"Yes, Mom loves cacti," she replies in her slow, reserved manner. "She likes the way they look."

"And they don't need a lot of care or attention, do they?" I say. "Don't they more or less live on air?"

She makes no response. She seems to be waiting for us to sit down on the pristine white furniture. So we do: Jóa next to me on the sofa and Björg on the chair facing us, with Pal on her lap. He seems at ease there.

"Are you a student at the high school?"

"No," replies Björg, fidgeting restlessly in her chair. She is clearly not used to media attention. "I dropped out last spring. I'm taking some time out to decide what I want to do. Maybe I'll go back to school. I don't know."

"In search of yourself, like the rest of us?" I ask with a smile.

"I suppose. I've been doing some work at my mom's architectural studio. Helping out."

"So your mom's an architect?"

She nods.

"Do you want to be an architect too?"

"I don't know what I want yet."

"Do you happen to know a girl at the high school, Sólrún Bjarkadóttir?"

She smiles wryly. "The one who made a fool of herself in your paper."

"Well, she was made a fool of. But it wasn't entirely her fault."

"I don't know her. But I heard she had a rough time in school last year. She had no friends and was alone a lot. I think maybe she's gotten into bad company."

"And bad company's better than no company?"

"I didn't say that," she says. I detect intelligence and a strong will behind her reserved exterior.

"OK," I say, starting the tape recorder. "Let's begin at the beginning."

The story began when she was walking down by the docks and saw some boys of about ten chasing a little dog. Björg recounts the whole story, articulately and complete with self-deprecating humor. While Jóa is taking photos I wander around the living room. Against one wall is an old piano. Among the cacti on top of it stand several framed photographs of Björg with an attractive woman, presumably her mother, at various ages: she is about the same height as Björg but with fairer skin and hair—worn up in all the pictures—but the resemblance is striking. Mother and daughter wear beaming smiles in every single photo. I suggest that Jóa takes some photos of Björg and Pal in front of the piano. As we take our leave, I ask Björg:

"You live here with your mother, do you?"

She nods.

"This Kjartan Arnarson," I ask, "the teacher who got into this embarrassing situation. What's he like?"

"I was never in any of his classes," Björg replies. "He looks a bit odd, but I've always heard that he's nice enough."

We wish her a happy Easter and set off for the car with Pal on his leash. The dog glances back toward the house with a muffled bark.

PAL'S ADVENTURE IN AKUREYRI
Once upon a time there was a little dog named Pal...

I start my heartwarming essay on the mutt and his savior. As I add the finishing touch to my account with the words *And they all lived happily ever after*, I find myself suddenly overcome with exhaustion. I swing my feet up onto the desk and light up. The back of my chair almost touches the closed door. So my closet of an office is, according to my rough calculations, about as long as my coffin will be. It's past five o'clock. I send in my piece and immediately feel better. I stand up and go to the break room. Ásbjörn, Karó, and Pal have gone upstairs. I can hear quiet barking through the wooden ceiling. Jóa has sent in her pics, and she says she's going to a movie. I'm going home to lie down. But I have a cup of black coffee without sugar all the same. I light another cigarette and return to my closet. On top of the pile is the third of the message slips, the one I couldn't identify. Karólína has written the name *Gunnhildur Bjargmundsdóttir* and a telephone number. I pick up the phone and ring.

"Hóll. Good afternoon," answers a woman's voice.

"Hóll?" I ask. "What's that?"

"Hóll is a care home."

"I see. My name is Einar. I got a message to contact Gunnhildur Bjargmundsdóttir. Is she a member of staff or a resident?"

"Gunnhildur lives here with us."

"May I speak to her?"

"That depends. For instance, on how she is. Or whether she's awake. If you'll wait a moment, I'll find out."

I wait for two minutes.

"Gunnhildur is asleep. She's had a difficult time for the past few days. Especially yesterday and today."

"Oh? Was it something in particular?"

"It's always hard to lose a child. Even when you're nearly eighty and sometimes a bit confused."

"What happened?"

"Her daughter died yesterday, after an accident. She fell into the Jökulsá River on Saturday and sustained a severe head trauma. She died without regaining consciousness."

"Would you let her know that Einar returned her call?"

"Yes, I will."

I thank her and hang up, wondering what Gunnhildur Bjargmundsdóttir can want with me. On top of everything else, can I have made some mistake in reporting the accident?

Then I go home to Polly, hastily clean and tidy the apartment to prepare it for my daughter's arrival, and try to put from my mind this day of joy and tribulation for Icelandic families.

6 WEDNESDAY/HOLY THURSDAY

"Hi, Dad," says Gunnsa's sweet voice.

"Gunnsa, darling. It's so good to hear you. Are you all packed for tomorrow?"

"Ahem," Gunnsa clears her throat. "I'm packing. But not necessarily for a flight to Akureyri. Ahem. Ahem."

I am so taken aback that I almost drop the phone. "What is it? Is something wrong? Are you ill? Are you going into the hospital?"

"No, no, no. Raggi's mom has invited us both to Copenhagen for Easter. There was some megadeal this morning, and our flight's this afternoon."

My heart drops at least five feet.

"Hello? Hello? Dad?"

"Yeah, I'm still here," I sigh. "I'm here, somewhere."

"Sorry, Dad," says Gunnsa, in her gentlest tone. "But I've never been to Copenhagen. I reeeeeally want to go. You've been, haven't you?"

"What? Yes, but not until I was eighteen."

"It was different back then. There weren't any megadeals."

I pick myself up off the floor of my closet.

"No, that's true. There were no megadeals then."

"Mom says it's OK with her. Please, Dad, say it's OK with you."

"But you've never been to Akureyri either." I'm flailing around for an argument.

"No, but I can come another time. Akureyri's in Iceland."

"There are loads of Danish houses here."

Gunnsa is taken by surprise. "Danish houses?"

"Yep, old Danish houses."

"You're kidding."

"Or houses in Danish style. They're really pretty."

She laughs. "Houses in Danish style in Akureyri. You're so funny, Dad!"

I'm about to tell her that Akureyri has its own Ráðhústorg, or Town Hall Square, just like Copenhagen's Rådhuspladsen, and the only pedestrian shopping street in Iceland, like Strøget. But then I realize that this is yet another lost cause. "Well, Gunnsa, sweetheart, it's all right so far as I'm concerned, but I have to say, I've really been looking forward to your visit."

"I'll come soon. Promise."

"OK. So it's just you and Raggi and Rúna going to Copenhagen?"

Gunnsa hesitates before answering: "Well, the three of us, and some guy Rúna's been seeing."

Now it's my turn to hesitate before saying, "Have a good trip, honey, and have fun. But take care in Nyhavn."

The worst that could happen has happened. I sit frozen in my closet with the conversation with my daughter like an albatross around my neck, crushed with self-pity and disappointment. Then I start trying to talk myself around: Of course it isn't the worst that could happen. Gunnsa's not dead. She's alive and kicking, happy and cheerful, on her way to Copenhagen for Easter with her boyfriend. When I was fifteen, wouldn't I have preferred to go to Copenhagen with my girlfriend rather than visit my old man in Akureyri? Admittedly, when I was fifteen I didn't have a girlfriend. And my dad wasn't in Akureyri. And back then Easter was a Christian festival, not a time of megadeals. But the answer to my question was nonetheless as clear as the view of the wall next door.

No, the second-worst thing that could happen has happened.

And then there's this thing about Raggi's mom, Rúna, and some guy. Why is that gnawing away at my cerebral cortex? It's all selfishness. Selfishness and importunity.

Einar, you're selfish and importunate, I say to the stranger reflected in the computer screen.

He makes no reply.

You're a free man, I go on. *Enjoy your freedom. Here in Akureyri. Over Easter.*

And the man on the screen replies: *Yeah. Enjoy the suffering.*
Ouch.

Who knows, maybe I'll be offered some megadeal of my own over Easter, here in Akureyri? I try to convince myself I'm doing all right and reach for the phone.

"Good morning. Hóll." A male voice this time.

"Good morning. May I speak to Gunnhildur Bjargmundsdóttir?"

"Just a moment."

I wait two minutes.

"No, I'm afraid Gunnhildur is having her bath. Can I take a message?"

I say no and thank him. No doubt the old lady has completely forgotten that she called some journalist called Einar—and even why she made the call. I consider contacting Kjartan Arnarson following the publication of Trausti Löve's prominent apology on today's front page. I decide against it. I kept my word.

Instead I return to the piece I'm hammering together about a press conference held at Hotel KEA this lunchtime, presenting the report of a project group on the future development of the local Eyjafjördur region. The minister for regional affairs was there, along with the mayor and the project board. They all shook hands and patted each other on the back and congratulated each other on finally reaching the conclusion that more diversity was required in the regional economy, with particular emphasis on *clusters in the fields of education and research, health care, tourism, and food production, in a family-friendly community that will be sought after for its good services, potential for education, and leisure activities, all grounded in a diverse, developed, specialized, and competitive economy with strong international ties...*Which is how the population and job opportunities are supposed to increase by an average of 2.3 percent per annum, so that by 2020 the population of the Eyjafjördur region will be twice what it is today, or around thirty thousand. Headline:

A WORLD-CLASS FUTURE

"I think this is the fifth or sixth report on regional development since I've been here," remarked my colleague on the *Morning News* with a cynical smile. He's been in Akureyri for years on end.

"They always launch them with a huge fanfare, then quietly file them away in a drawer. In the end, they don't want to spend the money."

Who knows? I think to myself. It's only a few weeks until the general election: that kind of pressure can work miracles.

In addition to the regional development piece, I send in a dramatic account of a crime wave in Akureyri. People with nothing better to do have been vandalizing park benches around the town, where tired townspeople have hitherto been able to rest their weary bones. There are about fifty benches in total, and as fast as municipal workers replace them, the vandals come back to kick them to pieces all over again. I type in the headline:

VANDALS ON THE BENCH

and switch off my computer.

"Is there no real crime here, Adalheidur?"

"Call me Heida."

Adalheidur "Heida" Heimisdóttir, editor and publisher of the *Akureyri Post*, raises a manicured hand with long nails, varnished blue to complement her pantsuit. She lifts a forkful of halibut and pasta to her reddened lips and takes a sensual bite with her white teeth.

Lucky fork.

She is about my age, not tall but curvaceous, with thick, shoulder-length red hair, and small horn-rimmed glasses perched on an upturned nose. I find her enchanting.

The white dining room at the Frederick V, which is named after its owner and chef and not after the Danish king of the same name, is full tonight. About half the guests seem to be speaking Icelandic; the other half is a discordant babble of other languages—and of course we know that *it is vital for the future development of the region to have strong international ties.*

"This is an excellent restaurant," I remark as she swallows. "Original and imaginative."

"Couldn't agree more," says Jóa, who is digging into a plate of lobster tails. "Just as good as down south."

Heida looks from one of us to the other, as if we were two-year-olds. "How can you possibly imagine that originality and imagination in cuisine are the sole province of the Greater Reykjavík Area? They have edible food in places like Paris and Barcelona, don't they?"

Jóa and I exchange an embarrassed glance. We have nothing to say. We've both dressed in our best—which, oddly enough, means we're wearing almost identical outfits. Black suits, white shirts. She is wearing a tie, I am not. Jóa's dirty-blond hair is still in a short ponytail, framing her bright, honest face, free of makeup.

"We have all the same crimes as down south," answers Heida. "Just on a smaller scale. Burglary, robbery, fights, rape, assaults, especially on weekends. Manslaughter or murder—but only rarely. Prostitution, but on a small scale. Most crime here is connected with drug abuse, and that's rising fast. Young people today see nothing wrong with popping an E-pill or two, or snorting coke or speed when they go out."

"There hasn't been much about that in the police reports since I got here," I comment.

"As you may remember, a group was formed to combat violent crime when people felt things were getting out of hand. It's had some impact. And hopefully led to a change of attitude."

"That sounds like wishful thinking to me," I reply. "To the criminal element, a change of attitude simply means they have to alter their tactics."

"We have Special Branch officers deputed by the National Commissioner of Police, under the command of the chief of police here in Akureyri," she adds. "They're supposed to deal with the most difficult cases."

"Yes, including the matter of the big industrial development projects here in the east? I think I heard something about action against organized crime in that context."

"That's right. But we've seen no sign of that here in Akureyri. Not so far as I know."

"Are there drug gangs here?" I ask. The halibut is long gone.

She nods her red locks. "Yes, but only a few. Sad to say, groups of youths rampage around the streets—maybe ten or fifteen of them—waving baseball bats and knives and even occasionally loaded guns. They collect drug debts by intimidation. A lot of people have been injured, and there has been an increase in suicides. It's just a question of time when they stop posturing and actually kill someone. The older generation is just beginning to see what's happening. But I'm not sure the parents really know what their kids get up to. And the police haven't managed to control the problem. The rate of drug-related crime is rising one hundred percent from year to year. Far too many young people—including those from so-called good homes, who are in school or well-paid work—take drugs for granted as part of their weekend fun. Just like us with a beer or a glass of wine. Some of them have been using for years." She falls silent and observes me for a moment. "Have you never drunk alcohol?"

"What? Oh, yes. I have been known to take a drink, quite often," I smile. "And in some quantity."

"He's taking a break," Jóa interjects. "Well, he had a great choice: the whiskey or the work."

"Yes, wonderful choice," I say. "I'm doing an experiment to see how long I can remain drunk by nature."

They share a bottle of white wine. I stick to Coke—with a capital C—and find myself gazing longingly at their glasses. Heida's glass, anyway.

"Everything in the bigger communities is also found in smaller places," I remark, because I can't think of anything more original to say. "Just scaled down. Miniaturized. It's true of the squares, the banks, crime, and drugs. Just think how the influx of people into Reydargerdi will increase the problems there: drugs, prostitution, violence. I spoke to the chief of police there the other day. He preferred to call them 'tasks' rather than problems."

"Yes, I read your article," says Heida. "It sounded like a complex business arrangement rather than a complex social dynamic."

"And now they're talking about heavy industry here in Eyjafjördur," says Jóa.

"Or Húsavík," Heida replies. "Or Skagafjördur."

"Isn't that a recipe for disaster?" Jóa asks.

"Where people see a prospect of profit, greed will always win out," I remark. "They forget everything else when they see a fast buck. Nature? To hell with it!"

"I heard somewhere that a person who thinks money can't buy happiness just doesn't know where to go shopping!" quips the local editor.

"And should read the ads more carefully."

"But who can be against better quality of life? Nobody says *no* to higher pay or lower taxes."

"But you can sacrifice one kind of quality of life by accepting another. It's a question of values surely?" I protest.

"No doubt," replies the editor. "And we'll never achieve a consensus on those values. Or any other value judgments."

"Don't you find it difficult to address these issues in your paper? In such a small community, don't you have to keep everybody's goodwill? Avoid offending the authorities and advertisers with uncomfortable truths?"

"I tread carefully," she gravely replies. "The paper is my living. And it has two other salaried staff. I've been doing this for six years, and it demands a certain skill."

It demands responsibility, without falsifying reality, I think to myself. I light a cigarette, and the minute I exhale my first puff of smoke a woman at the next table ambushes me.

"You can't smoke here. You'll have to go into the bar."

She gives me a look, as if I'm a filthy, disgusting, dangerous terrorist with a nuclear warhead in my mouth. I look around. No one else is smoking. As so often in recent times, I feel like a most-wanted outlaw, on the run with my weapons of mass destruction.

"Sorry," I say to the woman. "I didn't realize. I didn't mean to commit a crime against humanity."

Here comes the story of the Hurricane, voices are wailing in the bar.

The man the authorities came to blame
For something that he never done…

It's a trawler crew, ashore and looking for some fun after a fishing trip, a Dylan aficionado among them.

At another table, one man yawns mightily as his companion attempts to entertain him with comic verses. And here is an extended family celebrating the patriarch's eightieth birthday. A young couple sits silently at a corner table. She is pregnant, he is blind drunk. *What kind of a life will that child have?* I think as we take a seat at a small table.

I've treated Jóa and Heida to coffee and brandy and indulge myself in a cigarette. The editor of the *Akureyri Post* has generously imparted to us her knowledge of the vibrant social life of the town, the expansion of the university, high school, and technical high school, the construction of more student accommodations, improvements to the local theater, the high hopes of a director at the Akureyri Theater Company, record attendance at the swimming pool, increased tourism, a new preschool, large-scale construction, and a conference on renewal in the town center, which has been in decline as shopping malls have been built in the suburbs. It all sounds exactly the same as the news down south. Same situation. Same thought processes. *Strong international ties.*

At the end of the lecture, I ask her: "Do you know anything about the people involved in the accident on the Jökulsá River?"

"I don't know them personally," answers Heida, sipping at her brandy. "The Yumm candy factory goes way back. It belongs to the family of the woman who died, but it's been run for years by her husband, Ásgeir Eyvindarson. He used to be on the town council for the Center Party, and he was an alternate member of parliament."

"Good people?"

"So far as I know. I think I heard something about her being in poor health. Ásdís Björk."

"Are you from Akureyri?"

"Yes," she replies. "But I left after high school. I needed a change of scenery."

I light another cigarette and look around me at the people in the bar. "Akureyri people have a reputation of being distant with outsiders, or even hostile. I don't get it. They don't strike me as any different from other people I've dealt with."

"I think we've improved," she smiles. "But it's better to keep a low profile and not do anything to stick out. It's safer. And certainly not offend the townspeople's sense of decorum by driving around in a rusty or dirty car and parking it in the street. That will get you nasty looks."

So now I know where we stand, my car and I, in the eyes of our new neighbors.

It's nearly eleven when we emerge into Strandgata. After a warm day, a chilly breeze is blowing. Heida shivers.

"Well, I'm off. Thanks for an enjoyable evening."

I find it hard to conceal my disappointment. "Pleasure's mine," I manage to say and reach out to shake her hand. "I hope we'll meet again soon."

"Yes indeed," she says with a smile. "I'd like that."

She and Jóa shake hands and exchange a nod. Heida waves good-bye and crosses the street to the taxi parked on the corner.

Jóa and I share a look. "Now what?" I ask. "Can I buy you a drink somewhere?"

She thinks about it as she pulls on a blue parka over her black suit. "Oh, no, I don't think so."

"Come on, Jóa. The night is young."

"Yeah, but we're a little older."

I haven't brought a coat, and I feel the chill. "You! You're hardly thirty!"

"I'd rather go for a walk."

"Do you really mean it? You're going to leave me here, all by myself in a strange town?" I try to appear cheerful, but I'm already dreading being alone.

"You're a big boy, Einar. I'll see you tomorrow."

As she walks off in the direction of Town Hall Square, she calls back over her shoulder: "Thanks for dinner!"

Det var ingenting, I think in Danish: You're welcome. No doubt Gunnsa is strolling now on that other Town Hall Square, in Copenhagen, with Raggi and his mom and some goddamned guy.

It's a still, calm evening down by the fjord. Mass migration has not yet begun from parties, restaurants, and cafés to the nightspots of Akureyri. But the traffic is increasing; as in any small town, young people are cruising in their cars, to see and be seen.

So I don't have to fight my way through any crowds as I enter a spacious bar that is happily free of the latest in cool modern design. Ornamented with flashing fairy lights and prints of central European forests and mountains, the décor is completed with frilly pink curtains at the windows. I stand alone at the very long bar, draw my weapon, light the fuse, and order a coffee. A few people sit grouped around the room. On the dance floor are two girls dancing to a Beatles song performed by a four-man combo on the stage at the end of the bar.

A bad little kid moved into my neighborhood,
He won't do nothing right, just sitting down and
Looks so good...

At the bar I am joined by two couples, somewhat the worse for wear.

One couple—the man grossly fat, in a gray jacket several sizes too small, the woman wearing furs, swaying on her stiletto heels—are in the middle of a fight.

"You! Master Electrician Helgi Hámundarson! You're just a big fat zero!" the woman screeches at the man, probably for the thousandth time.

Master Electrician Helgi Hámundarson turns a deaf ear, no doubt for the thousandth time. He's got what matters: a double vodka and Coke.

The woman turns to me: "Have you any idea how much I hate this man?" she asks, looking right through me.

"No, actually, I don't," I mumble into my coffee cup.

She neither sees me nor hears me. "Even if you enjoy a sausage now and then, that doesn't mean you want the whole pig!" she remarks to no one in particular. Clutching a large glass of green liqueur, she totters over to the other woman, who is sitting at a table with a pint of beer.

The two men stand together next to me and share a toast. Master Electrician Helgi Hámundarson says to his companion, "Have you heard the latest pickup line?"

"Don't suppose so," slurs the other man.

"You say to the woman: *Do you like to smoke after sex?*

"And she answers: *Yes, I do, actually.*

"Then you say: *Then I'll have to remember to buy a packet of cigarettes.*"

They laugh themselves breathless. The invisible man, the Big Fat Zero, takes his leave. I'm thinking: *I wonder if these people have children? How do they feel? What can they be like?*

Driving home along Strandgata, I think I catch a glimpse of Agnar Hansen, with his blond ponytail, in the back of one of the cars cruising around the town center. But I'm not certain.

A man who had no shoes felt sorry for himself until he met a man who had no feet.

I wake up with that idea in my head, without knowing where it came from. It's 6:30 a.m. I dozed off over a local TV station, which was showing on a continuous loop a segment in which town officials and representatives of the ski area express their concern that their advertising campaign about plenty of snow for skiers over Easter is simply melting away into thin air, due to the unseasonably high temperatures.

Before that I'd watched *Chinatown* for the tenth time. I've always liked it, especially the scene where Polanski, playing the little rat of a crook, inserts the point of his knife into Jack Nicholson's nostril, asking: *You know what happens to nosy fellows?*

When I arrived home at about one in the morning, Jóa's bedroom door was closed. I blocked all exits, went into my own room, and opened Polly's cage. Then I sat on the sofa in the living room with a Coke and a bag of chips and switched the TV on. A few minutes later the bird came flying into the living room and perched on the curtain rail. Polly sat there for a while, singing and squawking. I was biting into a chip when she suddenly took to the air, swooped down on me, and settled on the back of my white shirt collar. She sat there, nibbling at the chips I offered her from time to time and occasionally pecking gently at my neck. Now, when I wake up, she has returned to her cage, where she is perched with her head beneath one wing. I close the cage door as quietly as possible so as not to disturb the only lady in my life. Then I start scraping the bird droppings off my shirt.

Peace still reigns when I wake up again just before midday on Holy Thursday. I feel rested and find myself surprisingly cheerful. Behind her bars, Polly coos and cackles when I bring her breakfast seed. Outside, the sun is shining, and out in the gardens children are playing ball. I go into the kitchen, put the kettle on, light a cigarette, and turn the radio on. The twelve o'clock news offers slim pickings, except for an announcement that catches my attention:

> *Skarphédinn Valgardsson, a student at Akureyri High School, is requested to get in touch with Örvar Páll or Ágústa at once. Phone numbers...*

I met him, I think to myself. I go into the hall, where the special Easter edition of the *Afternoon News* has been thrust through the door. I flick through until I find my article, under the headline:

MAKE MY WILL THY WILL
According to a new Loftur the Sorcerer from Akureyri, Jóhann Sigurjónsson's classic play is as relevant today as it ever was. Students at the high school premiere the play this evening in its historical setting, Hólar in Hjaltadalur.

Is the last part of the intro about to be proved wrong?

7 HOLY THURSDAY

"My desires are powerful and boundless. And in the beginning was desire. Desires are the souls of men."

Skarphédinn Valgardsson, nineteen-year-old student at Akureyri High School, spoke the words, written over a century ago by playwright Jóhann Sigurjónsson, with such passion and conviction that I almost felt he was articulating his own thoughts.

"Take Loftur's dialogue with the blind man in the first act," Skarphédinn had remarked during our interview in the lobby of the gym at Hólar College. "The blind man says he has prayed over and over again for the merciful hand of God to lift the darkness from his eyes. Loftur replies: *Indeed I know that human desires can work miracles. They have done so in the past and still do so today.* And I agree. If we know what we want, we can achieve our own miracles. And when the blind man says, a bit later, *I wished, until it led me into sin. When I gave up my wishing, my soul could finally be at peace,* he has been led by his perception of sin into giving up. He gained peace for his soul by giving up and accepting his fate."

"But," I had dared to ask, being quite unaccustomed to such high-flown literary debate, "Loftur makes a pact with the devil in order to fulfill his desires. Do you maintain that he was justified in doing that?"

Skarphédinn smiled at me. "Well, initially Loftur wants the devil to make his desires his own, in order to get what he wants. But later he wants to escape from the devil's control and be free. It's a matter of opinion, of course, how literally the pact should be interpreted. You can see it as a pact between a man and himself or between different aspects of himself."

"What do you think?" I asked.

After a brief pause for thought, he replied: "I just keep the options open. I feel it's up to the audience to decide for themselves—like so much else in the play. And in life. I play this character, and I do my best to portray him. I'm not about to sit in moral judgment over him."

"He comes to a bad end."

"Yes, well, that's the playwright's choice. He's in charge of what he puts down on paper, so he adds a moral dimension—perhaps he was bowing to the straitlaced standards of his time. I don't know. The theme is an ancient one. Faust, Nietzsche, the idea of the Übermensch to whom the usual rules of human behavior don't apply. In the play, Loftur says, shortly before his demise: *He who never commits any sin is not a human being. In sin lies a mystical joy. All good deeds are nothing but an attempt to reproduce that joy. In sin, one becomes one's true self. Sin is the wellspring of all new things.* I'm quite sure that the playwright was expressing his own view and reflecting his own experience. He puts them forward in contrast with other, opposing views, which were also his, and were in conflict with them. A dramatic tension between opposite extremes, which are all given the opportunity to prove themselves in the play—and that's what makes it such a powerful work."

This young man's pretty powerful himself, I thought to myself as the tape recorder spun. The deep, expressive voice exerted a subtle charm. The brown eyes sparkled. Shoulder-length dark hair with a center parting, above a handsome, masculine face with strong eyebrows. If Skarphédinn didn't shave for a few days, he would even resemble the traditional image of Christ in Western art.

Although dressed in historical costume, he was keen to stress the relevance of *Loftur the Sorcerer* to the people of today, or indeed of any period.

"Just think," he said, raising his arms to emphasize his point and revealing hairy, well-muscled forearms under his white shirt, "how issues of class and discrimination are constantly arising, for instance in Loftur's dealings with Steinunn. He's the steward's son, she's a housemaid. He gets her pregnant, then throws her over in favor of Dísa, the bishop's daughter. Or in his relationship with his boyhood friend Ólafur, who is also in love with Steinunn. And today, when the gap between rich and poor is constantly growing, and tension is increasing between native Icelanders and immigrants, people are dealing with exactly the same issues—even though we dress differently and use computers to communicate."

I had nothing to add.

"And what about the question of reproductive rights? In those days a desperate woman might leave her baby in the wilds to die. Today we debate abortion rights. It's essentially the same issue, isn't it?"

I nodded in agreement.

"Life is always a matter of the quest for happiness," Skarphédinn continued unstoppably. "Our efforts to make our dreams and desires come true and the methods we use to achieve them."

Loftur the Sorcerer was in full flood when a cell phone rang in his pocket. He answered the phone, which was in a tooled brown leather pouch, taking a break from his rhetoric. Or was he just an expert salesman?

What has happened to this promising young man? Why is there an appeal on the radio for him to get in touch, just hours before he is due to make his first entrance onstage?

I clearly remember an atmosphere of tension and anticipation among the young people who had recently taken over the Akureyri High School Drama Group. There had been talk of disbanding the group, but they had revived it, and their first production was to be this ambitious staging of *Loftur the Sorcerer* in its authentic setting at Hólar. "We wanted to do the first performance at this important historical and ecclesiastical site, which was the center of the church in north Iceland for seven centuries and de facto capital of the region. The rest of the performances will be at the old theater in Akureyri," I had been told by the chair of the drama group, Ágústa Magnúsdóttir.

After Jóa and I took our leave of them in the gym, where the stage set concealed athletics equipment and basketball goals, we were in agreement that this production of *Loftur the Sorcerer* seemed to be worth seeing. But now, when the chair of the drama group and the director, Örvar Páll Sigurdarson, have apparently lost their leading man, we can't be sure we'll have the chance.

Lost in my thoughts, I hear a key in the front door, and Jóa enters. I hadn't noticed her go out. The door to her room is closed, as it was when I arrived home last night. "Hi," I call out. "Have you been out for a walk?"

"What? No," she replies. She comes in wearing her parka and takes a seat at the table.

"Oh?" I ask.

Jóa looks a bit bleary. If I didn't know better I'd think she might have a slight hangover. She seems a little embarrassed, but there's a strange light in her eye. Then I notice that under the parka she is still wearing the suit and shirt she dressed in yesterday. But without the tie.

"Hey, hey," I say. "You're just coming home now!"

I look at the time. It's past 2:00 p.m.

I put on a disciplinary expression: "This will not do, young lady. We cannot allow such conduct here under this roof. We have a strict curfew, which must be respected."

She just smiles.

"Get lucky?" I grin.

The smile gets wider.

"Come on, tell Daddy."

Jóa makes no reply. But her eyes go a little misty.

"Who is it?"

She is reluctant to answer. I look her up and down. There's something she wants to say, but can't get the words out. I keep on looking.

And then it clicks. Something I'd sensed about 15 percent yesterday evening, but pushed aside in favor of 85 percent wishful thinking.

"Adalheidur Heimisdóttir, editor of the *Akureyri Post*!"

She nods.

"Whoopdedoo!"

The smile is back.

"And I was fool enough to have some silly hopes of my own," I say, feeling my surprise, embarrassment, and humiliation evaporate as I observe the happiness in Jóa's eyes.

"I knew," says Jóa, standing up and placing a friendly arm around my shoulders. "And I'm awfully sorry if you feel I spoiled your chance with her. It wasn't like that."

"Of course not, Jóa dear," I say as I stand up and give her a hug. "I never stood a chance against a foxy lady like you."

We both fall over laughing.

"You knew each other before," I say. It's not a question.

"Back in Reykjavík, Heida used to come to the odd gay event. So we knew each other by sight, but we'd never really met. Not until I moved up north."

"So when you've been taking your walks around town with your camera, and at the movies, or whatever, were you actually meeting her?"

"No, absolutely not," retorts Jóa. "We went to the movies, admittedly, but nothing else happened. Not until last night. I wouldn't lie to you, Einar."

"But does she keep it a secret here or what?"

"Yes. She hasn't dared take the risk yet. Because of the paper. The contacts. The ads. The readers."

"Secrets and lies, Jóa dear. Sexuality, gender, ethnicity, color, nationality, religion. When questions like that come up, there's a tendency not to be able to tell the forest from the trees. For whatever reason."

"That's just the way it is. Even today."

"So you thought it was better to bring a male along for cover? To counteract any misunderstanding? Avert any difficulties for Heida?"

Jóa shakes her head vehemently. "Not at all. Don't sell yourself short, Einar. You're not bad company, on your own terms. When you're in the mood."

I light a cigarette. I don't think the mood's been right for a very long time. But I let it go.

"But when you nodded to each other outside the restaurant yesterday, had you decided to meet up afterward?"

"Einar, sometimes you don't have to say anything. Sometimes you just get a feeling."

"Absolutely. Know what you mean. I'm an expert in getting a feeling."

Although the next edition of the *Afternoon News* isn't due for publication until the Tuesday after Easter, I'm in my closet at the office by late afternoon. Not from a sense of duty, but motivated by sheer curiosity.

Jóa and I had treated ourselves to coffee and cakes at Café Amor, appropriately named after the god who had shot his arrows of passion into my friend. Tables and chairs had been placed outside in the sun. The town was aglow. Town Hall Square was humming with energy and high spirits. Youngsters, frisky as calves in spring, were zooming back and forth on their skateboards, cheerfully falling over in all directions. For whatever reason, the town seemed to be full of young girls pushing strollers, all dressed, no doubt, in the very latest style from the fashion magazines. Most wore such deeply plunging necklines that even at a distance Jóa and I had no trouble discerning their heaving maidenly bosoms. At the tables around us sat the cooling remnants of last night's passion.

———

When I stroll across the square toward the red wooden building with its banner—*Truth Be Told*—I think of Gunnsa and her traveling companions, on that bigger town hall square in Copenhagen. I open the news website and find the radio announcement asking Skarphédinn Valgardsson to get in touch. I debate whether to ring Örvar Páll or Ágústa, and opt for the latter. She told me she was in her second year at the high school. A small girl, she was a bundle of energy, freckled and lively, with her hair cropped short. In the play she wore a gray wig, in the role of the wife of the Bishop of Hólar.

She answers the phone breathlessly.

"Hello," I say. "This is Einar at the *Afternoon News*. I wrote an article about *Loftur the Sorcerer* in today's paper."

"Oh, yes. Hello," she replies. Clearly she had hoped it was someone else on the phone.

"I heard the appeal on the radio at lunchtime. Has Skarphédinn turned up?"

"No. We've had to postpone the first night. We couldn't leave it any longer."

"Has a search started?"

"We've been looking for him all morning. And now the police are involved."

"What do you think has happened?"

Obviously upset, she breathes rapidly. "I don't know. There was a party after the dress rehearsal yesterday. He was there for a while, but he hasn't been seen since."

"And did anything out of the ordinary happen?"

"Nothing I know of."

"Couldn't he be sleeping it off? Or maybe he went out somewhere, and the party's still in full swing?"

"You don't know Skarphédinn. He's a hundred percent reliable."

"Where does he live?"

"He used to live at the high school dorm, but he moved out last fall and rented an apartment in town. He's not answering the door."

I thank her for the information, with the feeble assurance that we must hope for the best.

Then I call the police.

"We've put out an APB about him, and a search is beginning," says the woman who answers. "He hasn't been missing long, but the circumstances are certainly unusual. With the first night this evening, and all that."

"Have you been to the apartment where he lives?"

"I'm afraid I can't tell you any more."

On an impulse, I make one more phone call.

"Good afternoon, Hóll."

"May I speak to Gunnhildur Bjargmundsdóttir?"

"Just a moment."

Two minutes.

"Hello. Yes, hello."

A wavery, nervous voice.

"Hello, Gunnhildur. This is Einar at the *Afternoon News*. I got a message a few days ago asking me to call you. But I haven't managed to reach you until now."

A long silence.

"Hello? Gunnhildur?"

A massive throat clearing resounds down the phone. "Hrhuhrummmmm."

I wait while she clears her tubes.

"Sorry, my boy," says Gunnhildur, wheezing slightly. "When you're as old as me, everything gets clogged up."

"I gather that you're Ásdís Björk's mother. I'm sorry for your loss."

"Thank you. They often say you can never really grasp the reality of death until you bury your own child. That…That…"

It sounds as if the old lady is on the verge of tears.

"That is absolutely true," she manages to say.

"Is there something I can do for you?" I ask to keep her on track. "Why did you get in touch with me?"

"I don't know whether you can do anything for me."

"But…?"

"I've tried talking to the police. But they won't listen to me. They probably think I'm a senile old bat. Too many people assume all old people are daft and deaf and have lost their marbles."

"I'm sure that's right," I say, wondering if I am one of them. I realize that my remark was ambiguous and hasten to add: "That far too many people think that. It's nothing more than prejudice, of course."

"I don't envy people who think that way, when they get old themselves. Or hopefully not."

Although I don't want the conversation to develop into a discussion of old age, I playfully reply: "Why do you say that? You're not wishing those people an early demise, are you?"

"No, I'm just expressing the hope that no one need be humiliated or ignored just because of their age. The same applies to children. And teenagers. Everyone has rights."

"I'm with you there. But," I add, "why did you call me?"

Irritated, Gunnhildur raises her voice to a harsh and grating tone: "Because the police dismissed me! Just like that! Dismissed me!"

"Why?"

"I told them Ásdís Björk's death wasn't an accident."

"What?"

"And I won't have it!" she shrieks into the phone. "I won't be dismissed, not until I leave this godforsaken world feetfirst, in my coffin!"

"But why do you say your daughter's death wasn't an accident?"

She lowers her voice and whispers her secret to me with melodramatic emphasis: "Because, my boy, she was murdered. Murdered in cold blood. In the coldest of blood that flows through human veins."

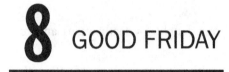

8 GOOD FRIDAY

In the beginning was the wish.

As Good Friday dawns, the main idea in my mind is the simple, sincere wish that I may get through this day without doing anything. Not a single damned thing. If I may use such language in the present situation. But, as we know, wishes are not always granted.

On the dining table I find a note: "Gone to meet You Know Who. Hope to see you later."

Next to the note Jóa has left a selection of pastries she has bought somewhere that remains open on this holiest of days. A gas station, probably. When I was young, gas stations just sold fuel for cars. Now they seem to be mainly for refueling the drivers.

Relishing Jóa's little treat, I open the door from the living room into the garden and sit at the table on the small terrace with my coffee and cigarette. I bask in the sunshine, which is as bright as yesterday. There's not a trace of snow, so the skiers who have made their way to Akureyri, hoping to swoop down the slopes, might as well have stayed at home. In the next-door garden, children are kicking a ball around. Even computers and high technology haven't managed to stop kids going out to play. Not yet, at least. After half an hour of luxurious indolence, I'm climbing the walls. I check that my avian roommate has plenty of food and drink to keep her going, then bid her farewell, reassuring her that I'll be back by dinnertime.

POLICE reads the sign over the entrance to a long, white two-story building on Thórunnarstræti, with a blue square beneath each window. The police station bears a strong resemblance to the stronghold of law and order in Reykjavík—though in miniature. I go to reception, and before long I am shown into the office of Chief of Police Ólafur Gísli Kristjánsson. He's a tall man with sharp features, going on forty, in a light-blue uniform shirt. He wears glasses in heavy black frames of the kind sported by Buddy Holly and other rock and rollers of the fifties and sixties. Below his shaven scalp, he has a strong Roman nose, a cleft chin, and a big gap between his upper front teeth. Gravely he waves me to a seat.

Not very welcoming. Behind the lenses, his eyes express distrust.

"I wanted to ask how the search for Skarphédinn Valgardsson is progressing," I say.

He crosses his arms across a barrel chest. *No entry*, says that posture. *You won't get anything out of me.* "Unfortunately it hasn't yielded any result as yet." He speaks in a deep voice with a lilting northern accent.

"Are many people taking part in the search?"

"We've called out all available manpower—both police and the volunteer rescue team. About twenty people in all." He leans forward on his desk, where papers are neatly stacked alongside a hefty desktop computer.

"Have you any clues as to what may have happened to him?"

"I can only tell you what I've told your colleagues from radio and TV and the *Free Times* and *Morning News*. We have no information that we can share with the media at this point in time."

After a moment's thought, I decide to push a little harder. I politely inquire: "Is that because you have no information? Or don't you want to share it with the media?"

Chief Ólafur Gísli Kristjánsson gives me a ferocious glare, jumps to his feet, and looms over me like a volcano about to spew fire and brimstone over the plains beneath.

"Who do you think you are?" he asks in a silky tone, disconcertingly at odds with his threatening posture.

"A jour-jour-journalist," I babble, struggling to my feet.

"I know who you are," he goes on. "You're a sensationalizing tabloid hack from the south, putting on your cosmopolitan airs and thinking you're going to dig up dirt here in Akureyri. But you've got another think coming."

"I didn't mean..."

"I know who you are," he reiterates. "You're notorious down south, the police know all about you. You don't respect the rules of the game. You ignore the usual channels of communication to go sniffing out information..."

"I just won't be told what's news and what isn't," I say.

"...and you think you're God's own seeker of truth..."

"It's for me to decide. We still have freedom of expression..."

"We don't need people like you here in Akureyri."

"...and freedom of the press in this country."

"However. Since you've seen fit to come here, there's just one thing that's stopping me from kicking you out."

I'm brought up short. "Really? What's that?"

He returns to his seat behind the desk. "No, probably two things. Firstly, my tolerant attitude to troublemakers of all kinds."

His smile is now so broad that through the gap between his front teeth I catch a glimpse of his uvula. "No, wait. There are three things," he smirks. "Secondly, my duty as a police officer to maintain good relations with the public and the media…"

He waves me to a seat.

"And thirdly?" I inquire, wiping cold sweat from my forehead.

"Thirdly, I shall, at least for now, give you the benefit of the doubt, because my friend Ásbjörn has vouched for you."

I find I am breathing more easily. "Aha. So you're Ásbjörn's friend on the force here?"

"I know the two of you haven't got on well over the years. So it just goes to show what a fine, honorable man he is, that he has asked me to show you as much consideration and understanding as possible."

I don't know what to say.

He glares at me again. "So what do you say to that?"

"Excellent," I reply with a smile. "I humbly thank you, and Ásbjörn, for your tolerance."

"Don't thank me. Thank Ásbjörn. I'm turning a blind eye, primarily out of my regard for him."

"Were you childhood friends?"

"We were classmates at the high school, and we soon became inseparable friends. I owe him a lot."

"Really? Like what?"

Ólafur Gísli removes his spectacles and polishes them on the tail of his blue uniform shirt. "I wasn't an outstanding student. Believe it or not." Smirk. "I was more interested in girls and parties. I might well have flunked out, ended up in the gutter. I could have finished up on your side of this desk. But I could rely on my best friend, of course. It was Ásbjörn, really, who got me through my high school diploma. After that we went our separate ways."

"Shall we start over?" I ask, offering him my hand across the desk.

He shakes it firmly. "Let's," he says, still smirking. "Ásbjörn warned me. He said you might push the envelope. But he also told me that you were to be trusted, if you gave a promise. That you aren't as bad as you look."

"I must remember to thank him."

"I still can't tell you any more at this stage than I have already about the search for Skarphédinn. But off the record, I have a bad feeling about this. Everybody seems to agree that he's a responsible young man."

"Where are you searching?"

"All over Akureyri and in the vicinity."

"And Skarphédinn doesn't appear to have been home the night before last?"

"We don't know. But it's definite that he isn't in the apartment."

He stands up again, calm and composed his time. "Duty calls."

Before I leave, I ask: "The death of the woman who fell into the Jökulsá River. Is that being investigated at all?"

He glares at me again. "Why do you ask?"

I consider telling him about my phone conversation with Gunnhildur Bjargmundsdóttir. But I conclude that I must maintain confidentiality. I owe no loyalty to Ólafur Gisli. Not at this point in time—as he would say. "Just asking."

"We're waiting for the autopsy results. It's Easter, and people are on vacation and so on. We should hear after the weekend.

But there's no indication that it was anything other than an accident."

His parting words are: "Remember you're not in Reykjavík anymore. Learn about your new surroundings. Even a bull in a china shop can learn to tread carefully."

In the deathly quiet of the *Afternoon News* offices, I'm starting to feel envious of the broadcast media, with their frequent news bulletins, not to mention the *Free Times* and the *Morning News*, which publish an Easter Sunday edition. But there's nothing I can do about that. Sometimes the last are, in the end, last. I pick up the phone and call Reydargerdi Police Station. I ask for Höskuldur Pétursson, Ólafur Gísli's fellow chief.

"Speaking."

"Hello. This is Einar from the *Afternoon News*."

"Oh, yes. Hello," he says, politely enough. But he sounds a little stressed.

"So. Did I succeed in displaying responsibility without falsifying reality?"

"It was all right. But the leader of the town council wasn't particularly pleased about the picture of his son."

"So I suppose he would have liked me to soften the truth a little?"

"I don't know. Jóhann's fond of the little beggar, naturally enough. Agnar isn't a bad kid, although he's getting off track in a big way just now."

"I think I spotted Agnar cruising around downtown Akureyri the night before last. Is that possible?"

"Oh, yes. Quite possible. He and his buddies were banned from Reydin, not for the first time. When that happens they generally go gallivanting off to Akureyri."

"So your brother Ásgrímur feels there's been enough negative media coverage of the conflict between the locals and the incomers?"

"Now, Ásgrímur...Hey, how did you know he's my brother?"

"Oh, you know. Small world."

He falls silent. I can hear a din in the background.

"So was there no trouble last night or the night before?"

"Night before last, no. Last night there was a bit of a ruckus. Just the usual. Nothing important."

The Hóll care home is in the northwestern quarter of Akureyri: a three-story building comprising two wings, designed in an unfussy but featureless style, like so many institutional buildings, inspired more by policy and economy than by any aesthetic vision.

Indoors, it is clear that the staff have done their utmost to make the best of what they have. Potted plants and vases of flowers enliven the lobby and corridors with warmth and color. Not unlike Hotel Reydargerdi, in fact.

Gunnhildur Bjargmundsdóttir is waiting for me in a spacious lounge, where gray-upholstered chairs and sofas are grouped around a large TV.

"Hello, Gunnhildur," I enunciate loudly.

"Shhhhhhhh," choruses from the gray chairs and sofas.

"Shhh."

On the TV screen a couple are acting out a dramatic scene in English. Deeply tanned, with bright white teeth and pretty-boy good looks, the man reminds me of Trausti Löve. The woman's an animated Barbie doll with silicone-enhanced breasts and big hair.

"How could you do this to me?" he says, pouting to express anguish. "With my own brother?"

"Oh, darling," she replies, eyes shining with glycerin tears, "I'm sorry. So sorry. I didn't mean to. It just happened."

"Oh, yes. It's all high drama here," Gunnhildur whispers. "*Guiding Light.* They're all watching *Guiding Light.* Now I'd prefer a proper blood-curdling murder story rather than this frothy nonsense. A classic British crime drama like *Morse* or *Taggart*, for instance. Whatever happened to them?"

I had wondered, after my phone conversation with Gunnhildur, whether the old lady might be living in an imaginary world of the British whodunit, where people are stabbed to death in grimy alleys or poisoned by a roast beef dinner on a country estate. Her remarks about her daughter's death seemed at odds with our reality. With the real world of Akureyri.

As she spoke to me on the phone, she became so distressed that a member of staff intervened and politely asked me to call back later.

And so I called back, sitting in the garden over my coffee and pastries. Gunnhildur wanted to meet me, and here I am, at the Hóll care home. I'm not about to dismiss elderly people, not until they reach the end of the road.

Gunnhildur Bjargmundsdóttir is a thin, lively, wiry little woman, with gray hair in a braid down her back. She walks with a cane but apparently has little need for it. Her limpid blue eyes are in constant motion, observing her surroundings. The skin of her face is rather leathery with age, yet remarkably unwrinkled. She has dignity. Life may have bowed her, but it hasn't broken her.

In men and women of Gunnhildur's years, old age seems to transcend gender. Neither specifically male nor female, they appear as human beings who have attained a kind of spiritual peace and inner beauty that nothing can disturb. Some battered more than others by life, their role is now to be observers rather than participants. They sit in the lounge, white-headed or balding, waiting for their departure to the final, inescapable destination, and watch *Guiding Light* to pass the time. Before very long—on the time scale of eternity at least—I'll be sitting there too.

No, I won't dismiss people because of their age.

But still, once we have fled the drama of *Guiding Light* and taken refuge in a little niche in the corridor, I catch myself speaking loudly.

"Keep your voice down, young man!" snaps Gunnhildur. "What, do you think I'm deaf? Do you want to bring the *Guiding Light* mafia down on my head?"

I'm confused. Is the old lady demented?

"No, God forbid," I mumble to myself.

"God!" she exclaims. "He's no use!"

"It's Easter," I continue in a whisper. "Aren't we supposed to be God-fearing at Easter?"

"Fearing?" Now it's Gunnhildur who's raising her voice. "How are we supposed to fear the One who made everything from nothing? And that's all that's left."

"What?" I whisper, looking around. "What's left?"

"Nothing," replies Gunnhildur softly. "Everything from nothing. In other words, nothing. Nothing from nothing."

I am, briefly, struck dumb.

"What did God do for my Ásdís Björk?"

"Um, I don't know."

"That's easy to answer. He did nothing. Not a thing."

"You mean…"

"All I mean is that God didn't save her from the danger she was in. He did nothing."

"What danger was she in?"

"From evil. Wickedness. Viciousness."

She leans forward to murmur in my ear. "Ásdís Björk was murdered. She was murdered in cold blood."

"In the coldest of blood that flows through human veins?"

She is taken aback. "Yes. How did you know?"

I decide to let it go. "So who killed her?"

"That scoundrel Ásgeir, of course. Who else?"

"You mean her husband? Ásgeir Eyvindarson?"

"Yes!" she shrilly exclaims. "Him. No one else!"

"Why would he kill his wife?"

"He's evil. Wicked. Vicious."

Gunnhildur's bright blue eyes are on me. She's daring me to contradict her.

"So how did he do it? She fell into the river in front of a crowd of witnesses. I'm sorry to go into unpleasant detail, Gunnhildur, but her face hit the rocks. She died of head trauma."

"Humph," she says, offended. "You're just like the police. I suppose you think I'm a loony old bat who's watched too much *Morse* and *Taggart*?"

At this precise moment, I can't think of anything to say to that.

"Not at all. It's just that it's easy to make allegations like that. What you're saying—where's the proof?"

"Proof?" she snaps. "How am I supposed to provide proof? An old lady stuck in a home?"

"Well, clues, then. Are there any clues?"

Gunnhildur places a wizened, liver-spotted hand on my knee. "Could it be a clue that Ásdís Björk had no intention of going on that goddamned wilderness tour?" she whispers. "Or that she and Ásgeir disagreed about how Yumm should be run? And that Ásgeir attended the company annual dinner while his wife was in hospital, fighting for her life?"

I consider what she has said. "Well, those could be clues to various things. A clue to conflict within the family firm. A clue about a disagreement over going on a wilderness tour. A clue to a managing director's sense of duty to his employees. But clues to murder? Not really, Gunnhildur."

"Well, then," she coldly retorts, withdrawing her hand. "I've no more to say to you. You can go now."

She is getting worked up again. "Why did you call me?" I calmly inquire. "I'm new in Akureyri, and I'm just finding my feet. You don't know anything about me."

"No, I don't know anything about you. But I read your articles in the paper about my daughter. And I saw what you wrote about those people who lost their dog. That's why I called you." Gunnhildur starts to weep. "But I see now that there was no point. Go away, young man. Leave an old woman to cry in peace."

On the evening of Good Friday, this is the news: Heida invited Jóa to dinner. Polly and I took a bath. Separately.

Then we watched a violent American action movie about the Passion of the Christ.

And as I tossed and turned through the night—pursued by Detective Chief Inspectors Morse and Taggart for the theft of a bottle of Jim Beam—at the Akureyri junkyard a body was found.

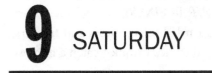

9 SATURDAY

What was it the clergyman said in his radio sermon on Palm Sunday?

If we wish to be disciples of Christ, we too must shoulder his cross and follow every day in his footsteps. The cross of suffering is an indispensable aspect of the life of all Christians. The events of Holy Week serve to help us understand the suffering in our own lives...

It's around midday on Easter Saturday, and Jóa and I are on our way to the junkyard at Krossanes, otherwise known as the Eyjafjördur Refuse and Recycling Scrap Metal Facility. At my first attempt I take a wrong turn, and we find ourselves down by the fjord at the Óseyri marina. But eventually we reach the dump, beyond the Krossanes fish factory.

The dump is enclosed by a fence, with a large central entrance gate. It is wide open, but on either side of it uniformed police officers stand guard. In front of the gate are five or six cars. By one of them I see a radio reporter with a little handheld outside-broadcast gadget, which always reminds me of a hip flask.

Another car bears the logo *Morning News*. On the other side of the fence is a shack, painted pale blue, with dumpsters and containers scattered around and a truck on which the slogan *SCRAP METAL IS OUR BUSINESS* is emblazoned. Plus two police cars, and one unmarked. They aren't painted with the slogan *DEATH AND DESTRUCTION ARE OUR BUSINESS*. Behind them I see huge stacks of tires, boxes, discarded refrigerators and freezers, and all sorts of garbage. In the distance I think I catch a glimpse of a car graveyard.

Jóa and I step out of the car, and she starts taking photos through the gateway, which is closed off by yellow crime-scene tape, and of the police and forensic specialists in their protective clothing. They are all preoccupied, many crouching over a half-burned pile of tires, from which dark-gray smoke is still rising into the motionless air in the bright sunlight.

I follow Jóa to the gate, where four reporters are clustered, brandishing their video cameras, mics, and tape recorders.

"What's happening?" I ask as I join them.

"We're waiting for a statement," says the *Morning News* reporter with a glance at his watch. "It's about time. I'm going to miss my deadline."

"What have we got?"

"Just that they found a body here at the dump last night."

"Is that it?"

I look around and spot a shiny white Citroën draw up by the other cars below the gate. Out of it steps Heida, editor of the *Akureyri Post*, wearing snug jeans and a summery white jacket.

She gives me a nice smile.

"Hi, and thanks for dinner the other night."

"My pleasure," I answer, looking around for Jóa.

She is still taking pictures. She turns around, and she and Heida politely nod to each other.

The local editor walks over to Jóa, taking from her pocket a small digital camera. As she takes pictures, she discreetly says something to Jóa.

We watch and wait, chatting casually to pass the time. After twenty minutes I see approaching us a big, sharp-featured man with a shaven head and heavy black-framed glasses. Chief of Police Ólafur Gísli Kristjánsson is in uniform. His manner is formal and distant as he ducks under the crime-scene tape to address the media.

"Good afternoon," he says as he glances over the group, pretending not to see me. "Unfortunately there isn't much I can tell you. Not at this point…"

This point in time, yet again, I think. What would the police do without it?

"…but here, at the Eyjafjördur Refuse and Recycling Scrap Metal Facility…"

Oh, the bureaucratic verbiage!

"…a body was found in the early hours of this morning. A search party of police and rescue volunteers made the discovery at around 5:30 a.m. A night watchman on his rounds had noticed smoke, which is not normal at that time of night, so he immediately got in touch with us."

The chief stops talking. He doesn't seem to have any more to say.

"Is the deceased a man?" asks the radio reporter, who is live on the air on the midday news.

Ólafur Gísli hesitates. "There are indications that it is, but we can't give a definite answer as yet."

"Is that because of the state of the body?" I inquire.

"I can't answer that question at this point in time."

"Is it unidentifiable?" I continue.

"No comment," he replies, putting on his glary face.

"Presumably we can deduce," I observe, "from the fact that we can see smoke here at the dump, that someone set fire to the body?"

"That is an inappropriate question at this point in time. We have yet to determine the identity of the deceased and then inform the next of kin. Until we have done so, such questions will not be answered."

"We can see a plume of smoke, apparently rising from a pile of tires over there," I say, pointing through the fence. "Can you at least confirm that someone set fire to the tires?"

"Yes, I can certainly confirm that."

"So would it also be unwise to deduce," asks the *Morning News* reporter, "that the body is that of high school student Skarphédinn Valgardsson?"

"Yes, that would be an unwise deduction," the chief replies, "at this point in time."

"But he hasn't been found?"

"No, he hasn't been found."

"So the search party that found the body was presumably looking for Skarphédinn?" asks the *Free Times*.

"Yes. But that doesn't necessarily mean that the body is that of the missing man."

"Has anyone else gone missing in the Akureyri area in the last few hours or days?" I ask.

"No," replies the chief. "No such notification has been received by the police."

The little group of reporters is growing restless.

"That's all I have for you at this point in time," says Ólafur Gísli. "Thank you."

"When can we expect more news?" asks the radio reporter, now off-air.

"When new information becomes available," the chief brusquely retorts. "The investigation is ongoing. We'll be working as quickly as possible. Thank you."

The chief is preparing to duck under the yellow tape again when he is accosted by reporters from state TV and *Vision 2*, who only arrived halfway through his statement. They want to film an interview, to which he reluctantly agrees. I wait around to eavesdrop on his interview. He adds nothing to what he said before.

The other reporters, including Heida, have all left by the time Jóa and I meet up back at the car.

"So what shall we do now?" she asks.

"Not a lot we can do. There's no paper till Tuesday. Let me drop you off somewhere. Have some fun."

She smiles at me, and her eyes go a little dreamy.

I hardly need to explain what Jóa's idea of fun is, in the present circumstances. As for me, I can't think of anything better to do than go to the offices of the *Afternoon News*. Ásbjörn is sitting at his computer. He jumps when I knock at the door and hurriedly closes the website he's looking at, but not before I notice spectacular images of sexual encounters, with gigantic cocks, voluptuous bosoms, and spread thighs. I pretend not to see. "So how're things?"

"Fine," he says, trying to appear cool in spite of his flushed cheeks.

"Where are Karó and Pal?"

"They're having a nap."

"I met your buddy, Chief Ólafur Gísli."

"Did you indeed? How did you get along with him?" he asks, sketching an ironic smirk on his red face.

"He started off by trying to throw me into confusion. And it worked. After that, I think we got along pretty well."

"Good."

"Yes, it is. Very good. And it's really invaluable to have the chief of police as a contact. Especially now, with this missing person case and the discovery of the body."

"It's a pity we aren't going to press again for another two days," observes the former news editor, wringing his hands. "Such a stroke of bad luck."

"Ásbjörn, I want to thank you for putting in a good word for me with Ólafur Gísli."

"It was nothing."

"You were under no obligation to help me. Do you remember the old movie *Casablanca*?"

Ásbjörn is taken by surprise. "I don't know. I don't know if I remember it. Why?"

"There are two characters in *Casablanca* who are at a standoff and distrust each other. At the end of the movie one of them says to the other: *I think this is the beginning of a beautiful friendship.* Remember?"

"Um, I think maybe it sounds familiar." His astonished expression is giving way to dawning comprehension. "What do you mean?"

"Nothing," I smile. "Or maybe…Perhaps I mean that in a movie it's important for the characters to be reconciled before *The End*."

How did *The Odd Couple* end, anyway?

I stare out of the window at the wall next door. Then I pick up the phone and punch in the number I've been given for theater director Örvar Páll Sigurdarson. He's a veteran actor, fiftyish, who hasn't been seen much onstage in Reykjavík in recent years. He got typecast in comedies and farces as he grew older and fatter and lost his hair. When I interviewed him at Hólar, I received the impression of a man who can't shake off the role of the clown and ends up being a clown himself. Always trying to raise a laugh. Unsuccessfully. His graying beard concealed most of a jowly face and a rather feminine little mouth with pouty lips. But the facial hair didn't add any appearance of intelligence or dignity, nor did it distract attention from the swollen red nose.

"God has always been hard on the poor," he quoted. That was about the cleverest remark he made, in answer to my question about why he had come north to direct the play. I suppose he must be better at directing than he is at telling jokes, I thought at the time, and still do. Like everyone else in that kind of interview, he commented, of course, that it was just so exciting working with these enthusiastic youngsters on this brilliant play. And so on.

"This is actor-director Örvar Páll Sigurdarson," enunciates the voice on the answering machine. "I'm busy achieving new triumphs in life or my art, or possibly both. Please leave a message after the tone, preferably making an offer I can't refuse. But if you're Spielberg, Coppola, or von Trier, just leave your name, and I'll get right back to you!"

Always the joker. I leave my name and phone number. An offer he can easily refuse. But of course he doesn't.

Within three minutes he's on the line. I ask if he can meet me to discuss the disappearance of Skarphédinn, and he is happy to do so. He says he's staying at Hotel KEA, so we agree to meet at the hotel bar in ten minutes.

"I'll be the tall, elegant gentleman in the gabardine suit," he says with a forced laugh. "If there are more than one, you'll recognize me by my diamond rings."

"It's quite appalling," he sputters as he gulps down half his bottle of beer and sets it back on the table with a shaking hand. "Appalling to find myself in this mess."

"Do you mean…"

"I mean that my contract was supposed to end today."

"Oh, that's what you mean."

He purses his feminine little mouth and takes another drink.

"So have you got lots of work waiting for you down south?"

"No, that's not what I said," answers Örvar Páll, draining the rest of the beer. "But it's appalling to be caught up in all this."

"It's worst for Skarphédinn, of course. And his family."

"Yes, of course. But I gather there's something a bit weird about the family."

"Really?"

He shifts forward in his seat, his big belly flopping over the edge of the table. He is wearing a blue turtleneck sweater and faded jeans. "I don't know much, really, about Skarphédinn's private life. But I know he didn't live with his parents. That's for sure."

"And what does that tell us?"

"It tells us he didn't want to live there."

"Surely that's quite normal? He's nearly twenty, after all."

"He'd been living in a student dorm before that."

"So you think his relationship with his family was strained in some way?"

Örvar Páll summons a passing waiter.

"I'm just mentioning it. After all, what do I know? Tell you what I do know—Bette Davis said: *If you've never been hated by your child, you've never been a parent.* Hahaha!"

"Would you like another beer?" I ask as the waiter hovers. In the restaurant is a crowd of people who have come to Akureyri to ski and been disappointed. So they're getting drunk instead.

"Now that's an offer I can't refuse."

"Do you have children of your own?" I ask as I order myself another Coke.

"Not yet. I'll have to choose the lucky lady who can demonstrate to me the truth of the maxim that the first half of your life is ruined by your parents and the second half by your children."

Örvar Páll gazes at me, hoping for a response.

I decide to indulge him and smile. "Did Skarphédinn strike you as an especially independent-minded young man?"

He thinks about it.

"That's the impression I got, on the one occasion I met him, at Hólar last Saturday," I add. "Independent. And unusually mature for his age."

"Yes, I suppose you could put it that way. He certainly had strong views. Sometimes rather too strong for my taste."

"Was he difficult to direct?"

He fidgets in his seat. The waiter brings the beer and Coke, and he eagerly seizes his drink.

"No, not at all. Not difficult. Determined. As a director, I like to work in a collaborative, collegial environment. I encourage all the members of the cast to make a contribution."

Maybe because you don't have much of a contribution to make yourself? I wonder.

"Did you get at cross-purposes?"

The silly old duffer stares at me as if I'd slapped him in the face. "Did someone say that? Who said so?"

"No, no. No one said it. I'm just asking."

He takes a drink and says nothing.

"Was he a good actor?"

"He was, as they say, promising. He had experience, of course."

"He did? What experience?"

Örvar Páll gazes his astonishment. "Oh, didn't you know? Do you remember *Street Rider*?"

"*Street Rider*...," I echo, trying to access my memory files.

"It was a teen movie."

"I don't remember whether I remember," I say, echoing Ásbjörn.

"Skarphédinn played the lead role."

"How long ago was this?" I ask, embarrassed that I don't remember *Street Rider*.

"It must have been about five or six years ago. Skarphédinn was fourteen or fifteen, I think."

"So he was a child star?"

"Child, or teen star," corrects Örvar Páll. "When they get pubic hairs, innocence goes out the window."

"I seem to remember reading that kids who have been child stars can have problems coping with life after their fifteen minutes of fame."

"Too much, too soon," he smiles. "Yes, we've seen a few cases of that."

"Do you think that's what happened to Skarphédinn?"

"Not so far as I know. As you said yourself, he gave the impression of being a determined, mature young man."

"Actually, what I said was that he gave me the impression of being independent and mature. You're the one who said *determined*."

He shrugs.

"So was that the sum of his acting experience? That movie and now *Loftur the Sorcerer*?"

"I believe so. I don't have a copy of his résumé," answers the director as he finishes his second bottle of beer. "I first made his acquaintance three weeks ago, along with the other youngsters in the drama group."

"Were you in *Street Rider*?"

Örvar Páll rolls his empty beer bottle between his palms. "Yes, actually, I did have a small part in the movie. I played a cop, I think."

Hmmm, I think. "But you said just now that you didn't know Skarphédinn before? Not until rehearsals started here in Akureyri?"

He gnaws at his dainty lip. The veneer of joviality has vanished. "If you want to be finicky about it," he says, "I said I first made his acquaintance three weeks ago. Before that I was on the movie set with him for one day, six years ago."

I give him a look. As inquisitorial as I can manage. I put on a glary face, like Chief of Police Ólafur Gísli.

"Look," he protests. "We've met. Twice. Would you say you know me?"

"All right," I admit. "I see what you mean."

"Just as well," says Örvar Páll with a guffaw. "Otherwise I'd have called the waiter over and asked for the phone book."

"What for?"

"To find a cheap lawyer." Örvar Páll is back in character.

I force a smile, call the waiter over, and ask him to bring, not the phone book, but yet another beer.

"Did you notice anything unusual or odd about Skarphédinn before he disappeared?"

"No, not really," he answers as he starts on his third beer. "Of course, I didn't really spend much time with the kids, other than at rehearsals."

"And the dress rehearsal on Wednesday went well, did it?"

"Just the usual. The odd problem. People dried up. Forgot their stage business. Some lighting that didn't work. That sort of thing. We went through it all after the rehearsal. Everybody seemed pretty happy with the dress rehearsal, so far as I could tell."

"Did you go to the party after the rehearsal, back here in town?"

"I just looked in briefly. Had a couple of beers. Then I came back here to the hotel and went to bed. I didn't approve of the kids having a party just before the first night of the show, of course. But it wasn't my place to tell them what to do."

"Where was the party?"

"At Ágústa's place. She's chair of the drama group."

"When was Skarphédinn there?"

Örvar Páll swills down bottle number three. "He arrived just before I left. About ten."

"And?"

"He seemed to be stone-cold sober. But…"

He falls silent and peers into the bottom of the bottle.

"But what?"

"He was wearing a dress."

———

114

The TV evening news and the Easter Sunday edition of the *Morning News* have nothing new to add about the body at the Akureyri junkyard, nor about the disappearance of Skarphédinn Valgardsson.

But they report that a public meeting has been called in Reydargerdi on Easter Monday, with community leaders and members of parliament for the region, to discuss the local "situation and prospects" in the countdown to the general election in May.

10 EASTER SUNDAY/EASTER MONDAY

"What pearl of wisdom came out of your Easter egg today, Trausti?"

"Oh, come on! Give it a rest, would you, buddy?" retorts the news editor.

"Could it be *No pain, no gain*?" I say.

"Ho, ho, ho. Very funny."

I have to admit I'm rather enjoying rubbing salt in his wounds and then twisting the knife. I know it's not big of me. *Little things please little minds* might have been the maxim from my egg. If I had an egg. I would have liked to come up with something funnier. But my childish glee is short-lived.

"You and Jóa must get over to Reydargerdi this afternoon or evening, to cover the public meeting at lunchtime tomorrow."

I exhale my cigarette smoke into the clear blue sky as I sit out in the garden, watching the neighboring children kicking a ball around.

Goddamn it to hell, I think to myself on this peaceful Easter Sunday when swearing is strictly forbidden, out loud at least.

"What kind of a slave driver are you?" I bark into the receiver. "You send us rushing around on a wild-goose chase, all over the country."

"News isn't confined to office hours, buddy. I thought you knew that."

"Can't we have one day off to relax?"

"I'm not relaxing," retorts the news editor. "I'm busy, talking to you. If you imagine I see that as relaxing, you're delusional."

"But I've got a missing person case and a dead body to cover. Just as examples. Isn't that more interesting than some politicians spouting the usual hot air, trying to drum up votes before the election?"

"You may well be right. But that meeting has got to be in Tuesday's paper. Things are heating up over there, and we've got to be there if and when they reach the boiling point."

He may have a point. But a thought crosses my mind and gives me pause: the new owners of the *Afternoon News*, alleged by their opponents to favor the Social Democratic Union and its leader, Sigurdur Reynir, may be quite happy to see in-depth reporting of the meeting in Reydargerdi, which is likely to consist of an all-out attack on the present government.

"So you're happy to pay for a hotel for the two of us for some stupid political bullshit meeting?" I ask, just to get in Trausti's face.

"Is it a matter of principle with you, to argue every point with the news editor?"

Only when the news editor is an idiot, I think. But I say, "You realize this means that the *Question of the Day* from Akureyri will have to be bumped over from Tuesday to Wednesday?"

He says nothing. Then: "All right. We'll handle it here. Now I really can't be bothered to argue with you anymore, buddy. Have a good trip."

Out of the kindness of his heart, Óskar has made up beds for us in two small and uncomfortable rooms in the basement, as the hotel is fully booked. After a mouthwatering dinner of Icelandic lamb with a Thai twist, Jóa and I make our way over to Reydin. It's past ten o'clock on this Easter Sunday evening, and the bar is half full. About forty people, most of them incomers. Tomorrow's public meeting isn't for them. They wouldn't understand the speeches, and nobody will be trying to win their votes. Yet the main reason for holding the meeting is the influx of these people and the consequences of their presence.

I glance around in search of Agnar Hansen and Co., but they are not here.

I go over to the bar and order a coffee for myself and a beer for Jóa from the same luscious bartender, who gives me a warm welcome.

"How are things?" I ask.

"Business is booming," she smiles.

"No business to do with Agnar?"

"He doesn't bring in much business. Not considering how much he drinks. He runs a tab here, which is paid—or not—by his dad."

"I heard he was kicked out of here?"

"Yeah, the owner had had enough trouble."

"What was the trouble this time?"

"Agnar sent some thugs to intimidate those Poles who beat him up last weekend."

"Didn't he go himself?"

"He wasn't in any state to do much."

"And he's accepted the ban?"

She nods. "He hadn't any choice about it. But he and his buddies have been running wild in Akureyri over Easter instead."

"So are they still there?"

"So far as I know. Agnar ceremoniously informed me that they were going to spend the holiday weekend skiing there."

"Yeah, well, I suspect that anyone trying to ski there at present will have a pretty rocky ride."

She smiles. "I'm sure he's stoned enough. And even when they're not banned from here, they always go over to Akureyri now and then, for some fun."

"Doesn't Agnar have a job?"

"Depends what you call a job."

I get the impression that she's not going to say any more.

"I promise I won't quote you. But is he dealing drugs here?"

"I can't answer that." Elín steps back from the bar and starts washing glasses in the sink.

"They say silence can mean consent," I say.

"Yes," she answers, with her back to me. "Sometimes it can."

When I join Jóa at the table, her beer has gone flat and my coffee is cold. I have second thoughts about Agnar: *If he's dealing drugs, why would he need to get his old man to pay his bar bill?*

"Pessimism has given way to optimism. We have come out of the doldrums into a time of high hopes for the future. And not hope alone. We now know for certain—we have reliable, indisputable evidence—that in this region, which means so much to us all, a new era of progress and prosperity has begun, in this community that has the resources to offer its inhabitants all the facilities and benefits that have hitherto been confined to the capital area and tended to attract our people away to the city. We see bright prospects for our children, our grandchildren, for parents and grandparents. For ourselves. For the future."

The members of parliament from the Conservative Party and the Center Party deliver identical speeches, more or less, then swagger back to their seats to an ovation from the packed convention room at Hotel Reydargerdi. At the table on the stage are representatives of all the political parties, plus the chair of the town council, Jóhann Hansen, and Mayor Anna Thóroddsdóttir, who is chairing the meeting. I met her on my first outing to Reydargerdi, last year. She seems to have put on weight since then. Her hefty frame is draped in a loose-cut black dress. In the front row is her uncle, Ásgrímur Pétursson, solemn in a gray three-piece suit. He is still as lean as ever, so far as I can tell. His hair is even thinner than when I saw him last. The members of parliament for the Social Democratic Union, the Radical Party, and the Other Party then get a chance to give their speech, which is:

"We can to some degree share the contentment of the parties in government, regarding the development in this region, which is boosting confidence and boldness in the local economy and the entrepreneurial spirit of this community; inaction has given way to action. But we ask you, people of Reydargerdi and the surrounding area, is this phenomenon real? Have employment opportunities improved in Iceland, in fact? Has the migration from the regions to the capital area been halted or even reversed? Hundreds of millions of *krónur* have been borrowed here. Have they benefited the local community or are they certain to do so? The answer is no, no, and no. In addition to which, we will have to face up to the unforeseeable consequences of a completely wrong-headed development policy, relying on heavy industry that will pollute the environment and hydroelectric plants that will wreak the worst damage to nature in the history of our nation. Government policy for this region is characterized by lack of imagination, narrow-mindedness, and short-termism, and the same is true of so many other parts of the country that have suffered the effects of the population drain."

And so on. And so on.

The opposition spokesmen garner little support and seem rather dejected as they return to their seats.

The chair of the meeting, Anna, declares that the floor is now open.

An awkward silence ensues.

The politicians on the stage seem to breathe more easily.

I'm about to whisper to Jóa, who's sitting next to me snapping pictures, that I could have written this article with one hand tied behind my back sitting in my office when I hear a voice from the back of the hall. I look around and see an elderly woman stand up, arm raised. She says she's a local housewife. "I've lived here in Reydargerdi all my life," she quavers nervously. "I've brought up four children, and I have eleven grandchildren. Of those fifteen, only three are still living here. I can accept that. It's the way things are. But I find it hard to accept that those of us who have stayed on here can't move around freely in our own community. We can hardly leave our homes at night, especially at weekends, for fear of aggression, intimidation, and threats, even violence, from drunk and drugged ruffians of all sorts—Icelanders and foreigners. We didn't have this problem before the days of what you choose to call *optimism*."

She is breathless as she finishes her speech, as if the nervous effort has exhausted her.

Then she adds: "I'm not addressing myself to the Martians from parliament. I'd like to hear what the town council has to say. Thank you."

Laughter. Haphazard applause begins, then spreads throughout the room.

The members of the panel shift uneasily in their seats.

Jóhann Hansen doesn't look happy. He passes a trembling hand over his smoothed-back graying hair and pulls at the neck of his dark red sweater. After a moment's thought he takes his place at the lectern.

"Thank you for your question. I understand your concerns," he soberly observes. "These issues are constantly under discussion among those who represent the community here." He pauses, then continues. "We will continue to scrutinize these issues and seek to achieve a solution that everyone will be happy with."

This doesn't raise much applause. Not even Ásgrímur Pétursson is clapping.

"Any more comments or questions?" asks Anna, desperately trying to keep control of the meeting.

"What are the authorities planning to do about all the illegal drugs that are pouring in here?" asks a man's voice from somewhere in the hall. "Whether they're to be sold up at the hydroelectric plant or on the factory site or here, in the streets and bars? How long is this going to be allowed to go on?"

Anna Thóroddsdóttir opts to answer this herself. "It would be naive to assume that major development projects like these, which have led to an influx of people from all over the world, won't give rise to any social problems. The unavoidable price..."

"Now who's being naive?" asks the same voice. "Weren't the municipal authorities naive in neglecting to take into account the *unavoidable price*, as the mayor chooses to call it?"

The whole meeting breaks into applause.

"If you'll allow me to finish what I was saying," resumes Anna, obviously disconcerted, "when a community undergoes such a huge transformation, there will inevitably be a price to pay. We may even call it a revolution. Here in Reydargerdi we have experienced, and are experiencing, a revolution in our standard of living..."

"Anna!" shouts a young woman. "Don't you know that traveling pimps come here regularly, with girls from down south for sale? Are the town authorities in favor of sex trafficking?"

A wave of applause. Mainly from women.

Two men give a wolf whistle. Some males in the audience exchange conspiratorial looks.

"Have the town authorities formulated a policy to respond to organized crime if it seeks to establish itself here in Reydargerdi?" asks an elderly man tranquilly. "I don't just mean the degradation entailed by bringing in cheap labor, as it's called—impoverished workers with limited rights, who are nobody's responsibility. I'm also referring to the marketing of amphetamines from Estonia and heroin from St. Petersburg and cannabis coming in by ferry from Scandinavia. And, like the lady who spoke earlier, I also mean prostitution and pornography and the sex trade in general. I ask again: Have the town authorities formulated a policy to respond to this menace?"

Anna Thóroddsdóttir looks at Jóhann Hansen, who in turn looks at Ásgrímur Pétursson. The expressionless face of the local boss gives them nothing to work with.

"So Jóhann Hansen thinks he's going to safeguard our children from drugs and violence, does he?" exclaims a woman.

There is no need to articulate the rest: Jóhann Hansen couldn't even safeguard his own son! And now our children need protection from his son!

A muttering spreads though the hall. Nobody is clapping. You can feel the toe-curling embarrassment. That was a blow below the belt.

Jóhann Hansen looks down at a sheet of paper and makes a note with a shaky hand. Then he removes his misted glasses and wipes them on the sleeve of his sweater.

The member of parliament for the Radical Party breaks the oppressive silence by calling from his seat: "It's encouraging to hear how many people here have realized what is really happening here and agree with the Radical Party's views. Right from the start, when the governing parties started paying court to the regions and dangling prospects of industrial development, we have been arguing that international finance will entail international problems..."

Though in full flood with his party political address, he is soon silenced by boos from the audience. And the public meeting in Reydargerdi on Easter Monday gradually deteriorates into a shouting match among the bigwigs from down south.

I switch off my tape recorder and stand up with a nod to Chief of Police Höskuldur Pétursson, who is sitting directly behind me, then make my way through the crowd to the hotel bar. A few teenagers stand in a huddle, smoking. Two middle-aged men are sipping beers. At the corner of the bar is a young man who looks familiar. I can't identify him until I've had a nicotine hit.

It's the guy who was sitting at Agnar Hansen's table at the Reydin bar. When I approached he stood up and left. He doesn't seem to notice me. Maybe he doesn't remember me.

A pale and distressed Jóhann Hansen gives the closing remarks at the meeting:

"I'd like to thank our local members of parliament and you, the people of Reydargerdi and the surrounding area, for attending this meeting and raising so many interesting points. I assure you that these issues will be given serious attention by the town council in the future, just as they have in the past."

"I declare this meeting closed," adds Anna Thóroddsdóttir, slipping a tissue down between her heavy breasts.

WHO WILL PROTECT OUR CHILDREN
FROM INTERNATIONAL CRIME?
asked Reydargerdi people at a heated public meeting yesterday.
Town authorities under attack.
Optimism about the future of the community
overshadowed by concerns over social problems.

That is my introduction to my article, which is ready to send in by dinnertime.

I take a breath and nibble at deep-fried chicken pieces that I picked up from a global fast-food franchise on my way back to the office.

Next on the agenda: Dead Body. Missing Person.

On the TV and radio news the police are saying nothing.

I call the police station, giving my name. I'm put through to a woman who tells me nothing.

I ring the station again and, without giving my name, ask for Ólafur Gísli Kristjánsson. He's unavailable.

I consider my options, then go out onto the stairs and climb the worn wooden steps to the third floor. I am met by a strong odor of cauliflower with a dash of garlic and fish. I hear muffled barking and a low mumble of the weather forecast on the radio. It sounds as if a cloudy night is expected, with falling temperatures.

I knock at the door.

Karólína half opens the door. "Ásbjörn Grímsson!" she calls out. "It's the intrepid Einar for you!"

And with that, she is gone.

I hear Ásbjörn apologizing to Pal because he's got to leave the room.

"I'm sorry to disturb you at mealtime," I say as Ásbjörn waddles to the door.

He makes no reply, chewing on a tattered toothpick.

"It looks as if the police aren't going to give any information about the body this evening," I tell him. "I can't get hold of Ólafur Gísli. He's not taking calls. I was wondering if you could do something?"

He keeps gnawing on the toothpick.

"Well?" I ask. "Can you?"

"Go down to the office. I'll call in a minute."

No, no, don't invite me in, I think as I make my way back down the stairs.

While I wait, I blow clouds of smoke out of the open window to the wall opposite.

The phone rings. "Wait a bit," says Ásbjörn. "He'll call you in a few minutes."

"Great," I reply. "Thank you."

"Actually, he said he thought you'd been rather argumentative down at the junkyard on Saturday."

"Argumentative? I was just asking obvious questions. He can hardly expect me to stop being a reporter just because you put in a word for me. Can he?"

"Calm down, Einar. Then he said it would probably be best if you were as argumentative as possible with him in public, and he'll argue back. That will make it harder for anyone, his lot or the other media, to pinpoint where your information is coming from. If there is any information."

"He's absolutely right."

"But everything has to go through me. Completely confidential."

"I agree to that."

I think to myself that this will give the former news editor a little bit of self-respect and influence. I can allow him that. So long as I get the news stories.

"Hey, Ásbjörn," I add before we end the conversation. "While I remember. Are you still getting those mysterious phone calls?"

"No," he replies. "Strangely enough, they stopped after I told you about them."

"Good," I say. "Then my intervention has worked."

I picture his perplexed expression. "What intervention?"

"Just let me know if the phone calls start again."

"What goddamned intervention?"

"I'm sorry, that's absolutely confidential. Everything has to go through me."

Then I hang up, with a silly smirk.

———

After waiting half an hour, with the news editor down south hassling me about missing my deadline, I receive information from my confidential source and write the following article:

BODY AT AKUREYRI JUNKYARD
BELIEVED TO BE SKARPHÉDINN VALGARDSSON

The body that was discovered on Saturday morning at Krossanes near Akureyri, at the scrap metal yard, is believed to be Skarphédinn Valgardsson, a 19-year-old student at Akureyri High School. He had been missing since Wednesday evening. On Holy Thursday the high school drama group was to have given its first performance of Loftur the Sorcerer *at Hólar, with Skarphédinn in the title role. An extensive search, organized by the Akureyri police, began around midday on Thursday and led to the discovery of the body nearly two days later. According to* Afternoon News *sources, preliminary indications are that the circumstances of the young man's death are suspicious. The body is believed to have been moved after death. Other aspects of the matter are, at this point in time...*

I delete the last few words and write instead:

Other aspects of the case remained unclear when the Afternoon News *went to press.*

11 TUESDAY

What happened on Good Friday?

Jóa and I stand shivering in the cold wind sweeping across Town Hall Square, trying to get some of the very few passers-by to answer the *Question of the Day* from Akureyri a day later than usual. The sky is overcast. The mountains, gray and forbidding. The waters of the fjord, ruffled. The passers-by are in much the same condition. Jóa and I too.

It takes us half an hour to get five answers.

A little boy: *Jesus died.*

A teenage girl: *Nothing in particular. I watched a video.*

A middle-aged man: *Something in the Bible...no, don't remember.*

An elderly lady: *Christ was crucified.*

A young boy: *I went to a party and then to the Sjallinn disco. Didn't open till after midnight. What is it with these weird rules about holiday openings?*

Yep. What is it?

I don't know. But what I do know is that events that took place two thousand years ago in Holy Week haven't helped us understand the suffering in our own lives. Whatever the clergy say. After sending in the answers to the *Question of the Day*, I do my best to put together some small local news stories. Shopkeepers in the town center are uneasy about plans for a new mall in the suburbs. Bench vandals caught red-handed. Ten drug arrests on Easter Monday.

My article about the body at the junkyard is all over the front page, and my piece about developments in Reydargerdi is featured on the back page, with the main article inside. Although it's always satisfying to get a scoop, I'm feeling a bit down. No doubt an effect of the gray weather, combined with the fatigue from my long working hours of late.

Just for something to do, I call Hannes.

"Excellent coverage today, sir," he says. Perhaps all I wanted was to hear him say that.

"But I'm getting tired of rushing back and forth to Reydargerdi," I protest. "Trausti seems to be obsessed with the situation there."

"Whatever the reason, you're writing good copy. Something is brewing there."

"True," I admit. "Something is brewing there. But isn't Trausti motivated purely by politics?"

"His motivation isn't your problem. You simply go there and write your articles, which are nonpolitical."

I want to try testing Hannes a little. Since the merger, when the *Afternoon News* became a part of the Icelandic Media Corporation, there have been allegations that Hannes, and by extension the newspaper, is a mere puppet of the Social Democratic Union, now in opposition in parliament. I've never asked Hannes before, although I've wanted to for a long time. I decide to jump in: "Tell me, Hannes, was Trausti Löve your choice as news editor? Did you press for him to be appointed?"

He buys himself time by lighting a cigar.

"An appointment of that nature, when new stockholders become involved in a media enterprise, will always be a compromise of some kind. There were various different views that had to be reconciled."

He's obviously not going to answer. "Why don't you answer my question, Hannes? Did you suggest Trausti?"

"Now, Einar, you know I can't discuss with you what happens at meetings between the editorial board and the owners."

"Would it be wrong of me to draw the conclusion that, if it had been your idea, you would tell me?"

"Well…"

"Did the Owner—with a big O—want Trausti appointed?"

"Fortunately the company has many owners—with a small o. And when they join forces, they can be big too."

"But not as big as the big one?"

"As I said, certain viewpoints have to be reconciled with regard to important decisions about the running of any paper. A person who gets his or her way on one issue will back down over another. That's the way it works. As one of the smaller stockholders, I exert my influence as I see best for the paper. That's the way it is, my good sir. Simply the way it is."

"Well, if that's the way it is, I would urge you to exert your influence as soon as possible to kick that clown out of the news editor's chair. You could keep Trausti Löve on to write about men's fashion or restaurants and wines."

He exhales his cigar smoke. "We shall see. Let's give him a chance. Like others have had. You've made mistakes of your own over the years, as we all have. And you were offered second—and third—chances."

I realize that my dislike and contempt for Trausti have gotten out of control. I've reached a point where I'd like to see him destroyed. *My desires are powerful and boundless. And in the beginning was desire. Desires are the souls of men,* said Loftur the Sorcerer.

In a white concrete building on Skipagata, a few minutes' walk from the *Afternoon News* offices, the *Akureyri Post* has its offices on the second floor, above an optometrist's shop. They seem to be on a similar scale to us. But their offices reflect that incomprehensible obsession in modern design with tearing down all partitions between individual workspaces, to create a single "large, bright, dynamic space." In practice it means that everyone is thrown together. You can't have a telephone conversation—in fact, you can hardly draw breath, let alone sneeze—without throwing the whole workplace into disarray. Or have a smoke. No doubt it's *as in the neighboring countries.* I'd rather have my own little private closet, thanks very much.

As I enter the "space," which is only a pretentious word for a room, I find Jóa sitting there with her feet up on Heida's desk. At two other desks, people are trying to work. The glass-and-steel desks with their steel-and-leather chairs would look at home in a nightclub. Everything neat and tidy.

"Hello," I whisper, as if I were in a library. "How's it going?"

"Fine," answers Heida with a smile, in her normal voice.

Maybe it is possible to get used to a "space" like this, I think.

Jóa is quite at ease. "Let's have a coffee," she says, pointing to a door at the back. Hey, one ordinary room has survived.

The coffee room at the *Akureyri Post* is five times the size of my office, painted white, with more steel/glass/leather furnishings.

"Did you do a promotional deal with the Furniture Store?" I ask Heida. "Furniture for advertising space?"

"Actually, that's exactly what I did," she replies as she starts the coffeemaker. "Necessity is the mother of interior decoration."

We sit on the steel and leather and discuss the latest local events.

Then I ask Heida: "Have you heard anything new about the Skarphédinn Valgardsson case? What do your contacts say?"

She looks me right in the eye. "Do you think I'd tell you? Let you steal my scoops?"

"Sorry. But I get the impression that the *Akureyri Post* isn't big on reporting so-called negative news. Raking up the dirt like we do down south."

"No, true enough. We want to present a positive picture of life in Akureyri. That's what our clients like. But of course we report on what happens here. And we'll have a story on the case in Thursday's paper."

"It's debatable whether it's responsible to display responsibility without falsifying reality."

"Hmmm…"

"But it's OK to soften it a little?"

She smiles. "You should try being me for a few months. You'd be a changed man after such a course of treatment."

"A better man?"

"A different man."

"Einar doesn't want to change," interjects Jóa. "He thinks all change is the devil's work."

"Nonsense!" I retort. "Look at me: I haven't had a drop of alcohol for two months."

"All right," Jóa continues. "Maybe it's more accurate to say that you see change as entailing a sacrifice of the accrued rights of your personality."

I can only laugh. "I think there's something in your analysis, Jóa. Maybe even quite a lot."

"But this Skarphédinn case," says Heida. "It's only just begun, of course. And as a weekly paper, we don't have much chance of a scoop, not in competition with you on the daily papers. Let alone radio and TV."

"You seem to be doing your usual thing, Einar," observes Jóa. "Crime scoops, when you've only just arrived in this sleepy little town. Where you go, trouble follows."

"So far as I can tell, there's plenty of trouble to be found all over the place. I can't be everywhere."

"But I can tell you one thing, if you haven't heard," says Heida. "Several sources have told me that a link is being suggested between Skarphédinn's disappearance and that Reydargerdi gang."

"His disappearance?" I ask in astonishment. "But what about his death? Are they supposed to have killed him?"

"No one's saying that, not yet. But they were here in town over Easter."

"Yeah, I know," I reply. "I heard that over in Reydargerdi yesterday. And shortly after our dinner on Wednesday evening, I caught a glimpse of the gang leader, Agnar Hansen, in a car cruising on Strandgata."

"Did you?" exclaims Jóa. "Did you see who was with him?"

"No, unfortunately not. He was in the back of the car. That's all I saw."

"Have you told the police about this?" asks Heida.

I'm taken aback. "No. Actually I haven't. It wasn't until yesterday evening that the body was identified, and it was said to be a suspicious death—as they say when they don't want to commit themselves to murder, manslaughter, or other variants of carnage."

We remain silent for a while.

"And in fact nobody suggested a connection between the Reydargerdi gang and the murder. Not to me. Not until you mentioned it just now, Heida."

"I'm not suggesting anything. Just passing on what I've heard."

"So you haven't got this from the police?"

"No, not at all. Just the classic rumor mill."

"The classic rumor mill can be unreliable, not to say slippery. It's always easy to lay the blame on outsiders when something unpleasant or unusual occurs."

Trausti Löve had better not hear this rumor from Akureyri. That would really put the fox in the henhouse.

Heida puts down her coffee cup, stands up, and makes ready to go on with her work.

"Yes. When the news is vague, not all of us can resist the temptation to speculate," she observes. Then she adds with a smile: "But here at the *Akureyri Post*, we never do that. We show responsibility without falsifying you-know-what."

In the afternoon I go and hang around the police station. I'm not expecting to get much out of it. I'm there mostly to show myself, see and be seen. Divert attention from a certain channel of information and make it known that I'm talking to more than one or two police officers. I'm muddying the waters.

I don't get any more out of my efforts. At the police station the atmosphere is so tense you could cut it with a knife. The police here haven't had to deal with a case like this for a long, long time. Some officers are polite but reserved, while others are brusque and skeptical of me and of the *Afternoon News*. When I've been loitering in the reception area for nearly an hour, trying to accost passing police officers, I decide that it's time to move on.

Chief Ólafur Gísli didn't pass through the reception area while I was there, so I decide to call on Ásbjörn's goodwill a second time.

"No, we have no suspects at this point in time," is Ólafur Gísli's answer to my first question.

"Any clues?" I try to elicit more without referring to the gossip about the Reydargerdi gang.

"There are always clues. We'll follow up on all information we receive. But it takes time. People must understand—especially you in the media—that investigation of a criminal case of such a serious nature is inevitably time-consuming."

I'm not quite ready to back down. "Isn't there a lot of gossip around town?"

"Of course. But we're not going to devote time to that, now are we?"

"No, no, God forbid," I reply.

He says nothing. I realize I've got my work cut out.

"Was our article in today's paper all right?"

"All right? Nope. It was not all right, let me tell you!"

Oh, hell. What did I do wrong now? "What was wrong with it?" I nervously inquire.

"There wasn't a damn thing wrong with it! That's what was wrong with it! I've been flailing around here, trying to find out who leaked that information. It's absolutely intolerable."

Someone must be overhearing him now.

"It's intolerable for the police not to be able to carry out their work without leaks that may endanger the progress of the investigation. You media people should take account of other interests than…"

I wait until he runs out of steam.

He half covers the mouthpiece, and I hear him say, "Yes… OK…Yes…Do that…Fine…" to someone who has entered his office. "No, I'll be with you in a minute…. Just need to finish this…"

I'm still waiting.

"Are you there, you bastard?" he asks.

"Mhmm."

"What we're trying to do now is to retrace the last hours of Skarphédinn Valgardsson's life. But I won't say anything about it now. At present, we're simply working on the case."

"So there's no news at this point? Nothing new?"

"Like what? What can you think of?"

"Er…" I try to think of something.

"Ask me something. Or I'll have to stop this bullshit."

"We reported today that Skarphédinn's body is believed to have been moved after he was killed."

"Yes. Call this journalism?"

I think the chief is having a laugh.

"Where do you think he died?"

"Good question," chortles Ólafur Gisli. Now he sounds like a politician trying to win time so he can avoid answering the question and answer another one instead.

"Were you thinking of answering it?"

"No, I won't. Not for now. Next question."

"Do you know any more about the cause of death?"

"Not quite such a good question. But indications are…I reiterate, indications are—as the final autopsy findings won't be available for another two days—indications are that he died as a result of head trauma, arising from a fall."

"So he had a fall? It wasn't a blow to the head?"

"You heard me right. He suffered brain trauma on the opposite side to the frontal injury. That indicates that his head struck an obstacle at considerable speed. So his head was not motionless, as it is when someone is struck on the head as they stand. In the case of a blow to the head, the internal brain trauma is generally in the same location as the external injury."

"Any broken bones, other injuries?"

"No fractures. The rest is still under investigation."

"Could he have fallen rather than have been pushed?"

"He either fell or was pushed."

"So it could have been an accident or suicide?"

"What did that goddamned article of yours in the *Afternoon News* today say?"

Hang on, I think. What's he talking about? "Do you mean the body had been moved?"

"Have you ever heard of someone falling to his death, by accident or design, then getting up, moving to another place, and setting fire to himself?"

"No, I don't think I have," I reply and find myself smiling inappropriately.

It's not easy to write an update on the investigation into the disappearance and death of Skarphédinn Valgardsson. I know, going on what my source has told me, that a number of police, forensics personnel, and other experts are aware of the facts I now know. Also the dead man's family. And no doubt others. But it's difficult to write the piece without getting into trouble. My continued access to information depends upon my writing this piece in such a way as to conceal the source of my information while displaying tact for the feelings of Skarphédinn's family.

After an hour at the computer, I think I've managed the task and send in my piece. Although it's cold out, I open the window and light a cigarette. Then the phone rings.

Expecting some new hell from Trausti Löve, I gently lift the phone and speak: "You have reached Einar's phone at the *Afternoon News*. I'm busy carrying out important reporting assignments on fashion shows and wedding receptions for news editor Trausti Löve, but if you leave..."

"Hi, Dad. Stop messing around."

"Gunnsa, sweetheart! Welcome home. Have you just landed?"

"Yeah, I'm calling from my cell. We're on our way into town from the airport."

"And how was it?"

"Ab-so-lute-ly awe-some!"

"Was it?"

"In-cre-di-bly cool!"

"Oh, I am glad. I thought you'd be bored stiff."

"I even saw loads of Danish houses."

"Well, well."

I can hear some muffled chatter between Raggi and his mom and some goddamned guy.

"I'll tell you more about it tomorrow. How have you been?"

"Awesomely cool, as always. I'll tell you more later."

"OK. Speak to you tomorrow."

Akureyri suddenly seems brighter—and Iceland too. Scandinavia, Europe, the world, the universe.

As I lie down to sleep, tired out, with Polly around eleven o'clock, for some reason another parent and another daughter enter my mind: Gunnhildur Bjargmundsdóttir and Ásdís Björk Gudmundsdóttir.

12 WEDNESDAY

The last hours of Skarphédinn's life?

On my way into town on a wet and windy morning, I can't think of anything better to do than retrace the police's footsteps.

"What do you think?" I ask Ásbjörn as we sit over a coffee at the *Afternoon News* offices.

He slurps his inky black beverage and frowns. "I don't know why you're asking me. News is nothing to do with me anymore."

"Yeah, but I'm asking mainly because your contact with Ólafur Gísli is crucial to our keeping ahead of the pack in coverage of the case. I mean, do you think he'll take offense if I start getting information elsewhere? Do you think he's expecting me to wait here patiently for him to feed me tidbits about the investigation?"

"He knows perfectly well who you are. How you work."

"So?"

"So you must do what you feel is right." He hesitates, then continues: "But I think you should keep me informed about what you come up with. Then I can pass information along to Ólafur Gísli if necessary. It's all the better if it can be a two-way street."

"All the same, I doubt I'll find anything out that the police don't already know. I'm sure they'll be a step, or several steps, ahead of me. It's inevitable."

"We'll see," says Ásbjörn, who's unusually cheery today.

I lean forward and take out a cigarette, without lighting up: "Do you miss being news editor, Ásbjörn?"

He waves an angry finger at my cigarette. "Don't you light that thing in here! I know you're always smoking in your office. And you know I don't approve. But I can't be bothered to argue with you anymore about your urge for self-destruction. Provided you leave the rest of us alone!"

"OK, OK, OK," I say, slipping the cigarette into my breast pocket. "I sometimes forget myself."

"And I've got nothing to say about the news editorship. You know that the matter was handled disgracefully."

"There's no honor left in modern business, Ásbjörn. Surely you know that."

He snorts.

"But let me tell you," he resumes. "I'm going to show how unfair and unjustified it was. I'm going to prove myself here in the north."

"Hannes told me they're already seeing results. Sales in the north are up—both retail and subscriptions. And they're selling more advertising to local businesses."

Ásbjörn wriggles. "I'm well aware of that." Then he gives me a straight look. "And we've got to keep up the good work."

I realize that Ásbjörn Grímsson is not entirely free of guile himself. He's helping me in order to help himself. And Chief Ólafur Gísli is repaying an old favor for the same reasons: he's helping me to help Ásbjörn to help him.

———

In my smoky little room, my head is filled with ideas. Where can I find out about the last hours of Skarphédinn's life? It would be inappropriate to contact his family so soon after his death. And since he had a place of his own, the family probably can't tell me much anyway. I can see no better option than to start with Ágústa, chair of the drama group. But first I must, reluctantly, make another call.

"Trausti."

"Hello. Einar here, in Akureyri."

"Buddy!"

"I just want to be clear that we've agreed that I can focus on the Skarphédinn case for the next few days and forget the trivial stuff for now."

"Depends what you call trivial. But the case is good for sales. So you can concentrate on that, as long as nothing more important comes up."

"OK."

"What have you got lined up for tomorrow's issue?"

"I don't know. I'm going to try to find out what Skarphédinn was doing before he vanished on Wednesday evening."

"Sounds good."

"But I may not have enough for a story for tomorrow's paper."

"Oh, yes, you will. And don't forget the police investigation. The autopsy. The crime scene. All that."

All that yourself, you trivial little moron.

Energetic little Ágústa is less perky than she was at the rehearsal at Hólar. She lives with her parents in a rather dilapidated detached house on one of the narrow streets off Strandgata. Facing me across the laminated kitchen table in the dead gray light with a glass of water in front of her, she seems to have aged several years since I saw her. The freckles that enlivened her face have faded into the pale skin.

"How are you doing?" is the first question that occurs to me.

"Not good, thank you very much," she answers in a small voice. "I haven't slept for three nights."

"Aren't they offering grief counseling at the high school?"

"Yes, if we want it. With the student counselors."

"Doesn't it help?"

"I haven't asked for it. Not yet. I'm not sure that counseling can replace the actual trauma."

"Replace? Isn't it supposed to help you get over the trauma rather than replacing it?"

"Oh, I don't know," she says, her cropped head hunched over the table. "Sometimes I think that traumas happen because they're meant to happen, that they're an important experience, even a valuable one, and we shouldn't try to minimize that or make it easier on ourselves. I just don't know."

I glance around. "You live here with your parents?"

She nods down at the table.

"Do they both work?"

"Dad's a fisherman, and Mom works shifts. She has a job in a bakery during the day, and then she works as a cleaner in the evenings and at night."

"I gather the party on Wednesday evening was here. So your parents weren't home, then?"

"They're not here much."

"Are you an only child?"

"I have a younger sister. She's away at boarding school."

Ágústa seems so unhappy that I can hardly bring myself to go on with the interview.

"Do you want me to leave?" I ask her.

She looks up from the table. "No. I'll do my best to answer your questions. Have you got a cigarette?"

I produce my cigarettes, offer her one, and have one myself.

We smoke for a while in silence. Outside the window the wind howls through the naked branches of the trees, blowing the washing horizontal on the line outside.

She's agreed to talk to me on the condition that I don't refer to her by name, but she makes no objection when I switch on my tape recorder. "How did the party come to be held?"

"It was simply that we'd all been working so hard. We wanted to relax a bit, put first-night nerves out of our minds. I knew my parents wouldn't be home, so I let it be known that there would be an open house here."

"When you say 'open house,' do you mean that the party wasn't only for members of the drama group or those who were actually involved in the play?"

Ágústa gives me a strange look: "Haven't you ever had a party?"

"Not for ten to fifteen years, I don't think. Why do you ask?"

"It's just that sometimes people turn up at a party without being invited. People bring someone with them. People drift in off the street."

"And is that what happened that evening?"

She stubs out her cigarette. "There were no admission tickets. People came and went. After a while you stop noticing."

"So people dispersed all over the house, without you seeing all of them. Or knowing all of them."

"I suppose. I was in the kitchen chatting for most of the evening."

"How many people do you think were here?"

She shakes her head. "I don't know. Up to about thirty, maybe. But as I said, I wasn't counting—or noticing."

"What about Skarphédinn? When did he arrive?"

She thinks for a moment. "The police have asked me all this, and I can only tell you what I told them. I'm just not sure. Maybe about eleven."

"And when did he leave?"

"I have no idea. There comes a point when you forget the time. And everything else."

I don't know what to make of her answers or lack of answers. Maybe that's simply what parties are like. Timeless. Amorphous. Incalculable. Unpredictable. But I venture to ask her: "Were your guests very drunk?"

A slight smile in her green eyes doesn't reach her mouth. "Could be."

"What about the hostess?" I smile back.

"I was just having a good time."

"Who arrived with Skarphédinn?"

"I didn't notice."

"Who did he leave with?"

"Didn't see that either."

"Were you two close friends?"

She glances out of the window. "We knew each other pretty well."

"Who were his best friends? Who else should I talk to?"

"Skarphédinn has…" She stops, then goes on: "Skarphédinn …had a lot of friends. He was very popular. I don't think I've ever known a person my age who knew such a lot of people."

"But who knew him best?"

She thinks. "I can't answer that. Skarphédinn had lots of groups of friends. All different."

"How did he get on with the director, Örvar Páll?"

Ágústa doesn't answer right away. "Not badly," she says, "considering that Skarphédinn had apparently given more thought to the play than the director had."

"Did he get in Örvar's face?"

"Well…Örvar was a bit nervous around him. I think Skarphédinn sometimes threw him for a loop."

"Why did Örvar get the job?"

"We contacted a number of people. But I think Skarphédinn suggested him—said he wouldn't give us any trouble."

"Give you any trouble?"

"Yes. And Örvar Páll jumped at the offer."

"He told me he didn't approve of this party, the evening before the first night. Is that right?"

"Yeah, he was grumbling about it to Skarphédinn. But he soon backed down."

"Did Skarphédinn have a difficult relationship with his parents?"

"Not that I know of," she says in surprise. "Why would you think that?"

"Well, maybe because he hasn't lived at home since he started high school. At first he lived in the dorm, and then he moved into his own apartment last fall."

"That was just because he didn't like to be dependent on anyone. That's simply who he was."

"Then I have to ask you one thing: On the phone the other day, you told me you hadn't noticed anything odd or out of the ordinary about Skarphédinn that evening."

"What about it?"

"I've been told that he arrived about ten o'clock..."

"Ten, eleven. What difference does it make?"

"No, it's not a question of the time. From what I've been told, he was wearing a dress."

Ágústa's melancholy expression suddenly gives way to hysterical laughter.

"If you think there was something odd or unusual about that," she chokes, tears in her eyes, "it shows you didn't know Skarphédinn."

"Really? Was he in the habit of wearing a dress?"

She reaches for a roll of paper towels, tears off a sheet, and dries her eyes. "He simply enjoyed being alive. He wanted life to constantly present him with the unexpected—and other people too. He was always doing the weirdest things."

"So he wasn't a transvestite, as such?"

Ágústa strives not to burst out laughing again. "Nope. Don't think so. He was just always looking for fun."

"And he wasn't gay?"

"Why would you think that?"

"Well," I reply, fully aware that I'm awfully old-fashioned and bigoted, "because he was wearing a dress."

Her pale and tear-stained face is turned down toward the table. She starts picking at some dirt that has collected at the metal edge. "So far as I saw, and remember, it wasn't just any old dress he was wearing."

"So what was it?"

"He was wearing a black robe, with a cord at the waist."

"Like a monk?"

"No, like a witch."

Back at work, I call Trausti Löve to tell him I need more time to reconstruct Skarphédinn's last hours. Ágústa—I'm sure she's hiding something—gave me the names and phone numbers of the leading members of the drama group, who also seem to have been the leading revelers at her party. But I can tell it's not going to be easy to put together a coherent picture of events. Trausti replies with encouraging words, such as: *Show what you're made of, buddy.*

I call Gunnsa, and we exchange tales of our Easter adventures. She promises to visit me one weekend, as soon as possible, whenever it's convenient. I call my parents, and they tell me how pleased they are to hear me sounding so cheery from Akureyri.

With Ásbjörn as intermediary, by dinnertime I have Ólafur Gísli on the phone.

"Is the picture getting any clearer?" I ask.

"Some of it is. Some isn't. What about you?"

"A few things. Mostly not."

"Some days are harder work than others."

"Yep, you're right there. Shall I ask you some questions?"

"Up to you. Would you rather I asked you?"

"Not unless you want to. Has the time of death been established?"

"Not precisely. But it looks as if he died between between three and six in the morning on Holy Thursday."

"Have you been able to confirm when he left the party?"

"About that party. We don't seem to have anything solid to go on. It's almost as if it never happened. Or to put it another way, it's as if no one who was there can confirm what happened."

"Have you spoken to all of them?"

"From the party? How many were there? Who were they? Nobody seems to know."

"Do you know anything about where Skarphédinn went after the party?"

"Not yet."

"Or who was with him?"

"Not yet."

"So you haven't got much in the way of clues?"

"No, I must admit. So far."

"At this point in time?"

"Couldn't have put it better myself."

"What about forensics? From the body? And from the scene where he was found?"

"It's way too soon for that. We won't have anything from forensics for a few days at least. Have you visited a garbage dump recently?"

"Not since I came up here to Akureyri. When I moved out of my basement in Reykjavík."

"If you cast your mind back to the bittersweet memory of your little pigsty, maybe you can imagine the trace evidence that shows up on things at the dump. And on a human body in among all the scrap iron and garbage."

"But where do you think Skarphédinn was killed? Was it a long way from the dump?"

"No. We think he died there."

"What have you got?"

"We found evidence—blood and other traces. The obvious conclusion is that he was shoved off the top of a large container on the site and took a dive onto the rocks below. He seems to have died instantly."

"And what was done to the body?"

"It was dragged some distance from the place where he died and covered with a pile of old tires. There were plenty of them scattered around the place."

"Well, well."

"Yes, indeed."

"That must have been quite a strenuous task. Do you think more than one person was involved?"

"Not necessarily. Depends. On how strong they were, for instance."

"If this happened during the night or in the early morning, shouldn't the night watchman have noticed the smoke much sooner?"

"He didn't notice anything on Holy Thursday. He wasn't on duty on Good Friday. And he spotted the smoke in the early hours of Saturday."

"Which means?"

"It seems to mean that the tires weren't set alight until Good Friday. Probably not before the evening, going on how much they'd burned by the following morning."

"That's odd. Why not set fire to the body at once? Why wait a day?"

"We don't know, at this point in time."

"Is it possible that the killer or killers, or whatever we call them, had second thoughts and decided to burn the body so it would be difficult to identify? Or something like that?"

"Bad question. Next."

I have a thought. "Maybe they wanted the body found? Don't tires burn for a long time and give off a lot of smoke? They can smolder for days, can't they?"

"That's a bad question too. At this point in time. But tires can burn for a long time. That is so."

I think this over some more. "Well then, I can't think of any more questions."

"What a pity," comments Ólafur Gísli. "I so much enjoy our little get-togethers on the phone."

"Ásbjörn and I appreciate your help. Much more than you know."

"Well, that's the object of the exercise. Send him my kindest regards."

"Oh, while I remember. Have you had the autopsy results on the woman who fell into the Jökulsá River—Ásdís Björk Gudmundsdóttir?"

"Oh, that case. Yes, hang on. They're here, somewhere." I hear him shuffling papers. "Yes, it's as I said. The woman fell overboard and hit the rocks face-first, sustaining major head trauma."

"Something like Skarphédinn?"

"I suppose so, now you mention it. But it was an entirely different case. Absolutely off the record, I can tell you she was off her face on prescription drugs and beer when she went into the water. The woman was an addict. It was something between an accident and a self-inflicted injury."

On my way home I stop at the video store and pick up the Icelandic teen movie *Street Rider*.

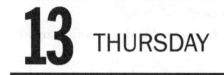

13 THURSDAY

Don't be trying to fool me…

As the final credits of *Street Rider* roll, the movie's theme song is sung, expressing the thoughts of the young leading lady, who's always had:

> *…A thing for guys like you,*
> *Ridin' on your bike,*
> *No fear in the world…*

Pretty much summed up the movie, I felt, as I watched it last night lying on the sofa with a supply of popcorn and Coke and Polly wandering around my shirt collar, depositing small black-and-white droppings as she went. So it was a pretty romantic evening, all in all, with accompaniment of the gale howling along the roof while the clothesline in the garden hummed.

Street Rider turned out to be a so-so romantic tale for kids, about puppy love between a beautiful girl from a wealthy suburban family and a rebellious kid from the wrong side of the tracks—if we had trains in Iceland, which we don't. He and his single mom are outsiders who have moved from some small regional town to live in one of the housing projects in the Reykjavík suburbs. Failing at school, he struts and preens and rides his motorcycle as the leader of a tough gang that communicates in code, as in all the best children's adventure stories. The girl's father does his best, of course, to break up the young lovers. But when the rich dad is threatened by real crooks, the Street Rider rides to the rescue with his gang and shows his true character. And they all live happily ever after.

Not too bad, as a watered-down Romeo and Juliet theme, I think as I have my first cup of coffee of the day. I'd probably have enjoyed it when I was the age of the main characters. I liked the rock-and-roll music on the soundtrack, which placed the events firmly in the early eighties.

And there was Skarphédinn—young, handsome, innocent, acting his little heart out, with his breaking voice and toned body—roaring around the mean streets on his motorbike. And I spotted Örvar Páll Sigurdarson in a small part as a fat policeman. Among the other kids I noticed a face that looked familiar, but I didn't manage to place it before I dropped off to sleep.

When I get to the office, Jóa is already there, sitting talking to Ásbjörn over a coffee. Karólína's not there. I haven't seen her in the office for a while, and Ásbjörn has been rushed off his feet, scuttling between his own office and the reception area, answering the phones, dealing with the delivery staff, retailers, and God knows what else. He's not looking good today—his hair is disheveled and greasy, and his eyes are red and sore.

Jóa, who is never at home anymore, remarks: "I've been given permission to stay on here for a while."

"Great," I say. "I haven't been looking forward to you leaving us. How long are you allowed to stay?"

"I've asked for Jóa to help me out in the office now and then," adds Ásbjörn. "Karó's not well, and I simply can't manage everything on my own."

"Fortunately I'm not too busy taking pics," Jóa continues. "I can easily add a few feathers to my cap. And I want to stay on for a while."

I give her a smile. "Of course you do. Polly and I don't see you anymore back at the homestead. Roughing it, are you?"

Jóa grins back. "It'll give Polly and you the opportunity to develop your relationship further. Explore new things."

Even Ásbjörn joins in the laughter, briefly.

Then he stands up and walks into his office.

"Is there something seriously wrong with Karó?" I whisper to Jóa.

"Don't know. Ásbjörn says the Lady Wife is tense, whatever that means. Didn't ask. I'm quite happy with the new arrangement."

"I'd be tense myself if I were married to Ásbjörn," I observe, then withdraw to my closet after asking Jóa to take photos of Ágústa Magnúsdóttir's house and the building where Skarphédinn lived, then pop into the high school and take some background pictures. I'm going to look in there this afternoon and try to have a word with the principal.

But as I sit down at my desk, my first task is to consult the phone book. Movie director Fridbert Sumarlidason is listed with a Reykjavík address, with both landline and cell phone numbers. There is no reply at his home, but he answers his cell.

I explain why I'm calling.

"*Street Rider.* Oh, yes," says Fridbert, who sounds as if he's about my age. "My first and only full-length movie. I haven't been given a chance since. I earn a crust doing commercials and TV work."

"Sorry to hear that."

"No, don't be. I'm doing much better now. In Iceland, movies are made only by masochists or fools. You can't help them. They seem to want to bankrupt themselves. Over and over again, preferably."

"I'm hoping you may be able to give me a comment on Skarphédinn. How did he come to be in the movie?"

"We just advertised for kids who wanted to be in a movie and held auditions. A huge number of youngsters applied. It took us three days to audition them all."

"And why did you cast Skarphédinn in the lead?"

"First, he had the look. He was the right type for a biker antihero. Second, he had that countrified lilting northern accent, which was just right for the lead character. He was an outsider among the prosperous Reykjavík middle class. Thirdly, he had a real talent for acting, although he was a complete beginner. And fourthly, he was so keen on playing the role. He convinced me that he would put his heart into it. And he certainly did. A bit too much, perhaps."

"Too much?"

"Yes, he sometimes butted in over things that were nothing to do with him. Not because he was pushy. He was just passionate about what he was doing. The boy was a born leader. The other kids in the cast knew that from the start."

"Especially the girls?"

Fridbert takes a pause for thought. "All the girls had crushes on him. Every single one."

"And did that get them anywhere?"

"Off the record?"

"Yes. I'll only quote what you said about his acting talent."

"All I remember is that there were some broken hearts."

"And you don't know any more about it?"

"No."

"In the movie, Örvar Páll Sigurdarson had a small role. He's been directing Skarphédinn in *Loftur the Sorcerer* here in Akureyri. It's a bit of a coincidence, isn't it?"

"You think so? Well, the Icelandic acting world is pretty small."

"So it was pure coincidence?"

"I can't imagine it being anything else."

"But Skarphédinn's violent death—you must have been shocked when you heard?"

"Absolutely. I would have bet money on that young man having a glittering career."

"Well, thank you very much…"

"But it's a strange coincidence…," he seems to be thinking out loud, then falls silent.

"What's a strange coincidence?"

"No, I just remembered something I heard a few years ago. Inga Lína, who played Skarphédinn's girlfriend in the movie, had a lot of problems after that, and died when she was only sixteen, I think."

Could that have been the face that seemed familiar? Would I have seen her photo in the papers? "How did she die?" I ask.

"I'm not sure. But I think she got into drugs or suffered from depression. Something like that."

"So both the leading actors in *Street Rider* are dead before they reach the age of twenty. That is a strange coincidence, as you say."

156

"Coincidence," echoes Fridbert Sumarlidason. "It seems more like a curse."

Akureyri High School is a cluster of buildings, large and small, dating from different periods and eclectic in style. The school is located on Eyrarlandsvegur, above the town center and the church. Instinctually, I assume that the principal's office will be in the oldest part of the school. It's an elegant wooden building looking out over the fjord, with gabled roofs, carved trims, and a flagpole. It reminds me of a ski chalet. Annexes and extensions have been added to the old schoolhouse bit by bit over the past hundred years. As I wander the corridors, I see sky-blue walls covered with mementos of the school's history: plaques, paintings of former principals, group photographs of graduating classes as they grow steadily bigger over the decades, from a handful of grave young men with bow ties to clusters of girls in their party dresses. A century of fashions is preserved here: crew cuts, brilliantine, beehives, Beatle mop-tops, long hippie locks, shiny disco girls, until we reach our own time when, once again, anything goes. And here are photos of productions by the school's drama group, in which the students express both joy and grief—but mostly joy, it seems to me. Will a picture from *Loftur the Sorcerer* make it onto this wall of remembrance?

After drifting around the corridors retracing history, it is time for the fifteen minutes the principal has said he can spare me from his busy schedule. I had the sense to mention the scandal about the *Question of the Day*, Kjartan Arnarson, and Sólrún Bjarkadóttir myself. I reiterated the explanation that had been given in Trausti's front-page apology. That precaution saved me from a long, predictable rant about sensationalist hacks and the irresponsibility of the media. But I still had to sit through the short version.

Stefán Már Guttormsson is fortyish, tall and slender, with receding hair, clean-shaven, with old-fashioned spectacles perched on his bulbous nose. He ponderously stands up and offers me a seat.

"What a tragedy," he says, slurring his words a little. "We're all in shock. We canceled all lessons on the first day of term. And we're doing all we can to help the students get over the worst of the crisis. Those who want help."

"Did you know Skarphédinn personally?"

"No, not really. He wasn't one of those students who have to be read the riot act. We maintain a high level of discipline here in the high school. We have a long tradition to uphold. This old schoolhouse was built on the estate of Eyrarland, which dates right back to the early settlers of Iceland, over a thousand years ago. We're very proud of our long and illustrious history. All the students' social events are required to be alcohol- and drug-free. At our annual dinner, for instance, we don't serve alcohol, and smoking is forbidden. Smoking is not permitted anywhere in the school or on school property."

Whew! I think. I wonder whether this glossy image of the school can possibly be consistent with the pattern of personal development that tends to take place at this age. And the way the principal describes the school is totally at odds with my own colorful experience of student social life in high school in Reykjavík. We strove to drink, smoke, and otherwise try out any substance that came our way.

I don't know whether my skepticism is obvious from my expression, but the principal fixes an even more ferocious glare upon me.

"Does that surprise you?"

"Yes, I must admit it does. Asceticism wasn't really a feature of my high school years."

He relaxes a little. "I'm not talking about asceticism, but self-discipline and moderation. We appeal to the students' sense of responsibility, but it's not as if we have moral police all over town enforcing our policies."

I nod, still dubious.

"And school authorities have an obligation to do what they can to counteract the negative influences on young people in society today and safeguard them. Don't you agree?"

"Uhh, yeah, I'm with you there. But I'm pretty sure that young people can never be safeguarded from their own curiosity about new things. All of us have to make our own mistakes before we find out what's right for us."

Stefán Már seems thoughtful. "I expect there's something in what you say. But it's our duty to strive to draw the attention of these young people in our care to the positive aspects of their surroundings and at the same time to counteract the attraction of the negative, dangerous, even life-threatening. Here at Akureyri High School we were, for instance, one of the first schools in the country to introduce a program of alcohol and drug counseling."

In my day in high school, an anti-drink counselor would have been laughed right out of town and up into the mountains, I think to myself. "But so far as you know, Skarphédinn Valgardsson had no need for such counseling?"

He shakes his head. "To the best of my knowledge, absolutely not. You can seek confirmation from the student counselor if you wish, although we naturally maintain confidentiality about individual students' personal affairs. Skarphédinn set a fine example for other young people. And that makes it all the more appalling that he should suffer such a tragic fate."

"Was he a good student?"

"So far as I know. He was majoring in social studies, and his grades were consistently high. But his teachers and the student counselors know more about that than I do. And I'd like to point out that Akureyri High School was the first Icelandic school to introduce student counselors. Unfortunately, as principal I haven't time to keep up with the progress of individual students at the school. They number well over five hundred. I tend to see the exceptions, students who find themselves in some kind of difficulties. We are proud that our dropout rate here at Akureyri High School is one of the lowest in the country. About two-and-a-half percent, so far as I remember."

The principal is getting antsy.

"I gather that Skarphédinn was a local boy. But he didn't live at home with his family after his first year at the high school. He moved into the student dorm and then into his own apartment last fall. Any idea why?"

"Why what? Why he moved into the dorm or why he moved out?"

"Um, both."

"No. It's not my business to go prying into the private lives of students. Akureyri High School is the largest boarding high school in the country. About half the students are local, the other half from other parts of the country. Where they choose to live is their business, provided they observe the discipline and rules of the school."

"So would it be reasonable to deduce that a student who chooses to live off-campus is looking for more freedom and less discipline?"

"If you like," answers Stefán Már curtly.

The principal's secretary gives me a list of school staff. I see that Kjartan Arnarson teaches in the social studies program. I call his extension at the school, but there is no answer. The secretary consults his schedule and tells me that he should be free in half an hour. The social studies program is taught in the school's newest building, Hólar, named after the old episcopal seat, Hólar in Hjaltadalur.

"Hólar is where Iceland's first scholastic establishment was founded, eight centuries ago," she remarks. "The Learned School, attached to the cathedral."

I carry on wandering the corridors. From the old schoolhouse a long passage leads over to Hólar, which I gather is the focus of student life. The proportions are different in the new building: bigger classrooms and workshops, a large library, a spacious hall on the lower floor, and the school reception area on the upper floor, where the students also have coat closet facilities and lockers.

The youngsters who are walking around or sitting over a drink or a snack all seem to have their own individual style in clothing and hair—because today anything goes. But I'm surprised to see so many of them wearing slippers. I've never been able to understand why people who wear slippers at work don't just stay home. But then, that's my problem.

I wait outside Kjartan's classroom until the door opens and the students bustle out, all appearing in a serious mood. When the last of them is gone, I squeeze past into the classroom. The teacher is wiping the board.

Kjartan is quite different from what I had imagined, going on his youthful voice and the nature of the scandal. He is about forty-five, below average height, wearing a worn brown corduroy suit. Around the ragged gray collar of his shirt is a shoestring-

161

thin bow tie. His small-featured face is pink, with a red goatee beard and bristly red hair.

Kjartan Arnarson looks more like a middle-aged nerd than a sex symbol for teenage girls. He glances up with a questioning look. I start by mentioning the embarrassing scandal, as I did with the principal. Kjartan gives me a strange smile. "You did what you promised. No more could be expected of you."

After we briefly discuss what a shock Skarphédinn's death has been for the school and his fellow students, I ask Kjartan whether he knew the dead boy.

"He was in my class last year. An exemplary student. Unusually mature and intelligent. Quite a Renaissance man, I would almost say. He was as much at home with computer science as with literature and other humanities."

"But what about personally? How would you describe him, his character?"

"I didn't get to know him much outside the classroom," Kjartan replies. "But he gave me the impression of being what is sometimes called an *old soul*. I know it's a vague term, but I can't find a better way to put it. He was deeply interested in the past, in Icelandic history…"

He perches on the edge of his desk. "In some ways Skarphédinn seemed to think almost like a person from the distant past. He was fascinated, for instance, by Hólar and its history as the center of north Iceland over the centuries and a citadel of learning, a forerunner of today's universities. He saw an unusually strong connection between knowledge and power and progress. By unusually strong, I mean in comparison with his contemporaries, who generally opt for high school and further education either to fulfill their parents' ambitions and pressure or simply because their friends are going and they can't think of anything better to do."

He falls silent and glances at his watch.

"I'm afraid I'm late for a meeting. Are we finished here?"

"Well, I'm not quite sure," I say. "Can I get back to you if I think of anything else?"

Kjartan takes his briefcase off the desk and walks to the door, slightly pigeon-toed. "I suppose so. But if you want to find out more about Skarphédinn's ideas about life, you could check the *Morning News* online archive. I remember he sent in a couple of articles last winter, one about regional development and the other about patriotism."

I walk out into the corridor with him and say in parting: "I hope that business in the paper hasn't caused you too much trouble."

Again he gives me that odd smile. "Just between you and me: after all the fuss and the way it was handled, I find I'm regarded as quite a hottie in my old age."

At the end of the day I don't send in any copy to the *Afternoon News*. News editor Trausti Löve alternately purrs and howls, like a feral cat. Meanwhile in Akureyri, Pal is wailing in distress on the upper floor. As I go downstairs and leave the building, I hear the sound of breaking crockery and screeching.

"Karó dear," says Ásbjörn. "Darling Karó. Please calm down."

14 FRIDAY

I want to consider the concept of "patriotism," if only in order that the process may awaken in my own heart noble feelings toward my native country and a desire to contribute what I can, in all good faith, to the welfare of the country and its people.

Those were Skarphédinn's opening words in his article in the *Morning News*. He went on:

> *True patriotism must, above all, entail sacrifice. We offer our energies, our health, our material goods and comforts—we give up all that is most precious to us—for the sake of our country. Even life itself. The object must be to teach our nation to know and to love the truth, and to conduct ourselves in accord with that knowledge in every way. We should do nothing in our own interest, unless we are sure that it is also for the good of the nation as a whole, our native land. All our interpersonal relations should put justice and love in first place. We must devote our energies*

to the quest to make Iceland the home of true happiness, personal and social development, equality, brotherhood and, perhaps above all, freedom.

If that exposition of patriotism is correct, it is obvious that young people—my generation—do not spend much of their time in service of that ideal. And I am no exception. I doubt that patriotism stirs in the bosom of any young Icelander today—except perhaps when one of our sports teams is doing well in international competition or when Icelandic entrepreneurs buy up foreign businesses. And in such cases patriotism is often manifested in its negative form, in other words as aggressive nationalism. It emerges in belligerence and arrogance toward other nations and not as a deep, sincere feeling toward our own people. I have come to the conclusion that nationalistic fervor is in fact the opposite of patriotism, just as selfishness is the opposite of love.

We must not settle for simply accepting the gifts our country bestows upon us in her bounty. We must give back to it all that we have. We must devote our whole lives to making ourselves into a nation of true patriots.

Shades of a young Jack Kennedy? I think.

The second article is concerned with the regions and migration to the capital area:

It is painful for young people in the regions to watch their so-called saviors—large conglomerates in commerce, services, industry or fisheries—buying up everything of value in the rural areas for small change and pretending that they will continue to run the enterprises there, then sucking out all the profit and closing them down, or transferring them to other places, where they merge into larger production units, or to market areas where a bigger profit is to be made. Is such a pattern of behavior likely to increase young people's hopes that they can stay on in the region for a good life? No, of course not. And that is not the object of the exercise. The object is to make the rich richer and to leave the poor and vulnerable to fend for themselves. That is the end that justifies any means. In truth, it is surprising that young people still want to live in rural areas and fishing villages. The reason, one hopes, is that in spite of everything they know in their heart of hearts that the closer we move to the capital, the farther we go from the regions, the farther we have departed from our origins, from the essence of what makes us Icelanders.

Under both articles he is credited:

The author is a high school student in Akureyri with a sincere interest in the future of the Icelandic people.

The articles were written nearly a year ago. There is something about this call for self-sacrifice that is hard to reconcile with the individualism that Skarphédinn had advocated with such passion in our interview about *Loftur the Sorcerer*. This youthful idealist, so deeply concerned for this country and the regions, seems at first glance to have little in common with a young man who chooses freedom over discipline and turns up at a party dressed as a witch. But then I remember, of course, how rapidly opinions, lifestyle, and philosophy can change at that age.

Maybe Skarphédinn simply liked to have fun, as his school friend said. Maybe he felt the urge to try out new roles all the time. Or maybe he meant every word, sincerely and deeply. Maybe I'm just not seeing the connection.

But I remember that when Jóa and I were driving back to Akureyri after our expedition to Hólar, there was a request on the radio played for Skarphédinn and the other kids in the drama group: *Season of the Witch*, which was about the need to be all sorts of different people.

> *So many different people to be*
> *That it's strange, so strange…*

One thing's for certain: nothing's certain.

Since I've got the *Morning News* archive open, I enter the name Inga Lína in the search engine. I can't remember her last name. And Inga Lína may be a diminutive. Anyway, I get no hits. I think I ought to rent *Street Rider* again and take a closer look.

Today is Ásdís Björk Gudmundsdóttir's funeral, and so there are three commemorative articles about her in the paper. I read them with interest but don't learn much. They're typical obituaries:

Ásdís Björk was a fine woman, who made a good home for her husband and son, and also played an active role in the management of the family firm, the Yumm candy factory. Just in case, I jot down the son's name: Gudmundur Ásgeirsson. Age: 25. Economist.

167

Jóa is a jill of all trades at the office today. Ásbjörn looks in now and then, with a face like a storm cloud, just like the ones outside. He hardly speaks before disappearing back upstairs.

I seize the opportunity and smoke all over the office, as much as I like.

But that doesn't dispel the clouds from my brain.

I'm still reluctant to approach Skarphédinn's family. I take another look at the list of members of the drama group, with phone numbers, that Ágústa gave me. On the first number I get voice mail, but I don't leave a message. On the second number there is no reply. The third won't talk to me. The fourth person on the list is Fridrik Einarsson. His character in the play is called Ólafur: Loftur's boyhood friend and assistant to the steward at Hólar. He's not willing to meet me, but reluctantly agrees to answer some questions on the phone. I tell him I'm writing an article about the dead boy and the last hours of his life.

"Skarphédinn was my friend," he says in a hoarse voice. "If I can do anything to help figure out what happened to him, I won't say no. But I've already told the police what I know—which isn't much."

"Maybe an article in the paper—whenever it gets published— may spark some memories or produce some clues. Who knows?"

"Who knows?" He replies. "Nobody knows nuthin'."

"Quite. So how would you describe Skarphédinn?"

"In many ways he was a very strange guy..." He falls silent. "No, wait. I'd better not say it like that, not on the record. I'll start again: Skarphédinn was in many ways a very unusual person. He was especially good to his friends—nothing was too much trouble. And he was incredibly bright, man, really incredibly. He'd read everything. Literally. He was a walking fucking encyclopedia..." He stops again. "Don't write *fucking*."

"How did you meet?"

"We went to elementary school together."

"Was he from Akureyri originally?"

"No idea. Skarphédinn never talked about the past. He was a here-and-now guy. Right here, right now—that's how I would describe him."

"Was he popular?"

"He was *The Man*. You know?"

"The Main Man?"

"Oh, yeah. When he decided something should be done, it got done. And if anyone didn't want to join in, it was just: *Fuck you!*"

"Fuck you? Is that what Skarphédinn said to people who didn't want to join in?"

"No, no, don't write *Fuck you*. But he had no time for wimps and assholes. Get it?"

"Was it Skarphédinn who got you to join the drama group?"

"Yeah, of course. I'd never have thought of joining otherwise. And Christ has it been a blast, man!"

"Did he have a girlfriend?"

"No shortage there. He could take his pick. They were all over him, drooling. Girls. Young women. Even old bats of forty were dropping their panties."

"But when he died? Did he have some particular girlfriend at that time?"

"Why should Skarphédinn have settled for just one girl at a time? He sampled the goods, like anyone would in his place."

"Is that what he said? Are you quoting his exact words?"

"I think so. He was quite cool about it."

"Did you notice anything unusual that day or the evening before he disappeared?"

"No. But he was on a roll."

"Was that unusual?"

"Are you crazy? No, he was always the life and soul of the party."

"Was he drunk, that evening at Ágústa's party?"

"He was just having fun."

"Did he take drugs?"

Fridrik is, for the first time, disconcerted. "If he had, I would never say so. Never."

"But what about this dress he was wearing?"

"The witch's robe?"

"Yes. Why was he wearing it?"

"He just felt like it. I asked him, and he said: *Tonight I feel like a witch, and that's why I'm dressed as a witch.* He was in his element, man!"

"So he danced and drank and so on, did he?"

He makes no reply, but goes on: "He jumped up on a table and howled out over the crowd: *I bear the Terror Helmet above you all!* I didn't get what he was on about. What's a terror helmet, anyway?"

"Um, I'm not at all sure I know. Did he do anything else that night that you didn't get?"

"Don't remember. I was a bit wired myself, you know?"

"So…"

Fridrik interrupts: "Hey, yeah, there was one thing. I remember he reached under the robe and pulled out a pubic hair." He bursts out laughing. "Fuck, man! Reached under the hem and pulled out a pube! What a guy!"

"What? What are you talking about?"

"Just that. He was an unbelievable guy, Skarphédinn. Fucking incredible."

"Yes, it sounds like it. But why would he do that?"

"I dunno. He just did."

"So wasn't he wearing anything under the robe?"

"Buck-naked or wearing underpants. How would I know? I didn't suck his dick that night."

That night? I thought. Maybe some other night, then. But all I asked was: "And what did he do with this pubic hair?"

"We went into the bathroom. Skarphédinn pulled out an eyelash, put both hairs in a little bowl and set fire to them. Then he swept the ash into the palm of his hand. He went back to the party, walked up to some girl, and slipped the ash into her drink. Hahaha!"

"And…"

"Without her noticing. She had no fucking idea."

"What girl was this?"

"I don't remember. Just some bitch."

"Did you tell the police about this?"

"No. What's to tell? Skarphédinn was just having a joke. He was always doing weird stuff."

"So it just slipped your mind?"

"Fucking right. It slipped my mind."

"Did you know everyone at the party?"

"Don't remember. To start with, it was just the kids from the play. And that asshole, the director, I can never remember his name."

"Örvar Páll."

"Örvar Páll, yeah. And they were arguing, as usual."

"Örvar Páll and Skarphédinn?"

"And Skarphédinn had the last word, as always."

"What was the argument about?"

"The play, I guess. The asshole director was nagging that we needed to be well rested for the following day—the first night and all that. He was trying to shut the party down."

I recall the director saying that he had only seen Skarphédinn arriving when he himself was on his way out. I ask Fridrik, who has grown gradually more agitated as the interview has progressed: "Are you sure Skarphédinn got there before Örvar Páll left?"

"They met at the door and got straight into an argument."

"Did they argue a lot?"

"Skarphédinn could always shut the old fart up. No problem."

"Did he argue with anyone else that night?"

"How should I know? I wasn't breathing down his neck all evening."

"So everything was peaceful and quiet, was it?"

"Hey, yeah, some guys turned up that I didn't know. But Skarphédinn knew them somehow. He chucked them out."

"Skarphédinn threw them out?"

"Fucking right. Chucked them out on their asses."

"What were they like?"

"Like? How would I know, man? One of them had blond hair, in a ponytail. He was all cuts and bruises, bent over so he could hardly walk. With rabbity teeth."

"Did you tell the police about them?"

"Yes, I did."

"When did Skarphédinn leave the party?"

"The hell I know. I was in one of the bedrooms with some bitch. All the rooms were occupied, man. Ágústa fucking in her mom and dad's bed. Really wild."

"And who was she fucking?"

"Do you think I'd tell you, if I knew? Forget it."

"How do you know she was fucking in her parents' bedroom?"

"I could hear the noises."

"Couldn't she have been having sex with Skarphédinn? Since you don't know when he left?"

Fridrik, about whose reliability as a source I am beginning to have serious doubts, at least at this point in time, says nothing.

"Well," I say. "It was good to talk to you, Fridrik. Thank you very much."

He sniffs. What, I don't know.

Suddenly he seems nervous. "You mustn't quote me. Nothing. Get it?"

"No problem," I assure him. Then I ask this student, who appears to be the opposite of the model his principal has described to me: "So how are things at school?"

"Don't talk to me about that fucking high school. Skarphédinn always got me through tests and assignments." He falls silent and sniffs again. Maybe he's just upset. "I don't know what I'm going to do now. Without him."

Who was Skarphédinn Valgardsson? The more I hear about him, the further I seem to get from the truth. The more I know, the less I understand.

I try to get this into Trausti Löve's head. I tell him I'm far from being ready to publish a profile of Skarphédinn, and I've no idea when I will be. Trausti's reaction is predictably predictable.

I get so fed up with the hassle that I call Hannes. Not so much to complain about Trausti, more to get the go-ahead from a higher power to do my work on a sensible basis and not as a pissing contest.

"I'll have a word with Trausti, sir," says Hannes. I think I hear him sigh with exhaustion, or as a response to the constant aggravation. "You focus on that case, exclusively. For the time being. Until otherwise decided."

Considering the state Ásbjörn is in today, I hardly dare call him or go upstairs to ask him to do his usual mediation with Ólafur Gísli. I'm giving some thought to my predicament, with the help of a nicotine hit, when I hear a low whining from the reception area. Ásbjörn appears at my door with Pal on his lead. He looks frazzled, and the little dog too.

"Einar," he says, "could you smoke a bit less? It's driving Karó crazy. She says she can't open a cupboard or lie down in bed without being overwhelmed by the smell of your smoke. She sees it seeping up between the floorboards."

I don't know whether to laugh or fly into a rage. "I'm sorry. Have you seen these clouds of smoke yourself?"

He hangs his head. "I'm not sure. But she's in a very fragile state, Einar. Anything can set her off."

I chuck my cigarette out the window at the wall next door. "Is there something in particular that's troubling her? Other than my air pollution, that is?"

"Yes, there is something. But I don't know what it is. She's so sensitive, Karó."

"So I'm being deprived of my last and only pleasure?"

"No, no," protests Ásbjörn.

"OK, no problem. It's just one more thing."

"Just try to be a bit discreet with your damned pleasure. You're not alone in the world, Einar."

"Sure of that, are you?"

"A person who's always ranting on about pollution of the natural environment and the way it's abused by mankind should be able to show a bit of consideration for the human beings around him."

I must admit, I hadn't thought of it quite like that.

But Ásbjörn has more on his mind than raking me over the coals.

He pats the trembling little dog. "She comes around quite often now, Björg, the girl who found Pal. She drops in to see him. He's very fond of her. But it upsets Karó. She nearly faints with distress after the girl has gone. I really don't know…"

I've been wondering about the agitation on the upper floor. I'm sure it's about some emotional issues. It started shortly after Skarphédinn died. I've been told that he was a ladies' man, a magnet for females of all ages. Could Karó have been stepping out? Best to change the subject.

"Ásbjörn, I need to get in touch with Ólafur Gísli, to ask him about something I heard today."

I tell him about my interview with Fridrik.

I leave out the naughty bit. About the pubic hair.

When I finally get to speak to the chief at about ten that evening, there is no news on the investigation into the death of Skarphédinn Valgardsson. Ólafur Gísli is at home. "It's the first time for more than a week that I've gotten home before midnight," he sighs and tells me about the delicious meatballs his wife heated up for his dinner and which he is now comfortably digesting.

"My roommate heated up a seed ball for me," I counter. "Wonderful, this old Icelandic home cooking. Rich in fiber. Keeps you regular."

He doesn't respond to that. Just as well. I suspect he's counting his blessings.

"Ásbjörn told me about your interview with Fridrik. What did you think of him?"

"Not the sharpest knife in the drawer. And I have a feeling he may have been indulging in something a bit stronger than cough drops."

"I tend to agree," observes Ólafur Gísli. "But we're seriously looking into these delinquents from Reydargerdi. We know—and from independent witnesses, apart from our young friend—that they were at the party and got into a scuffle with Skarphédinn."

"Any idea what that was about?"

"No, that's still pretty vague. You mustn't breathe a word of this. We don't want them to get any hint that we consider them suspects."

"Are you close to making an arrest?"

"Not just yet. We may be bringing them in for questioning. We'll see. You won't be publishing any of this yet. Nothing I've told you this evening."

His last remark is not phrased as an order. More of an indisputable fact.

"Sir, no, sir! I will follow you through thick and thin," I respond. "May I ask a question?"

"If it's a bad enough goddamned question."

"Do you know any more about whether Skarphédinn was on anything when he died? Drunk, drugged?"

"Not at all. He appears to have been as clean as the proverbial whistle. Next question."

"And I assume you can't tell whether he had sex shortly before he died?"

"Doesn't seem to be possible. Not by forensics, at any rate. The body was too badly burned."

"What was he wearing when he was found?"

"Wearing? Have you forgotten he'd been set on fire?"

"So were his clothes burnt to a crisp?"

"Not quite to a crisp. We found scraps of some kind of coarse-weave black fabric."

"Which could be part of the dress, or robe or whatever?"

"Entirely possible."

"Did you find anything else?"

"Also entirely possible. White adhesive tape had been stuck to the fabric, forming some kind of symbol. Crossed lines with tridents at the ends."

"What the hell is that?"

"Our forensics people put us in touch with an expert on runes, and I spoke to him this evening. He says it's probably a magical sign of some kind. I faxed him a photo of the symbol, and he called back."

"And what did he say?"

"He says it's definitely a magical sign, known as the Terror Helmet."

"Anything else?" I ask.

"Nothing for the record. We were called out to the scene of yet another suicide today."

"What suicide?"

"Depression and drugs. Drugs and depression. Same old, same old. A tragedy, as usual."

"Who was it?"

"A young student at the high school. Sólveig, Sólrún, something like that."

15 SATURDAY

Sometime before I got to high school I learned the lesson that somehow I can never take for granted, that when you add two plus two the answer isn't twenty-two. Bearing this in mind, I start my day at work by calling the police station and asking for the officer who is handling the investigation into the suicide of Sólrún Bjarkadóttir, the high school student who answered my *Question of the Day* on Town Hall Square. I am put through to a policewoman who I think I ran into when I was putting in an appearance at the police station the other day.

"She took an overdose," she explains. "We gather that she'd been using for the last year or so."

"What did she take?"

"We haven't got the tox results yet. But we found empty containers for sedatives and some E."

"Had the pills been prescribed by a doctor?"

"Some of them."

"What about drugs that aren't prescribed? Where do they come from?"

"There's a vast amount of prescription drugs in circulation. No less than the illegal ones. Some doctors are careless about prescribing large amounts to addicts. And a lot of prescription drugs get onto the market illegally. For instance, a few weeks ago a load of medications were stolen from a pharmacy here in town. And drugs disappear from hospitals. And then there's smuggling. Misuse of prescription drugs is as common now as use of illegal substances."

"Were there no signs of violence? No indication that it was anything other than suicide?"

"In Sólrún's case? No, nothing like that."

"Where was she found?"

"In her room at the student dorm."

"Was she from Akureyri?"

"No, from Reykjavík."

I can't think of anything else to ask, so I thank her for her help. "I won't write anything about the suicide, naturally. I'm just looking into the drugs market up here in the north."

"Knock yourself out," answers the policewoman. "You've got plenty to work with."

So what now? I ponder, and get several possible answers.

Should I call Kjartan Arnarson the high school teacher? Or Björg Gudrúnardóttir, who knew a little about Sólrún, but not a lot? Should I try to track down the other two girls who were with Sólrún on the Day of the Question on the square?

At present, I don't see much point in continuing down that path. Drugs and suicide. Suicide and drugs. Routine. A waste of time, as dopey Fridrik might say. But I can't help feeling sad that a lighthearted young girl who made one silly mistake should have been overcome by the conviction that her life was a waste of time.

———

"The Terror Helmet? Why on earth is the sensationalist press suddenly taking an interest in ancient magical signs? Haven't you got any real news to report?"

On the phone is an aged professor emeritus of Icelandic language. I got his name after making a load of phone calls to members of the academic community.

I do get tired of the *sensationalist press* thing. "I'm just looking for some information."

"Why?" demands Professor Ingimundur Kjaran. "Is anyone interested in anything these days, if it's not about money?"

"Well, I don't know that there's any money in magic. Not these days. But I'm asking because some high school students here in Akureyri have apparently shown an interest in the Terror Helmet symbol. And shortly after declaring that interest, one of them was found murdered."

Ingimundur says nothing for a moment.

"Do you mean the young man they found at the dump at Easter?"

"That's the one."

"Good heavens above."

Yep. Fucking shit.

"So what can you tell me about this sign? The Terror Helmet?"

"Well, there's quite a lot, if you're interested." Ingimundur speaks slowly. "In the first place, the Terror Helmet is not necessarily a magical sign. The word can also be used to mean, quite literally, a helmet or mask that strikes terror into the enemy. But a magical sign named Terror Helmet is mentioned in many sources, especially in the seventeenth century. A variety of different powers and qualities are attributed to it. But as a rule the Terror

Helmet consists of two crossed lines, each ending in three points. What did this poor schoolboy do with the Terror Helmet?"

"Unfortunately, I don't know precisely. But at a party he declared that he *bore the Terror Helmet* above all the rest."

"Did he, indeed?" The professor titters. "Now *that* usage has nothing to do with the magical sign. The phrase to *bear the Terror Helmet over others* simply means to excel, to be better than others or superior in some way. Is that all? Was that all you wanted to ask me about?"

"I know the phrase and what it means," I say, "but I've got some more questions. He was dressed in some kind of robe or gown, onto which he had stuck the magic sign."

"What nonsense is this? Some boy dressing up for a joke?"

"No, there was more to it than that. It wasn't as if he put on a Santa suit or a Superman costume."

He waits. I'm not at all sure he knows who Superman is.

"He reached under the robe and pulled out a pubic hair."

The professor's breathing becomes ragged.

"Then he pulled out an eyelash, set both hairs alight, and slipped the ash into a girl's drink."

Silence.

"Without her noticing," I add.

"Now that is more interesting," comments Ingimundur after a pause for thought. "But it seems likely that the young man was using some superficial knowledge of magical signs as a party game for his own purposes. So far as I know, the boy's acts, as you describe them to me, would be some kind of aphrodisiac spell, with the intent of attracting or seducing a girl."

"Like the way people will spike drinks today?"

"I wouldn't know about that. I don't move in such circles," sniffs Ingimundur, who seems to think he's being asked the question as an expert witness on contemporary social mores. "For such purposes, the Terror Helmet was used quite differently and in a more complex manner. A person who wished to use magic to seduce a woman was supposed to fast and then draw the sign with his own saliva in the palm of his right hand. Then he was to shake the girl's hand, and the power of the sign was supposed to work through the physical exchange of humors. It has been suggested that the saliva signifies semen, so that the handshake symbolizes sexual intercourse. So you can see that the boy was no expert. Or at any rate, he chose to do something showier. He probably thought it was cool, as they say these days. But the intention of the ritual was probably the same."

"To hook up with a girl?"

"If you want to put it that way. Just a moment while I look it up."

I wait a few minutes while Ingimundur does his research.

"Here it is. *The Book of Magic*, as it is called, a seventeenth-century manuscript, says the following about the Terror Helmet: *'Item, make with thy fasting saliva this sign in thy palm, when thou greetest the maid thou wouldst have. It shall be the right hand.'* Yes, it's as I remembered. But your young man didn't follow that formula?"

"Not so far as I know."

"There are many more examples of ancient aphrodisiac spells, but I won't go into that. But the Terror Helmet was regarded as a uniquely potent magical sign. Not only for such aphrodisiac effects, but also for the more general function of breaking down resistance for the sorcerer's purposes. It might be the resistance of an evil power or an enemy, no less than the resistance of a woman he wished to enjoy. So the Terror Helmet was not simply a way to induce lust," he continues. "It was also said to be used for medicinal purposes. I remember there was a man who claimed to have used the sign to cure disease in livestock. In fact, he wound up being burned for what they called *forbidden medicine* in the seventeenth century—poor fellow. These days they call it *alternative medicine* and rake in the cash."

"Burned at the stake?"

"Oh, yes, burned at the stake. That's how they used to send witches and warlocks over to the other side." The professor titters again. "I don't suppose it will be of any assistance in solving your present-day murder case. But…"

"Yes…?"

"It is undeniably remarkable, if that young man really believed in the potency of magic in general and the Terror Helmet in particular—a magical sign that had the paradoxical powers of inducing fear or passion or curing the sick. But he was probably just having fun, as they say."

"He was actually due to play the lead in a production of *Loftur the Sorcerer* with the high school drama group."

"I see. That could explain his interest in the old lore. Very likely. That makes more sense."

But I'm far from sure.

Finally he inquires, "Just as a matter of interest: How did things go for the boy? With the girl?"

That afternoon, news spreads from the police station that a twenty-year-old man from Reydargerdi has been brought in for questioning in connection with the death of Skarphédinn Valgardsson. It's Agnar Hansen.

"He denies everything," says Ólafur Gísli. "Naturally."

"But surely he doesn't deny being in Akureyri or at the party?"

"No. He can't deny that. But he denies any involvement in Skarphédinn's disappearance and death."

"How did Agnar know Skarphédinn?"

"He hasn't said anything about knowing him. He claims that he and two others heard there was a party there, at Ágústa Magnúsdóttir's place, and simply crashed it."

"So they just followed their noses?"

"Pretty much, yes."

"What about the other two?"

"Agnar's still refusing to tell us who they are. Claims he's forgotten."

"So he's the only one who's been identified? As a gate-crasher at the party, I mean."

"So far. But we've got some leads on the other two. We'll be bringing them in within a few hours."

"Are they from Reydargerdi too?"

"Yes, indeed. It's a little clique of Agnar's. A sort of wannabe gang."

"Will you be taking Agnar into custody?"

"We're working on it. We should be ready to go this evening. And not a word until then."

"No, of course not. What does Agnar say he remembers from the party?"

"He says he sang some song for the other partygoers: *Who put broken glass in the Vaseline?* Or some such."

"*Who put broken glass in the Vaseline?*"

"Yep. Good question, isn't it? Who the hell put the broken glass in the Vaseline?"

We allow ourselves a brief, dry laugh.

"Is that all he says he remembers?"

"Selective amnesia, I think they call it," quips the laughing policeman. "But he does say he got in Skarphédinn's face. Making fun of him about that robe or dress or whatever it was he was wearing."

"Was this after the Vaseline business?"

"Yes. And he says that's why Skarphédinn threw them out."

"Could he be telling the truth?"

"I don't believe a word of it. But with luck we'll find out more, once we put some pressure on him and his hangers-on."

"He seems to have been rather a complicated person, this Skarphédinn Valgardsson," I say. "I've been trying to put together a proper picture of him, and all I get is more and more fragments."

"Same here."

"What about his parents? I've been reluctant to contact them. It's still too soon, isn't it?"

"Yes, I think so. They're grieving, and they haven't even buried their boy yet. Apparently they didn't have much contact recently. But it's still a huge shock."

"Maybe even worse because they were estranged?"

"Yes, you may well be right. They're just a quiet middle-aged couple, who can't grasp what happened to their son. What kind of violence led to his death."

"What do they do?"

"He's disabled. I don't remember what he used to do. But they got into some kind of difficulties, ten or fifteen years ago, and lost everything. She's a nurse. A hard worker, so I hear. And of course she's supporting the whole family."

"Was Skarphédinn an only child?"

"No, they have another son. Younger. About sixteen, I think."

We don't speak for a while.

"Can I ask a bad question?" I ask.

"Absolutely."

"Have you looked into this Örvar Páll at all?"

"The director of the play?"

"Yes. He got into some kind of spat with Skarphédinn at the party."

"I know. Örvar said he'd been trying to convince the cast that it was good idea to do the first performance without a hangover. So there wouldn't be too many disasters onstage or vomiting into the audience. Understandable, don't you think?"

"Oh, yes. Have you got any witnesses that confirm he left the party at about ten, as he claims? And that he got back to his hotel shortly after that?"

"The witnesses from the party are unreliable, as you know. And at the hotel nobody noticed him in the lobby. They were very busy, with all those people who came here for the skiing and found there was no snow. He says he had his room key in his pocket, so he didn't need to go to the reception desk. Sounds reasonable enough, doesn't it?"

"I suppose."

"Out with it!"

"It's just that I found out that Skarphédinn's and Örvar Páll's paths had crossed before, about five years ago. Skarphédinn played the lead in a kids' movie, *Street Rider*. Örvar Páll had a small part. He played a cop, actually."

"*Street Rider*?" echoes Ólafur Gísli, and suddenly bursts into song: "*Speeding along on his new Honda, helmet shining like fire...*"

"That's the one."

"*Tearing up the tarmac, shakin' and wakin' up the neighborhood...*"

"My goodness, you're quite an expert on the golden oldies."

"I'm an expert about everything of importance. But, with all due respect, how is that relevant?"

"It probably isn't. I spoke to the director of the movie, and he told me that the leading lady, a young girl, Inga Lína, died a few years back."

"How did she die?"

"He didn't remember exactly. But he thought he'd heard she'd been depressed, or got into drugs."

"That's not the only young life lost to those."

"No. I'm just trying to get a handle on it. The two youngsters who starred in the movie are dead, and Örvar Páll is the only person involved in this case who knew both of them."

"In this case, true. But the death of the young girl a few years ago is another matter. Let's keep the two separate, shall we? I can't see any tangible connection."

"No, nor can I," I mumble stubbornly.

After dangling my leg almost out of the window of my work-closet as I exhale my noxious fumes, in an effort to be a good conservationist, but even more to avoid offending Her Upstairs, I reach the conclusion that my only option at present is to wait for confirmation that Agnar Hansen is to be taken into custody. I shuffle through the papers piled on my desk and arrange my notes into some semblance of order. I come across the name of Gudmundur Ásgeirsson, economist.

He's Gunnhildur's grandson, the son of the late Ásdís Björk and her husband, Ásgeir Eyvindarson. For something to do, I look him up in the phone book. He isn't listed in Akureyri, but in Reykjavík.

A small child answers.

"Hi. Is your daddy there?"

"Daddy! Daddy! Man on the phone!"

After assorted crashes and bangs as the kid drops the phone on the floor, a man's voice says: "Gudmundur."

"Hello. My name's Einar. I'm a reporter for the *Afternoon News* in Akureyri."

"Oh?"

"Yes. I'm sorry to disturb you. And my sympathies for the loss of your mother."

"Thank you," he replies, surprised or wary. Or both.

"The thing is I had a phone call the other day from your grandmother, Gunnhildur."

"Oh?" he says again.

"And, at her request, I visited her at the care home where she lives."

"Oh?"

"Yes. Um, I don't quite know how to say this. But what she wanted to tell me was that she believed the death of her daughter, your mother, wasn't an accident. That she was killed."

No reply.

"I haven't known what to make of what she told me. But I haven't been able to put it out of my mind. So I decided to call you."

I have the impression than he says nothing for a full thirty seconds.

"Is this an interview? Are you going to publish what I say?"

"No. I'm simply trying to get a clearer idea of what's going on here. Or, perhaps, if anything's going on here."

"Look, what's going on is that dear old gran has lost her marbles. She can't face the truth."

"What truth is that?"

"The truth that my mother suffered from an illness. Hypochondria."

"What does—"

"Daddy! Daddy!" a shrill little voice calls. "I've gone poo!"

"Excuse me. I've got important work to do here," Gudmundur babbles hurriedly. "But that's all you need to know about my gran."

"Do you mean Gunnhildur is a hypochondriac herself?"

"No…Not exactly. I'm not sure…"

"Daddy! Poo on the floor!"

"Sorry, I've got to go," he says. "Did Gran say Dad killed Mom?"

"Well, she implied as much."

"For goodness' sake, take no notice of her. She's a poor old worn-out, bereaved woman."

"OK…"

"Ooooh," the little voice resounds. "Poor poo."

"Good-bye," says the economist. "Dirty work to do."

"Look, Daddy! I'm drawing with the poo…"

There's dirty work, and then there's dirty work.

In the evening I try to persuade Trausti Löve to stop the front page and redo the layout to make room for a report that a twenty-year-old man has been remanded in custody in connection with the investigation into the death of Skarphédinn Valgardsson in Akureyri. He explains to me, quite gently, that it is Saturday evening. There is no paper tomorrow.

16 SUNDAY

After Friday comes Saturday, followed by Sunday. I learned that once upon a time, even before I went to high school. But it seems to have slipped my mind in the busyness of my new life, exciting personal affairs, and vibrant social life. It's not so very long ago that weekends and days off were what I most looked forward to. Sometimes they were all I looked forward to. Now they don't seem to matter anymore.

I start that Sunday by changing the newspaper in the bottom of Polly's cage and giving her a cracker to peck at as a Sunday treat. Then I stand at the kitchen window for a long, long time, with a cup of coffee in one hand and a cigarette in the other, contemplating what to do. It still looks wintry outside, and I think I even spot the odd snowflake drifting down, just as a reminder that in these times of prosperity and optimism we're still living in chilly old Iceland. Times may change, but place remains the same. In the neighboring gardens there are no children playing ball today. I look through the CD collection left behind by the owner—I didn't think to bring my own music with me. There are a lot of operas and symphonies. Then I come across a CD of

R.E.M. As *Man on the Moon* fills the room, I feel I'm home. On my own private moon:

> *Now, Andy, did you hear about this one?*
> *Tell me are you locked in the punch?*
> *Hey, Andy, are you goofing on Elvis?*
> *Hey, baby, are you having fun?*

Then the phone rings.

"This is Ásgeir Eyvindarson," says a grating male voice. "Who am I speaking to?"

"Einar."

I can tell that he's struggling to control himself, without much success. "My son, Gudmundur, tells me you called him yesterday, making ridiculous and slanderous allegations against me."

"Not at all. That's a misunderstanding."

"Repeating the ravings of a demented old woman. How dare you treat a grieving family this way?"

"All I did was tell your son what your mother-in-law alleged to me. And she's grieving too, of course…"

He abruptly abandons the grieving family angle and starts threatening legal action. "Surely you realize the gravity of these allegations. They're slanderous!"

Now he's shouting.

I feel my temper rising. "Didn't you just say that Gunnhildur was senile and nobody could take her allegations seriously?"

"Of course she is. That malevolent old witch has always had a grudge against me, ever since I married Ásdís Björk."

Gleefully, I ask, "Oh, really? So it's not a new thing, because she's senile or demented, or whatever you call it?"

"Now you're adding insult to injury!"

"I haven't published anything about this, and I never intended to. And I don't see what all the fuss is about. I just felt that Gunnhildur had a right to her opinion, even if she is old. I simply wanted to explore the facts a little better. That's all there is to it."

"I'm warning you," says Ásgeir Eyvindarson, his voice like a taut bowstring.

"What are you warning me against?"

"I'm warning you to stop snooping into a family tragedy of people who've done nothing wrong. I'm warning you not to go sensationalizing…"

And there it was!

"…about people's private lives, just so you can sell that pathetic little rag that thinks it's a newspaper. Don't—"

"I don't like being threatened," I reply. I'm quite calm again.

"—imagine that I don't have influence. Don't think you can treat me like any Tom, Dick, or Harry you drag down into the gutter. Your boss, Ölver Margrétarson Steinsson, is a piece of shit and a punk who thinks he can use his ill-gotten gains through the media to buy political power and respectability. A gangster who buys up all the competition and then forces the rest to knuckle under. It's…"

"What has your wife's death got to do with one of the owners of the *Afternoon News*? Or political issues?"

With a gulp of rage, Ásgeir Eyvindarson hangs up on me.

It seems a huge leap from the pleasant, polite son to the hysterical, threatening father. Before my delightful phone conversation with the bereaved husband, I'd been wondering how hypochondria, as described to me by Gudmundur Ásgeirsson, could relate to his mother's death when she fell out of a boat into the

Jökulsá River. The poor woman actually died: surely that couldn't be hypochondria?

I've still got my conversation with Gunnhildur at the back of my mind, and it occasionally pops up to the surface when things calm down a bit. Now, for instance.

"Oh my God! Oh my God! Oh my God!"

"You can say that again."

"Thank you. Oh my God! Oh my God! Oh my God!"

Gunnhildur tosses a gray braid. "I don't know how they can be bothered with such drivel."

We're sitting out in the corridor, but we can't avoid the sound of an American sitcom that's enthralling the *Guiding Light* mafia.

"Maybe they can't find anything better to do," I suggest, offering Gunnhildur a chocolate from the box I have brought her as a peace offering.

A gnarled, wizened index finger hovers over the tray like a small helicopter. Then she finds what she's looking for: a bottle-shaped chocolate, with alcohol-laden filling.

"Old people are getting to be just like the younger ones," she observes. "They don't read, they don't talk. They just sit and watch those stupid American idiots make fools of themselves for a million dollars, or whatever it is they get paid."

The leathery face dissolves into a smile as the chocolate bottle bursts in her mouth, releasing the boozy contents.

"Delicious, my boy. Even though it's not from the Yumm candy factory."

I can't help envying her. I make do with a caramel that's so chewy and sticky that I'm afraid I may have no teeth left by the time I leave the Hóll care home.

"So you didn't write off an old woman," says Gunnhildur, looking at me out of limpid blue eyes. "Here you are again."

"Yes, I wanted to meet you again, talk a bit more."

I tell her about my dealings with her grandson and her son-in-law. I don't go into details about what they said about her.

"That's Ásgeir to a T," she says. "He's full of…"

"Evil, wickedness, and viciousness?"

"Yes, that's right. How did you know?"

"Oh, just something I heard. And of course I've had the dubious pleasure of speaking to him myself."

"Evil. Wickedness. Viciousness. That's Ásgeir." She picks out another little chocolate bottle. "Maybe you're not so silly, my boy. There's enough silliness about." She jerks her head toward the *Guiding Light* mafia, with a swing of her braid.

"But I haven't really made any progress about what you said— that your daughter's death wasn't an accident."

"But why on earth did you go and ask Ásgeir? Surely you didn't imagine he'd simply fold and confess, then go and turn himself in to the police? If you hadn't brought me these lovely chocolates, I might think you were a little bit silly."

"Um, I'm sure you're right."

"Haven't you seen Detective Chief Inspectors Morse and Taggart at work on the TV?"

"Yes, of course I have," I reply.

"It takes them a whole episode, or sometimes more, to break the murderer's resistance, gather evidence, get them to confess."

"But…"

"Of course on television they compress it into an hour. I know that. They edit it, days of work by those conscientious detectives, and make one hour of it. Of course they have to sleep and eat, and go to the bathroom, like the rest of us. But they needn't show us everything. You know that, my boy, don't you?"

"Yes, yes."

"And you spoke to our poor little Gudmundur? He's not a bad boy, although he's so desperate to be richer than other people and much richer than his scoundrel of a dad. They've got greed in their blood. It's all in the cells, as they say these days."

"In the cells…"

"He didn't get that greed from my Ásdís Björk. That greed came straight from cold blood, as cold as any that flows through human veins."

"I'm sure."

Gunnhildur's eyes have been darting around, but now she fixes me with her gaze. "So you spoke to poor Gudmundur, to find out whether I was a crazy old woman?"

"Well, I couldn't simply make the assumption that Ásdís Björk was murdered just because you said so."

She looks at me with a strange light in her eye.

"Would you believe me," I go on, "if I told you the pope had been murdered by a mad prostitute?"

Gunnhildur shakes her head. "You really are a bit silly, my boy. A prostitute—let alone a mad one—would never be admitted into the Vatican. Ha!" She squeaks with glee. "That was a good one! Hahaha!"

"My point was that we can't take things for granted."

"And the poor old pope, pale as the ghost of a ghost! Really!"

"It was just an idea."

She tries to stifle her giggles. "You can be quite amusing, even if you are a bit silly."

"Well, I'm glad you think so."

"Have you got a cell?" she suddenly asks me, with no trace of a laugh.

"Cell?" I parrot, thinking: *What the hell am I doing here?*

"Yes. A cell."

"Well, I certainly hope so."

"Can I borrow it?"

"Borrow a cell?"

"Yes. I'm going to make a phone call for you, to someone who can answer all your questions. There's no point calling the murderer up and asking if he did it. That will get you nowhere."

"You want a cell phone?"

"Yes. What else, my boy?"

I reach into my pocket for my cell phone and hand it to her.

Awkwardly Gunnhildur fiddles with the phone in her gnarled hand. "These new cells are made for spiders to use. The buttons are much too small for ordinary people to see and press the right ones." She passes it back to me. "Dial for me, would you?"

She recites a phone number, which I punch in before returning the phone to her.

"Hello? Ragna, dear? It's Gunnhildur."

She waits.

"Hello? Hello?" Turning the phone back and forth in her hand, she glares at it. "The damn thing's stone dead."

I reach out and turn the phone around so she is speaking into the mouthpiece. She tries again.

"Hello? Ragna, dear? It's Gunnhildur...How are you?...Is it low down or further up?...The small of your back?...Oh, yes... Just the same as I had the other year...The same year as the Reagan-Gorbachev summit in Reykjavík...I think it was the only thing that resulted from that summit...Yes, I'm sure I got it sitting in front of the TV hour after hour, waiting for something to happen…"

I stand up and stretch. Have a chocolate. And another.

"Look, Ragna, dear. There's a young man here with me…No, no, no, nothing's go on between us…Noooo…Too young and delicate…Ragna, dear, I'm going to send him over to see you… No, no, none of that…None of that, with him…I just want you to answer some questions from him…About my Ásdís Björk… And that goddamned wilderness tour…No, don't be put off. He's a bit silly, but he means well…Thank you, my dear…No, Lord, no, don't go to any trouble for the boy. He brought me a box of chocolates…No, these boys are made far too much fuss of…I'll tell him to bring you chocolates, or you won't talk to him…Oh, fair to middling, my dear. Fair to middling…He's on his way…"

Yep, I'm on my way. On the road again. And now, after my second visit today to the expensive confectioner's shop, my next destination is a small single-story concrete house with a red roof, not far from the high school campus. I had imagined Ragna Ármannsdóttir being around Gunnhildur's age, but she turns out to be a young thing of only sixtyish, with long black hair—obviously a dye job—wearing a green floral-patterned dress and a blue-striped apron. She is of average height and weight, but with a stack of chins beneath her broad, smiling face. She's obviously just put her makeup on, and from the kitchen drifts an aroma of pancakes. I ceremoniously present the chocolate box to her, and shortly afterward Ragna and I sit down to coffee and pancakes at her old varnished dining table. She watches me stuff my face and smokes slender Capri cigarettes, as she recounts to me how fond she is of dear old Gunnhildur.

"I started working at Yumm as a messenger. That was while Gunnhildur's husband, Gudmundur, was still alive. Gunnhildur treated me like one of the family. I've worked there ever since. At first I had a summer job during the school vacations, and then I started fulltime after I graduated from Commercial College. I've been the office manager, in practice, but without the job title."

"And how have you liked working under Ásgeir's management?"

"I don't want to speak ill of Ásgeir. He came into this old family business, which had been run with the emphasis on *family* rather than *business*. He wanted to introduce new management methods, marketing strategies, and so on. A huge amount was spent on all sorts of evaluations and management analyses and advertising campaigns and strategic plans, but he didn't manage to turn the business around. And that's all I'm prepared to say about Ásgeir. He had grand ideas, but his plans didn't work out."

"Gunnhildur doesn't think much of him."

"When old Gudmundur died, Gunnhildur wanted Ásdís Björk to take over the business, but she refused. She wanted her husband to get the job. She pointed out that he had specialist qualifications in business administration, which is absolutely true. Gunnhildur gave way, but she's found it hard to forgive Ásgeir for what's happened to the business. But it's not fair to put all the blame on Ásgeir. There's been fierce competition in the Icelandic candy market for years now. Not only between Icelandic companies, but also with imported candy from huge and powerful multinationals. Established products and trademarks drop out of favor, and new ones are launched. That's just the way it goes."

"Tell me a bit about this wilderness tour."

"We've gone on trips like that, ending up with our annual dinner, for the past three years. I can't say I like it. But it's awfully popular to organize that kind of thing. It's the latest craze in management and human resources policy. *Human resources policy*, just think! What's that supposed to mean? Isn't it enough to treat your staff like human beings? We've been on a glacier trip, snowmobiling, dogsledding, snow games, mountain biking, and kayaking. And, on this occasion, white-water rafting, which ended so horribly. What I think is extraordinary is that the objective is supposed to be to promote solidarity, encourage people to get to know each other, stimulate enterprise, but the way it's done simply leads to competitiveness and rivalry. This time we were supposed to clamber up a cliff fifteen feet high, then jump off into a deep pool of water. They have safety procedures, of course, but the idea is to prove yourself, show how tough you are. And if you're not prepared to get into that, you're humiliated. I've seen two excellent members of staff, of the older generation, who gave up after trips like that. They felt they weren't up to the job anymore."

I'm now full of pancakes. I light up, to keep Ragna company.

"I assume the trips were Ásgeir's idea?"

"Oh, yes. The other aspect of the wilderness tours is the question of where, when, and how the drinking will come to an end."

"So there's a lot of drinking, is there?"

"Not supposed to be. But people bring some beers along and sneak a drink when the guide isn't looking. And then, when they get back to town, that's when they get going. Everybody goes along to a fine dinner, tired out and hyped up on adrenaline, excitement, and frustration, and they really let go. That's when things go wild."

"Except this time?"

"Yes, except this time." Ragna twists her cigarette in the ashtray.

"Gunnhildur said that Ásgeir attended the dinner although his wife was lying unconscious in hospital?"

"He stayed for an hour or two. Everybody was so traumatized after the accident that most of us decided not to go. But Ásgeir wanted the program to go on. He didn't want to cancel. He felt that was what Ásdís Björk would want. Which is actually quite true. I knew her well enough to know that. And at that point we didn't know how serious her injuries were."

"What was their marriage like?"

"I'm not in a position to tell. I can imagine what Gunnhildur must have said about it. But no outsider can know what goes on in a marriage. Only the two people who are in it. I know what I'm talking about. When I got divorced, about ten years ago, nobody understood why. Not even my closest family and friends. Some of them couldn't grasp how I could let go of such a good man after thirty years together. Others couldn't fathom how I had put up with such a tedious boor for so long. And then there were those who felt my husband was lucky to be rid of me." She smiles warmly. "But I will say that over the past five or six years Ásdís Björk has been much less involved in the business. She's hardly been seen in the office, let alone in the factory. She stayed home, mostly. Ásgeir never said anything about their private life, but I gathered from Ásdís Björk—from the little we spoke to each other—that she was very ill."

"What was wrong with her?"

"It seemed to vary. First one thing, then another. She used to be a beautiful woman, but she'd put on a lot of weight in the last few years. Maybe because of her poor health."

"Did you see her fall into the river?"

"No, I was in the boat ahead of them. I just heard all the shouting and screaming. We've talked about it a lot, of course. Especially that evening, at the restaurant. I got the impression that no one actually saw her fall. She was sitting in the stern, and she seemed to have stood up, lost her balance, and fallen overboard. Ásgeir was sitting in front of her, and he immediately jumped in after her. He was quite a hero, really."

As I take my leave of Ragna, darkness is falling. I remember another question: "Gunnhildur told me that Ásdís Björk and Ásgeir had a disagreement about the running of Yumm. Do you know anything about that?"

She hesitates. "Not exactly. But I've noticed over the past few years that Ásgeir has sometimes had meetings in his office with intimidating men carrying briefcases and shown them around the factory. Whatever that may mean."

"I've been told that Ásdís Björk had an addiction problem?"

Ragna looks at me in astonishment. "I've never heard any such thing. But, as I say, there's so much we don't know about people and their private lives. And even less that we understand."

As I have said before, two plus two doesn't make twenty-two. Nonetheless, Chief of Police Höskuldur Pétursson in Reydargerdi informs me, off the record: "There are people here, actually quite a few people, who think these arrests are purely political."

"Do you mean the Akureyri police are investigating Agnar Hansen and his gang for political motives?"

"No, I'm not suggesting anything myself. And the police don't get into politics. I just heard a rumor that people think it's likely that the political opponents of the bosses here in Reydargerdi are exploiting the opportunity to cast suspicion on those young men."

"Why on earth would they do that?"

"To muddy the waters about the alleged disorder and strife that's taking place here as a result of the industrial development. Could be convenient now, just before the election."

"It sounds far-fetched to me," I say.

"Perhaps. But why have they picked on those kids while the rest of the people at the party get off scot-free?"

"Because they were gate-crashers and made trouble?" I ask.

"Or because one of them is the son of the head of the town council and one a foreigner, to boot?" retorts Höskuldur.

But none of that gets into my rather threadbare piece for the Monday edition on the progress of the Skarphédinn investigation. My article concludes:

> Skarphédinn's funeral will take place today at
> Akureyri Church.

17 MONDAY

"Bullshit," says Trausti Löve. "It's just the same old bullshit."

"I'm just saying what the chief of police at Reydargerdi told me last night," I object, sitting in my closet, shortly before midday.

"And the guy is Ásgrímur Pétursson's brother," Trausti irritably snaps. "It's a desperate attempt to distract the public and the media from the real issue. Political conspiracies, my ass! Now do you see why it was so important to cover events in Reydargerdi properly?"

"There's every chance you may have been right there."

"Every chance? You should have the grace to admit I was right, without reservation, buddy. I was man enough to own up to my mistake the other day, about the *Question of the Day*…"

"Only because you were forced to."

"…and you should be man enough to do the same about Reydargerdi."

So it's back to the old tug-of-war. "All right," I say. "You were right. But I warn you, the *Afternoon News* had better not make a big splash about this Reydargerdi gang, Agnar Hansen and his buddies, being guilty. They haven't made any admissions, and there's no proof they did anything at all. All the police have got is that they were there, at that party, for part of the evening—like plenty of other people. We can't jump to conclusions—it'll come back to bite us."

"We've got to report what happens. All three of them are in custody, aren't they?"

"Yes, two of them were picked up this morning. But they can only hold them for four days."

"Then you have to provide more information about these guys in tomorrow's paper."

"Are we supposed to publish the names and personal details of people who haven't been convicted of anything?"

"I say again: we report what happens. The guys are in custody. No one else. We should say who they are."

I don't like this. "Surely you're not expecting me to identify Agnar Hansen by pointing out who his dad is?"

"Of course I am. Jóhann Hansen's a public figure. Our readers have a right to know about the relationship."

"But Jóhann's not a public figure in this specific case. He's head of the town council in Reydargerdi, who happens to be the father of the young man who's in custody here in Akureyri. Do I have to spell it out to you, as news editor?"

"No need to spell anything out to me, buddy," rages Trausti. "Just do what I tell you."

"No, I won't," I firmly reply. "If we do that, we're only going to encourage the idea—even confirm it—that someone's trying to make political capital out of a completely unrelated matter. And it's a serious matter. A murder investigation. Are you completely off your goddamned head again, Trausti?"

"Just do it. For days on end you've been doing your own thing, snooping around Skarphédinn's background and character, without producing a single bit of copy. Not one line."

"It's a complex case."

"What isn't complex, so even you ought to be able to understand it, is that our readers have a right to information about a case that's on everybody's mind and everybody's lips. And that's that. So fuck you!"

I must admit, I'm beginning to feel like a little kid who's always running to Daddy to tell tales on his big brother. "Hannes," I say, after having explained the situation, "Trausti's way off base, again. And I won't do as he says."

"My dear Einar," pronounces the editor.

This doesn't look good.

"My dear Einar, you must see the bigger picture here. The young men are in custody because they're suspected of being involved in this case. And the fact that they're being held has led to some political strain in Reydargerdi. The *Afternoon News* had nothing to do with that. Surely we have an obligation to report on it?"

"I'm not at all sure that it's led to any political strain in Reydargerdi. It may just be some personal speculation by a few individuals, perhaps just one or two. Isn't it likely that someone's got their own agenda? That they're trying to lead the paper into a political trap? To make these kids into political martyrs? And confuse the readers? Shouldn't we stick to the facts of the case instead of repeating rumors and inventions from people who have nothing to do with the case?"

"Rumors and inventions can be worth reporting too, sir."

I decide to change my tactics: "If you had a son, Hannes, or if Trausti Löve had a son—God forbid—and if that son were to be arrested in connection with a major criminal case, would you regard it as normal and correct for other media, or even the *Afternoon News* itself, to publish his name and add that he was the son of the editor or news editor of this paper—which is completely irrelevant? Do you find that a comfortable prospect?"

He doesn't seem to need any time to think it over: "Facts are facts, whether or not we find them comfortable. It isn't our job to sort out the comfortable ones from the others, which aren't. This is an ugly world, Einar. Do you think we should be prettying it up?"

"So you're on the side of the idiotic news editor?" I ask, disappointed and annoyed.

"I agree with him in principle," Hannes replies. "But the principle can't always be applied in exactly the same way."

"What on earth is that supposed to mean?"

"Just this, sir. If we can get hold of the names of the three men, we should publish them. If we can find some Reydargerdi people who are willing to be named saying that there's a nasty political smell about the case—and preferably more than just two of them—then we should publish what they say."

I think about his arguments for a moment.

"I had a phone call last night," the editor says, interrupting my chain of thought. "From someone called Ásgeir Eyvindarson. You know the name, I take it?"

"Oh, yes," I reply. I tell Hannes about my side of my conversation with Ásgeir and why he had called me.

"The man was seething with rage. I told him you were a journalist who wouldn't be tempted into libel nor sensationalism and that threats would not impress you. Nor the *Afternoon News*."

"And?"

"He was a little less agitated by the end of our call."

"I find it very strange," I remark, "that both he and that Reydargerdi crowd blame political persecution. What nonsense is that?"

"Well, isn't it always the way? People who find themselves in a position of weakness—often due to their own mistakes—will claim they're being victimized. Either personally or politically. It's human nature to blame others for our own misfortunes."

"All right. But what about this Reydargerdi nonsense? Isn't that exactly what you were talking about? What am I supposed to do about that?"

"I've told you where I stand, sir."

"Trausti seems to have the IQ of a radish. He dismisses the political allegations as bullshit, to quote his exact words. But we're still supposed to report on them. So are we meant to publish what we *know* is bullshit?"

"We can't tell," replies Hannes. "We should simply report on what people think, whether or not we personally think it's bullshit."

"I'm having serious doubts, Hannes, about whether I belong on this paper anymore."

"Perhaps your doubts are, in the end, a matter of whether we belong in this society anymore. I sometimes have doubts about it myself, sir. Even serious doubts. But we can't pretend it's not happening. Then where would we be?"

The elegant church on its hilltop site above the town center is crammed with people by the time I arrive, ten minutes late, for Skarphédinn's funeral. I scuttle out onto the steps and wander back and forth for a while in the chilly wind before giving up and strolling down the hill into the arty Listagil district. I go into a café, and for half an hour or so I think things through over a cappuccino, then take my phone out of my pocket and make four calls. The first is to the Akureyri police station: I am informed that the names of the three men in custody will not be released to the press.

Good.

The other calls are to Reydargerdi: to the police station, the hotel, and the Reydin bar. Nobody is willing to be quoted about political overtones to the case.

Good.

What is not quite so good is that I get the three names from the innkeeper and from Elín, the bartender at Reydin. And Chief Höskuldur confirms that information—but off the record: Agnar Hansen, Gardar Jónsson, and Ivo Batorac, who is of Croatian origin.

What the hell am I going to do with these names?

I can't just sit there. I climb the hill back up to the church and hang around for five minutes until the doors open. The pallbearers are six young people—three boys, three girls. I recognize one of them—Ágústa Magnúsdóttir, chair of the drama group, deathly pale and stony-faced. The others must also be schoolmates of the dead boy. Maybe one of them is Fridrik. Following the coffin out of the church is a stricken trio—a middle-aged couple with a teenage boy. The man is gaunt-faced and emaciated, wearing a suit that is far too big for him, with a white shirt and black tie. His thick dark hair, swept back in a wave from his face, is graying at the temples. His shaven face shows dark stubble, and dark glasses are perched on his straight nose. The woman, tall and sturdily built, is wearing a black coat. Her oval face is thickly coated in makeup and painted with a red slash of a mouth, like on a mask. Wearing black high-heeled shoes, she seems unsteady on her feet, or perhaps she's simply unaccustomed to heels. The boy has long hair and heavy brows like his brother, but he is not as tall. On his handsome face are round glasses. He appears uncomfortable, walking awkwardly alongside his parents with his head bent. No doubt he would rather be anywhere else than here.

As the coffin is placed in the hearse, I observe the mourners leave the church.

Jóa is here with her camera, taking photos of the procession. I was reluctantly permitted to take her out of the office, where she has been hard at work doing Ásbjörn's job for him.

The whole high school appears to be here, plus half the town. Skarphédinn was clearly a popular young man.

But are those responsible for his death safely behind bars?

Or are they here—right here—to see him off?

I recognize some faces in the crowd.

Here's the principal of the high school.

Örvar Páll sees me, but pretends not to.

Kjartan Arnarson nods gravely to me.

I manage to have a word with him before he disappears out into the cold. I ask if there will be a funeral reception.

"Yes, the school's holding a reception in Kvosin."

"Where's that?"

"It's the assembly hall in the Hólar building."

The rituals we've developed to deal with death have always been hard for me to grasp. Funerals, eulogies, obituaries, fine. Showing the deceased respect and dignity—deserved or undeserved—at the final hour. But the wake? Doesn't the compulsion to see the dead person lying in a coffin betray some kind of guilty conscience? Or masochism? Doesn't it imply a lack of imagination?

Surely it should be enough for us to say our farewell in our minds? Think about the person, thank him or her for happy times—or even not so happy ones? I just don't know. But what I do know is that I have never met anyone who found it good, or helpful, to go to a wake. And no one asked the dead guy.

Funeral receptions are much the same. Unlike the wake, the reception's a public event, a sort of celebration of the deceased. The bereaved have to pretend they're coping, thank the guests for their sympathy, chat about their dead relative, how they're doing, and generally share. Then coffee is drunk, cakes and sandwiches are devoured, and every single person is desperate to make their escape.

I just don't know. But what I do know is that funeral receptions make me feel as if I'm stuck in the coffin with the dead person and everyone he or she ever knew in life. There's not much room to breathe in there.

I hover restlessly at the edge of the spacious assembly hall. What am I doing here, anyway? I'm a gate-crasher. I didn't know the guy at all. But I'm striving to write about him and his demise. That's probably what I'm doing here.

I'm very far from happy with it.

Out of the corner of my eye I notice Skarphédinn's brother, who is standing away from the crowd. Next to him, Ágústa from the drama group is bending his ear. He seems distracted or uninterested in what she is saying. In among the guests his father sits like an insensate object, all alone, white as a sheet, staring into space, or possibly asleep. He's still wearing the dark glasses, so it's hard to tell. His wife is close by, surrounded by guests and trying to take part in the conversation. Then she leaves her guests, goes over to her husband, and whispers in his ear. There is no reaction. I'm wondering if I should seize the opportunity to try to speak to her. But there's something in her weary yet stony expression that deters me.

I'm about to leave when a young man walks past who seems as uncomfortable as me. Skarphédinn's brother strides off in the direction of the toilets. I follow, and before I know it we're standing side by side at the urinals.

Today's *Morning News* devoted nearly a whole double-page spread to obituaries in praise of his brother's manifold talents and virtues. From them I gleaned the information that the younger brother's name is Rúnar, and he's a high school student too. Since he's sixteen, he's presumably in his first year.

I glance over at him, desperately trying to give the impression that I'm not just pretending I have to pee. He stands there in his black suit, white shirt, and black tie, head bent, absorbed. I think of running water. Nothing happens. I think of billowing, gushing waterfalls. Still nothing. I think about the Jökulsá River. A trickle.

Thank you, God.

He's drying his hands as I walk over to the sinks.

I automatically offer my hand as I say: "Sorry, Rúnar. I just wanted to…" Then I realize what I'm doing and pull my hand away. "Sorry," I say again. "Better wash first."

He can't help smiling as he finishes drying his hands. Then he hovers awkwardly by the sinks as I wash and dry my hands.

I offer my hand once more. "I'm sorry for your loss. I only knew your brother slightly. I just met him once, in fact. But he made an impression on me. My name's Einar. I'm with the *Afternoon News*."

We shake hands, moistly.

Initially Rúnar says nothing, but observes me from under his heavy brows. "Thank you," he murmurs.

"I interviewed Skarphédinn over at Hólar, a few days before he died. About the production of *Loftur the Sorcerer*."

He says nothing, heads for the door.

I follow. When we get into the corridor I summon the courage to say: "As I'm sure you're aware, your brother's death has made him a public figure, because it's the subject of a criminal investigation."

He stops dead, staring down at the floor.

I have the impression he's about to speak. I wait a moment.

"Skarphédinn was determined to become what you call a public figure," he slowly says.

I nod. "But not like this?"

To some extent Rúnar strikes me as a typical insecure teenager in pain. But in other ways he gives the impression of being mature beyond his sixteen years.

"I've been assigned to find out about your brother and write an article about him and his life," I quietly tell him. "I've talked to various people who knew him. But I must admit I haven't managed to put together a full picture of him."

Rúnar looks toward the assembly hall.

"Until now, I haven't felt I should approach your family. And really I feel it's inappropriate to be ambushing you here. But would you mind meeting me? We can just talk. I won't quote you, if that's what you prefer. But I need some reliable information."

Head bent, he makes no response for a while. Then he says: "All right. But don't call me at home."

I make a note of his cell phone number, and promise not to get in touch for a few days. Then he returns to the assembly hall, to try to survive his brother's funeral reception.

———

AKUREYRI CASE—THREE IN CUSTODY
Three young men, all residents of Reydargerdi, have been
placed in police custody in connection with the investiga-
tion into the death of high school student Skarphédinn Val-
gardsson in Akureyri...

That is how I start my article. My conscience is not at ease when
I conclude the piece by giving the names of the three young men.
I state in my article that their involvement in the case remains
unclear and that the period of custody is short. My conscience
isn't clear, but it could be worse. Not a word about political spin.

In order to ensure that my piece gets into print in that form,
without any artful editing or editorializing by Trausti Löve, I call
Hannes and ask him to keep an eye out. He gives me his word. He
also gives me permission to continue to focus on my article about
the dead boy.

I've asked Ásbjörn to tell his old buddy, Chief Ólafur Gísli,
what I'm doing.

I had to call Ásbjörn on his cell phone. The landline seemed
to have been unplugged.

"Ólafur Gísli has no objection," he says, leaning against the
doorway of my closet. "He says everything we print is our responsibility anyway."

"Did you get the impression he thought they'd got the right
guys?"

Ásbjörn writhes against the doorpost, like a horse scratching
its itchy back. His puffy face is so flushed and weary that it is almost bluish. "No, I wouldn't say so. But it sounded as if they were
beginning to talk. He wouldn't say any more."

"Not at this point in time?"

"No, not at this point in time."

I observe Ásbjörn. "Hey, Ásbjörn, you're not looking too good. You almost remind me of me in the mirror on a Monday morning."

He shakes his sweaty, disheveled head. "That's quite possible. Maybe I should start drinking like you used to. Maybe that would make it more bearable."

"What's wrong, Ásbjörn?" I ask, standing up.

"I think Karó's having a breakdown," he says in a shaky voice. "She's a nervous wreck. She doesn't sleep. She roams around the apartment all night, crying. Pal's a bundle of nerves. And I can hardly get any work done. I've unloaded everything onto Jóa. I don't know what I'd do without her. Probably I'd go on such a bender that I'd never come out of it."

I feel moved to place a comforting hand on his shoulder. "Won't you tell me what's upsetting Karó?"

"I only wish I knew that myself. I ask her and ask her and beg her to tell me what's wrong. But she just cries even more. Isn't that what they call hysteria?"

Weird idea, hysteria, I think to myself. *Based on the theory that a woman's womb can drive her mad.*

Ásbjörn shrugs his shoulders in despair.

"Have those mysterious phone calls stopped?"

"Yes, they've stopped."

"Do you think it's got anything to do with them?"

He gives me a questioning look. "What do you mean?"

"I don't know."

"You said you'd intervened. I suppose you were yanking my chain, were you?"

"Um, yeah," I admit shamefacedly.

"So you don't know anything?" he asks in an accusatory tone.

"No, I don't know anything. You and I are both rather square at the edges, Ásbjörn."

He looks at me again, even more bewildered. "Square at the edges? What the hell is that supposed to mean?"

"Have you been unfaithful to Karó?"

Ásbjörn flushes red. "How dare you? How could you think that?"

Maybe because I'd have trouble being faithful to Karólína, I think to myself. *Or to Ásbjörn, for that matter.* But I say: "Well, it just occurred to me. And what about her? Couldn't the state she's in indicate that she's been up to something herself?"

He claps both hands to his greasy head. "I can't believe that. We're not like that, Karó and I."

"That's what a lot of people think, without knowing."

"Karó is more interested in Pal than she is in men," observes Ásbjörn tonelessly.

"Do you really want to know what's happening?"

"Of course I do. This situation is intolerable."

"You're sure?"

He seems about to explode from the tension. "Yes! Goddamn it! Yes, I do!"

"Then I'm going to find out how square at the edges my mind really is. But don't blame me if it turns out to be wrong, or if you don't like it. But I really shall intervene now."

18 TUESDAY

This wheel's on fire,
Rolling down the road,
Best notify my next of kin,
This wheel shall explode!

Julie Driscoll is on the radio, singing good old Dylan's unsettling song.

I take Thórunnarstræti toward the police station; so far as I can see in the rearview mirror, my wheels aren't on fire. Not these tires, not my wheels.

Jóa is out in front of the police station with her photography gear when I arrive. Ásbjörn had woken me at eight o'clock this morning to tell me that the Reydargerdi Three would be released within the next few hours. "All Ólafur Gisli would say was that they didn't think it would serve the interests of the investigation to hold them any longer."

"But the custody order is still valid for another few days?"

"Yes, but that's all he said."

"Have you seen them yet?" I ask as I get out of the car. The temperature has risen. The morning air is humid, and a veil of mist curls at the foot of Mount Hlídarfjall. "Have they been released?"

"No," she replies. "Not yet. I hear they'll be out in the next few minutes." Wrinkling her nose, she asks: "Am I really supposed to take a photo of them when they're released? Is that the kind of picture we're publishing now?"

"Yes," I reply without enthusiasm. "We published their names when they were arrested, although I'm certainly not happy about that. But under the circumstances, we really have to report the fact that they're being released."

"But with pics?"

"There was a photo of Agnar with the report on the disturbances in Reydargerdi, and we published his name when the arrests were made. It's old news, really."

"But what if they don't want their photo taken?"

I shrug. "Well…"

"Or if they conceal their faces?"

"There's not much we can do about that. But I don't really think these guys are likely to shun the limelight. Let's see what happens."

Fifteen minutes later the doors of the police station open, and three young men emerge.

Agnar Hansen is in the lead, wearing brown leather pants, a blue denim jacket, and a black T-shirt with the legend *Born To Be Wild*. His long blond hair is not in a ponytail this time, but sticking out in all directions. With a laugh he comments to his companions, whom I have not seen before: "Fucking assholes. We'll get them."

Catching sight of Jóa and me, he stops dead in his tracks, and the other two crash into his shoulders, one on either side. Ivo Batorac is the darker of the two, wearing black jeans, a black T-shirt, and a black leather jacket. He is short in the leg, chunky, with a shaven head and earrings, a scarred, flat face like a pancake, and big, bluish hands with fingers like sausages.

Gardar Jónsson looks a little older than the other two, twenty-five perhaps. His face is lopsided, and his lanky frame is graceless. He has no coat on, and with his blue jeans he wears a white T-shirt with black lettering: *White Power!* He too has a shaven head.

"Well, well! If it isn't the paparazzi," sneers Agnar, revealing his long, yellow teeth.

"Nice of you to turn up."

"Morning, Agnar," I say. "Can we do a short interview with you and take a photo?"

Agnar Hansen walks slowly over to us, his two sidekicks close behind. The sneer is still on his battered face, and his stance is intimidating.

"What do you think, guys?" he asks his sidekicks. "Shall we kick the shit out of them or talk to them?"

"Let's kill them," replies Batorac, his voice heavily accented.

"Surely not?" I observe. "Not when you've just been released from jail? You'd find yourself behind bars again in no time. And you might not get out again so quickly."

Agnar walks right up to me so the silver tips of his boots touch the toes of my worn shoes.

He stares coldly into my eyes.

"I will say, on the record," he articulates into my face with a blast of foul breath, "that the Akureyri police are a gang of stupid idiots…"

"Isn't that a redundancy?" remarks Jóa. She doesn't generally get involved in my conversations with interviewees, but the scorn in her face is obvious even to Agnar.

He goes up to Jóa and adopts the same threatening pose, right in her face. He must have learned it from watching American movies about bad boys in the hood. "*Redun*-what? What are you? A she-male? Or just a typical frigid bull dyke?"

Jóa isn't intimidated. She's stronger and more muscular than he is. "How could I be both frigid *and* a typical bull dyke?"

Agnar grimaces horribly, but can't think of a comeback.

"And," adds Jóa, "it would be enough to make anyone frigid to smell your stinking breath. Don't they have toothbrushes at the police station?"

This is getting out of hand, I think and approach Agnar with a big smile on my face. "Now, now, Jóa. The boys have been held in isolation. Hey, Agnar, wouldn't you like to say a few words about your arrest and your release?"

The tension drops for a moment. He walks over to his companions, stands between them with his arms round their shoulders.

"OK, take a photo of us, bull dyke. And you, motherfucker," he remarks to me, "you can write under the photo that the Akureyri police are way out of line, bullying innocent outsiders who were just in Akureyri for some fun. We haven't done anything wrong. We have never done anything wrong." He claps his friends on the back with a laugh. They respond with guffaws of laughter, as if on command, as Jóa snaps a photo.

"Well, guys," says Agnar. "Let's celebrate. Have a snort and then find something to fuck."

Sniggering, they make their way to a brand-new black Honda. I recognize it. I saw Agnar cruising downtown in that car on the fateful night before Holy Thursday.

"*Speeding along on his new Honda...*," as the theme song of *Street Rider* said.

Gardar Jónsson takes his place at the wheel, Batorac in the passenger seat, and Agnar in the back, like a VIP with his chauffeur and bodyguard. As they drive past us, Agnar rolls down his window and shouts: "I've always wanted to rape a fucking bull dyke. See you later!"

Jóa and I exchange a look. I'm stunned, but she simply shakes her head.

There's a vague uneasiness in my gut as I drive down Oddeyrargata into the town center, past the library, and turn left onto a short street named Hólabraut. This is where Skarphédinn lived. Rattling around in my mind is the little I know about the case, and I am constantly discovering how much I don't know. I park my car and look up at the three-story white concrete building. This was his home. So?

After a few minutes' indecision I take out my phone, ring directory assistance, and ask for the phone number of Skarphédinn Valgardsson in Akureyri. A landline number is recited in my ear. I call it.

No reply.

What did I expect? Did I think he would pick up the phone and say: *Skarphédinn?*

Perhaps I was hoping someone was in the apartment. Or maybe an answering machine would share some clue with me. At least the phone hasn't been cut off. I get out of the car and walk over to the building. It's a stately building, well-maintained. The uppermost doorbell is marked *3rd floor and attic, Skarphédinn.*

Just for the hell of it, I press the doorbell. There's no response, of course. I'm about to head back to the car when something else occurs to me. I ring the doorbell for the first floor. No answer. I try the second-floor bell. After a short wait, the entry phone crackles and a young girl's voice speaks.

"Hello?"

"Hello. My name's Einar. Is your mom home?"

"Nope."

"What about your dad?"

"Nope."

Not much of a talker, this one. "Um…"

"They're both at work."

"What's your name?"

"Ösp."

"That's a nice name."

"Nope, it stinks."

"How old are you?"

"Twelve."

"I knew Skarphédinn, on the floor above you…"

"He's dead," the girl says.

"I know. Did you know him?"

"Nope."

"So…"

"Well, he used to give me candy sometimes."

"So he was nice to you, was he?"

"He was all right."

"Did your parents know him well?"

"Dad couldn't stand him."

"Really? Why was that?" I ask her, feeling that this entry-phone conversation is getting a bit long—and weird. But I daren't ask the girl to let me into the building. The way things are today, God knows what deviant urges I could be accused of.

"Cos Mom thought he was cute."

I think about that for a moment. "And what did you think of him?"

"He was OK. Rúnar's much hotter."

"So you know Rúnar?"

"He's going to move into Skarphédinn's place."

"Is he indeed?"

"Yeah. I'm not going to talk to you anymore."

A click and a crackling on the entry phone tell me she's gone.

"I hope Ragna was nice to you?" asks Gunnhildur when I call her at the care home.

"She was fine. Very pleasant," I say as I count the cracks in the wall outside the window of my closet.

"Did she make pancakes for you?"

"She most certainly did."

Gunnhildur sighs on the phone. "What a life, my boy. I can't even make pancakes for my visitors. What kind of a life is that?"

"But isn't it a relief? Being free of all that stuff?"

"Let me tell you, I used to make much better pancakes than Ragna's." She falls silent, and her thought fades away as she adds, "Used to."

"Gunnhildur," I say. "Who was your daughter's doctor?"

"Why on earth do you want to know that?"

"Well, I thought I'd ask him about her health."

"Health? Ásdís Björk was in excellent health. She was fit as a fiddle. Until Ásgeir murdered her, in…"

"What's the doctor's name?" I interject.

"It's that Karl."

"Karl who?"

"Karl Hjartarson. They've known each other since high school."

I thank her and say good-bye, before she can start grilling me about the progress of my investigation into her daughter's death.

Then I look Dr. Karl Hjartarson up in the phone book. My finger is raised, ready to dial, when the phone rings.

"Good work!" remarks Trausti Löve curtly.

"Thanks very much."

"What about the question?"

"It's looking for the answer," I reply, just to say something.

"I've had it up to here with your clowning around. What..."

"Why don't you just spit it out?" I ask. I've no idea what he's talking about.

"What about the *Question of the Day*?"

Oh, that.

"It was supposed to be in today's paper, buddy. Is it really so difficult for you to remember?"

"Talk to Hannes about it," I reply. "I'm focusing on the Skarphédinn case, with his permission."

"You should still be able to find fifteen minutes for the *Question of the Day*. It's not as if your investigation into Skarphédinn's case is giving us daily scoops. I'm beginning to think you must have fallen off the wagon. Gone on a binge."

For some reason, I find myself engulfed with rage.

"Think what the hell you like. I don't care. You're an expert in misinterpretation, whether you're drunk on your vintage wines or stone-cold sober."

"Tut, tut," remarks Trausti. "You're obviously getting a bit tense, buddy. Isn't that usually a sign that someone's fallen off the wagon, or is about to?"

"You'll get a piece for tomorrow's paper about the Reydargerdi gang who were released this morning. And a pic. So you can shove it…" I get a grip. "And next week I'll remember to send in the answers to the *Question of the Day* from Akureyri. The *Question* is: *Who's Iceland's sexiest moron?* Good-bye!"

"I can't talk to the press about a patient," protests Dr. Karl Hjartarson when he returns my call two hours later.

"But Ásdís Björk Gudmundsdóttir isn't your patient anymore," I point out. "She's deceased."

"That makes no difference. I won't answer any questions about her." He stops. "Not without permission from the family."

"What family? Would her mother, Gunnhildur Bjargmundsdóttir, be able to grant permission?"

He thinks about it. "No, I'm sure the permission of her husband and son would be required."

I make one more attempt.

"Her son told me she was ill. That she had hypochondria."

"I can't confirm or deny that. What does it matter, anyway? Why is the press interested?"

"Well, Gunnhildur got in touch with me. She told me she believed her daughter had been killed."

After a pause, the doctor responds: "That would be a matter for the police, surely. But I gather they have no such suspicions. Do you know what hypochondria is?"

"It's when you imagine you're ill, isn't it?"

Karl Hjartarson loudly clears his throat, but says nothing.

"Are you implying that it's her mother, Gunnhildur, who's a hypochondriac?"

"I'm not implying anything of that nature."

"Is hypochondria an illness that runs in families?"

"I'm not implying anything like that, either."

"So what are you implying?"

"I won't say anything. Not unless Ásdís Björk's husband gives his permission."

And that's that.

The Internet, fortunately enough, is more willing than Dr. Karl Hjartarson to divulge its secrets.

A person with hypochondria is obsessed with thoughts and worries about his/her health, according to an article by an American doctor. *A diagnosis of hypochondria can be made if a person has been convinced for a continuous period of at least six months that he/she is suffering from a serious disease, in spite of being assured by a doctor, or even many doctors, that this is not so. The prevalence of hypochondria is equal among men and women, and it is found in all social groups and people of all ages.*

According to another reference: *A patient with a headache, stomachache, dizziness, or fatigue may misinterpret, or over-interpret, those symptoms as indications of a far more serious illness than is actually the case. To the patient, a headache may be a sign of a brain tumor, not simple stress or migraine. Chest pain means a heart attack, not stiff muscles. And any discomfort is seen as another confirmation of life-threatening cancer.*

An article in a British medical journal states that risk factors for hypochondria include mental conditions such as depression, anxiety, and personality disorder, as well as childhood physical, sexual, or emotional abuse and, last but not least: a family history of hypochondria.

Hypochondriacs, I learn, may consult doctors over and over again—sometimes even several times in one day—and undergo repeated tests of the same symptoms, seeking medical confirmation of their fears by consulting more and more specialists. In some cases, unscrupulous people will exploit the hypochondriac's fears for profit. The patient tends to become withdrawn—which is consistent with what Ragna told me about Ásdís Björk's behavior toward the end of her life.

Hypochondria, apparently, is curable. But it's a long process and not always successful. Medication can be helpful, especially antidepressants. And cognitive behavioral therapy is sometime effective. Many specialists in the field are of the view that the condition of the hypochondriac, and the obsessive thinking, are an unconscious response to stress factors.

It's all very interesting. I've learned something about hypochondria. But I know absolutely nothing about Ásdís Björk's medical condition. And I have even less idea where to go or what to do now. The Internet is no help there.

I have the impression that Chief Ólafur Gísli is in much the same position.

"The stupid little dimwits were at least clever enough to deny, deny, and deny everything," he says when we speak on the phone in the evening. "They'd obviously agreed among themselves to get their story straight and stick to it. They say they were thrown out of the party and then went drinking in town. They don't remember where."

"But don't you think at least one of them would have broken down under questioning, if they were involved in Skarphédinn's death? That Gardar Jónsson looks pretty ineffectual to me."

"Gardar? Totally brain-dead."

"But why didn't you hold onto them until the custody order expired? You had a few more days, didn't you?"

"Yes, we did. The main reason we released them was that a witness came forward yesterday evening saying he'd been with the little idiots from about 3:00 a.m. on Holy Thursday until about eight that morning."

"Who's the witness?"

"Our old friend, Fridrik Einarsson."

"Well, well. He must have pulled all the stops out to manage to remember what he said he'd forgotten."

"True. He says he remembers bumping into the Three Stooges somewhere downtown, after he left the party. He says he got into their car and invited them back to his place to carry on partying. They had plenty of booze, he said."

"But why do you believe him? Fridrik struck me as a twerp and a tweaker."

"I quite agree. The problem is that he still lives at home with his parents, and his mom, who's eaten up with worries about her little darling, hangs around at the kitchen window until he comes home."

"And she corroborates his story, does she?"

"That's not all. She didn't get a wink of sleep all night because of her worries and also because of the noise they were making in the basement, with music blaring at full volume. About eight o'clock she woke her husband up, and he went rampaging down to the basement and threw the idiots out. They were pretty much wasted."

"And he corroborates the story?"

"Yes. It was the parents who made Fridrik come forward. And that left us with nothing to use against the Three Stooges."

"Did they say anything about what went on between them and Skarphédinn that night?"

"Only that he insulted them at the party. Made racial slurs against the Croatian boy."

"That's odd. I've never heard anything to indicate that Skarphédinn was a racist. He seems to have been an old-style nationalist. A patriot. But racism? That strikes me as highly unlikely. He was far too mature and intelligent for all that nonsense. And Gardar Jónsson himself was wearing a *White Power!* T-shirt this morning. What little I thought I got, I really don't get."

"You're not the only one."

"But what's their motive supposed to be? Why would they want to kill Skarphédinn?"

"Idiots like that don't need a motive. They're completely out of touch with reality. They think they're living in an American crime movie. And if they're drunk or high, there's even less need for a motive. We see it a lot. In the past, the present. Here, there, and everywhere."

"Do you know whether they're involved in distributing or peddling dope or debt-collecting?"

"We have reason to believe they are. But there's no solid proof. Our witnesses, who are their clients, of course, somehow develop amnesia. They won't testify. Or are afraid to."

"So what's next?"

"Next we're going to go back over all the evidence. Trawl through everything yet again."

———

As I'm turning off my computer to head for home and Polly, I notice a photograph in the pile of stuff on my desk. It's an enlargement Jóa has made for me. As I emerge onto the landing, I hear Karó shrieking upstairs and Ásbjörn's soothing responses. I decide that the next step in the case can wait until tomorrow.

The photograph of a young girl and a middle-aged woman is added to the large collection of unanswered Questions of the Day in Akureyri.

19 WEDNESDAY

"Oh my God!"

Ásbjörn drops the photo I show him on my desk and seizes his puffy face in both hands.

I say nothing.

"Oh my God!"

I continue to say nothing.

He picks the photo up again in trembling hands and gazes at it, transfixed.

"Do you know the woman?" I ask.

Ásbjörn is standing in my closet-office, unable to tear his eyes away from the photo of Björg, intrepid savior of Pal, with her mom, Gudrún. The photo's a bit blurry. Jóa used her magic tricks to enlarge it from a photo she took of Björg and Pal in front of the piano where framed photographs were displayed. But the pic is obviously clear enough to Ásbjörn.

Clutching the photo, he sways. I stand up from my desk chair.

"Have a seat, Ásbjörn, before you pass out."

He collapses into my chair.

"Who's the woman?" I ask after a lengthy silence.

Ásbjörn looks up. His forehead is pouring with sweat, and his eyes are brimming with tears. "It's Gudrún," he groans. "Gudrún."

"But you knew Björg's last name was Gudrúnardóttir, so her mother's name was obviously Gudrún."

"But I didn't make the connection. I'd forgotten…"

I wait. He clasps his hands together and looks down. "We were together for a little while here in Akureyri. Shortly before we graduated from high school."

"And?"

"We just went our separate ways. I moved down south to Reykjavík to work as a journalist on the *People's Press*—as you know. She got a place at some university abroad to study architecture. I never heard from her again."

I wait.

He shakes his head, downcast.

"You do realize, don't you," I remark, "that based on Björg's age you could be her father?"

He says nothing. I hear a quiet barking in the reception area. Maybe Pal isn't Ásbjörn's only baby.

"You could be. But it's not necessarily so."

"But why didn't Gudrún tell me?" Ásbjörn sighs. "Why did she never get in touch?"

"I've got no answer to that. But the two of you obviously need to make contact now."

"Do you think that the mysterious phone calls, and the way Pal…"

"What about it?" we suddenly hear from the doorway.

We spin around. Karólína is staring hard at Ásbjörn, who sits hunched, still holding tight to the photograph.

"Karó dear," falters Ásbjörn.

She walks over to her husband and gives him a searching look. Then she spots the photo and snatches it away from him.

"What on earth...?" she exclaims. Then the blood drains from her face. "That woman..."

Ásbjörn gets shakily to his feet.

"What woman?" asks the husband.

"It's the woman who asked me for directions, up by the church, while Pal was running about in the grass. Before he vanished."

Ásbjörn and I exchange a look.

"Ásbjörn Grímsson," says Karólína, who is now trembling as much as he is. "Who is that woman?"

Before Ásbjörn Grímsson answers her question, I feel it wise to withdraw from the scene.

As I stroll down the near-deserted street toward the Bautinn Grill, I consider my next move...The road seems to be long, with many a winding turn...

The investigation into the death of Skarphédinn—my inquiries and the police work—seems to be getting nowhere. And what about the death of Ásdís Björk?

At Bautinn I sit down at a table and order a coffee and a phone book.

Once I've looked up the Yumm candy factory and made a note of the number, I light a cigarette. I'm instantly informed that this is a nonsmoking zone. I finish my coffee and flee the scene. I feel like a refugee from my own life. As I stand outside on the corner, I'm seized by an overwhelming need for readmission. So overwhelming is the feeling that I crumple the damned cigarette pack and stuff it into the nearest trash can.

While I make my call, I perch on the low stone wall below Hotel KEA. I ask for Ragna Ármannsdóttir.

"Yes, hello. How are you today?" she warmly greets me.

"Can I ask you something about that wilderness tour? Going on what you told me about Ásdís Björk not being around much recently, wasn't it unusual for her to go along on that sort of trip or attend the company dinner?"

"Yes, it was. I don't remember seeing her on any of the company jaunts for at least three years."

"And how did she seem? Was she her usual self?"

"Not like she used to be. Back then she was lively and cheerful. But she'd become quite withdrawn, hardly said a word anymore."

"Did she seem to be drunk or anything like that?"

"It's hard to say. We were in the same vehicle, but she sat at the back with Ásgeir. She was wearing sunglasses. She didn't speak."

"Did she take part in the cliff-jumping or water sports and whatever?"

"No. But she got out of the SUV and watched. And I did get the impression she was walking very slowly and with difficulty. I thought she must be ill. But then she went on the white-water rafting with us. It was so unexpected that we all gave her a round of applause. And Ásgeir gave her a kiss and…"

She falls silent. I think she's on the brink of tears. I reach into my pocket for my cigarettes.

"I'm sorry," I say as my hand comes up empty. "I shouldn't have asked you to go over it again."

She's regaining control. "It's all right. It just happened. There's nothing to be done about it."

"Did Ásgeir seem to be pressuring her to join in?" I venture to ask her.

"I don't know. They were sitting at the back of the SUV, and they were talking before they got out. That's all I know."

"Um," I mumble as I stride across the street to the trash can. "Is Ásgeir in today?"

"Yes, he is. Do you want to speak to him?"

I reach down into the bin. "Hmm, I'm not sure."

"I'll put you through to his receptionist again. I'd better not put you through to him myself. I don't want him finding out…"

The damned cigarette pack is a long way down. "No, I see. I'll call again. In a little while."

I thank her and abandon the idea of retrieving the cigarettes. As I withdraw my hand, a hundred-*krónur* coin is pressed into my palm. A well-dressed elderly lady smiles at me as she passes, with an expression that combines pity and encouragement.

"No, excuse me, madam, there's no need!" I call after her.

Too late. She waves a gloved hand, without looking back.

I head for the nearest store to buy another pack of cigarettes. I never claimed to be perfect, did I?

In the industrial district north of Glerárgata is the Yumm candy factory, an uninspiring white-painted two-story building in the low-key style-less style so beloved of Icelandic builders. Build fast. Build cheap. And start cashing in.

I sit in my car in the parking lot, guiltily smoking and counting the minutes until half past three.

Surprisingly, Ásgeir Eyvindarson has agreed to meet me during his coffee break.

It was, admittedly, not quite that simple. I'd called his son, Gudmundur, and assured him yet again that it had never been my intention to make a fuss about his mother's tragic death. But, I told him, her history of hypochondria had got me interested.

And the *Afternoon News* too. People in Iceland didn't know much about the condition, and I wanted to find out more about it. The question was would he or his father be willing to talk to me about the experience of a family member of a hypochondriac—in order to inform the public about the disease? He said he would talk to his father about it, and shortly afterward he called back and said Ásgeir was prepared to meet me for half an hour.

The Yumm offices are on the upper floor of the building and the factory on the ground floor. A sweetly mouthwatering chocolate fragrance wafts around the entrance and stairs. The reception desk is piled with samples of the company's wares: chocolate bars and chocolate cookies, crème-filled confections, bags of hard candies, liquorice, and a multicolored array of gummy shapes.

There is no receptionist at the desk, and three offices stand with open doors, apparently deserted.

I knock on the reception desk. "Hello! Einar here!"

"Come on in. I'm in the end office," I hear from beyond. I follow the direction of the voice.

At the eastern end of the building is a large, bright office with a stunning view of the fjord and the mountains. Ásgeir Eyvindarson puts down his square gold-rimmed glasses, stands up from his mahogany desk piled high with papers, and offers me a seat on an imposing mahogany sofa, upholstered in pale yellow to match the curtains. On dark wood-paneled walls hang paintings by the luminaries of the modern Icelandic art world: Tryggvi Ólafsson. Tolli. Helgi Thorgils. So far as I can tell.

"I'm sorry," he says, gesturing toward reception. "They're all on coffee break."

"No problem," I answer with a big smile as I sink into the depths of the sofa. "I'm just grateful that you're willing to give up your own break."

Ásgeir sits facing me in a matching armchair and gives me a searching look. He's quite a dashing-looking man of middle age, wearing neatly pressed black pants and a freshly ironed shirt in light blue with a dark red tie. He's tall and well-proportioned, putting on just a little weight around the waist. His facial features are strong, with a pointed nose and gray mustache. His graying hair is combed forward over an almost unwrinkled brow, and as he leans forward I see that his hair is thinning slightly on top. A confidence-inspiring figure, in short.

"That's absolutely fine," he replies, pushing toward me a bowl of candy. "I may have been a little hasty the other day. I do apologize."

"Nothing to apologize for," I assure him, helping myself to a chocolate cookie and thinking: *My goodness, what a polite conversation. Really civilized. A credit to us both.*

"I'm sure you realize that people who've been through such a painful experience as we have, in our family, can be rather touchy about prying, not least from the media."

"I quite understand. And I didn't mean to cause you any more pain. But I'd had that phone call from Gunnhildur and…"

He makes a face and waves my excuses away. "Not a word more about that. No more about all that nonsense. My son tells me that the positive side of all this is that you're interested in learning more about hypochondria?"

"That's right."

"And that's why I agreed to meet with you. People simply can't imagine how difficult it is for the family of people who suffer from that bizarre disease."

"Surely it's most difficult for the patient?" The words pop out of my mouth as I switch on my tape recorder.

Ásgeir apparently isn't listening—which is just as well.

"But I want to read the interview before it's published. And I may prefer to remain anonymous."

"All right," I say. "But this kind of interview generally has greater impact if people are willing to be named."

"Perhaps," he answers thoughtfully. "But it has to be my decision."

I nod.

He starts telling me about hypochondria in general terms, stroking his mustache from time to time, as if to focus. He adds nothing to what I've already learned from other sources.

I try to steer him in the right direction: "When did Ásdís Björk first start to display symptoms of the illness?"

Without missing a beat, he continues in the same helpful tone: "It was soon after the birth of our son. In fact, she had already shown a tendency to obsessive behavior during the pregnancy. It was all she could think about. She was always worried that something might be wrong, whether the baby was normal, whether she should avoid some particular kind of exertion, go out in a car, eat a certain food. But I gather that it's not uncommon for first-time mothers to have such concerns. After Gudmundur was born, her anxieties became more focused on herself. She was always tired, complaining of stomach cramps, shortness of breath, insomnia. She started going to the doctor every week for a checkup, then twice a week. And when he assured her that she was fine, she couldn't accept it. She maintained that only she knew how she felt. She thought our doctor was careless—or incompetent. But he was an old friend of ours from school, and she'd had complete confidence in him until then."

"Karl Hjartarson," I add.

He stops short and looks me in the face. "Yes. How did you know that?"

"Gunnhildur told me," I reply, as guilelessly as I can manage. "Because you and I had got off on the wrong foot, I got in touch with Karl to ask about hypochondria. But he wouldn't speak to me without your permission."

Ásgeir nods. "If you want to talk to him, I'll give you permission. But only to talk about the illness. Not about our private family affairs."

"Of course."

He gets back to his story: "Karl and I both did our best to convince her that, since he could find nothing wrong with her, nothing was wrong. He thought it was some form of postpartum depression. And her obsessive behavior gradually died down. When Gudmundur was growing up, she had many good years when she was focused on motherhood. And she was a wonderful mother." He falls silent, and for a moment he seems to be holding back tears before adding: "And a marvelous wife."

"So when did the problem recur?"

"When Gudmundur was in his teens, she was very anxious about him. She had no reason at all to be. He was careful not to upset her or cause her worries. He was a conscientious student and a good boy. That was when she started to obsess about her own health again. We both noticed that she was taking her pulse several times a day. She thought her heart rate was much too fast. If she felt her heart skip a beat just once, she would go into a panic. She went to Karl over and over again, but he found nothing wrong. And a few months later she started having heartburn and assumed she must have a stomach ulcer. And then headaches, which she attributed to a brain tumor. And aches and pain and so on and so on.

"After Gudmundur left home and moved down south, things went from bad to worse. For the past four or five years, it's hardly been possible to induce Ásdís Björk to leave the house, except to go to the doctor. Or doctors, in fact. Karl had no option but to refer her to specialists of all kinds—oncologists, cardiologists, surgeons, dermatologists, gastroenterologists, pulmonologists, immunologists, otolaryngologists—all depending upon what she thought was wrong with her at the time. For the last few months of her life she was convinced she had leukemia."

"But what about psychiatrists or psychologists? Since it was primarily in her mind?"

"Yes, indeed. We tried all sorts of psychiatrists and psychologists. And sometimes they gave us hope of improvement. She would manage better for a few months. But then she would revert to the same state."

"Is it true that she...?" I start again. "But what about medication? From what I've learned, antidepressants can sometimes be effective in treating hypochondria."

"Yes, that's right," answers Ásgeir as he takes a candy from the bowl, apparently without thinking. "We tried various medications. Some seemed to be effective, but never for more than a few months."

"Did she overmedicate?"

He stares at me as he crunches his way ferociously through the candy. "Yes, I think it's true to say she did. She tended to take more than the recommended dose. She seemed to think she would feel better the more she took. And the medication was affecting her looks. She piled on more and more weight..."

"What was she taking before she died?"

He glares at me. "Why do you want to know that? I thought you were going to write an article about hypochondria? Or are you planning to write about the accidental death of my wife?"

"Surely we have to see her accidental death as a consequence of her hypochondria?"

After a brief pause, he replies. "I see what you mean. Yes, of course that's right. I wasn't aware of everything Ásdís Björk was taking, but recently it was mainly Prozac. And she took sedatives sometimes. Valium, or something like that."

"I've read that some hypochondriacs feel better if they have a drink."

"Oh, really?" he replies. "Ásdís Björk didn't often drink, but she enjoyed it, and it made her feel better. She had become so withdrawn. That's true."

"How did the alcohol mix with the medications?" I ask. "Did she know her limit?"

"It was a very rare occurrence. She wasn't a drinker at all."

"On social occasions, then? Parties and so on?"

"She didn't really do that anymore. And if she did attend, she preferred to go home early. So I suppose I would have to say she knew her limit."

I realize I'm on thin ice now, but I ask anyway: "On the wilderness tour, people were drinking beer, weren't they?"

"Oh, yes," he replies frankly. "We always serve beer. Not a lot. It wouldn't be appropriate. On that last trip she had some beer. But not much."

I decide to leave well enough alone. For now. He glances at his watch. I do the same. We've run well over the half hour he promised me. I switch off my tape recorder and thank Ásgeir for his time.

"I've been thinking about what you said," he remarks as we stand up. "About interviews having more impact if people speak in their own name and not anonymously. I think you're right. I've noticed it myself when I read the papers. And apart from anything else, there's so much gossip and rumor flying around here in Akureyri. Especially if people start believing Gunnhildur's fantasies. So it's probably best for me to speak in my own name. Then people will know the truth of it."

His expression is determined, but also searching.

"That sounds good to me," I reply. "I think it will work better that way."

He goes to the door of his office. "But you'll let me read your article before it's published. You promised."

"I will."

"When will it be published?"

"Well, if Karl can speak to me tomorrow, we ought to make the Saturday edition."

"I'll call Karl and let you know later today. Can you meet him any time?"

"I don't even need to meet him. I can talk to him on the phone," I answer. I don't know what to make of the helpfulness of this man who, only a few days ago, raged at me, threatened me, and slammed the phone down. We shake hands. As he closes the door I notice that his light-blue shirt is now damp under the arms.

On my way out I pass through the reception area, where a young girl is now sitting at the desk. In one of the offices I spot Ragna Ármannsdóttir, focused on her computer screen. On the inside of the door to the stairs is a poster for the production of *Loftur the Sorcerer* by the Akureyri High School Drama Group.

I come to a halt. On the poster is a photo of Skarphédinn in the title role, wearing a collarless white shirt and a black waistcoat and gazing intensely at a book with a black cover. At the bottom of the poster are three corporate logos identifying the sponsors of the show. In this case Hotel KEA, the Bonus low-price super-market chain, and the Yumm candy factory.

I turn to the receptionist and ask: "Are you sponsoring the high school students' show?"

"Yes," she replies with a smile. "But the leading actor has died. The play's been postponed until after the exams in the spring."

My evening chat with the chief of police in Akureyri is along these lines:

Me: "What's new?"

Him: "Lovely cheeks."

"What cheeks? What are you up to?"

"Lovely cheeks. Delightful. Have you never tried them?"

"Er..."

"Just can't stop."

"Well..."

"*Slurpslurp*. So what are *you* having for dinner?"

"Oh, I see what you mean. *Cod* cheeks. Nothing. I've eaten too much candy today. I took a chance on calling you direct, not via Ásbjörn, just this once. I don't want to disturb him. Have you heard from him today at all?"

"No. Why do you ask?"

"Well, I'd rather you heard it from him. But I think he's in need of a friend this evening."

"Oh? Is something up? Anything serious?"

"I'm not sure. Maybe what's up is perfectly fine."

"How can something be up if it's fine? Is that one of your funny southernisms?"

"Give him a call."

"I will."

"But there's nothing new then, apart from the cod cheeks?"

"No, we're reexamining everything from the start, as I said. And there's one thing I want to ask you—just for a change."

"Oh, good. Ask away."

"You met Skarphédinn at a rehearsal and interviewed him, didn't you?"

"That's right. On the Saturday before Easter. At Hólar."

"Did you notice whether he had a cell phone?"

"Yes, I did, actually. His phone rang just at the end of our interview."

"Hmm."

"What?"

"We've searched high and low for a phone, but we can't find it. And no cell phone is registered in his name."

"No, well, you can buy a cell phone without Big Brother knowing about it. You can buy them anywhere, not just in ordinary shops here in Iceland. In other countries or in the duty-free store or from anyone."

"Yes, yes, I know that. Don't go twisting my words. There is no SIM card or cell phone number in Skarphédinn's name anywhere. And if you're going to rant on about it still being possible to buy a SIM card without Big Brother's knowledge, then save it. Even if the bosses down south want to make it compulsory to show ID in order to buy a SIM card so that the name and number can be traced, they're not doing it for my benefit."

"Really? Isn't it being done at the request of the police?"

"Quite possibly. But nobody asked me."

"What a scandal!"

"Just the usual. They don't call me before they go off half-cocked. And I'm in the phone book, after all."

"So you think it's unnecessary for people to be registered when they buy a SIM card?"

"It's not unnecessary. It's insulting and demeaning for ordinary people."

"But it would make the police's job easier, wouldn't it?"

"I've never asked anyone to make my job easier. I want police work to be difficult. It isn't supposed to be easy. What kind of a country is it, where police work is easy?"

"A police state?"

"Quite. I don't want to live in a country where the government bases its actions on the criminal. I want to live where the government treats people like people."

"Hear, hear."

"If the government bases its actions on gangs of crooks, it will finish up, sooner or later, as a gang of crooks itself."

"Hear, hear."

"Are you making fun of me, you bastard?"

"Far from it. You really aren't the Bad Cop, are you?"

"I can be the Bad Cop. If I need to. I just want to be a policeman, not a spy or a soldier. Anyway. Do you know the number of Skarphédinn's cell phone?"

"No, I never got it. What about all his friends and acquaintances and family?"

"That's what's so odd. You're the first person who's said he had a cell phone. Everybody else says he was so old-style that he didn't like to carry one. It seems far-fetched."

"Not really. Not going on what I've heard about his character. Or, to be more precise, going on some of what I've heard. And I'm a bit old-style that way myself."

"But you did see him with a cell phone?"

"Yes. But I suppose he could have borrowed it."

"Who from?"

"No idea. But what about the landline? Presumably you've checked the calls on that line?"

"Yes. But we didn't get much out of it. He doesn't seem to have used the phone much."

"A modern man rebelling against modernity?"

"Your guess is as good as mine."

On my way from the Yumm candy factory down into town, I'd visited a second-hand bookshop and invested in a dog-eared old paperback copy of *Loftur the Sorcerer*.

Now I'm lying on the sofa in the living room with a cushion under my head and my roommate perched on my shirt collar. She sings and chirps as I page through the old play, which has, for whatever reason, sprung into life once more.

I read about a man who longs to be master of his own life, to control all around him, taking no account of any other person, or of anything other than his own will, or, as the play puts it, his own desire. And I read about the timeless theme of the love triangle.

I'm too sleepy to get any further than the middle of the first act. I stop at a line spoken by Ólafur, who is in love with Steinunn, the peasant girl impregnated by his friend Loftur. I fall asleep over that line and wake up to it in the middle of the night as Polly pecks at my neck:

He who feels that he has wronged another, will often find that
he hates him.

20 THURSDAY

"They say you shouldn't go to a doctor who has dead plants in his office."

I don't know what to say.

"Very sensible of you not to risk it."

"Pardon?" I'm lost.

"Oh, I'm sorry," says Dr. Karl Hjartarson. "Just being frivolous. Inappropriate, I know."

"That's…" I manage to say. "That's all right."

"Just fooling around. Doctor jokes aren't to everyone's taste. But at any rate, I've just been watering my plants, trying to resuscitate them. But without success."

I think of the cacti in Björg and Gudrún's home.

"I suppose you can't think of everything when you're busy keeping patients alive," I remark.

"Even that doesn't always work," he replies with a sigh. "Whatever. Ásgeir said it would be enough for you to talk to me on the phone?"

Can this be the same man who, only the day before yesterday, put on a mask of professionalism, claiming to be gagged by his Hippocratic oath? People are unfathomable.

"Hello?"

I'm abruptly jerked from my thoughts.

"Yes, yes, I'm still here. It's this article I'm researching about hypochondria. I'm wondering if you can help me at all?"

"Yes, hypochondria. I almost feel I've become a specialist, although it's a field not covered by any medical specialty."

And he gives me a long lecture about the illness, research from other countries, symptoms, and theories. A variation on a familiar theme.

"And was Ásdís Björk's case unusual, in light of what you've learned about the condition?" I ask when I can get a word in edgeways.

"No, I wouldn't say so. She was fairly typical of the most difficult cases. No treatment seemed to help her, except in the very short term."

"I gathered from Ásgeir that you tried a number of medications?"

"That's right."

"Were you aware of her misusing the drugs? Or overmedicating?"

"At times, yes. But I can't go into details. Ásgeir's permission doesn't extend to making their private affairs public."

"No," I say, trying to find a subtle enough way to pose my question. "But toward the end of her life, what medications seemed to be most effective? I mean, what was the result of the treatment you prescribed?"

"Unfortunately, we can't really call it a *result*. The only real result was Ásdís Björk's untimely death."

"Was she on medication at the time of her death?"

He doesn't answer immediately. "Well, I suppose it's all right to tell you that she was on Prozac. That shouldn't do any harm."

"Only Prozac?"

"Yes, only Prozac. Antidepressants were generally the most effective treatment for her. They reduced the anxiety and helped distract her from the obsessive thoughts. For a while, anyway."

I thank him for the information. I wish I could ask him if taking Prozac might have made Ásdís Björk so woozy that she could have lost her balance and fallen overboard. But I know that will get me nowhere. I say:

"The more I learn about Ásdís Björk, and this illness—or imaginary illness…"

"Oh, it's not an imaginary illness," the doctor interjects. "For the patient, it's absolutely real. You must make that crystal clear in your article."

"Yes, of course. Sorry, I put that wrong. But from all I've learned about hypochondria, it seems to me that it springs essentially from mental distress. Profound unhappiness?"

"In my view—and you must not, absolutely must not, quote me—you're quite right."

"You were old friends, weren't you?"

"Yes. I'd known Ásdís Björk ever since high school. Back then, she showed no sign of that kind of unhappiness. I think perhaps her Achilles' heel was really that she had such a sweet personality—she had a profound desire or need to please others, to make them happy. I had the impression that behind it all lay a certain lack of security or self-esteem. But I've no idea where that could have come from."

"But this unhappiness or distress—what did that entail? Didn't she ever tell you, or the specialists who treated her, what was wrong?"

"If she did, I couldn't share that with you. That would be a step too far over the boundaries of confidentiality."

"No, of course. But would it be fair to say that her hypochondria was, in a sense, an unconscious cry for help?"

"A cry for attention, at least."

Before we say good-bye, I find myself saying: "It sometimes seems that the whole of society is making an unconscious—or even conscious—cry for attention. Don't you think this society is attention-seeking?"

He laughs. "You could say so. That's not a bad diagnosis."

"Or maybe even hypochondriac? A whole nation of imaginary ills?"

He is silent for a moment. "No, I wouldn't go so far as to say that. But medicalization, as the medical profession sometimes calls it, is certainly real. And it's cause for concern."

"All these personality disorders. Don't we all have one? Is anyone normal anymore?"

"Well, it depends how you look at it. Psychiatry isn't my field, although I've learned a lot about it of late. In a British journal, for instance, I read a paper about a disorder that you could attribute to a whole society and not just individuals. It's called *narcissistic personality disorder* or NPD. Of course the idea comes from the Greek myth of Narcissus, who fell in love with his own reflection. In narcissistic personality disorder, the person exhibits obsessive self-admiration, leading to the complete lack of morals or conscience. I read a quote from a British specialist who said that a diagnosis of NPD crops up in almost every major criminal case these days."

A society of narcissists, I think. *Ancient mythology thriving in the reality of the modern world.* What was it Jóa said?

Who knows when we may rediscover Atlantis.

And what was it that brought Atlantis down?

"Why are you always asking about that accident?" inquires Ólafur Gísli when I eventually make contact with him via Ásbjörn.

I decide it's time to tell him about Gunnhildur and her suspicions.

"Oh, that," says the chief. "I've talked to the old lady myself. Immediately after the accident, she was on the phone all the time. But there's nothing to it. Not the slightest trace of anything. Surely you're not planning to write about these wild delusions of hers?"

"I'm working on an article about this illness Ásdís Björk had, hypochondria. I'm planning to publish it at the weekend."

"But the woman didn't die of hypochondria. She died of injuries sustained when she fell in the river. Full of a mixture of all sorts of pills."

"All sorts of pills? I've been told that she was only on Prozac at the end."

"Who says so?"

"Her doctor. Karl Hjartarson."

"Oh, yes. That's what he told us too. But druggies tend to get their pills from more than one place. They have lots of sources."

"And do you know what drugs she'd taken when she fell in the river?"

I hear a rustle of papers. "It was quite a cocktail, I can tell you. Yes, there's Prozac. But there were also sedatives like Valium. And sleeping pills...Hang on, I can hardly make out the names...Oxazepam...Triazolam...Zopiklon...I'm not even sure all this stuff is available on prescription in Iceland. She'd even taken Ritalin. And then she'd drunk beer on top of it all."

"And what did her husband have to say about it?"

"He just said, as the families generally do in these cases, that he'd had no idea his wife was taking so many drugs, let alone where she got them from."

"Were the pills packaged legally?"

"We didn't find anything like that. But that's often how it is. Illegal pharmaceuticals are rarely in the proper packaging. And never with a doctor's prescription."

"Did the autopsy reveal any signs of physical disease?"

"No. The woman was physically fit as a fiddle—apart from the effects of drug abuse."

"Have you found the can, or whatever she was drinking from on the wilderness tour?"

"No. We've searched high and low. But they were drinking out of throwaway containers, which have gone without trace. Straight to the dump."

"No hope of finding them there?"

"Are you out of your mind?"

"So you don't think there's anything fishy about the case?"

"Anything fishy? What's fishy about this case is that god-damned drug peddlers are cashing in on unfortunates and their urge for self-destruction."

And now I must undertake a difficult conversation. So difficult that I decide to go in person to the Hóll care home, rather than making a cowardly phone call.

"My dear Gunnhildur. Her doctor says she had that illness, and lots of specialists back him up."

Gunnhildur is enraged. We are sitting in the niche, an irritating buzz from the television in the background.

"It will be interesting, educational, for people to read about it. It will make them more aware—"

"And to think I was happy to see you, young man," Gunnhildur interrupts. She seems to be speaking more to herself than to me. "I thought you'd finally got to the truth. And then all you have to say is that you're going to do a hatchet job on my Ásdís Björk."

"No, not at all. It won't be a hatchet job. Just an article about the disease and an interview with Ásgeir about the family's experience of—"

"An interview with that goddamned man will only blacken my daughter's name," shrieks Gunnhildur. People turn to see, and the *Guiding Light* mafia prick up their ears.

"Gunnhildur," I say, placing a reassuring hand over hers, "it won't blacken your daughter's name simply to report on her illness."

She jerks her hand away. "She wasn't ill. She was just unhappy. She didn't have any disease, apart from that awful, evil man. That goddamned Ásgeir was her illness."

"But I can't write that. You must understand."

"Oh, you can't, can't you? You believe him, and write what he says. You don't believe me, or write what *I* say."

Once again, I'm lost for words.

"I'm just a batty old woman!" she shouts. Her eyes rest on me with such pain and reproach that I have to force myself not to look away.

"Not at all," I quietly reply, hoping that she will also lower her voice. "And I've made a real effort to find out whether you're right about your daughter's death. But the fact is no one else believes it."

Gunnhildur seizes her walking cane and rises painfully to her feet. "I should never have gotten in touch with you, young man. It's just made things worse," she mumbles. "Just made things worse."

I stand up and place my arm around her shoulders. "The article I'm writing," I whisper in her ear, "is certainly not going to blacken Ásdís Björk's name. You've got to face up to the fact that she had this illness, Gunnhildur. The article will simply help people understand it better."

She shakes off my arm and will not look at me.

"But," I add, "I'm far from convinced that the illness was really the cause of her death. The only way I was able to approach the case was on the pretext that I wanted to find out more about the hypochondria. I had no other option."

Gunnhildur turns toward me, her eyes filled with tears. "What exactly are you trying to tell me, you young rascal?"

"I'm trying to tell you that I'm going to go on looking into the case."

She shuffles off, leaning on her stick.

"I'll do as much as I can," I say to her retreating back, which expresses neither friendship nor trust. It's the back view of a person who feels utterly defeated.

I feel awful as I sit down in my little closet to start writing my informative feature about hypochondria. I couldn't bring myself to tell the old lady that her daughter had been an addict who swallowed handfuls of prescription medications before she went into the water. Nor could I say that I had no idea where to look next.

I get a grip on myself and continue writing the article. By late afternoon I've finished the feature, together with an interview of a family member of a hypochondriac—Ásgeir Eyvindarson. He's read the article and approved it. I send it in, along with a photo of Ásgeir taken by Jóa in his office and another of him and Ásdís Björk with their son when he was a little boy. A happy family snap. Ásdís Björk was a very attractive woman, dark-haired, slender, with a brilliant smile on her face.

Hannes is pleased with the feature for the weekend edition. "But what else is new, sir? Aren't there any developments about the murder of the high school boy?"

"Not at present, Hannes. The investigation seems to be running out of steam. I've got an excellent informant in the police. All thanks to Ásbjörn, I must admit."

"Really? Well, I'm delighted to hear that our former news editor, and your dear friend, is participating fully. The Odd Couple seem to be getting along famously."

"I won't argue with you there."

"But it's certainly becoming a problem that he's been off work so much lately. We weren't planning for Jóa to stay up in the north this long."

"Yeah, he's having some family problems. But I hope that will all be settled before long. He was at work this morning."

"Excellent. So Jóa can be getting back to Reykjavík before long?"

"I wouldn't care to say. She..." I think about this for a second. "She's enjoying being here so much, I think she'd like to stay on a little longer."

"That's all very well," replies Hannes. "But we can't afford to keep our staff here, there, and everywhere just because they like it."

"I don't think it would be wise to recall her just yet. We'll be plunged into chaos if anyone gets ill. And Jóa's doing a great job. She's familiarized herself with the local area and the office. And someone has to take the pics. It takes time to get settled here."

"Hmm," muses Hannes. "We shall see. Let's wait and see for a little longer. You've all made a good start, I'm happy to say. But another scoop would be very welcome. As soon as possible, please."

"Well, I'll do what I can. I've been researching a piece about the dead boy, as you know."

"Yes, I know. Trausti feels you're taking a long time over it. And I'll admit I'd like to see some copy myself."

"The problem is that the more I learn about Skarphédinn, the less I feel I know about him. The victim is even more of an enigma than the identity of the killer."

"And when that puzzle is resolved, will it also solve the other?"

"I don't know, Hannes. I have a feeling that the mystery of the killer will be resolved before the question of the victim's character is clarified. Maybe his death is the last piece of a puzzle that is never supposed to be solved."

"Very philosophical, my good sir. But I would prefer some copy."

"How are things?" I ask Ásbjörn, closing his office door behind me. He sits hunched at his computer, but as he turns to face me I detect a new energy. The dark smudges under his eyes tell their tale of sleepless nights, but in his eyes there is some spark of life that wasn't there yesterday.

"The situation is unclear," he replies.

I perch on a chair in the corner. "Do you mean the past or the future?"

"The future. Karó is absorbing what's happened. Me too, for that matter."

"And what has happened?"

"Yesterday evening we both went over to see Gudrún and Björg. And I must say it's been a huge relief."

"So was it Gudrún who asked Karó for directions the other day?"

He nods.

"To distract her while Björg grabbed Pal and took him home?"

"Yes." He shakes his head, as if he can't make sense of the events.

"Why?" I ask, although I suspect I know the answer.

Ásbjörn continues to shake his disheveled head. "It was her way of making contact with me. Through Pal."

"Whose way? Gudrún's or Björg's?"

"Björg's. Or maybe both."

"Are you her father?"

"Yes," answers Ásbjörn with a trace of a smile. His weary face expresses something like pride.

"Didn't she know about you until recently?"

"When we opened the new office here, we published a piece about it in the paper, with a picture of me. And you."

I frown, recalling my opposition to that photo.

"But why did Gudrún never get in touch with you all those years ago? Why didn't she let you know you were the father of her child?"

Now Ásbjörn frowns. "That's the thing. All the time we were together—which wasn't long—she kept going on about not wanting any commitment. She meant to go abroad to study. To learn about life, she said. She didn't want any man spoiling her plans. The last thing she said to me was, *Thanks, Ásbjörn. Now forget all about me.* And it took me a long time to forget her. So when she found she was pregnant, she felt there was no going back. And really, I think this is the way she wanted it. On the rare occasions when Björg asked about her father, Gudrún gave her the impression that she had been conceived after a one-night stand with some foreigner. But now she felt she couldn't conceal the truth any longer. Gudrún told us that Björg's been going through a difficult time lately. She dropped out of high school, and she was always asking about her father. Gudrún's in a new relationship now, and she's pregnant. And the upshot was that when the photo of me was published in the paper, she told her daughter..." He corrects himself: "...our daughter that I was her father."

"So the mysterious phone calls, day and night, were from Björg?"

"Apparently she became quite obsessed with what she had learned. It was all she could think about. Her mom knew nothing of the phone calls until she caught her one time. Then Björg admitted she'd been calling me."

"But she never said anything? She hung up every time?"

"Yes. I understand why. She really wanted to make some kind of contact. Hear my voice, as she told her mom. She couldn't just blurt out: *Hi, my name's Björg, and you're my dad.*"

"No, I suppose not."

"Karó remembered that Björg had come into the office once, to buy a copy of the paper—although they have a subscription to the paper. Karó asked why she'd come all the way here instead of buying the paper in a shop, and Björg hurried out. She started spying on us, without our noticing, when we were out and about. And Pal. That's how she got the idea."

"To pretend to rescue a lost dog?" I ask. Pal is the closest thing Ásbjörn and Karólína have to a child of their own.

Ásbjörn is shaking his head again. "The poor, dear child," he says, drying his eyes. "She sat there, while her mother told us the whole story, in a state of shock!"

"And she got her mother to help her fake the rescue?"

"Gudrún said she had no choice, really. Björg was so determined to make our acquaintance by doing something good for us. Then I—her father—would appreciate her." He buries his face in his hand. "Poor, sweet girl."

"And how did Karó take it all?"

A flood of tears cascades from Ásbjörn's bloodshot eyes.

"Karó had sensed something. Not me, not the Tin Man, so square at the edges—as you put it, Einar. All Karó's distress, the tension and agitation, especially after young Björg started dropping in, ostensibly to see Pal—it all sprung from Karó feeling that something was not right here. I think she sensed it, although she never said it explicitly. I even talked about hysteria, didn't I? But when she heard the truth, a calm came over her. She took the initiative. Stood up and hugged Björg. I just sat there, dazed and confused. Like the Tin Man of Oz I am." He dries his eyes on his shirt sleeve. "The two of them stood there in Gudrún's living room, crying and hugging. Before I knew it we were all in tears."

He looks up at me and smiles. Ear to ear, through his tears.

"Now," I say to Ágústa, chair of the drama group, on the phone. "I hear you've set a new date for the premiere, after the exams?"

"Yes. We didn't want all our work to go to waste. And we plan to put on more performances in the fall semester."

"Have you found a new Loftur the Sorcerer?"

"No. Örvar Páll will be here at the weekend, and we'll consider the possibilities. We've got an idea about it."

She doesn't seem keen to talk. "And there's no progress on the case? The guys from Reydargerdi were simply released?"

"Not my problem."

"No, of course not. Was there something between you and Skarphédinn that evening?"

I pose the question baldly. It seems to take her by surprise.

"Who said so?"

"Just a rumor I heard," I lie, freely interpreting what Fridrik said about sex antics in her parents' bedroom.

"Is it Agnar and Co. saying that?" she snaps. "Are they trying to drag me into this mess?"

"So you know Agnar Hansen and his merry men?"

She cools down. "I know who they are." Ágústa says nothing for a while. Then she speaks: "Skarphédinn threw them out long before anything happened in any of the bedrooms. They know nothing about who was with who."

"And who were you with?"

"None of your business."

"What about Skarphédinn?"

"I don't remember." Amnesia to the rescue, again.

"All right. Sorry. By the way, have you got Skarphédinn's cell phone number?"

"What kind of a question is that? He's dead! What do you want his phone number for?"

"It's just that I saw him with a cell phone when I interviewed him, but according to the police he didn't have one."

"That's right. He didn't have a cell."

"Why not? Everyone—especially everyone your age—has a cell these days."

"Have you considered that maybe he just didn't want one?"

"No doubt. I tend to feel the same way. So what cell phone was it that I saw him with?"

"Dunno."

"OK. Well, I mainly wanted to check up on what was happening about the play. Won't it be difficult, without Skarphédinn?"

She seems to breathe more easily. "Yes, of course it will. It was his baby, really."

"His baby? Who picked the play *Loftur the Sorcerer*?"

"He suggested it. He felt that it was the obvious choice. He had read a lot more than the rest of us."

"I see. And he was the Main Man in the production?"

"Well, we all had our own tasks. But most of the ideas came from Skarphédinn. And I'm sure he wouldn't have wanted us to abandon the production."

"Probably not. And you'd raised funding for the production, found sponsors and so on…"

"Yes, we don't want to let the sponsors down. Especially because we want to go on with the drama group next year. Skarphédinn wouldn't have wanted that."

"Was it Skarphédinn who found the sponsors?"

"He was the only one in the drama group who had connections. And he made a good sales pitch."

After some routine housework, and general care of my roommate, I have an early night. I manage to read as far as the second act of *Loftur the Sorcerer* before I drop off to sleep. Perhaps Ásdís Björk, Gunnhildur, and Ásgeir Eyvindarson are at the back of my mind as I read, over and over again, Steinunn's line:

The most painful thing of all is to find out that the one who possesses you, heart and soul, is evil.

Or maybe it's something quite different on my mind. Or nothing at all.

21 FRIDAY

The advantage of the emotions is that they lead us astray is the Quote the Day on one of the websites I come across. Those words of wisdom are attributed to Oscar Wilde in *The Picture of Dorian Gray*. Oscar certainly had a way with a witty quip—and contrived to sound profound as well.

If it's an advantage to be led astray, then I think I'm suffering from a lack of emotions. I don't feel I'm moving in the right direction. Nor the wrong one. I am, somehow, nowhere at all. Nothing's happening. Why is no one, and nothing, leading me astray?

There's not much to raise my spirits this morning. Not even the sun, which, yet again, has brought a breath of summer to the town center, conjuring up happy children, leisurely pensioners, and half-dressed girls with bare midriffs to enjoy the warmth. It strikes me that there's nothing wrong, really. I'm just bored. And I have a feeling of restlessness, emptiness, and edginess that are old, familiar companions. In the old days I'd have taken a firm hand with them by having a drink. I can't do that now. I must do something else. And as I open the window with its view of the opposite wall and light up, the solution is plain to me. I pick up the phone and call Gunnsa. She's at school.

"Hi, Dad. I can't talk for long now. Morning break is almost over."

"Just wanted to hear your voice. How's it going?"

"Fine. We start studying for exams next week."

"Oh, yes. What do you think of that?"

"Not too good. But I'll do my best. I'm determined to get a place at high school."

"Since your old man made it, I'm sure it'll be a breeze for you."

I hear her smile. What a great feeling.

"And Raggi's doing the same, is he?" I ask.

"Yes, he's got it down. We're going to study together whenever we can."

"Good, good. So I suppose this means you won't be coming to visit me anytime soon?"

"No, not till after the exams. Then I'll come, I promise."

"Thanks, honey. You've made my day."

And she has. I get to work and make some phone calls about routine news items. Then I call Trausti Löve, determined to apply my newfound positive philosophy of life.

"Hello, my dear old Trausti."

"Who is this?"

"Your friend Einar, of course. In Akureyri."

"Sounds as if you're on a bender."

"Why do you say that?"

"You're just not your usual self. Not the way you've been recently, anyway."

"Can't I be nice to my news editor without being accused of intoxication?"

Trausti's silence tells me he doesn't quite know how to take this.

"I wanted to let you know that I've sent you some news items. You were complaining that I wasn't submitting any copy, weren't you?"

"What? Yes."

"And Trausti, I want you to know that I'm striving to do my best for you and the paper."

"Are you sure you're not drunk?"

"That's pretty much the only thing I am sure of."

No reply.

"My cup runneth over with the milk of human kindness."

"And you'll remember to send in the *Question of the Day* from Akureyri on Monday?"

"Absolutely. And I'll even do more than that."

"Oh? What's that?"

"I'll send you the answers too!"

"Good."

"Yes, it is good, isn't it? Quite splendid, in fact?"

He doesn't know what to say.

"Finally, my dear Trausti, I want to say, have an enjoyable weekend, in the company of beautiful women and outrageously expensive vintage wines."

"Thank you," he brusquely replies. "And fuck you too." He hangs up.

Strange how people can be so weird and graceless and ungrateful.

After my exercise in Christian charity, I feel so good that I go out into the sunshine, stroll over to Café Amor on the square, opposite the office, and order a cappuccino at an outside table.

The young girls wheel their strollers past, midriffs bare—even the ones who really oughtn't—and belly buttons on show.

Just after boys stopped walking around with their jeans falling off and their shorts showing, the fashion world succeeded in convincing girls it was their turn to walk around half-undressed. And so it goes on. Once upon a time, I used to keep up with fashion. Now fashion doesn't keep up with me.

How can you make a girl believe that a muffin-top of naked blubber sagging over her waistband is sexy? It may be kind of cute, and relaxed, and remind us that we all have a tummy. But *sexy*? And what about the boys walking around with their hairy ass cracks on show, thinking there's something cool about it? How can that happen? Is there anything that isn't possible? I wonder as I smoke my cigarette.

Then I give some thought to my irresistible urge to be at odds with news editors. Now, when Ásbjörn has finally been induced to accept that he's not right for the job, and he and I are managing to get along all right in our new roles, another idiot is appointed, far worse than Ásbjörn ever was. And of course I get at cross-purposes with him from the start. How is that possible? Do I imagine I know more than anyone else about being a news editor—regardless of who's trying to do the job? And then, when I'm offered the position myself, I turn it down!

Is there no limit to what's possible?

I wouldn't like to be the manager of me. Maybe it's the idea of being managed I don't like. We should all be colleagues—that's the right term.

Would I want to have me as my boss? Absolutely not! I'd be in contention with me in no time.

A young man walks by, not in a sunny mood, anymore than the first time we met. Rúnar Valgardsson is wearing the same black suit, white shirt, and black tie as at his brother's funeral. His long hair is ruffled by the breeze as he waits for a gap in the traffic so he can cross the road.

I stand up and walk over to him.

"Rúnar, hello. Remember me?"

He's taken by surprise. "What? Yes," he replies. He looks at me out of the corner of his eye, still observing the shining cars passing by.

"I was planning to call you. I wanted to leave it a few days after your brother's funeral. Have you got time for a chat now?"

"No, I'm afraid not," he answers, shoulders hunched.

"That's a pity."

He says nothing.

"You must be on your way to school," I say, although his clothes tell a different story.

"No. I just haven't got time to speak to you now."

He's not hostile, but seems a little tense.

"When can we meet?"

"I really don't know."

"What about Sunday? No school or anything?"

"OK. Call me on Sunday."

"One thing. I've been wondering who Skarphédinn's oldest and best friend was. Your brother seems to have been very popular and had lots of friends. But who was his closest friend?"

It's clear that he would much rather cross the road than answer me, but another car comes along and saves the day.

"Apart from you, I mean, of course. You were close, weren't you?"

He nods. "Mördur, I suppose."

"Where does he live?"

"In Reydargerdi. He moved there last year."

"OK, thanks. What's his last name?"

"Njálsson."

"Mördur Njálsson. Thank you."

A gap opens in the row of cars. "You're dressed for a party. It's a bit early in the day, isn't it? Even for a Friday?"

Rúnar strides out into the street. He seems relieved to get away.

"I'm not going to a party," he mutters. I can hardly distinguish his words. "I'm going to a funeral."

A funeral? I think as I return to my seat outside the café. *Did he mean that literally? Or is he still in mourning for his brother?*

I beckon the waiter, order another cappuccino, and ask if they have a copy of the *Morning News* for customers to read. Within a few minutes I have a fresh cup of coffee, a cigarette between my lips, and a copy of the *Morning News.* I turn to the Obituaries page, to see whose funeral is taking place today. Only one person has been moved to write in commemoration of Sólrún Bjarka-dóttir, the high school student who in a moment of high spirits made a joke about her favorite place to party and in the lowest of spirits took her own life.

I'm ashamed to admit, even though it's only to myself, that the poor girl had quite slipped my mind.

Knowledge and innocence cannot be reconciled, a wise man once said. My dear Sólrún, I know that you, like others, were finding it more and more difficult to cope with your painful experiences in life. Those experiences were at odds with your own intrinsic innocence, your faith in the good. Sólrún, you weren't a strong person—not in the sense of being able to resist the temptations that seem, for a time, to make life more bearable. But you were stronger than most in that important aim in life of giving of yourself, contributing to the happiness of others, and encouraging them. Then the day came when you could not go on. Not because you had no more to give, but because your gifts were misconstrued and desecrated. And although the knowledge of other people that you acquired in your life ultimately became unbearable for you, the place you have in my heart glows with joy and gratitude for the privilege of having known you, gratitude that you allowed me to know you. You will remain there, in my heart, forever, and the memory of you will be a source of strength for me.

    R.

Although the obvious conclusion seems to be that the obituary must have been penned by Rúnar Valgardsson, I remind myself that I may be completely wrong. It may have been written by a woman—a friend, perhaps one of the girls who were with her the other day on the square. Or someone else entirely—male or female.

But by comparison with the flood of obituaries when Skarphédinn was buried, the obituary, though expressing beautiful sentiments, seems a sad and lonely memorial. What does that say about the life of Sólrún Bjarkadóttir?

Surrounded by sunshine, the scent of spring, and bustling Friday traffic, once again I'm feeling downcast. I take out my phone, get the number for the high school, and ask to be put through to Kjartan Arnarson.

"He's out. He won't be back today. He's gone to a funeral," the telephonist informs me.

"Right. Were lessons canceled today for the funeral of Sólrún Bjarkadóttir?"

"No, only for her class," is the answer. "It's so close to exams that we couldn't give the whole school a day off."

I thank her. I consult the paper and see that the funeral started at one thirty. I set off for the church.

Breathless from the effort of climbing the long stairway up to the church, I quietly slip inside. It's two o'clock, and the funeral ceremony is well underway. In contrast with my previous visit to the church, there is plenty of room. The pews are about one-quarter full, and the mourners are spread sparsely around the church. As I stand at the doorway, I spot Rúnar Valgardsson sitting three pews in front of me, crying. Suddenly I'm overwhelmed by a feeling of discomfort, almost claustrophobic in its intensity. I discreetly sneak back out of the building.

As I walk, deep in thought, back down the stairway to heaven, I notice Pal running about on the grassy hillside, chasing after a ball. He finally catches it and runs with it toward a young girl, who claps her hands in pleasure. Pal proudly presents his trophy to Björg.

Quite a heartwarming moment. I feel better already.

Back at the office, Ásbjörn is in the reception area, chatting to a visitor over a cup of coffee. He's looking a touch less frazzled than he has of late. Our visitor is his usual smooth self.

"Well, here he is," says Ásbjörn, rising from his chair. He goes into his office and shuts the door behind him. Ásgeir Eyvindarson stands up and greets me warmly.

"I was wondering if there was any chance of seeing what the article will look like in the paper tomorrow."

"That's rather unusual," I answer. "As a rule, interviewees don't get to monitor the whole process."

"That may well be," he politely counters. With a smile, he adds: "But rules are made to be broken. I gather that you may have broken one or two before."

What's Ásbjörn been telling him? I wonder. But I'm well aware that it's a good idea not to offend Ásgeir, all things considered.

"All right, then. But you'll have to come into the 'production department' with me."

I offer Ásgeir a seat in my closet-office and switch the computer on. I open the layout system and find the relevant pages.

ALL IN THE MIND?

is my headline for the main feature. The interview with Ásgeir is headed:

SHE ALONE KNEW HOW SHE FELT

"There you are," I say.

He puts on reading glasses, peers at the screen, and strokes his gray mustache all the while as he reads. I don't know why, but I've always had reservations about men with mustaches. Maybe because they seem to be equivocal about their facial hair, unwilling to go the whole hog and grow a proper beard.

I don't know. *What ridiculous prejudices I harbor,* I think as I observe Ásgeir Eyvindarson stroking his mustache. This constant urge to classify people as *good* or *bad*. It's never got me anywhere.

Ásgeir removes his glasses and folds them into a leather spectacle case.

"Reading this," he says as he puts the glasses away in the breast pocket of his jacket, "one can't help thinking that perhaps it was a blessed release for Ásdís Björk, an end to her sufferings."

I gaze at him, speechless.

"Yes, I know it's a strange thing for me to say. But nothing could be done for her. There was no prospect of a cure. She would simply have gone on suffering and desperately searching for new ways to assuage her pain."

"So you mean that her death was a relief? For her, or…"

"A relief, in a sense, yes. For her." Lost in thought, he gazes out of the window at the opposite wall. "I just hope your article will help people understand this illness better and…"

He leaves the sentence hanging and walks out of the room.

"Um, Ásgeir," I say, following him, "I saw on a poster that you, or the Yumm factory, are a sponsor of the high school drama group's production of *Loftur the Sorcerer*."

"Yes, that's right," he says, continuing toward the door. "We give some support to local cultural events from time to time."

"It's certainly praiseworthy when the private sector makes the effort to sponsor the arts."

He looks me up and down. "Why do you ask?"

"I was wondering if you knew a young man named Skarp-hédinn Valgardsson?"

"Skarphédinn Valgardsson? Isn't that the boy who was found dead at the dump?"

"Yes, that's him."

"I don't think so."

"Wasn't he the one who called you to ask you to sponsor the play?"

"Quite possibly," he replies. "Some young man called and asked for sponsorship. Was that him?"

"I think it must have been."

"So?"

Without waiting for an answer, he disappears down the stairs.

Not that I could have said anything.

No landline is listed for Mördur Njálsson in Reydargerdi. I call information and get his cell phone number.

It goes straight to voice mail:

"This is Mördur. Leave a message."

As a rule, I have to force myself to comply with such churlishly worded orders. This time I haven't got the energy to make myself speak.

I call Óskar at Hotel Reydargerdi and ask how things are around town.

"Much the same," he answers. "We're as busy as ever, and everything's topsy-turvy."

"Any news of Agnar and Co. since they got out?"

"Much the same too," he laughs. "They're pretty busy, keeping themselves topsy-turvy."

"Are they behaving themselves?"

"No, they never behave themselves. They run wild in the evening, complaining of injustice one minute then boasting about getting the better of the Akureyri police. Those boys are just a total mess."

"Have they been allowed back into Reydin?"

"They haven't been barred, I don't think. But they get thrown out on a regular basis. I just heard they're off to Akureyri for some fun this weekend."

"That's something to look forward to, then."

"Not really. I hear they've been muttering about revenge."

"What revenge? What for? And against whom?"

"I don't know. I doubt if they know themselves. It's just some kind of revenge, for something, against someone. That's all a pack of idiots like that need."

"Well, well. By the way, do you know someone called Mördur Njálsson?"

"Mördur? Sure."

"Who is he?"

"He's just a kid, about twenty, who used to live in Akureyri. He moved here to study for his high school exams. He's an extramural student. And he's also writing something. He wanted some peace and quiet to work."

"It's debatable whether there's more peace and quiet over there at present, surely?"

"No, he's got a little house at the edge of the village, very peaceful. He's a quiet kid."

"Do you know where I can get in touch with him?"

"No, I don't. But he dropped in a couple of days ago for a coffee. He said he was driving south to Reykjavík and staying the weekend, so far as I remember."

"*Bon voyage*," I savagely mutter.

Before I go home to Polly to give us both a bath, I call the head office in Reykjavík and ask for my friend Guffi. He has moved on from his old job in foreign news and been promoted to the business section, after being admitted to the hallowed ranks of MBA students at trendy Reykjavík University. Guffi is better informed than anyone else I know about developments in business, the machinations of investors, and the pursuit of worldly pleasures— having moved on from the radical Marxism of his youth. I suppose that's what they mean by progress.

"Well, well, old buddy," says Guffi, who's about to close up shop and head home to domestic bliss. "What is this? It's past five on a Friday, and you're not propping up the bar yet."

As I hear his words, I am overcome by the desire to be, actually, at a bar. I imagine the multicolored glow of the liquor bottles and the shining glasses just waiting to be filled, drained, and filled again. I reach for my coffee cup, but spit out the cold, muddy drink after my first sip. Instead I light up.

"What?" Guffi exclaims. "Is that what the fresh northern air has done for you?"

"Yep, pretty much," I say, inhaling greedily.

"Maybe we should try marketing it," he continues. "Get ahead of the game for once, and sell fresh Akureyri air in cans."

"Better get a move on. They're already planning how to pollute it."

"That's one way of selling the fresh air, I suppose. But it's a bit ambitious for me."

"Guffi, listen. There's still some old-style food production here. Do you know the Yumm candy factory?"

"Of course. Doesn't everyone?"

"Have your highly attuned ears heard anything about it being up for sale?"

He needs no time to think this over. "Well, there's been a rumor for quite a while that it might be for sale. But a few days ago I heard that negotiations are underway with Treat in Reykjavík."

"Merger. Consolidation. Economies of scale and all that?"

"Exactly. These old family firms are generally far too small to meet today's demands for profitability. Their time has passed, really."

"These negotiations, how far have they progressed?"

"Not so far that I can report on them. But they're ongoing."

"I won't keep you. You'll be late getting home to your wife. And I'm late for my roommate too. I'll be in touch."

"Oh, is there someone? Tell me more! Hello? Einar? Hello? Damn…"

With a silly smirk, I hang up.

She is a little shy in this unfamiliar environment of Heida's apartment and doesn't say much. I understand. She isn't used to being invited out to dinner.

"I think it's love," says Jóa. "True love."

I nod. "She's certainly given me a fresh perspective, added a new dimension to my life. It was about time."

"But you weren't too happy about it to start with. You thought she was a pain," Jóa says.

"That's true. I admit it, I'm immature."

We each sit in an armchair, deep and white and cozy, watching Polly on her perch in her cage, standing on a round dining table draped in a white cloth. With her head under her wing, she's pretending to be asleep. But I know she's listening.

Heida appears from the kitchen with a tray and offers us coffee. She and Jóa have a Bailey's liqueur. I'm feeling restless. I get up and wander around Heida's white-painted loft on Adalstræti in the center of town. There are potted plants in every corner, picturesque dormer windows, old but elegant furnishings. I stop by the CD rack and hear Jóa and Heida chatting and laughing, but I can't distinguish what they're saying.

I find a *Best of Muddy Waters* CD and put on *I'm Your Hoochie Coochie Man*.

In the soft light of two floor lamps, I see how happy these two beautiful women are: happy to be together—happy with each other.

I've got a strong feeling that I'm about to fall off the wagon. We've had a delicious meal: avocado and prawn starter, followed by pork filet. So I'm not hungry. I'm well fed. But it's that goddamned thirst in the soul. That thirst is more overpowering than it has ever been since I came here to the north.

Since I woke up this morning, I've been seesawing between optimism and pessimism, between despair and energy. As so often before, I try to suppress that oh-so-familiar feeling, but it pops up to the surface, again and again.

"Ladies," I say, lifting my cup to share a toast with them. "What a delightful evening this has been. And I desperately want to get roaring drunk with you."

Jóa, who's glowing this evening in her pale color pantsuit, and has even put on makeup for the occasion, is horror-struck.

"Oh, no, Einar, you mustn't. That would spoil everything, and we'd regret having invited you."

"You and Polly," smiles Heida. She looks just as fine, in a short figure-hugging blue dress.

"No, no. No worries," I assure them. "It's just the way I feel. I've been on edge all day."

"It's just something you've got to work through," says Jóa. "You've been learning new things, and you need time to digest them. Trust me, I've been there."

"God, I wish you were right. I wish it weren't the same old thirst. The same old self-pity and the same old escapism."

"Here," says Heida, handing me the cigarette pack that has lain untouched on the table since Polly and I arrived. "Have a smoke. One cigarette won't kill us."

———

As I drive home through the town center around midnight, the great migration has begun. On the streets and sidewalks, there is an air of anticipation, mixed with the undefined tension, desperation, and aggression that are typical of Icelandic nightlife. At cafés and bars, the fun is about to start. The mild, windless evening presages a wild night.

A man carrying a parrot in a cage wouldn't fit in. Perhaps that's the reason I took Polly along. Perhaps on some level I realized that my responsibility for the little bundle of feathers was the one thing that would keep me on the straight and narrow.

Perhaps I realized that my own mistakes, and those of others, will never be an effective deterrent: the recollection of awful pick-up lines; stupid, desperate efforts at witty repartee; and a totally bogus persona as the life and soul of the party.

When we I arrive home, I turn to Polly, who on the drive home has been swaying back and forth, firmly clinging to her perch, and is patiently waiting to be carried indoors:

"What do you think, honey? Is there something I've got to work through?"

22 SATURDAY

What lies were not told about the Iraq War? Conflicting weather prognostications in Dalvík. Icelanders gain a majority holding in Marks and Spencer. Bookmakers predict Icelandic victory in the Eurovision Song Contest.

The newspapers are crammed with news items. I turn page after page, but nothing catches my attention. The investigation into the death of Skarphédinn Valgardsson has all but vanished from the media since the Reydargerdi Three were released.

The Akureyri offices of the *Afternoon News* are deserted this Saturday afternoon, but outside the town center is buzzing with cheerful people with spring in their hearts. I switch my computer on and set out to try to put together, from my notes and audio recordings, the fragmentary knowledge I have gathered about the dead boy. As I expected, they don't make up a clear picture, however many times I draft and redraft my article. I'm well rested and thinking pretty clearly—by my standards at least—but whatever I do there are gaping holes in my story.

I start by making a phone call to Reykjavík. Then I see that I can no longer put off what I've got to do. It's been on my mind ever since I woke up, and it won't leave me alone until I respond. I switch the computer off, pick up a copy of our weekend edition, and heavy-hearted with apprehension I walk out onto the sunny square.

"Gunnhildur isn't up," I'm informed at the Hóll care home. "She wouldn't get out of bed today."

Not good, I think. "Do you think it would be all right if I looked in on her?"

"Well, she hasn't said she doesn't want visitors. Not that she has a lot, anyway."

"Oh? Don't many people come to see her?"

"No, more's the pity. Not since her daughter died. She generally came twice a week in recent months. She used to visit every day, but apparently she was unwell."

"Yes, so I've heard."

"I see you've brought the *Afternoon News.* There's an article about her daughter in it."

I'm not sure what to say. Awkwardly, I ask: "Really? I haven't read the paper yet. Is it an interesting piece?"

"Oh, yes," is the reply. "There's so much we don't know. But I mainly found it very sad."

I ask for Gunnhildur's room number and get directions. As I stand at her door, I can hear quiet groans from inside the room. I knock.

No answer.

I cautiously open the door and peer inside. There are two beds in the room. Gunnhildur is standing there, dressed in her slip. She has put her head through the neck opening of a plain gray dress but is having trouble getting her arms into the sleeves. I go into the room and help her find the right openings.

"Thank you," she says without seeing who I am. When she realizes who I am, her aged but beautiful face hardens.

"Oh, it's you, is it, you young rascal? Who said you could come in here?"

"Well, no one said I couldn't," I say in an attempt to lighten the atmosphere.

"This is my home. I may not have much control over what happens here, but I will damn well decide who is allowed in. It's up to me who I see."

I groan with frustration.

"And I don't want to see you."

I pass her the paper. "But I wanted to show you the article in the paper, so you can see it's quite harmless. It may even do good…"

She shoves it away. "I've seen the darn thing. I haven't had a moment's peace from all the people here, the *Guiding Light* mafia—I haven't been able to lie here in bed without being constantly interrupted, and all because of your goddamned article!"

"What have they been saying?"

"What they've been saying? Just expressing their sympathy and pretending to be all understanding. I can't stand the hypocrisy and fawning!"

"Oh? I should have thought it would be a good thing, if people have gained some insights…"

"*Oh, dear Gunnhildur, I had no idea!*" she mimics a sympathetic voice. "*Oh, how hard it must have been for you with Ásdís Björk! It's just so sad!*"

"Um…," I say.

"Goddamned ridiculous nonsense. And the lies that bastard Ásgeir tells. Just trying to make himself look good. I can't believe you've done this to me!"

She shakes her gray braid.

"But the article's based mainly on medical information—"

"I don't believe a word they say, those quack doctors. I know what I know." She folds her arms across her meager chest, as if to say that she won't be persuaded.

"Would you like to come out into the sun?" I ask, hoping to change the subject. "We could have a little walk outside."

She gives me a searching look, then shrugs. "When you don't have many options, none of them are good."

I help her into her coat, and she places a scarf around her neck. Then we stroll arm-in-arm, step-by-step, out into the garden of the care home. Residents are out and about. Three women and a man stand in a little group, enjoying a smoke. I'm thinking of lighting up too when my companion points to the smokers and observes: "There are plenty of ways to kill yourself—and others."

I change my mind, cram my hands into my jacket pockets, and keep a firm hold on the cigarettes.

She looks up, squinting into the brightness. "Goddamned sun! Is it going to kill us off too? You can have too much of a good thing!"

We walk for a while without speaking along the path around the outside of the building.

"This seems a nice enough place?" I observe, just to say something.

Gunnhildur scoffs. "It's like living at an airport hotel, surrounded by people you've nothing in common with, except that you're waiting for the same departure. Just you wait, young man. Your time will come."

"Yes, that thought has occurred to me."

She starts questioning me about where I'm from and who my family are, how old I am, what I've studied, and where I've worked. I try to answer her questions without getting into anything too complicated. And there's plenty of that. We have completed our circuit of the care home when Gunnhildur halts at the entrance, gazes sharply at me from her limpid blue eyes, and says:

"Right. I've survived our little stroll. Now tell me whatever it is you've been wanting to say."

I decide that honesty is the best policy. "I've been feeling bad because you feel I've let you down. That really wasn't my intention..."

She shakes her braid without speaking.

"I still haven't found anything to prove that your daughter's death was anything but an accident, which resulted from her illness..."

Gunnhildur sighs and stamps her foot. "That's enough, young man. You've said all that before. If you've come to me hoping for absolution, you've had a wasted journey."

I continue, refusing to be distracted: "But I found out yesterday that Ásgeir is negotiating to sell the candy factory. So you were right about that."

Her face brightens. "Well, well. It's about time."

I raise a finger to stop her. "And before I came here to see you, I made a phone call to your grandson, Gudmundur, down south. I implied that I was interested in hearing what he thought of the article in today's paper—since I'd got in touch with his father through him. He was fine with it. Before I said good-bye, I said I'd heard rumors in the business world that he and his father were planning to sell Yumm. And he said that was correct."

I take my notebook out of my pocket. "Then he said, without prompting—I'm repeating it word for word—*The time had come long ago for us to get out of the business and cash in. It was a constant struggle to keep the company going. But Mom was always absolutely against selling. She felt it would be a disgrace for her and for the family. We've been entrusted with running the company, she always said, and it's our duty to nurture it and enhance its value. But the truth was that we never got any real profit from the company, and we even had trouble meeting the payroll. As I say: it was time.* That's what your grandson, the economist Gudmundur Ásgeirsson, said to me. Off the record, admittedly."

Gunnhildur is lost for words.

"None of this proves that Ásdís Björk's death was caused by her husband, Gunnhildur. Not at all. But I haven't given up. That's what I came to tell you."

She grips my wrist tightly in her hand. "I told my dear Ragna that you were a bit silly, my boy, but that you meant well."

She lets go.

"It turns out I was right, after all."

She turns and walks slowly into the Hóll care home, head held high.

When Gunnhildur Bjargmundsdóttir feels better, I feel better. Simple as that. I call Jóa and invite her and Heida out to dinner at the Fidlarinn restaurant.

I enjoy the bright panoramic view out over the fjord as I wait for my guests in the green-upholstered penthouse bar. I have a smoke and a Coke. Life seems pretty much OK. My overwhelming thirst has gone. For now.

Over our meal we chat about this and that—including the mouthwatering French venison we're eating. Afterward we return to the bar. Why would anyone need to go to Copenhagen? Or Reykjavík, even?

Jóa and Heida have just started on their coffee and cognac when my cell phone rings.

"Hello," I answer.

"Is that Einar the newshound?"

"Who is this?" I ask.

"This is Chief of Police Ólafur Gísli," answers a voice I have now identified.

Jóa and Heida are chatting as I speak.

"It sounds to me," comments the chief, "as if you're enjoying female company."

"It's not what you think. And not what I might hope."

"Excellent. I think you should leave your present location and move on to the next."

"Oh? What location is that? Has something come up?"

"Yes."

I'm instantly alert. "Do you mean a crime location?"

"A crime scene, that's right."

"OK. Where shall I come to?"

"The offices of the *Afternoon News*, on Town Hall Square."

"What's happened there?"

"I can't, and won't, tell you on a cell phone."

"I'll be there. Right away."

I end the call, then sit for a few moments, motionless. Has there been a break-in at the office? Arson? Has the place been trashed? Has someone been murdered there?

"What?"

I'm startled out of my thoughts. Jóa and Heida are looking at me like two question marks.

"I don't really know. A teddy bear just called and—"

"Teddy bear?" queries Heida.

"That's what Einar calls his anonymous informants," Jóa whispers to her.

"…and he said I should go right away to our offices. Something's happening there, according to him. Or has happened. Or God knows what."

I summon our waiter and ask for the bill. "Sorry, girls, duty calls. And Jóa, I think you should come with me. We may need pictures."

"But my gear is all there, at the office," Jóa points out.

"Well, let's hope the place hasn't been vandalized, and your stuff hasn't been stolen, or…" I comment.

"And I'm all dressed up," grumbles Jóa.

It's a quiet evening on the square as Jóa and I walk hurriedly over from the restaurant. It's not yet eleven o'clock, so the night is young. We stop at the square and look up at the building. Ásbjörn and Karólína's apartment on the top floor is dark, but the lights are on in the offices on the floor below. I glance around. The only vehicle I spot nearby is a black car on the pedestrian street.

"That's odd," I observe. "I don't see any police cars or anything."

Jóa says nothing.

As we walk over to the building and quietly mount the stairs, I feel my heart beating faster. When we reach the landing outside the office I glance at Jóa. She is deathly pale. I put my ear to the door and hear a low rumble of voices inside. I summon up courage, seize the doorknob, and open the door. There's no one in the reception area. I cautiously enter one step at a time, followed by Jóa.

The door to Ásbjörn's office is ajar.

"…and that's how they came to call him Hákon!" Ásbjörn brays with laughter.

"Hahahahaha!" howls the chief of police.

I shove the door open.

Ólafur Gísli and Ásbjörn appear startled by our sudden appearance. They are sitting there in their shirtsleeves, feet up on Ásbjörn's desk. Rosy-cheeked, they are drinking glasses of Coke-and-something. On the desk is a half-full bottle of vodka. Pal is lying on the floor, snoring.

They make a quick recovery and raise their glasses to us.

"Cheers!" exclaims the chief. "Cheers to the investigative journalist. Welcome to our crime scene."

"Hahahaha," giggles Ásbjörn, grasping his jiggling belly. "Ahahahahah!"

Ólafur Gísli smirks. "Just testing your response time." He glances at his watch. "Four and a half minutes. Not bad."

"Not bad," slurs Ásbjörn. "Almost as quick as the emergency services. Hohohoho!"

I look over at Jóa. "Crank call, Jóa. Just these two drunks having a joke at our expense. Let's get back to HQ."

Ásbjörn jumps to his feet. A bit too quickly—he sways on his feet. "No, not at all, my dear Einar," he says, stumbling toward me. "Now, now. We're just havin' a relaxin' drink together, me and my ol' buddy Ólafur Gisli. We wanna ask you to join us. We thought you'd be all alone."

"That's very nice of you," I reply, as drily as I can manage—the state of the two of them is, I have to admit, a pretty funny sight. Ásbjörn in particular.

"My dear Einar," rambles Ásbjörn, "you're nowhere near as bad as I always thought. Really, you're…you're…"

He's looking for the right word. Then his unfocussed eyes light up with an idea. He envelopes me in a hug. The smell of his perspiration wafts up into my nostrils.

"Really, you're all right. Yes, thass what you are. All right."

Ásbjörn places his hands on my shoulders, looks at me with unusual affection, and turns to face Ólafur Gísli, who is smirking.

"Ólafur Gísli. Thass what Einar is. He's absolutely all right."

I burst out laughing. Jóa too.

"But he keeps it secret," mumbles Ásbjörn. "Why's it such a well-kept secret," he asks me, "how all right you are?"

"Maybe it's because it sometimes slips my mind that I'm quite all right. Do you suppose that's it?"

He doesn't hear me. He's hugging Jóa now. She makes a grotesque face.

"And you, dear Jóa. My darlin' Jóa. What would I have done without ya?"

"I don't know," answers Jóa.

"What the hell would I have done without ya? Jóa, lemme give you a drop of vodka..." He turns toward me. "I know I can't offer you a drink, Einar. Wouldn' be appropriate. You've been doin' so well. Ólafur Gísli, give Jóa a drink, and get a Coke for Einar. And Einar, you know..." He stumbles and almost falls. I hold him by the shoulder. "Look, I'm blind drunk, and you aren't. You're stone-cold fucking sober! Einar, my friend..."

Suddenly he is completely serious. "I'm just celebrating with my friend Ólafur Gísli—my very best friend, although you're really quite all right too, Einar, aren't you?...I'm celebrating a turning point in my life. A crossroads. A whole new chapter."

After a dramatic pause, Ásbjörn declaims: "I have a daughter!"

He lifts his glass. He is red-faced and sweaty.

"My dear friends. Share a toast with me. I have a daughter. A beautiful, delightful daughter."

"Cheers!" we chorus. They toast in triple vodkas. I toast in octuple Coke.

"An' my darlin' Karó," he mumbles, mostly to himself. "Karó, my sweet, dear Karó…"

"Yes, how is Karó taking the news?" asks Jóa.

Over dinner at Fidlarinn I'd recounted the story of the long-lost daughter to Jóa and Heida.

"Karó? Jóa, lemme tell you how Karó's takin' it. She's gonna take Björg like our own daughter, that we haven't been able to have. Like the daughter we haven't been able to have! Just think! That's how Karó's taking it. Isn' that wunnerful?"

He dries his eyes. "Yes, it's quite wonderful," he answers his own question.

"And where's Karólína this evening?" I ask.

"She's popped down to Reykjavík to tell her parents all about it," replies Ólafur Gísli, who's been wearing a lopsided smile during his friend's monologue. He adds, suddenly quite sincere: "Their childlessness became more and more difficult for her to cope with over the years. Ásbjörn was getting deeply concerned about how unhappy she had become. He felt he had nowhere to turn—until Pal joined the family."

Ásbjörn flops down into his chair, panting for breath.

"We were sitting here swapping jokes before you arrived," the chief tells us. He swigs from a fresh bottle of vodka. "We've made a habit of it since we were in high school."

Ásbjörn wipes away his tears and sweat and drinks deeply from his glass. "Yes, it's your turn. Tell us a joke."

Ólafur Gísli strokes his cheek. "Yeees, let's see. Now then: A city girl was once sent to the country to spend the summer on a farm. On her first day, she was out in the farmyard with the farmer, who asked her if she knew any country skills. How about milking? he asked. She replied that of course she knew how. She sat on the milking stool by one of the cows and started fiddling with the udders. The farmer felt she was taking a long time and asked her: Aren't you going to start milking? Then the girl answered: I'm waiting for them to get hard!"

Ásbjörn Grímsson guffaws and rolls about laughing. Ólafur Gísli joins in. I burst out laughing too, at the sight of Jóa trying not to.

Shortly after that we leave the two old buddies to their drinking, at the scene of the crime.

I say to Jóa: "Hannes just mentioned it the other day. I think I managed to convince him that there were plenty of good reasons for you not to return to Reykjavík just yet. I hope so, anyway."

As we got into my car at the parking lot, Jóa had mentioned her plans for the future.

"I hope so too," she says. "I really don't want to leave yet."

"So is this the Real Thing?" I venture to ask her as I drive down Skipagata toward the square. Young people are out cruising by now, and the town center is crammed with cars.

"I'm in a good place" is all Jóa will say.

And that's enough, really.

Café Amor on the corner is overflowing with people as we slide slowly past and into Strandgata. Café Akureyri looks much the same.

"What about you?" Jóa asks.

"I've been fine. Broadly speaking."

"But what about the broads? Not so much?"

I look at her out of the corner of my eye, eliciting a smile.

"Broadly, I'd say I'm going through a dry patch."

"Taking a break there too?"

"I don't know, Jóa. I just…"

Goddamn! That car's too close behind us. He seems to be tailgating us.

"I just don't think I'm ready to get into something that may be too much for me. It's a full-time job keeping the thirst at bay. One thing at a time, Jóa."

"You're awfully averse to commitment, Einar. I think it must be some kind of phobia. Really!"

"Quite possible," I say.

As I speak, there's a bump from the rear of the car.

"What the hell is that?" asks Jóa, glancing back. "Did the bastard rear-end us?"

We're nearly at the end of Strandgata, passing more nightspots—Vélsmidjan and Oddvitinn. At the corner I pull over without warning and stop the car.

"Son of a bitch!" I exclaim as the car that's been following us inches past. It's the same car that I saw when we went into the newspaper offices. The same one that was still there when we came out. Agnar Hansen sneers at us from the open rear window, giving us the finger as he passes by. The black Honda screeches to a halt, the doors are flung open, and Ivo and Gardar jump out.

"Holy shit!" I say, scrambling back into the car and forcing my way out into the passing traffic. I head up Strandgata, back toward the square.

"What is it?" asks Jóa in alarm. "Who were they?"

"It's the Reydargerdi gang," I explain. I don't tell her what Óskar at Hotel Reydargerdi said to me about the threesome being out for revenge in Akureyri.

Jóa looks back. "They're still following us. They're a few cars back."

As I reach the corner of Strandgata and Glerárgata, I'm not sure what direction to take. I don't like the idea of being stuck in the downtown traffic with those lunatics, so I turn right onto Glerárgata. I drive as fast as I can, and before we know it, we're in the Hlídar district. When we reach my place and Polly's—which was briefly Jóa's place too—I park, but not in my usual space. I choose a spot a little farther down.

"Jóa," I say, trying to light a cigarette with hands that are trembling. "I know Heida's place is in the other direction, but I don't think we should tempt fate. Come in with me. Let's wait and see whether we've managed to shake them off."

Silently we get out of the car and listen. The district is quiet— a dormitory suburb, peacefully asleep.

Then we hurry indoors, close all the curtains, and switch on the bare minimum of lights.

Jóa calls Heida to let her know what's happened, and I go into the bedroom to check on Polly. She's asleep with her head under her wing.

"I do envy you, little Polly," I remark. "You're so safe and care-free, in your cage."

23 SUNDAY

You shake it to the left,
and shake it to the right,

resounds from the speakers—a simple but catchy sixties hit,
by what wasn't at that time called a girl band.

Was life ever that simple?

Jóa has dug up from our landlady's music collection a CD
called *Girls with Guitars*. For some reason that makes me think of
Girls with Guns—a very risky juxtaposition. It's nearly 4:00 a.m.
We've been sitting talking, listening to music, and completely forgotten the danger we seemed to be in a few hours ago.

Now Jóa's in her room and I'm alone, reclining on the sofa
in the living room, enjoying a cigarette and listening to the girls
armed with their guitars.

They are the lonely, sing Pat Powdrill & the Powerdrills. Never
heard of them. Good song, though.

I'm not certain, but I think I hear a noise from the room I
share with Polly.

No one in this world of confusion
*Tries to understand...*the girls go on.

Suddenly the bedroom door flies open and Gardar Jónsson is standing over me, lanky and ungainly, wearing his *White Power!* shirt.

Electrified, I stumble to my feet.

There are those who know
What heartache can bring.
They are the lonely...

Gardar hobbles over to the audio system and switches it off.

"Fucking teenybopper shit you're listening to, motherfucker," remarks Agnar Hansen as he enters the room. His hair is tied back in a ponytail, and he's wearing black leather pants and a matching jacket. He takes a seat in the armchair facing the sofa with a joint in his mouth.

From the bedroom I hear shrieks of terror. Agnar and Gardar share a look of complicity. I'm frozen to the sofa.

Ivo Batorac stands in the doorway, his heavy frame dressed in black as before. His bluish fist is raised, and between his sausage-like fingers a tiny head peeps out. Polly is silent now, but her head is rhythmically bobbing, and her beak is wide open. Ivo and Gardar take up their positions on either side of the seated ringleader.

"So you're fucking a parrot are you, you little queer?" sneers Agnar. The light gleams on his orthodontic retainer and yellow-ish teeth.

"You're right as usual, Mr. Hansen," I say, willing my voice not to shake, although my heart feels as if it's going to explode in my chest. "But she's a girl bird. Polly."

They cackle with glee. Their dilated pupils and wired posture tell me they've taken something other than sedatives tonight.

"Since sex is the first thing you think of when you see a parrot," I go on, tempting fate, "I'm not surprised you've got complexes."

Gardar charges over to me and kicks me hard in the shin. A current of agony shoots up into my head like a bolt of lightning.

"Come, come," I say, gritting my teeth against the pain. "Must keep a sense of humor. And it's nice of you to drop in, boys. The door's behind you—just as a matter of interest. There's no need for respectable guests like you to be scrambling in through the window and out again the same way." I think: *They must have got the address from directory assistance. But how could I be so careless as to leave the window open!*

"We'll leave when we want to. And by whatever way we want to," Gardar replies.

"Why on earth didn't you ring the doorbell? I'd have invited you in and served up tea and cakes, no trouble at all. I'm quite forgetting my manners. What would you gentlemen like?"

They're not sure what to make of this.

"Well," I say, speaking louder. I focus on poor little Polly, who is lying quietly in Ivo's ham-like fist.

"To what do I owe the honor, and pleasure, of this visit? What can I do for you?"

"We were looking for someone else here in Akureyri," Agnar informs me. "But we couldn't find him, so we thought we'd drop in on you."

"How delightful."

"Who ratted us out to the cops?" he asks.

"How would I know?"

Gardar Jónsson prepares to whack my leg again, but Agnar stops him with a gesture.

"It's obvious from your articles that you've got contacts. You really ought to tell us what you know. Otherwise you'll be left with an ex-parrot to fuck."

They snigger.

I'd like to tell him I'm surprised to hear that he can read. I'd like to point out that people who commit violence against a parrot ought to go back to their usual hobby of tearing the wings off flies.

"Well, I simply assumed it must have been someone who saw you at that party," I loudly announce, trying to think of the next move in this dangerous game.

"Don't assume. Just tell us who it was."

I can't think of my next move.

"Ivo, squash the bug," Agnar orders him, his gaze unflinching on me.

Ivo instantly obeys. Polly squawks in pain, or terror. The shrill sound cuts through me like a knife, as if I were the one caught in Ivo's fist.

"No, no!" I shout. "I'm just trying to remember whether I heard anything about it."

My raised voice has yielded the desired result. Behind my three unwelcome guests, I see the door to Jóa's room opening. She stealthily moves down the hall in her stockinged feet.

"Wait, wait," I stall. "Could it have been that Fridrik Einarsson?"

Jóa silently draws closer.

"No. No way. We own that moron. We own all that crowd."

"So who—"

Suddenly Ivo and Gardar are thrown off balance as Jóa swings a foot into the back of their knees. She bashes both in the neck, and they collapse in a heap on the floor. Ivo automatically puts out both hands to break his fall, and Polly makes her escape. She flutters up to the curtain rail, where she perches, angrily screeching. Next Jóa turns her attention to Agnar Hansen, sitting lumpenly in his chair. She grabs him by the neck and hauls him out of the chair without any resistance. I jump to my feet to help her. Together we drag Agnar over to the sofa and dump him there. Jóa sits on his head to restrain him. He struggles and kicks, but soon gives up, as his head is held immobile under Jóa's formidable rear.

Gardar struggles to his feet and over to the window, where he tries to recapture Polly, who is scampering back and forth on the curtain rail. Ivo seems dazed, but he raises himself up to a sitting position. He grasps his pancake face in both hands. I walk over to him and pick up a weighty cut glass ashtray from the table. I hold it threateningly above his shaven head.

"Excellent work, Jóa," I say.

"Those martial arts courses finally came in handy," she comments with a broad grin.

"Gardar," I say in my best laconic drawl, in keeping with the American thriller I seem to be living in at the moment, "stop that. Leave the bird alone. Or I'll smash your boss's head into pizza, and spread Ivo's brain matter on for relish. And then I'll make you eat it. I think I've got some parmesan cheese in the fridge to go with it."

"OK." A strangled cry of pain from Agnar. "Back off, guys."

Gardar stops dead and stands awkwardly at the window. I walk over to him and kick him in the shin. He winces in pain.

"You stay there," I say to Gardar, then return to Ivo, who is cowering on the floor. I place the ashtray against the back of his head so he can feel the weight of it. The vibration of his tense muscles indicates that he is recovering. "You. Ivo. Cool it."

I turn back to Jóa, who is sitting on Agnar Hansen with an ironic smile on her lips. I think she's enjoying this.

"Look out!" she shouts.

At that moment, Ivo reaches up with both hands and grabs me by the throat. I have no option but to slam the ashtray down on his head. He bellows like an elephant and drops to the floor. The ashtray is not broken by the impact, but Ivo is bleeding from a cut to the scalp.

"Cool it, I said," I scold him. I quickly dash to the bathroom and fetch a towel. Ivo seems to be out of it, but when I place the towel on his head he automatically grasps it.

"Now then," Jóa cheerfully observes. "I think we've had enough of the party games, haven't we?"

Agnar groans his agreement.

"Einar, shouldn't we be calling the guests of honor?"

"The police?" I ask, brandishing my phone.

"No! No! Please, man, don't call the cops. Please, fucking please!" Agnar whines.

"Listen, lamebrain," Jóa counters, "do you think you can break into innocent people's home in the middle of the night, make violent threats, take one of the family hostage, and then just walk away?"

"Please, ma'am," whimpers Agnar. "We're sorry. Please."

"I know you losers are involved in collecting drug debts," I say. "I'm sure you're proud of yourselves. But if you think you can treat us the way you treat those poor fuckers who owe you money for drugs, then you've got another think coming."

"Nobody owes us any money," says Gardar, still standing motionless at the window. Polly has taken up a position directly above him on the curtain rail. "We don't sell drugs."

"No. I'm sure idiots like you three are users rather than pushers. Am I right?"

Gardar makes no reply, but Agnar mumbles something that sounds like agreement.

"So you collect drug debts for other people now and then?"

Agnar is silent.

"Mostly to work off your own debts?"

Another mumble from Agnar.

"Ugh! Fucking fuck!" exclaims Gardar. A small dropping has landed on his nose. He looks up. On the curtain rail sits Polly, tail feathers gracefully raised.

Swearing, Gardar wipes Polly's little gift away with the back of his hand. Jóa chortles, bumping up and down on Agnar's head. He gags, and black slime seeps from his mouth onto the sofa cushion.

"Jóa, honey," I observe with a smile. "I think you've squashed Agnar's skull so much that the drug-addled mush of his brain is leaking out his mouth."

"Stop it! Stop it!" howls Agnar in between coughing and gagging.

"Who are you collecting drug debts for?"

Ivo's head moves. Just as a precaution, I lightly tap the cut on his head with the ashtray. He stops moving.

Nobody seems to want to answer the question.

"Agnar, you said just now that you owned all that crowd at the party. Why is that?"

Agnar says nothing.

"Jóa, do you know, I think Agnar's falling asleep over there. Don't let him get too comfortable."

Jóa bounces up and down again.

"Ow, ow. Don't...," groans Agnar, and dribbles more black slime.

"What's this?" says Jóa. "I thought you said you'd always wanted to get intimate with a bull dyke?"

"Come on, I want answers," I say.

"All that crowd. They owe money for shit," mutters Agnar. "But they don't owe us. We've only collected from them now and then."

"So you were just talking big?"

"Yes," he whispers.

"Who do they owe? And who do you owe?"

Agnar says nothing.

"If I tell you, I'm a dead man," he finally says. "Go ahead, finish me off, here and now."

Not really an option. Unfortunately.

"Who were you looking for tonight? Who is it that you think ratted you out to the cops?"

Jóa bumps up and down on his head.

"Rúnar!" screams Agnar Hansen. "Motherfucking Rúnar!"

"What? Skarphédinn's brother?"

He nods, as far as he is capable.

"Why him?"

"Like you said, it must have been someone from the party. He's the only one who doesn't use. So he's the only one who'd dare..."

"Was Rúnar at the party? Are you sure?"

"Yes, of course. He was around."

"So you know him, do you?"

"Never spoken to him."

"What about his brother?"

"I'll tell you what I told the cops: he got in our face and threw us out."

"How very inconsiderate of him."

Silence.

"You were giving him a hard time about that costume he was wearing, weren't you?"

More silence.

"Well?" I ask.

"He got in our face before that," says Gardar Jónsson. "He was hassling me about my shirt." He indicates the words *White Power!* "He said Ivo was lucky not to be black—although he's dark-skinned. Or something like that."

"And what did you have planned for Rúnar?"

"Just a bit of fun," says Gardar. "Teach him not to get involved with what's none of his business."

"His brother's death—that's none of his business, is it?"

"That's not what I meant. I meant he had no right to drag us into it. We weren't there."

"Did Skarphédinn use drugs?"

Agnar says nothing.

"If you wouldn't mind, Jóa, a little persuasion."

She bumps up and down on his head.

"Oooww. Don't! All I know is he was acting completely crazy."

"The police theory is that you were collecting a drug debt from Skarphédinn and finished up killing him. That's right, isn't it?"

"No! No! No way! We had nothing to do with it. We don't know anything."

"Where have you been looking for Rúnar tonight?"

"Around town. And we went to his place."

"And?"

"He wasn't there. His mom told us to get the hell out of there, or she'd call the cops."

I ponder this. "I'm with her there. Get the hell out of here. If you so much as look at Jóa or me sideways, we'll be reporting you to the police for burglary and assault."

"We're the ones who got assaulted," grumbles Gardar. "Not you."

"So we invited you here to a party and then beat you up, did we?" says Jóa. "If you think the police will believe a word of that, you're even stupider than you look."

"If that's even possible," I add.

"No, no, fuck it," gabbles Agnar. "We'll leave you alone. It was all a mistake. Sorry! Sorry!"

"You'd better keep your word and leave us alone," I say. "You know you're at our mercy now. Just like a little bird in the palm of our hand."

In a little while they're gone. Jóa and I sit in silence, mentally and physically exhausted. Polly swoops down from her curtain rail and settles on my shirt collar. Now and then she pecks gently at my neck. Then, without a word, Jóa and I simultaneously nod, stand up, and set to work to eradicate all traces of the three wingdings from the east, who came bearing their gifts of vomit, violence, and fear.

I press the doorbell for *3rd floor and attic, Skarphédinn*. On this occasion I'm buzzed in. I open the door and enter.

After driving Jóa over to Heida's place, I tried to get some sleep. But every nerve in my body was humming, my muscles so tense that I couldn't relax. Polly had refused to return to her cage. She fluttered wildly around, crashing into the bars. So I decided to allow her to snuggle on my shoulder as I lay in bed. She fell fast asleep there with her head beneath her wing, but my shoulder didn't get a lot of rest. Polly didn't stir when the shoulder slipped out of bed, made coffee, switched the radio on, and read the Sunday papers until lunchtime.

Then I found my note of Rúnar Valgardsson's phone number and dialed. He answered. As I suspected, he'd been staying at his brother's apartment. I told him about our nighttime visitors. He said his mother had also called him about them during the night. So he'd decided not to go home but to take refuge at his brother's place.

He is waiting for me at the door, wearing jeans and a long white shirt, untucked. He looks more like his brother than ever.

"Hi," I say as I enter the parquet-floored entrance hall. "I heard you were planning to move in here. Take over your brother's apartment."

"Who told you that?" he asks in surprise.

"A young lady here in the building. Her name is Ösp, and she hates it."

He smiles halfheartedly.

"It sounded as if she was really looking forward to you moving in. She thinks you're much hotter than Skarphédinn."

"She's a nice girl," says Rúnar gloomily.

"And talking of nice girls," I jump in, "I didn't realize you knew Sólrún Bjarkadóttir."

He doesn't answer. And it wasn't really a question, anyway.

I try to put it better. "You must have been close. Your obituary was a beautiful tribute to her."

He glances up at me. "How did you know it was me?"

I shrug. I didn't know, until now.

"We were pretty good friends," he says.

Rúnar leads the way into a spacious, bright living room, with tall windows, white-painted walls, and parquet flooring. The furniture is modern, tasteful, in pale colors. On the walls are old photographs of various places around northern Iceland. One shows Hólar.

"Wow," I observe.

"Yes," agrees Rúnar. "It's a good apartment."

I have to ask: "Are your parents wealthy?"

He shakes his head. "Not at all."

"So how could Skarphédinn afford to rent a place like this?"

Now he shrugs. "It belongs to a friend of his."

"You mean Mördur Njálsson?"

"Yes, he moved to Reydargerdi and offered the place to Skarpi while he was away."

"*Skarpi*, you say. You're the only person I've heard use that nickname. Was he called *Skarpi* as a rule?"

"Only by me and our parents."

"And now Mördur's lending the apartment to you?"

He nods. "Yeah, until he comes back here."

"So the move to Reydargerdi isn't permanent?"

"I don't know how long he plans to stay there."

"He must be well-off?"

"I suppose," replies Rúnar.

Not a chatterbox, Rúnar.

"Does everything here belong to Mördur?" I ask him.

"Everything but the pictures," he says. "They're…They were Skarpi's. Mördur used to have contemporary art on the walls."

I take a walk around. There are no bookshelves anywhere, only a gigantic flat screen. Beyond the living room is an equally spacious dining room, furnished with a blond wooden dining table and eight chairs and a massive matching liquor cabinet. Off the dining room is a big kitchen with state-of-the-art fittings. Between the kitchen and dining room are two doors. One leads to the bathroom, the other to the attic.

"Can I take a look upstairs?"

After a momentary hesitation, Rúnar goes up the stairs ahead of me.

It's as if he does so not because he wants to, but because it's what I want. Passive, not active. But it would probably be unwise to draw too many conclusions from the limited signs of life Rúnar's displaying.

A light is on in the attic. It's a long room, the sloping roof wood-paneled like the loft of an old farmhouse. At one end is a roomy sleeping area with a four-poster bed, and at the other a workspace, with a desk placed under a dormer window. On it stand a computer and a printer, along with piles of papers. Books fill the bookshelves and overflow into stacks on the floor. I see an audio system with CD racks, and atop the CD player an old-fashioned turntable. Vinyl LPs are arranged in an old wooden crate that once contained soda bottles.

This is quite a different world from the glossy rooms downstairs. The lighting is muted, the ambience somehow older, denser.

"I imagine that Skarphédinn made his mark up here?"

"Yes. This is more his style."

"You don't need to stay up here with me. I just want to have a quick look around."

He dithers, but then seems relieved. "All right," he says and sets off down the stairs.

I wait a moment before going over to the desk and starting to examine the papers there. They seem to consist of all sorts of notes for essays or articles. One printout reads:

Children who are constantly bombarded with stimuli from movies, TV, computer games—and, perhaps not least, news of real-life violence in all its forms such as murder, mutilation, rape—will, sooner or later, feel the impact of those stimuli. The form that it takes is a function of genetics and nurture: will the child reject the reality presented in those media or identify with it? Most Icelanders are resistant to the idea of killing another person, and that reflects cultural and educational influences. Here in Iceland, we have no military tradition, no glorification of weapons, such as exists in various forms in many other societies and systematically undermines that instinctive resistance. But even in such societies, only a minority, a tiny minority, lose that resistance. They tend to be the children of uncaring parents, who have grown up without boundaries, discipline, or love. A yet smaller minority, a fraction of a percent, make the conscious decision to do exactly what they want, regardless of their environment, family, or society— regardless of anything but their own desires. Parents and other environmental factors have no influence: only the individual's reasoning.

There's no context. Just some ideas. They could be part of an article for the press, like the ones written by Skarphédinn that I found in the *Morning News* archive. The style is similar, at any rate.

I move the mouse that's lying on the desk by the computer. The screen comes to life:

The Adoption of the Christian Religion in Early Iceland
An essay by Rúnar Valgardsson.

The title is followed by details of Rúnar's class and of his teacher: Kjartan Arnarson. Then the essay begins. I see no reason to read it all, but the style is nothing like the printout I've just read.

The CD rack contains an eclectic range of music, new and old. The vinyl LPs are classic rock of the fifties and sixties. Curious, I push the play button on the CD player and turn down the volume. From the first notes, I instantly recognize the song:

> *Please allow me to introduce myself,*
> *I'm a man of wealth and taste,*

sings Mick Jagger smarmily.

> *I've been around for a long, long year,*
> *Stole many a man's soul and faith.*
> *And I was 'round when Jesus Christ*
> *Had his moment of doubt and pain.*
> *Made damn sure that Pilate*
> *Washed his hands and sealed his fate.*

I glance over the bookshelves. The selection is as catholic as the music. Literary classics, Icelandic and foreign: Jón Trausti, Thorgils Gjallandi, Grímur Thomsen, Jónas Hallgrímsson, Jóhann Sigurjónsson, Halldór Laxness. I notice a number of books about witchcraft, witch hunts, and the occult, including works by an English mystic, Aleister Crowley, who I've read about, and *Malleus Maleficarum* by Heinrich Kramer.

> *Pleased to meet you,*
> *Hope you guess my name.*

But what's puzzling you
Is the nature of the game...

I've never really liked the Stones' *Sympathy For The Devil*. Not until now. I've no idea whether it's been there since Skarphédinn last pushed *Play*, or whether his brother picked it.

Does it mean anything?

"Good song, *Sympathy For the Devil*," I remark, back in the kitchen with Rúnar, who's taking a Coke from the fridge.

"*Sympathy...*?" he repeats, bewildered.

"Oh, I just happened to touch the *Play* button on the CD player. And it was that old Stones song."

He shrugs. "Skarpi must have been listening to it."

In a half-open drawer I notice a cell phone in a tooled brown leather pouch. I've seen it before. Or another one just like it.

"Would you like a Coke?" he asks as he drinks from his bottle and closes the drawer.

"No thanks," I answer. "I'd better be going."

I go into the living room. He follows.

"Is it all right if I smoke?"

"I don't care," says Rúnar.

I stop in front of the TV, which stands on top of a shelf unit holding a digital decoder, a DVD player, and a video recorder. Below them is a row of videocassettes. I light up and bend down to look at the videos. I pick out one I recognize.

"*Street Rider*. I remember this. Your brother played the lead role."

"Yes. He did."

"Skarphédinn seems to have wanted to be the star of the show." I stand up, holding the cassette in my hand. "In all situations?"

For a few seconds Rúnar says nothing. "It wasn't a question of wanting. He simply was. Everyone wanted him to be."

"Yes. A born leader."

"Yes. That's what he was."

"And I suppose he meant to make his mark on public life?"

No reply.

"I gather that your brother's cell phone hasn't turned up. I wonder what can have happened to it?" I ask as I kneel by the TV.

"Skarphédinn didn't have a cell phone."

"Oh, that's right. I heard that somewhere. Hey, can I borrow *Street Rider*? I'd like to take another look at it."

"I don't mind."

"I won't keep it for long."

I head for the door, smoking. "Thanks for letting me drop by."

"I thought you wanted to talk about Skarpi," says Rúnar.

"Yes, I do. Absolutely," I reply. "But I had such a rough night I don't think I can manage it now."

"And it was my fault that they came after you…"

"Not really. They're such a bunch of idiots. Better that they inconvenienced me than you. You must be very busy. Finishing essays, studying for exams?"

"Yes…," replies Rúnar remotely. "But it's hard to focus at present, as things are. At least I've got peace and quiet here."

"Are you interested in social issues and history, like your brother?"

"Yes."

"Following in his footsteps?"

No reply.

"Yes, it was very sad. A tragedy." Kjartan Arnarson is happy to speak to me when I call him that evening. But he speaks gravely.

"After that business of the *Question of the Day*, you told me that Sólrún was upset. But did she seem to be in such a bad way?"

"Not really. Of course I wasn't all that aware of how she was feeling. Not all the time. But I've heard she was deeply affected by Skarphédinn's death."

"I see. Because of his brother, Rúnar."

"No, no. Because of Skarphédinn himself."

"Skarphédinn?"

"Yes, apparently she was hopelessly in love with him."

Now I'm lost. Yet again.

"But weren't she and Rúnar close?"

"They were good friends. I know that. But it was the elder brother she was obsessed with."

"Well, well" is all I can say.

"I gather that, according to Sólrún's friends—those two who were with her that day and probably weren't the best company for a sensitive soul like her—the joke about me was her misguided attempt to attract Skarphédinn's attention. To elicit a public response, make him jealous."

"Well, well," I say again.

"I just don't know," he observes. "It's all quite bizarre. Bizarre and complicated."

Couldn't agree more.

"You teach Rúnar, don't you?"

"Yes. He's in my first-year class."

"Is he like Skarphédinn?"

"Both very bright. But Skarphédinn was totally extroverted, while Rúnar is very introverted. He seems to be terribly oppressed, somehow."

"Maybe because his brother was so successful and popular?"

"Maybe. Or it could be something completely different."

———

After watching *Street Rider* again, back home with my little Polly, I find I've run right out of energy. But my vague impression the first time I watched the movie, that there were more familiar faces in addition to Skarphédinn and Örvar Páll, is confirmed. And so at midnight, I'm still awake. Sólrún Bjarkadóttir is listed in the closing credits as an extra. She has a nonspeaking part among the gaggle of girls who flock around the leading lady, the little princess born with a silver spoon in her mouth, played by Inga Lína, now deceased. Sólrún is slimmer than when I met her, her pretty face open and unformed. In her brief appearances on the screen, she seems to be overacting in a desperate bid for attention. Saying what she shouldn't: *Here I am! Look at me!*

Still wide awake at 1:00 a.m., I reach for my tattered copy of *Loftur the Sorcerer* on the bedside table. I start on the third act and come across a sentence spoken by Loftur. I've seen it before, in Sólrún's obituary:

Knowledge and innocence cannot be reconciled.

24 MONDAY

Ingibjörg Sigurlína Adalgeirsdóttir.

Last night I made a note of the full name of Inga Lína, the leading lady of *Street Rider*. Like Sólrún Bjarkadóttir the extra, Inga Lína has made her final exit. Both girls have moved on to another stage, where every actor is equal, and there are no stars and no extras.

I go back six years in the *Morning News* online archive and enter her name. There are three obituaries published when Ingibjörg Sigurlína died and favorable comments in a review of the movie: "The young novice actors in the leading roles, Skarphédinn Valgardsson and Ingibjörg Sigurlína Adalgeirsdóttir, play their parts convincingly. Their enthusiasm makes up for their lack of experience," writes the critic. "These young people show great promise."

Less than a year after the review was published, Inga Lína was dead. The obituaries are of the usual kind: a bubbly, sociable girl, with many talents and a promising future. "But the race is not always to the swift, nor the battle to the strong," writes one biblically minded obituarist. "Inga Lína lost her way in the jungle that modern life has become for so many, young and old…"

I don't recognize any of the names of those who have written about her. Nor her parents' names. She appears to have been an only child. In the phone book, I look up her father, who is listed as a master housepainter, with both landline and cell phone numbers.

"Adalgeir's Painters," is the answer on the cell phone against a hubbub of voices and workplace noise in the background.

I introduce myself and explain that I'm calling about his late daughter.

He's taken aback. "Inga Lína? Why on earth? It's been six years since she died!"

"I know," I reply. "But two more young people, who were also in *Street Rider*, have just recently died." The background noise grows fainter. He's moved to a more private location.

"Two? I read about Skarphédinn. But who was the other one?"

"A girl who had a walk-on part. Sólrún Bjarkadóttir."

He says nothing, then repeats: "Sólrún Bjarkadóttir? I don't know anything…"

I wait.

"Unless that was the name of the girl who…"

He stops.

"The girl who…?"

"The other girl who fell for that boy, Skarphédinn. I think she and Inga Lína got into some kind of spat over him."

"So were Skarphédinn and your daughter a couple?"

"A couple? That's hardly the word I'd use for kids embarking on their first relationship. But I must say my daughter was very badly affected by the whole experience."

"You mean being in the movie and becoming a star?"

"That was part of it. All the attention. And then she was broken-hearted about that boy, when it was all over and the kids went their separate ways. She was a sensitive girl. She didn't seem to see that life goes on when a certain period, or experience, is over. But..."

I wait.

"But the worst of it was that the kids started messing around with drugs. That sealed Inga Lína's fate. After that, it was as if there was no going back. But she was never able to tell her mother and me everything. She was secretive."

"Teenagers tend to be secretive, at least to their parents. They want to keep their own business to themselves, have some privacy. Surely that's just part of growing up and demanding more independence. Part of trying to grow up?"

"Of course. I remember it well enough from when I was in my teens. But somehow you forget all that when you're a parent yourself and trying to live up to the responsibilities. You tend to lose your memory, and empathy, about adolescent mood swings."

"Was Inga Lína depressed?"

"She never was before that. But with the dope, she got into bad company, and she just lost all hope. She tried to get off the drugs. She went into rehab programs several times. But she never stayed. She would run away almost as soon as she got there. Her mom and I tried everything..."

It's obviously hard for him to go on.

"Was her death an accident or..."

"She overdosed on that filth...I don't know, we'll never know. Was it accidental? Or the ultimate act of desperation and despair? That's never been clearly determined. And I think that's part of what eroded our marriage away from the inside, until there was nothing left but an empty shell."

"So you and your wife are divorced?"

"Three years after we lost her. It was the only way. And now, when I'm just beginning to regain my balance, a reporter calls, opening up old wounds."

He doesn't sound angry, just surprised by the unexpected course of events.

"I'm really not looking to open old wounds. But it's certainly odd that these three young people, who spent time together all those years ago, are now all dead."

For a little while he says nothing.

"Yes, it is odd. But I hope you're not going to bring up my family's tragedy in your paper."

"Only if it proves to be unavoidable, in connection with the two recent deaths."

After giving him my usual assurances about handling information with all possible discretion, I thank Ingibjörg Sigurlína Adalgeirsdóttir's father and say good-bye. And as I put the phone down, I realize how grateful I am not to be in his place.

"This is Mördur. Leave a message."

It's the same abrupt instruction as before on Mördur's phone. Maybe he doesn't use the phone much. Or perhaps he screens incoming calls. Or both.

I put my feet up on my desk, grab the phone again, and call Hotel Reydargerdi. Óskar answers.

"Yeah, Mördur was here at lunchtime for a meal. He'd just driven back from Reykjavík."

"Is he there now?"

"No, no. He went on home after he'd eaten."

I check the time. With a bit of luck and effort, I can get to Reydargerdi by five.

In reception Karólína is working, singing away in her sawlike hum. She doesn't look up when I get myself a coffee for the road. Jóa's with Ásbjörn in his office, planning sales strategy for the region. When I catch sight of Jóa, I suddenly remember I've still got to do the *Question of the Day* and send it off for the Tuesday edition. A few minutes later, Jóa and I are on Town Hall Square, and I induce five passers-by to answer the important question: *Do you play the lottery?*

On my way out, having sent in the answers, I meet young Björg and Pal on their way in. Pal and Karó have a heartwarming reunion, and Björg and Karó share an affectionate hug. It looks very much as if everyone is living happily ever after. Like the end of a Disney movie.

I shake Björg's hand. After a friendly greeting, I have a sudden inspiration and go back into my little closet. I open the obituaries about Sólrún Bjarkadóttir on the *Morning News* archive, and find her parents' names. Sólrún was from Reykjavík. I look up her parents in the Reykjavík phone book. Then I have a discreet word with Björg.

After driving through Reydargerdi and getting directions from Óskar at the hotel I find Mördur's house easily enough. At the eastern end of the village, it stands apart, surrounded by neglected grass. The once-white concrete walls are scarred with weather damage. Rusty relics of old farm equipment, hubcaps, and moth-eaten steel barrels are dotted around on the grass. In front of the house is a gleaming silver-gray Mercedes-Benz, a sign of the boom times. I park my heap of rust next to it, as a reminder that *sic transit gloria mundi.*

I approach the house, which is on two floors. The basement looks uninhabitable and seems to serve for storage. The concrete steps leading up to the front door are crumbling under the assault of wind and weather, although today there is a definite hint of spring in the air.

Where there should be a doorbell, a couple of wires stick pointlessly out of the wall. I knock at the door.

A young man answers. I've seen him before. He was sitting at the table with Agnar Hansen the first time I met him, at Reydin, and stood up and left when I addressed Agnar. And I saw him in the hotel bar when I was in Reydargerdi for the public meeting. If I hadn't seen him twice in succession like that, I doubt if I'd have remembered him. In brown corduroy pants and a blue shirt, Mördur looks quite ordinary. Average height, average build, clean-shaven, short hair. His features are regular, unremarkable, like a child's drawing of a face. Gold-rimmed round glasses give him a surprised look.

"Sorry to disturb you," I say. "My name's Einar. I'm with the *Afternoon News*."

He nods. "I know who you are."

"I'd like to talk to you about your friend Skarphédinn. I'm researching a piece about him."

He glances around. "You haven't brought a photographer? I don't want any pictures."

"No, I don't need a photo. Just information."

He doesn't smile. He doesn't frown. The bland non-responsiveness reminds me of a politician or a faceless bureaucrat.

"What would you like to know?"

"To start with—how long had you known each other?"

"We met about six years ago."

"In Akureyri?"

"No, Reykjavík."

He doesn't seem to be thinking of inviting me in. I try to peer past him, but all I can see is the grubby wall of the hallway.

"That must have been at the time when Skarphédinn was down south, acting in *Street Rider*?"

"That's about right."

"Were you involved in the movie?"

"No, not at all. We just got to know each other around town, as you do."

"So you're from Reykjavík, are you?" I ask.

"Yes."

"And how did you come to become such close friends?"

"We just hit it off."

"So did you have the same interests?"

"The same philosophy, mainly."

"And what was Skarphédinn's philosophy? It could hardly have been fully formed at that age. You two were only fourteen or fifteen back then."

He stares at me. His eyes behind the lenses are green.

"It doesn't matter how old you are when you discover the simple truth that life is to be enjoyed."

I stare back at him. Neither of us speaks. I sense a hidden antipathy behind his surprised expression.

"So that was the secret of your philosophy, and Skarphédinn's? That life is to be enjoyed?"

A twitch at the corner of his mouth. "Deep, no?"

"Possibly deeper than it seems."

He shrugs.

"When did you move up north?"

"Three years ago."

"To be near your friend?"

"If you like. But you said you were looking for information about him. Not me."

"Can't have one without the other. I gather you were his best, his closest friend."

"From my point of view, he was my best, my closest friend."

"So were you at high school together?"

"I started there. But then I left and enrolled as an extramural student."

"Like a true friend, I suppose Skarphédinn helped you with your studies?"

"Absolutely."

"I understand that he was helpful to others too."

"I'm sure. Skarphédinn was generous, happy to share his abilities and his feelings."

I don't seem to be getting very far here. "Generous, you say. And you lent him your apartment in Akureyri when you moved out here, into the country?"

"Yes, I was happy to."

"That's a very nice place you have in Akureyri. And you've bought this house too," I remark, molding my face into a naive smile. "I only wish I had your talent with money!"

"I bought at a good time. I picked up both places dirt cheap, really."

"And times have certainly changed. The property market's booming. The value of your properties must have shot up!"

"It's quiet and peaceful here. For studying and writing."

I keep up the innocent look. "Are you writing something not related to your studies? A book, maybe?"

"Whether, and what, I'm writing is my business."

"Well." I'm starting to feel a bit ridiculous, standing there on the doorstep. "Is it true that Skarphédinn was one of the few people of your generation who didn't carry a cell phone?"

"He didn't want one."

"Yes, I know. But I saw him with one all the same."

"I wouldn't know."

He stands at the door, arms akimbo, steady as a rock.

I clear my throat, trying to think of some strategy.

Then I plunge straight in: "What do you think happened to him?"

Mördur appears, at last, to be thrown by my question.

"I can't answer that."

"The police must have spoken to you?"

"I went in and made a brief statement. I couldn't help them, really. I was in Reykjavík over Easter."

"Not on Easter Monday, you weren't. You were at the public meeting, here at the hotel."

"I left on Wednesday and got back here on the evening of Easter Sunday."

"Do you go down to Reykjavík a lot?"

"Now and then. My mother lives there. She's in poor health."

"So you've no idea who killed your friend?"

There's a glint of something in the green eyes.

"Ideas aren't evidence. Not until there's something solid to go on. There's no point is guesswork. A jealous husband? Who knows?"

"A jealous husband? Now there's an idea. Skarphédinn was apparently quite the lady's man, if you'll pardon the politically incorrect language."

He's still standing there with hands on hips, silent.

I bait my hook. "He played the field, didn't he? Had more than one woman at the same time?"

Another little twitch of the mouth. But he says nothing.

I plunge in. "Was he sleeping with the woman on the floor below your apartment in Akureyri?"

"I've got nothing more to say about it. Except that Skarphédinn didn't see human relationships as commitments. In his view, people had relationships if they wanted to, and they were responsible for that desire."

"Are you talking about sex?"

"That's one aspect of human relationships, isn't it?"

"What about love?"

"Love is a blood tie. It applies only to family. Apart from the relationship between parent and child, love is nothing more than a pretense."

"So you and Skarphédinn were in agreement, philosophically?"

"Mördur," says a voice from indoors. "Shut the door, it's cold."

Mördur glances back over his shoulder. A young girl wearing only a towel appears in the hall. Startled to see a stranger on the doorstep, she retreats in confusion. But not before I've identified the face: it's one of the girls who was with Sólrún Bjarkadóttir that day on the square.

Unperturbed, Mördur turns without a word and goes inside, shutting the door behind him.

It's nearly ten in the evening by the time I get back home to Polly. She's thrilled to see me, which is cheering, as I'm feeling disgruntled after going such a long way for so little.

That's what I like to see in a roommate. Welcoming me home, however useless I may be.

Or am I? There's something to it. Some damn thing to it.

I'm considering whether I should try to reach Ólafur Gísli, maybe share some of this stuff with him. But I don't think I've got much for him.

I call Gunnsa to see how she's doing. She's studying hard.

Next I call Björg. I can only hope that my plan has worked out. She said I should call her at home at ten thirty. I do so, on the dot.

"It worked," she says.

"Who did you talk to?"

"Sólrún's mom."

"What did you tell her?"

"That I was a friend of hers from high school…"

"Not an absolutely black lie," I say.

"A white one, anyway."

"You knew each other."

"Yeah. Sort of. As you asked, I told her that a mutual friend of Sólrún's and mine, Rúnar, was searching for his brother Skarphéðinn's phone. I said it would be helpful if we had his number, but Rúnar had lost it."

"And?"

"She said she knew nothing about it. Then I asked if she had Sólrún's cell phone. And she did. It had been sent to her with the rest of Sólrún's things."

"And?" I ask with rising excitement.

"She looked up the *Contacts* on Sólrún's phone, and there it was."

"Great!" I exclaim.

She recites to me the number I've been trying to find for so long, then says: "I felt kind of guilty after I talked to her. Sólrún's mom started to cry. She said that if Sólrún hadn't gone chasing that boy up north, she'd still be alive."

"*That boy?*"

"Yes."

"Who did she mean? Skarphédinn or Rúnar?"

She thought about it for a little while. "I think she must have meant Skarphédinn. She was talking about some movie they were both in—Sólrún and someone she called *that boy*. After that her daughter was never the same again, she said."

"Did she explain what she meant?"

"No. And I couldn't ask. Just couldn't. I was feeling so guilty about tricking her."

"Don't go feeling guilty about that. What you did will probably be crucial to revealing the truth about their deaths."

"I certainly hope so," sighs Björg.

"Have you ever thought of being a journalist when you're grown up? Even more grown up, I mean."

She laughs. "Well, as I've recently found out, it could be in my genes, right?"

I don't play the lottery. That would have been my answer to the *Question of the Day*. Short and clear. Whatever my sins, I don't gamble. But the old saw is probably true: *Nothing ventured, nothing gained*. My bright idea was that a dead person might be the only one not trying to conceal that fact that Skarphédinn had a cell phone. Sólrún has nothing to hide anymore. But what is everybody hiding? And why?

I've calmed down again, after the excitement of our little ruse. I look at the number I have finally managed to get hold of. Then

I have a cigarette. And give Polly her bath in the washbasin. And have a shower myself. These small, erotic moments are truly the spice of life.

Around midnight I'm sitting on the sofa in the living room, dressed for bed and deep in thought. I'm wondering whether I should go to bed and finally get a good night's sleep after reading a few pages of *Loftur the Sorcerer*, or...

Nothing ventured, nothing gained?

I pick up my phone and punch in the number.

It rings.

And rings.

And goes on ringing for a long time.

I'm about to ring off when I hear a click: "Hello?"

The voice resonates with tension and pain.

"Hello?" again.

"Rúnar," I say. "It's Einar."

"Yeah," he murmurs. "I recognized your number. That's why I answered."

"Is something wrong? Where are you?" I ask.

"At the apartment."

"Skarphédinn's apartment?"

"Yeah."

"Answering a phone he didn't have?" I sarcastically remark.

Silence.

"Rúnar?"

A strange buzzing noise breaks the silence.

"Rúnar!"

The buzz continues, with rhythmic interruptions.

I realize it's a doorbell buzzing.

"Rúnar! What's happening?"

"I've got to get out of here... They're—"

"Hello! Rúnar!"

The call is cut off.

I redial.

And again.

And one more time.

Then I start over. Now I ring Rúnar's own phone, again and again. Nothing.

The phone may be switched off or out of range, or all channels may be busy. Please try later.

25 TUESDAY/WEDNESDAY

Three possibilities:

Phone switched off. Out of range. All channels busy.

That's no answer.

If the phone's been switched off: Why?

If it's suddenly out of range: Why?

And how could all the channels be busy at this time of night?

Do they call this a phone service?

After contemplating these questions for some time without finding any answers, I decide it's time to stop entertaining myself with my own dumb thoughts.

I've been pacing and smoking and calling every five minutes. But now I've got to do something sensible. Take action.

As in the case of the phone company, there are three possibilities: Call the police. Call the parents. Go there myself.

Press one for police. Press two for parents. Press three for trouble.

I choose the third option. Of course.

I check all my windows before I leave. Twice. They're all shut. I leave lights on in every room. Finally I check that Polly is asleep. She is.

As I start the car, I think yet again how nice it would be to be an innocent little parrot. Or an unblemished babe at rest in its mother's arms.

Too late. Too late.

As things are, a gun in my pocket would probably make me feel safer.

At one o'clock on a Tuesday morning, the streets of Akureyri are all but deserted. As I turn onto Hólabraut, a black cat suddenly materializes in my headlights. I slam on the brakes and pull over a few houses down from Skarphédinn's place, formerly Mördur's place, now Rúnar's. I suppress my superstitious thoughts about black felines and bad luck and take a look at the building. The lower two floors are dark, but a faint glow is visible at the third-floor windows.

There's no sign of the black Honda, and nobody seems to be lurking around.

I get out of the car, approach the building, and ring the third-floor doorbell. Press it again and again. No response. I go crazy, leaning on the bell. Still nothing. I wonder if I should ring the doorbells on the lower floors, but can't face the hassle.

Now what?

I go back to the car and call information. I get the address of Rúnar Valgardsson's parents. They live in the Hlídar district. Like me. I open the glove compartment, dig out my map of the town, and find their address.

Kristín Rúnarsdóttir and Valgardur Skarphédinsson live on the fourth floor of a modern apartment block. I summon up courage and ring the doorbell.

I don't have to wait long before I hear a woman's shrill voice on the entry phone:

"Rúnar?"

"No, my name's Einar. I'm a journalist with the *Afternoon News*. Sorry to disturb you at this hour. But I spoke to Rúnar earlier, and he seemed to be in some kind of trouble. And now I can't find him."

A gasp. "What? Isn't he at Skarphédinn's place?"

"He was there. But now he's not answering the phone or the door."

Silence.

"Can I come in?"

"Yes, come on up." She buzzes me in, and I walk upstairs. On the fourth-floor landing, one of the two apartment doors stands ajar. I knock quietly at the doorframe.

Kristín comes toward me, wearing a gray toweling robe over a pink nightgown. The oval face, which at her son's funeral was thickly plastered with makeup, is deathly pale and finely wrinkled. Below her brown eyes are dark smudges. Her graying hair is permed into a rigid helmet.

"I hope I didn't wake you," I say.

"I haven't been home long," the woman replies. "I work shifts at the hospital."

She walks ahead of me into the kitchen, to the right of the front door. Beyond it is a dining room with a black wooden table and chairs, and on the other side a living room with big, heavy furniture upholstered in dark red. It's crammed with porcelain and knickknacks. To the left is a passage with three closed doors and an open door to the bathroom, which is tiled in green. The whole apartment seems to be painted the same muted shade.

Kristín switches a kettle on. "Would you like some tea?"

She doesn't seem at all disconcerted by my turning up here in the middle of the night.

But people's reactions to the unexpected can be unexpected too.

I sit down on a wooden stool by the small plastic-covered kitchen table. "If you're having one."

She takes two cups from the dish rack.

"Were you expecting Rúnar here tonight? Since you thought it was him at the door?"

"I wasn't sure," she replies. "But I was hoping he'd come."

"Have you heard from him in the past few hours?"

"You just don't know what your kids are getting up to when they reach his age," she says, as if she hasn't noticed my question. "I suppose you have to be grateful if they stay in touch."

I think of Gunnsa and count my blessings yet again.

"I'm sure you're right. Skarphédinn had moved out long ago, hadn't he? First into the student dorm, then to his friend Mördur's place. You and your husband must have been upset when he flew the nest?"

"There are so many things we have to deal with in life," she says, her back still toward me. She places tea bags in the cups and rests her hand on the kettle, as if it will boil faster like that.

"Skarphédinn seems to have been a remarkably independent young man, according to what I've been told."

"Yes, he changed when he became a teenager."

"Was that when he went down south to be in the movie?"

"It was then, yes," she slowly replies.

I say nothing.

"But," she adds, turning toward me and leaning against the table, "he's not my concern now. Rúnar is."

"Of course," I mumble. She has a strange way of putting it.

Her expression is severe, almost harsh, as she stands with her arms crossed, glaring at me.

"Why are you here?" she asks.

"Because I think there are some nasty characters out there who are out to get Rúnar."

"And what do you think that has to do with you?"

I'm floored by her question. "Well, there's the fact that they busted into my home on the night before last and raised hell. They said it was because they couldn't find Rúnar."

The kettle's boiling. She turns away and pours water into the cups.

"Milk and sugar?"

"Just sugar, please, if you've got it."

Kristín pushes the sugar bowl and spoon toward me and places the cups on the table. I notice that her fingernails are bitten to the quick. She takes a teaspoon and prods the tea bag with it for a long, long time.

"Why were they after you?"

"I don't really know," I tell her as I stir the sugar into my tea. "They're nuts. High most of the time. And they can be dangerous."

"They came here that night, looking for Rúnar. What did they want with him?"

"I can't answer that. You'll have to ask him. Or them."

"Is it anything to do with his brother?"

"I'm not sure. It may be."

She gazes into space.

"Have they been here tonight?"

"I only just got home. My husband doesn't answer the door."

Silence reigns for a while at the kitchen table. We sip our tea, which has a refreshing lemon flavor.

I break the silence. "What does your husband do?"

She looks up from her teacup. "He's disabled. An invalid."

"So you care for the sick at work, then come home and do more of the same?"

No comment.

"What did he do before he was ill?"

"He was a pharmacist."

"And you're a nursing graduate. Did you meet at college?"

She lifts her cup as if in confirmation and takes a sip.

I've had enough of this stalling. "Where do you think Rúnar could be?"

"Couldn't he be at the apartment?"

"That's possible. But he's not answering the phone or the door."

"Could be asleep."

"I don't think that's likely. He sounded pretty upset when I spoke to him less than an hour ago."

"I have the feeling," she says after a brief pause for thought, "that Rúnar's all right." She goes on: "We reap what we sow."

"Was that true of his brother?"

She says nothing. But an undefined tension is added to her obdurate expression.

"Shouldn't we contact the police?" I ask. Down the corridor, I hear a door opening.

"This is none of your business. You ought to go home and get some sleep. Me too. My days are long and my nights short."

She stands up.

I do the same.

"Thank you for your concern about my boy," she says hastily as she sees me to the door.

On the way out we run into her husband, Valgardur Skarp-hédinsson. Blue-striped pajamas flap on his wasted frame like laundry on a clothesline. His thick hair is sticking out in all directions and his unshaven face bristles darkly. Lethargically he walks toward us. His bony face is expressionless, lifeless. The eyes, concealed by dark glasses at his son's funeral, are blue, dead. It's as if he doesn't see us.

As his wife propels me out of the door, I hear her say: "Valli, dear, you should be in bed."

After my rather unsettling encounter with Skarphédinn and Rúnar's parents, I have a better idea of why the two brothers wanted to move out as soon as they could. Not a happy home. By three thirty I've driven around most of Akureyri, calling both cell phone numbers every fifteen minutes. I decide to call it a night and head home. When I get there, everything seems fine. Before going indoors, I make a final attempt.

Skarphédinn's phone is answered.

"Einar?" asks a strangled voice I recognize as Rúnar's.

"Where are you?" I ask.

A pause. "At the dump," he murmurs.

"You mean the junkyard?"

No answer.

"What are you doing out there?"

"I knew they'd never find me here."

"Wait there. Don't move. I'm on my way right now."

And with that, my phone is off, out of range, or all channels busy.

———

The night is cold and bleak as I step out of my car in front of the padlocked gate of the junkyard. With the engine running, I flash the headlights three times, then walk to the gate. Almost at once a hunched figure looms out of the darkness, wearing blue jeans and a leather bomber jacket. Rúnar stands for a moment silent and motionless in front of the gate, then swings himself up and climbs nimbly over. He's shaking like a leaf, either from the cold or sheer terror.

"You could have found a less extreme hiding place," I remark as I sling an arm over his shoulders and steer him toward the car. He obediently goes with me like a well-brought-up little boy. Back in the car, I light up.

"I wanted…," says Rúnar.

"What?" I ask, rolling down the window and blowing my smoke out.

"If they…if they found me and killed me…" He falls silent.

"Are you trying to say that, if that were to happen, you wanted to die here, in the same place as your brother?"

Rúnar nods, gazing straight ahead at the mountains of rusty iron, garbage, and tires.

I drive off.

"What happened after I spoke to you earlier?"

"They'd been coming over all evening, again and again, calling and ringing the doorbell…"

"You mean Agnar and his thugs from Reydargerdi?"

"Yeah. I wouldn't let them in. I threatened to tell the police…"

"And?"

"They said I could try that, if I dared."

"Why didn't you?"

He hesitates. "I have my reasons."

"That you're not going to tell me?"

Silence.

"OK. Then what?"

"I knew they'd just hang around outside until I came out. I'd have to go out sometime…so I called Ösp downstairs on her cell and woke her up. I went downstairs and she let me into their apartment, and I climbed down into the back garden from her bedroom window."

"There was no one there when I arrived about one o'clock," I say.

"Yeah, I asked Ösp to wait for fifteen minutes after I left and then wake her dad up and tell him there were some suspicious people lurking around outside." A faint smile lights up the handsome face. "I called her afterward, and she said her dad woke up with a shock and went ballistic. He ran downstairs and gave them a good yelling at. She said they didn't stick around."

"So you walked all the way out here to the dump, did you?"

"I flagged down a taxi and it took me out to the Glerá bridge. Walked from there."

"Why didn't you go to your parents' place instead?"

Rúnar gives me a grave look. "Not possible."

"You don't want to add to their troubles?"

He looks away.

"Rúnar, what do those guys want?"

No answer.

"Why are they after you?"

Still no answer.

"They told me they were going to make you pay for ratting them out to the cops."

Rúnar shrugs.

"That's not why, is it?"

No response.

"Because you didn't rat them out. Someone else did. You weren't at the party. Not officially, anyway. Didn't you want to be questioned like the rest of them?"

He shrugs again.

I park the car outside my place and Polly's and turn to face him. "They're after you because they want Skarphédinn's phone."

No question mark at the end of that. But he answers with a muted, "Yes."

"Why don't you just hand it over to them?"

After a brief pause, he says: "It's not their phone. It's mine."

"So was it your phone all along? Or do you mean it's yours now, since Skarphédinn died?"

"Both."

"How's that?"

He looks around. "Where are we?"

"This is where I live. Me and my life partner."

He seems bewildered.

"Don't worry, they won't come here," I reassure him. "Not for now, anyway."

It's daylight by the time I can induce Rúnar to lie down in the middle bedroom and try to get some sleep. I ordered a pizza and tried to talk to him. Tried to get him to say more. But he always jumped up again immediately and started prowling around like a caged animal. I tried to persuade him to call his mother to let her know he was all right, but he said he didn't want to disturb her—she needed her sleep. I somehow doubt that she's sleeping, all things considered. Speaking for myself, I can't get a wink of sleep if I think Gunnsa may be in trouble. But what do I know about other parents?

It's nearly nine o'clock in the morning. I'm overwhelmed with exhaustion and nerves—much like my overnight guest. But I've forced myself to stay awake for three-quarters of an hour until I'm sure he's asleep. I sneak up to the door of his room and listen. Hearing slow, regular breaths, I cautiously open the door. Rúnar is lying curled up under the quilt, fast asleep.

His bare left arm lies on top of the covers. It's crisscrossed with cuts and scars, which look recent. I've read that self-mutilation is a growing phenomenon among young people. I can't begin to understand the pain that drives them to it.

Rúnar's jeans lie draped on a chair, and the leather jacket is slung over the back. I grope in the pockets with both hands, looking for the phone. I find one in each. I slip quietly out of the room and close the door behind me.

Back in the living room I sit on the sofa, examining the two phones. One is in the tooled leather pouch I saw Skarphédinn using that day at Hólar. The other is in a plain black cover. I put the plain one down on the table and check out the *Contacts* list in the other. There are names like *Mom, Sólrún, Skarpi, Einar journo. That's odd*, I think. *Why would Skarphédinn list his own Top Secret phone number?* And I never gave him my number.

I pick up the other phone. I realize that Rúnar has been more devious than he seems. He's switched covers.

If someone got hold of the tooled leather case, they'd have the wrong phone.

I turn to the other phone, in the plain case. There is no *Contacts* list. The *Call registers* have been deleted. I check the *Messages*. Same story. Everything's been deleted.

So what's all the fuss about? What's the big secret about this phone? What is so important that a crazed gang of idiotic thugs are chasing around looking for it and threatening all and sundry?

My mind's buzzing but getting nowhere. There's a wall of exhaustion between me and my objective. I get up, go into the kitchen, and make coffee. Then I light up and return to the sofa. I'm no expert on cell phones. It's my own stupid fault. Goddamned stick-in-the-mud. *Think clearly*, I say to myself. *Think clearly*. But my mind doesn't obey.

I start fiddling with the buttons. OK. *Messages*. Nothing. *Call register*. Nothing. *Profiles*. What the hell is that? I press some more buttons and find *Conference call*; something called *Outdoor*; something called *General* and *Silent*. Nothing. *Settings* leads me to *Alarm, Time settings, Call settings, Lock keypad, Ringtone settings, Security*. I try them all. Nothing. *Games*. I can select a game, *Game services* and *Game settings*. All these damn settings. But they're not the right settings. They're just unsettling.

Calculator. I can add and subtract, multiply and divide, convert currency and God knows what. Thank you very much. Then I hit the jackpot: *Calendar*.

Or what?

There are entries for every day, for months back in time. The most recent was entered on the day of Skarphédinn's death. But each entry is an incomprehensible string of letters and numbers.

I give up. I'm running on empty.

I've got to sleep. Recharge my batteries.

Before going to bed I call in sick, then sneak back into Rúnar's room and replace the phones in his pockets. But not until I've removed Skarphédinn's SIM card from the phone and place it under my pillow. I'm instantly asleep.

I wake up to the angry shrieks of my roommate, who is understandably upset that room service is hours late. It's past four in the afternoon. I jump out of bed to see to Polly. Under this roof, the campaign for equal rights has not progressed further than the good old rule of *Ladies First.* Although I've only had six hours' sleep, I feel rested and refreshed.

Rúnar is gone. On the dining room table is a note: *Thanks for your help.*

After a strong coffee, accompanied by a chewy old pastry with hardened icing I found at the back of the fridge, I'm ready for anything.

Or I think I am.

I get my cell phone, remove the SIM card, and replace it with Skarphédinn's.

The strings of letters and numbers in the *Calendar* remain as impenetrable as ever. I can't make head or tail of them. Frustrated, I sling the phone down on the table, open the garden door, and have a cigarette. Then I close the door again, return to my room, and open Polly's cage. Enjoying her freedom, she flies into the living room and perches on the curtain rail. Standing in the middle of the room, I look around me at the bookcase, CD racks, and TV. I'm so absorbed in my thoughts that nothing makes an impression. Short-term memory is slugging it out with long-term memory. Somewhere at the intersection, a vague idea is emerging.

I slump onto the sofa and light up another cigarette. I pick up the remote and check what's on TV. Nothing.

And there's the answer. Staring me in the face. The *Street Rider* cover is on top of the TV.

I press *Play,* then fast-forward to the scene that introduces the secret code used by the teen gang, led by motorcycle antihero Skarphédinn Valgardsson. Of course that was before the days of cell phones, at a time when the words *code* and *encryption* were mostly identified with international espionage. In the movie, the kids exchange written notes containing coded messages. I remember secret codes like that in children's books I read as a kid. In *Street Rider*, the kids use a simple substitution code: letters for numbers, numbers for letters. A becomes 1, B is 2, C is 3, D is 4, and so on. For numbers, the process is reversed.

Well, well, I think to myself. I'm rather pleased with myself—even though codes don't come much simpler.

I pick up the phone and pen and paper. I trace my way back, day by day, decrypting letter by letter by letter, digit by digit by digit, back for weeks and months in the cell phone record of the life of Skarphédinn Valgardsson.

Just before midnight, I call a halt.

I decide to do a spot check on my decryption method. I pick a series of digits that looks like a cell phone number. On the landline, I dial the number.

"What?" answers a grumpy voice, rudely awakened. It's Ásgeir Eyvindarson of Yumm.

I hang up.

26 WEDNESDAY

MURDER SOLVED BY THE VICTIM

A text message sent by an eight-year-old Belgian girl just before she was murdered led to the apprehension of her killer. The girl's father, who was traveling at the time of his daughter's death, did not see the message until the following day. The girl had written that her father's girlfriend was trying to kill her. The father immediately contacted the police, who arrested the perpetrator.

Wow, that was an easy case for the police, I think as I read the article in the paper. It's all in the cells, as Gunnhildur said. But my case isn't quite so straightforward. There are too many possibilities—not least in view of the affection and respect Skarphédinn apparently enjoyed. A jealous husband from downstairs? A young high school girl in love, spurned and out for revenge? A respected businessman who wanted to cut loose from the encumbrances of personal life and then conceal the evidence? Addled debt-collectors? Desperate stoners?

I'm spoilt for choice.

With the idea of clarifying the picture a little, I call a DJ on Akureyri local radio. I tell him I heard his show on the Saturday before Palm Sunday, when he played a request, *Season of the Witch*, for Skarphédinn and the other kids in the Akureyri High School Drama Group.

"Yeah?" he asks.

"I was wondering if you could tell me who sent in the request for the song? Whether you have a computer record or anything?"

"No need for a computer," he replies. "If the boy hadn't disappeared a few days later and then turned up dead, I'm sure I'd have forgotten it by now. But I remember."

"And?"

"It was some guy who rang up. Said his name was Mördur."

Oh, yes. Indeed.

I'm rudely awakened from my thoughts by Ásbjörn barging into my closet. He's been cheerful for the past few days, and this has been manifested mainly in the form of excruciating comic stories and appalling jokes. The only thing to do is the smiley face: force the corners of my mouth upward and share his happiness.

"Einar," he eagerly asks, "have you heard the one about the pastor baptizing the child?"

Ugh, I think. *Please, no*. "No, Ásbjörn, I'm sure I haven't heard it. Why do you suppose that might be?"

"Because I haven't told it to you, of course!"

"And now you're going to?"

"Absolutely! Right now," he replies, glowing with pleasure. "There was a pastor who was asked to baptize a little boy. He was a little older than the usual age, about three years old. The boy was quite calm throughout the ceremony, not crying and wailing like infants often are when they're baptized. The pastor was pleased, and he suggested that perhaps it would be a good idea not to baptize children until they were old enough to understand. Then the pastor poured the baptismal water on the child. The boy glared at the pastor and said: *Why did you splash me, asshole? Ha-hahahaha!*"

Ásbjörn watches for my reaction.

"Haha," is all I can manage. "Odd that I've never heard that one before. It's such a funny story."

"I got it from Ólafur Gísli. He knows hundreds of hilarious stories like that."

"Hilarious," I say, gravely. "It's wonderful that the two of you are upholding the old tradition of comic storytelling."

Ásbjörn's happy expression gives way to a more anxious look. "But there's one thing we've got to deal with, Einar."

"Only one?"

"There have been much fewer news articles and features from Akureyri in the paper recently."

"I do the *Question of the Day* every week," I counter.

He doesn't allow me to distract him. "It's really nothing to do with me, except that it gradually has an impact on sales. Retail sales are down."

"You know I've been focusing on these big cases. They're going to sell loads of papers when the time comes."

"When the time comes. That's the thing. I gather from Ólafur Gísli that the case is going nowhere at present."

"You know, I disagree. I think the case is going to be solved before long."

"Have you got something new?"

"Not quite yet. But soon. Hopefully."

Ásbjörn shuffles uncertainly.

"You must be sure to let Ólafur Gísli know about anything important. That's what we agreed, isn't it?"

I nod.

"But since you're tied up on that case, and Jóa's helping out in the office, I've written a few news items."

He hands me three pages of printout: reports on road-building, a twin-town event, and a prediction that numbers of tourists in north Iceland will be up this summer.

"Great," I say. "That'll solve the sales problem for now."

"But you'll have to use your byline. Trausti will never agree to let me send in any news from here."

Well, that's the end of my professional reputation and prospects, then.

And now it's time for action.

Unlike the little Belgian girl, Skarphédinn didn't identify his killer on his cell phone. Nor did he leave a detailed record of his last minutes on earth. But he wrote plenty of clues. All I need is some more information for the clues to be transformed into evidence. And the source of that information is a young man who is teetering on the brink of desperation.

"You stole my SIM card."

Rúnar sits facing me in Mördur Njálsson's elegant living room. I'm soaking wet, having been caught in a typical northern wind-whipped rainstorm. The downpour is battering at the windows, drumming on the roof, in a heavy rhythmic riff to accompany this painful conversation. It's good for the vegetation, anyway.

"It wasn't your SIM card, it was Skarphédinn's."

He gazes down at his hands.

"Why did he get you to buy a cell phone and SIM card for him?"

No reply.

"Because," I answer my own question, "he was covering his tracks. He used the cell phone to keep his records. He wanted to be sure there was nothing to connect it to him. So he made you an accessory."

Rúnar looks up.

"The phone isn't only his 'little black book' of all his sexual conquests and that kind of thing. It's really quite a dangerous collection of information. For some people, anyway."

The recalcitrant expression vanishes to be replaced by astonishment.

"How do you know?"

"I managed to break the code."

"How? I didn't get anywhere with it. It's just strings of letters and numbers."

"The solution was in an old teen movie."

He stares at me.

"The teen movie you lent me."

"*Street Rider*? How on earth? I haven't seen it since I was a kid."

I explain to him how his brother used the code to encrypt information about his extensive dealings in legal and illegal drugs.

"Rúnar," I say. I'm being as friendly and unthreatening as I know how.

He's shaking from head to foot.

"Rúnar, it's over."

He shakes his head.

"This is a good thing for you," I go on. "You can relax now. Those sharks who've been after you for the phone will have other things on their minds. And they were just minnows playing at being sharks. The king of the sharks is someone else entirely."

A wave of tension passes visibly across his fresh, childlike face.

"The real shark is the owner of this apartment you're living in."

Slowly, he nods in agreement.

"Why did you point me toward Mördur?"

Rúnar's trembling fingers are drumming on the tiled top of the coffee table.

"You must have wanted him to be caught?"

He looks up at me with moist eyes. "When we met, when I was on my way to Sólrún's funeral, that was the way I felt. I hated him, and I hated Skarpi."

"For what they did to Sólrún? The drugs?"

"I wasn't thinking clearly. I shouldn't have…"

"Yes, you should. It was the right thing to do. And that's why you did it."

Tears are pouring down his face, like the rain outside the window.

"How did it start?"

He sniffs.

"It started down south, didn't it? When Skarpi went there to act in *Street Rider*?"

Rúnar gets a grip on himself. "Yes. It started there. I was only nine, but I remember it all as if it happened yesterday. When Skarpi came home, he was a different person. It was as if he'd decided to become a different person."

"What kind of a person?"

"Someone who does exactly what he wants. Someone who gets other people to do what he wants."

"Did he become addicted to drugs?"

He shakes his head. "Skarpi never took dope. Never drank. Never smoked."

"So he was a fine role model? He was the natural leader, respected by all?"

"He didn't want to do anything that might weaken him. He wouldn't allow anything to make it more difficult for him to become what he wanted."

I recall Dr. Karl Hjartarson's description of narcissistic personality disorder. It didn't strike me then, but it does now. He told me NPD manifests as an absence of morals or conscience, along with delusional ideas about the nature of success, power, and talent. "There was a recent case of a British teenager, an outstanding student, convicted of murdering his parents, who had done everything for him," the doctor told me. The adoring parents had the audacity to criticize their son for being careless with money, and they didn't like his girlfriend. For that he beat them to death with a hammer, then stabbed them twenty or thirty times with a kitchen knife, so the bodies were almost unrecognizable when they were discovered some six weeks later. The son had gone off on a long vacation abroad, using his dead parents' money. He was planning to enter medical school on his return. "Instead he found himself serving a life sentence, with a diagnosis of NPD. He had given the impression of a completely normal, promising young man," Karl told me.

"I went to your place the night before last," I tell Rúnar. "Your dad's addicted to drugs, isn't he?"

He looks down. "Dad's a loser. A loser and a junkie."

"He worked as a pharmacist before he got ill—I suppose he got addicted to his own drugs?"

No answer.

"He was no role model for Skarphédinn. He's a poster boy for what not to do. Do you think that's why your brother became what he was?"

"I don't know. But his experience down south convinced him that he could control people by exploiting their weaknesses. And then they would do whatever he wanted."

"And he met someone who thought the same way he did? Mördur Njálsson?"

"Yes."

"And Skarpi encouraged Mördur to move up here to the north, so together they would get rich and powerful? Gain control of young people here in Akureyri and, in due course, older people too?"

"Yes."

"And then they cast their net wider, to the east as well. Bigger market. Globalization. All that."

He says nothing. It wasn't a question.

"Skarphédinn recorded all his triumphs on the cell phone. But did he tell you everything too? Did he keep you informed throughout?"

"Right from the start. He started stealing medications from Dad and selling them. And he'd drop in on Mom at the hospital and steal more drugs there. And Mom…"

"Your mother got caught in his net. Stuck between your father's drug abuse and her son who was also making illegal use of drugs, but in a different way. And she covered for both of them."

His eyes fill with tears. "Mom couldn't…And then Skarpi started bringing the stuff in from all over…"

"He must have needed more, a larger range of wares. And Mördur went down to Reykjavík to pick the stuff up?"

Rúnar nods.

"Your parents lost everything ten or fifteen years ago. Was that because of your father's drug abuse?"

"Yes."

"Was Skarphédinn planning to help them out financially, with the blood money he got from his drug dealing? So that drugs, which had destroyed the family, could rebuild it again?"

"Mom wouldn't take anything from him. They had a furious fight. She called him a merchant of death."

"Did Skarpi tell you everything, as a rule?"

"Yes. Too much, sometimes."

"Were you always close, the two of you?"

"As close as any two people can be. He was always good to me, did all he could for me. And that didn't change."

"So he was your role model? Your big brother? Your protector?"

Now tears are flooding down his cheeks. "Yes. That's what he was. That's it."

I can just imagine how their mother must have felt about the situation.

"Until…?" I ask.

"Until…Sólrún was…"

He starts crying.

I stand up, go over to Rúnar, and put my arm around him.

"They met when the movie was being made," I say. "Sólrún fell in love with Skarphédinn. Head over heels. And he had sex with her. But he was also having sex with his leading lady. He introduced both girls to drugs. One survived longer than the other. But now they're both dead."

He's racked with sobbing.

"Sólrún never got over him," I say. "She never got over the way he dumped her, and she clung on to her hopes of winning him back. But she was hooked on drugs by then. She came up north and enrolled in high school here, just to be near Skarphédinn. Then what happened?"

I return to my seat, facing him, and leave him to weep for a while. I know all about this story, really. I'm familiar with the main points. The disparate threads have been coming together in my mind, bit by bit, slowly but surely. All that's missing is the denouement.

"Sólrún was supposed to be my girlfriend," Rúnar suddenly says. "Skarpi introduced us. He wanted us to be a couple."

"To get her off his back?"

He gazes at me through his tears. "Maybe." After a moment's silence, he adds: "Maybe he was doing it as a favor to me too. I try to believe that."

"So do you think she was only with you so she could be near him?"

In a voice full of pain, he replies: "Maybe."

"But maybe she really did like you? That's quite possible. You should think of that too, Rúnar."

He sniffs but says nothing.

"I think," I observe, "that the catalyst was the death of Ásdís Björk Gudmundsdóttir. The woman who fell into the Jökulsá River. Am I right?"

He's staring down at his hands again. Then he says:

"Skarpi had never done anything like that before. He sold drugs to people for their own use. He claimed he was just a facilitator—helping people who were bent on self-destruction. That they submitted to him of their own free will."

"Now that's debatable," I comment. "It's a rationalization. But not entirely illogical. Your brother appears to have been a chameleon, changing his ideas according to his own convenience. He seems to have had fun confusing people, giving a false impression, substituting one mask for another. That was the significance of the Terror Helmet—power over others. But OK, go on."

"He and Ásgeir at Yumm had been in contact before...done business, I suppose you'd say. To do with his wife. And...No, I can't...It's too horrible..."

He's on the brink of tears again.

"You don't need to say any more, Rúnar. It's all in the calendar on the cell phone," I assure him. "Ásgeir got in touch with Skarphédinn. He was tired of his wife and her resistance to selling the company. And the business was in trouble. Ásgeir and Skarphédinn came up with a plan to get rid of her while avoiding any suspicion of foul play. And it was easy, with Ásdís Björk's medical history. Skarphédinn provided the drug cocktail. Ásgeir slipped it to her in a drink. He probably didn't even have to give her a push overboard. And in return, Skarphédinn got a load of cash. Some to him personally, the rest as sponsorship for the play, *Loftur the Sorcerer*. Ten million *krónur*, according to the company accounts. It wouldn't take Ásgeir long to claw that back, once he could sell the business and cash in."

"The production was Skarpi's dream come true. He longed to play the part of Loftur. It was all he talked about for weeks."

"Why?" I ask, although I think I know the answer.

"I'm not entirely sure. But he said to me once: *What Loftur did by old-style sorcery, I'm doing with modern-day sorcery. If Loftur were alive now, he'd be doing the same as me. Loftur and I are human beings who become our own gods.*"

"And it destroyed both of them?"

He looks away.

"Now they want me to play the role," he says.

"To play Loftur?"

"Do you think I should?"

"Well, there would be a certain irony to it," I reply. Then I add: "And maybe there's a kind of poetic justice there, somewhere."

Rúnar is silent.

"Then what?" I ask.

"It was murder!" he exclaims, slamming his fist down on the table. "My brother took part in a cold-blooded murder!"

Yes, murder, I think. Murder, in the coldest of blood that flows through human veins. "I suppose anything was for sale, if the price was right?"

"He wouldn't listen to me," Rúnar continues, incandescent with righteous rage. "I told him he had to stop it from happening. He just said: *I'm above all laws. I decide for myself what I do. Other people decide what they do.* I got…I got so angry, I went for him. But he just laughed and patted me on the head, like a little puppy."

"Judging by the calendar on the cell phone, he seems to have got a kick out of the risk? The danger?"

Rúnar looks at me in surprise. "Yes, that's it. That's exactly it. He loved taking risks. Loved to see how far he could go. No matter who he hurt along the way."

"And I saw from the cell phone that you told your mom what he had done."

He says nothing.

"And she was convulsed with rage and despair."

"She told Skarpi he'd crossed the line. That he'd completely lost touch with reality. She said she hadn't raised her children so they could become killers. He just laughed at her too."

"That evening, the night before Holy Thursday, you were at the party with Skarphédinn."

"I went with Sólrún. Skarpi was acting like a raving lunatic. Wearing that stupid witch's robe and…"

"Those idiots from Reydargerdi were making a nuisance of themselves, and he responded with some racist insults."

He shakes his head.

"They were just fooling around. They had to pretend not to know each other, so they put on a show. Skarpi enjoyed that kind of thing."

Rúnar falls silent, deep in thought.

"If I were to say that Skarphédinn fell off his pedestal that night, would that be a long way from the truth?"

He looks at me. His surprise is giving way to trepidation.

"What do you mean?"

"Your brother performed some kind of aphrodisiac spell. He pulled out a pubic hair…"

He's taken aback.

"…and an eyelash. He set fire to them, then slipped the ash into a girl's drink at the party. And a little while after, he was in bed with some girl. I can't be sure who it was, but…"

"He didn't need any aphrodisiac spell. Sólrún would do whatever he wanted."

"Was she high?"

"She was using every day by then. And she was high at the party. But maybe she didn't need to be high. Maybe that was exactly what she wanted. What she wanted more than anything else." He buries his face in his hands. "She was pregnant by him."

I can hardly go on myself. I can't remember ever feeling so bad. Or seeing another person in such pain. After a long silence, I ask him: "Why did you and Skarphédinn go out to the dump?"

He pauses, then answers: "I asked why he did it. Why he did that to me. Why he did it to Sólrún. Do you know what he said?"

"*I did it because I could*?" I say.

Despite all his grief and pain, Rúnar is dumbfounded with surprise.

"How did you know that? What is it with you, anyway?"

"Um," I say. "It's my job to keep my finger on the pulse of life here in Iceland. And actually, your brother's calendar entries give a pretty good idea of his mind-set."

For a long time, Rúnar gazes at me. Then he seems to reach a decision.

"I broke down completely at the party. He put his arm around me and said: *Come on, brother of mine, let's get the hell out of here, leave these losers behind.* I saw that Sólrún was lying in the bed, dead to the world, off her face. I said: *Shouldn't we take Sólrún home at least?* Skarpi said: *Relax, man. You're master of your destiny. Other people must look out for themselves. You've got to face up to what Loftur said: I am silver alloy—fragments of evil, fragments of good.*"

I recall what Skarphédinn said in our interview, reveling in the hidden joy of his sins.

In sin, one becomes one's true self.

At about the time he spoke those words to me, a woman was falling into the cold waters of the Jökulsá River. Pushed by him. Although he wasn't there.

"Then he drove like a madman out to the dump," Rúnar continues intently. "I thought he was going to kill us both. He stopped the car at the gate to the dump, and I asked: *What are we doing here?* He didn't answer me. He gestured for me to follow him, and we climbed over the fence. He said: *I'm going to show you my king-*

dom. We walked on into the junkyard, and he showed me an old, crushed, rusty wreck of a motor. That was where he kept his stuff. Drugs in all the colors of the rainbow. *This is where my power is hidden,* he said. Like he was playing Loftur the Sorcerer."

He falls silent.

"I thought he'd gone mad. Talking like a character in some old book. Then he said: *Rúnar, you're the only one I can trust with my power and my dominion. You're the only one who knows. The only one who has the power.*"

Rúnar shakes his head.

"He jumped up on top of the wreck, spread his arms wide, and howled: *I am the Lord! I am the Master!*"

Once again he falls silent.

"Next to the motor was a container and a stepladder. He climbed up onto the container and kept on roaring that wild nonsense over the piles of garbage, scrap metal, and waste. I was in a state of confusion—angry, hurting, desperate. Maybe I was as crazy as he was. But all I knew was this: it couldn't go on."

I wait for the inevitable.

"I climbed up the stepladder and pushed him off."

We stand in silence for a moment.

"But why did you come back on the evening of Good Friday and set fire to the tires? Were you meaning to burn him at the stake, like the witch he claimed to be?"

"That didn't occur to me. I just thought he was less likely to be found in among all the burning rubbish."

"Leaving nothing but bones and ash?"

"I didn't realize tires would burn for so long. Didn't know that."

"And what happened to all the drugs?"

"They went first of all."

He gazes at me intently. His expression says: *That's the story. And now it's over.*

I wait a moment, then light up and say: "That was the story. And it's over. Except that there's one thing wrong with it, Rúnar."

Surprise and trepidation appear on his tense face.

"Your brother made entries on the calendar as interesting things arose."

"What are you getting at?"

"The final entry was made about half an hour before he died, according to the police's estimate."

The anxiety in his face is turning to naked fear. I retrieve my transcript. "This is the entry, decrypted:

Mom mad about my deal w/ Ásgeir about his wife. Rúnar told her. Fucked Sólrún to remind Rúnar who's boss."

I stop reading. "That's not all he wrote. In fact, your account of events is broadly true, but it wasn't just the two of you at the end of the story—not in the car, and not at the dump. You told your mother what was happening. She insisted on joining you, and your brother relented. She was there."

I take a breath and go on.

"And it wasn't you who pushed your brother off the container."

Rúnar has the look of a condemned man, waiting in the stocks for his turn on the gallows.

"It says here: *R went whining to Mom. I told her to mind her own business. She said I was a monster! That I'd burn in Hell! And she'd make sure of that, right now!*

"You both knew that Skarphédinn had to be stopped somehow. But she's the one who pushed him. You couldn't. And she acted. And after that you and your mom worked together to cover it up."

"There's more in the calendar," I add. "But I won't read it to you."

Fortunately, I don't find myself having to read out to Rúnar the final sentence of his brother's final entry:

I'm going to tell them the whole truth. Idiots.

27 SEVERAL WEEKS LATER

I have given you so much that I cannot let go of you. You must be kind to me, Loftur. My family are magnanimous—and melancholic. I do not know if I could bear it if you were to betray me... I think I would kill myself.

The young actress in the role of Steinunn, the abandoned, pregnant maidservant, is giving a heartfelt, emotional performance. Eternal love triangles form and re-form on the stage as much as off. I know the play so well by now that I find myself mouthing the words with the actors. And when Loftur declares, a little while later, a dead look in his eyes:

I wish you were dead!

I inevitably find myself thinking of the young man who longed, above all else, to stand on this stage and speak those words.

My desires are powerful and boundless. And in the beginning was desire. Desires are the souls of men.

Skarphédinn had quoted those lines of the old play.

I glance back over my shoulder and see Chief of Police Ólafur Gísli with his comely wife in the row behind me. He's obviously absorbed in the play and doesn't notice me.

He's made good use of the SIM card I formally handed over to him, accompanied by the key to the code. Mördur Njálsson is behind bars. The Three Stooges too. They will all be submitted to the justice of their fellow men.

The most painful thing of all is to find out that the one who possesses you, heart and soul, is evil...

When Steinunn speaks these words to her lover, I find myself glancing at the lady on my left—one of two I have invited to the play this evening. Gunnhildur is all dressed up and wearing lipstick in honor of the occasion. She seems to be totally caught up in the play—not unlike the *Guiding Light* mafia in front of the TV, back at the care home. I smile to myself as I recall the moment when I told her that her son-in-law, Ásgeir Eyvindarson, had been arrested on suspicion of causing the death of his wife. Not because it was a particularly happy moment, but because, before my eyes, the old lady was suddenly transformed. No longer old and senile, confused, unreliable, she was Gunnhildur Bjargmundsdóttir, a functioning member of society, whose word was worth something. Not written off. Not dismissed. And, above all, she was a mother who had won justice for her murdered child.

"How did you solve the mystery, my boy?" she inquired.

"It was a matter of a cell," I replied.

Gunnhildur brightened. "Aha," she said with satisfaction, raising a wizened finger. "Didn't I say so?"

"Yes, that's what you said."

"That's the way it is today. All in the...the..."

"Cells?"

"That's it. Absolutely."

I nodded. "The answers are always in the cells."

Gunnhildur leaned toward me, placed a weatherbeaten hand over mine, and whispered to me: "Considering how silly you can be, my boy, I'm sure that good old Inspectors Morse and Taggart would be proud of you now."

That was nice to hear.

And the old lady looked at me from her bright blue eyes, nestling in the wrinkles of her beaming face. "Do you know, I think I'm even a little bit proud of you myself."

That was even nicer.

"My dear Gunnhildur," I said, placing my other hand over hers, "don't forget that Morse and Taggart would have been nowhere without their trusty confederates."

On the Day of Judgment you will come face to face with a visage that is exactly the same as yours, but contorted by sin and passion, Steinunn says to Loftur.

A look at my other companion, on my right. My daughter Gunnsa's face shines with innocence. On the Day of Judgment, will her face be like mine, bearing the scars of life's sins and passions? In the first row, in front of us, sits Kristín, mother of Skarphédinn and Rúnar.

The back of her head has a tense, flinty look about it.

He who with all his soul wishes death upon another shall bow his head and look at the ground, and say: "Thou who livest in the eternal darkness. Make my will thy will! Kill this person! And I swear, in the name of the mighty trinity—in the name of the sun, which is the shadow of the Lord; in the name of the fire in the earth, which is thy shadow; and in the name of my own body, which is my shadow, that my soul is thine, for ever and ever."

Rúnar speaks the final words of the second act with such passion that the crowd bursts into a torrent of applause. His mother turns her head and I see that her lips are touched with a smile that is full of pride. But it's also full of sorrow.

Her elder son's death remains unsolved—according to the laws of man, at least. But there are other laws.

I think back to the day, over a month ago, when I sat with her son and a story was told.

At the end of the story I held up the cell phone to show Rúnar the final entry—but without the final sentence.

"I really don't know much about these gadgets," I said. I selected *Options.*

There were several *Options.*

One of them was *Delete note.*

On the keypad, my finger somehow slipped.

"Oops," I said.

Skarphédinn's final comments vanished.

"Human error."

Was it an error? Should I have allowed justice to take its course?

When Rúnar and I went over to his parents' home that evening, I still hadn't made up my mind. But as I observed his mother taking care of the living corpse that is his father, I abandoned my doubts.

The most painful thing of all is to find out that the one who possesses you, heart and soul, is evil was said about a lover. But what if it's your own child? She had decided to have that child. And she decided that the child's time had come. The season of the witch had come—and gone.

The mother embraced her younger son and wept. But her eyes were dry.

Then she said one sentence. She didn't look at me, but her words were meant for me:

"I had no option."

Do we sometimes have no option? I am brought back to the present when Kristín glances over her shoulder at me. Our eyes meet briefly. What passes between us cannot be put into words.

Except perhaps these words:

Holy Week calls us to join Christ on his final journey and share his pain, for suffering is part of human life. And his story assures us that suffering is not pointless—not his, not our own. Jesus said: "Father, forgive them, for they know not what they do." And those words have meaning for all of us sinners.

Fridrik Einarsson, playing the tortured loyal friend, Ólafur, speaks the final line of the final act.

Curtain.

The gym at Hólar College erupts into applause. The ovation goes on and on. The cast, led by Rúnar in the title role, take curtain call after curtain call. Director Örvar Páll makes an entrance onstage to bow in all directions, as if he thinks he's master of the universe.

TV cameras hum, radio station mics pick up every sound, and photographers bustle forward with clicks and flashes. Jóa's there among the media pack and gives me a wave. Next to her is Heida, editor of the *Akureyri Post*, doing her job.

I have to say that yours truly, journalist on the *Afternoon News*—Akureyri Office—has played some part in all this media hullaballoo. My articles and features on the many and varied events of last Easter, and the hidden network of the merchants of death, was not only a hit on the newsstands. It also cheered Ásbjörn up no end. I borrowed the overall title of the series from that request on the radio the day it all began: *Season of the Witch.*

The premiere of the Akureyri High School Drama Group production of *Loftur the Sorcerer* is followed by refreshments in the college assembly hall. Ásbjörn approaches me, red in the face, clutching a glass of white wine. The reception is not—God forbid—hosted by the school itself, because alcohol is being served, and that would be contrary to all the high school rules. Instead, the drinking is at the expense of the sponsors: Bonus supermarkets and Hotel KEA. Not the Yumm candy factory, however, due to supervening events.

"Cheers, my dear old Einar," says Ásbjörn. "And thank you for everything." With him are Karólína and Björg, who join him in toasting me.

I lift my glass of Coke to share the toast with them, as well as Gunnsa and Gunnhildur, both drinking white wine. I made myself bite my tongue when I saw Björg discreetly passing the wine to my underage daughter: all things considered, it's not such a big issue.

Outside, the sun is shining in a clear blue sky. Fields of grass have turned from withered yellow to rich green. The horses are no longer standing around like statues in the freezing wind, but run friskily about the verdant pastures.

"Have you heard about Dad's sweetheart?" Gunnsa asks with a wicked little smile.

They all turn to me expectantly.

I say nothing. Glare at my daughter.

"We were getting dressed earlier," Gunnsa goes on. "For the play. Dad had put on his good white shirt and was searching for his tie, which he couldn't find, naturally—because he doesn't own a tie and never has. Then Polly came swooping down off the curtain rail in the living room and perched on his collar. Dad was trying to smooth his hair down in front of the mirror, but Polly suddenly started rubbing her rump up against his collar. Back and forth, to and fro, faster and faster. She spread her wings. She trilled and squawked. She got more and more excited…"

Gunnsa stops and looks at me. I glance over the people gathered here in their Sunday best. There are many familiar faces. High school principal Stefán Már. Sociology teacher Kjartan Arnarson. Local councilmen. A handful of members of parliament—most from the majority party, thrilled to be entrusted for another term with the welfare of the country.

I look at Gunnsa and put on the gravest possible face. I wouldn't be surprised if there were a touch of suffering in my expression. Just a smidgeon.

"Then, all at once," Gunnsa continues, "Polly stiffened up. A tiny little penis peeped out from under the feathers and…and…"

Gunnsa takes a pause for dramatic effect, enjoying the stunned expressions, then says:

"I hope I'm not offending anyone's sensibilities here, but—she shot her load!"

The speechless silence and gaping mouths are so priceless that I simply can't keep a straight face anymore. I grasp my shirt collar and pull it forward to display, with exaggerated pride, a microscopic speck on the white fabric.

"Yes, ladies and gentlemen," I declare. "My sex appeal is a many-splendored thing."

As they collapse into giggles and guffaws, I put a nuclear warhead in my mouth, seize a glass of white wine, and with a smile I stride out into the summer.

Out of the wilderness, into the next adventure.

ABOUT THE AUTHOR

Photograph © Philippe Matsas

Arni Thorarinsson grew up in Reykjavík, Iceland, channeling his childhood interests in film, music, and writing into a career as a journalist. He cofounded and edited Iceland's first independent weekly, and covered stories big and small, local and international, for the nation's largest magazine and the weekend editions of two major newspapers. In addition to print journalism, he has worked regularly in radio and television. In the mid-1990s, he stumbled upon a penchant for writing screenplays and crime novels, including *Blue Moon*, *The Seventh Son*, and *Angel of the Morning*. *Season of the Witch* was nominated for the Icelandic Literature Prize.

ABOUT THE TRANSLATOR

Photograph © Eddie Lawrence

Translator Anna Yates grew up in London and Paris. After earning her history degree from Bristol University, she traveled to Iceland in search of her roots and never left. She studied Icelandic at the University of Iceland and worked for several years as a journalist and translator for the *Iceland Review*, the nation's leading English-language publisher. She has translated academic writings, legal documents, museum texts and guides, arts and tourism publications, CD cover notes, advertising copy, folklore, and fiction. The author of *The Viking Discovery of America*, she lives and works in Reykjavík.